COUGAR

A SAM RIVERS MYSTERY

CLAW

Also by the author

Gunflint Burning: Fire in the Boundary Waters
Opening Goliath
Lost in the Wild
Wolf Kill

PRAISE FOR *COUGAR CLAW*

"In this highly anticipated second novel in the Sam Rivers series, Cary J. Griffith delivers another finely researched and compellingly written thriller. Both the beauty and the savagery of our natural world form the heart of a Griffith story. In this case, it's the predatory habits of cougars. When the killing of a Twin Cities man in an apparent cougar attack brings Sam to the Minnesota River Valley to investigate, what follows is a gradual and fascinating revelation of not just the predatory nature of cougars, but that of humans as well."

—William Kent Krueger, Edgar Award–winning author of
This Tender Land

"Griffith—and his very engaging hero, Sam Rivers—both know the Minnesota wilderness inside and out. But be careful. After staying up all night to devour *Cougar Claw*, you may find yourself listening for a low growl the next time you're alone in the forest."

—Brian Freeman, *New York Times* best-selling author of
The Deep, Deep Snow

"A deadly threat from the wild comes far too close for comfort when an urban bicyclist is found mauled to death by a cougar. In this second book in the Sam Rivers mystery series, Cary Griffith takes this U.S. Fish & Wildlife special agent on a hair-raising hunt to find the cougar—and the truth. Mixing deep knowledge of the natural world with the twists and turns of the best suspense novels, *Cougar Claw* is a thoughtful and thrilling story."

—Mary Logue, author of the Claire Watkins mysteries and
The Streel

"*Cougar Claw*, the second installment in the Sam Rivers series, sends the U.S. Fish & Wildlife special agent to the scene of a grisly cougar killing on the outskirts of the Twin Cities. As usual in Sam Rivers's world, all is not as it seems. Griffith doubles down on his strengths in this series, giving us another vibrant cast of allies, suspects, and a misunderstood predator, while navigating a path between animal rights and human fears of the natural world. I can't wait for Sam Rivers's next assignment.

—Mindy Mejia, author of *Everything You Want Me To Be* and *Strike Me Down*

"From the first page to the last, *Cougar Claw* blends high suspense with the quiet observations of the predator's predator, Sam Rivers. Between Griffith's descriptions of Minnesota's natural beauty and the human nature of his characters, this is a book you won't want to end."

—Debra H. Goldstein, award-winning author of the Sarah Blair mystery series

COUGAR

A SAM RIVERS MYSTERY

CLAW

CARY J. GRIFFITH

Copy editors: Kate Johnson, Mary Logue, and Kerry Smith
Proofreader: Emily Beaumont
Cover design: Travis Bryant
Front cover photo: John McLaird/Shutterstock
Back cover photo: July Flower/Shutterstock

Library of Congress Cataloging-in-Publication Data
Names: Griffith, Cary J., author.
Title: Cougar claw : a Sam Rivers mystery / Cary J. Griffith.
Description: Cambridge, Minnesota : Adventure Publications, An
    imprint of AdventureKEEN, [2022]
Summary: "The sighting of a cougar in the Minnesota River Val-
    ley, outside the Twin Cities, is incredibly rare. A deadly cougar
    attack on a human in this area is about as likely as getting struck
    by lightning—twice. Yet when wealthy business owner Jack
    McGregor is found dead, the physical evidence seems incontro-
    vertible. In *Cougar Claw,* natural history writer Cary J. Griffith
    brings back Sam Rivers, the predator's predator, and pens a puz-
    zling mystery filled with suspense and intrigue." —Provided by
    publisher
Identifiers: LCCN 2021052057 (pbk.) | LCCN 2021052058 (ebook)
    | ISBN 9781647550813 (pbk.) | ISBN 9781647550806 (ebook)
Subjects: GSAFD: Mystery fiction. | Suspense fiction.
Classification: LCC PS3607.R54857 C68 2022 (print) | LCC
    PS3607.R54857 (ebook) | DDC 813/.6—dc23
LC record available at lccn.loc.gov/2021052057
LC ebook record available at ccn.loc.gov/2021052058

For Anna, life partner, playmate, and confidante

PART 1

PROLOGUE

September 2, Savage, Minnesota

Marlin Coots, McGregor Industries' gap-toothed, splay-footed nighttime security watchman, was making his morning rounds at the company's remote shipping facility. He loved this part of the day, when he could step to the edge of the minimum-maintenance road and gaze down into the Minnesota river-bottom woods. Sometimes he'd see a raccoon scurry into brambles, or an opossum's slow climb up a tree. You never knew what the Savage woods would give up, which is why Marlin always took a moment to pause and look down.

The perimeter road was always empty, particularly here, where a huge oak anchored the landward side of the pair of dirt ruts. The other side of the road dropped 15 feet to the bottoms. On this morning, Marlin was startled to see a large brown animal lying on its side, its neck twisted at an unnatural angle.

A white-tailed deer. The kill was too primitive for a poacher.

Marlin backslid down the embankment. The carcass was barely cold. Its chest cavity had a clean incision from neck to belly. The ribs were parted and its heart and lungs were gone. When he looked around, he noticed a paw print the size of a fry pan.

"What the . . . ?"

His dad had told him there were serious predators in the Minnesota River Valley. Marlin's father had spent most of his adult life hunting and fishing this wild stretch of river, from Mankato all the way up to Savage on the edge of the Twin Cities. Marlin didn't share his dad's enthusiasm for shooting game, but he loved seeing the animals in his neck of the woods. So he rigged a motion-activated game camera with an infrared flash, setting it up near the deer kill.

The next day, Marlin's camera confirmed the presence of a cougar, one of the images clear enough to print. Since this part of the valley was considered an outlying Twin Cities suburb, the local media picked up the sighting. "Big Cat Returns to Minnesota," the *Star Tribune* reported. One of the more dramatic TV news channels asked, "Are you safe in Minnesota's woods?" The coverage reported that over the last 10 years, out West, there had been dozens of human–cougar encounters, "and in some instances people were stalked, killed, and eaten."

The Minnesota Department of Natural Resources tried to place the sighting in perspective. Though cougar attacks were known to happen—even some in which humans were killed—in Minnesota people had a better chance of being struck by lightning.

The DNR suspected this cougar was someone's rogue pet, though no one came forward. If it was wild, they surmised, it was extremely rare for Minnesota, with only a handful of confirmed sightings in the last 50 years, none near the Cities.

In any case, there was no need to worry. A big cat's customary food source was deer, which could account for why this cougar had come to Savage. Along the suburban section of river, the white-tailed fattened on Kentucky bluegrass, backyard hostas, and tulip greens. Deer hunting was irregular or nonexistent, and the deer herd was prodigious.

The kill, the tracks, and the photo made for good TV, which is why, three days later, one station ran a follow-up piece on cougar hunting habits, noting they often returned to feed on kills a second, and even a third, time, sometimes several days later.

"So if you're heading into the Minnesota River Valley," warned the anchor, "be careful out there."

CHAPTER ONE

September 23

Jack McGregor pumped hard through the bike's lowest gear, his thighs burning. He neared the top of his quarter-mile climb, maintaining his bike's progress up this last steep grade. The black coffee he had finished before 6 a.m. was finally taking hold. He glanced at his heart monitor and watched the numbers spike from 156 to 157. Sweat dampened his tight yellow bike shirt.

Twenty yards, he thought, which was about all he could manage, trying to keep his ragged breathing steady. He rabbit-pedaled through the last short rise and finally crested the hill.

He appreciated the quiet half hour before dawn when the world slept and the second-summer air hung still and pungent. His heart rate peaked at 164 and he managed a stiff grin.

He took in a long breath and smelled witch hazel, he guessed, the odor of weeds heavy with seedpods and a faint wisp of river more than a mile below. It was a wet metal smell. And maybe there was the trace of something fetid beneath it; a car-struck deer decaying in a ditch, or a snake flattened across the blacktop? *Something...*

Over the last couple days, Jack had felt uneasy. He assumed it was his pending business deal. But there was something else, the vague feeling he needed to be vigilant or wary or just plain cautious. And it was annoying because Jack McGregor, the 51-year-old owner, president, and chief executive officer of McGregor Industries, was a stranger to unease.

Chester Drive formed a T at the top of Wannamake Circle. The hill dropped down into Savage and the Minnesota River Valley, where it connected with Highway 13 more than a mile below. In another hour, the blacktop would be busy with morning commuters, emptying the exclusive neighborhoods up on the hill. But from Jack's acme, at this time of morning, he had the road almost entirely to himself.

He turned onto Chester and crouched low, reducing his wind resistance so the air coming out of the valley wouldn't pick him up like a sail. Not that there was much of a breeze a half hour before dawn. Jack liked to feel aerodynamic. He liked to travel fast. As his bike picked up speed, he put his nagging doubts behind him and peered ahead, grinning down the dark thoroughfare.

Jack's Cannondale RZ One Forty mountain bike had been a 51st-birthday present. Carla accused him of a midlife crisis before finally accepting and then indulging his effort to stay fit. She bought him the most expensive bike she could find, making a big deal about its carbon alloy frame and phenomenal suspension. And no doubt about it, the bike could fly. His best birthday present came later that evening.

Carla was 37, and a mix of fortuitous genes, hard exercise, and no children kept her in the kind of shape Jack liked to see and feel in a woman. And the seasoning she'd experienced through her 20s, when she'd married one creep and then another, helped cultivate a particular appreciation for Jack.

The speedometer hit 22. He looked up and saw the road empty all the way to 13, not a car in sight. When he glanced down again, the speedometer read 25.

It was still too early for predawn light, which was why Jack squinted down the path in front of him. At this speed, traveling near the tree edge, it was foolhardy to look anywhere but directly in front of you. Deer frequented the wilder parts of Chester Hill. And plenty of nocturnal animals chose this final hour of darkness to hunt for a safe place to bed down and sleep for the day. Or to search for one last unsuspecting prey.

The wild country was one of the features that had charmed Jack and Carla about Savage. They could have chosen a big house in Edina, Excelsior, Shorewood, or just about any other place they wanted. But Carla liked the unpretentiousness of Savage. She appreciated the secluded, country feel of Wannamake Circle and their remote cul-de-sac, where she wouldn't run into anyone from the Club and where she could buy milk at the local Cub grocery without having to dress up or put on.

Speedometer: 27.

Up ahead something stirred. Under a sumac patch. Not a deer; the movement was too furtive and close to the ground. At his current speed, he would hit it head-on in a matter of seconds.

Jack yelled, the dark creature froze, and Jack hurtled by in a blast. He glimpsed a skunk hunkered down in the grass.

Just a few seconds either way, rodent or man, and Jack might have been a stinking pile of . . .

Focus on the tree edge, he reminded himself. It was a brief part of the hill, and he watched as its shadows flew by and opened onto empty pasture. His near brush with calamity rocketed his pulse. His bike speed climbed to 33. He glanced in front of him. The pools of light from the gentrified streetlamps were clear all the way to the bottom, and Jack flew.

The white Ford Focus—a rental out of Brooklyn Center—approached the entrance to the dirt road.

"Here's the turn," Benedict said.

"I know," John said, tired of taking orders.

They wore dark camo, head to foot. John wore a camo baseball hat with CABELA'S emblazoned above the bill. Benedict wore a bucket hat. They were edgy in the predawn.

John did what he often did, knowing there was bad business ahead. He put himself past it. *In 2 hours, I will be back at my place . . . showering . . . getting ready for work. Just another day.*

But given the task ahead, focusing on what came after was difficult.

This stretch of Highway 13 was mostly open country, separated by occasional remote storage facilities and grain elevators. Farther north, Savage gave way to Burnsville and single-family homes, apartment complexes, and a string of busy retail outlets crowding either side of the highway all the way to Interstate 35W.

Travel south and you passed more open country until the Valley Fair Amusement Park and Shakopee, the next suburb over. But here, in between the park and Burnsville's stores, the river bottom was vacant and wild, except for McGregor Industries and its potash and fertilizer facility.

John glanced in his rearview mirror. He saw one pair of headlights, a quarter mile behind him. At this hour, there was nothing up ahead. He signaled, turning onto the narrow dirt lane. It was empty and dark and rose to a pair of unmarked railroad tracks. On either side, the weeds were high and overgrown, and the car rumbled over the rails, leaving a faint cloud of dust. The car dropped over the hill and John turned onto the frontage road, pulled over beside a stand of river maples, and cut the engine. The headlights darkened.

They each glanced at their watches. They would sit in the car for exactly 5 minutes, waiting for the dust to settle and the crickets' *screedle-screedle* to return in the dark.

The first time John met Benedict was a week ago Saturday at the Black Angus truck stop on 169 outside Mankato. That was before any of them had names.

John thought driving 60 miles south when they could have met anywhere in the Twin Cities was a stupid precaution. He'd entered the truck stop, glanced at the handful of customers, and recognized Benedict as the guy sitting at the end of the counter, sipping coffee.

Benedict said he would be dressed in green khaki camo, like others in the diner—a hunter getting a jump on the grouse season. He wore his hat and dark aviator sunglasses and a bristly mustache John guessed was fake, but a good fake. His hair was loose and wild under his hat. John thought it, too, might be fake, but he wasn't sure.

John sidled up to the nondescript counter, keeping a seat between them. He was hungry for eggs, hash browns, and buttered toast with maybe a side of medium-hot salsa and some extra bacon. His normal custom would be to slip into some easy conversation, probably talking about the best-looking woman in the café, though this morning the selection was poor.

Benedict stared straight ahead into the mirror behind the counter. "You're late," he whispered, harsh.

A waitress approached.

"Coffee?" she asked.

"Why, thank you . . . Nancy," John said, reading her name tag and flashing a smile. John had perfect teeth. His brown hair was short and carefully trimmed. He wore slick warm-ups and black tennis shoes that marked him as not from around here and not interested in fitting in. An old girlfriend once called him *smarmy*. After he looked it up, it ticked him off because it was true.

Nancy smiled and poured his coffee. "Hey, sugar."

He had that effect on women of a certain kind. Normally he would have told her his real name, which wasn't John. But the man sitting one stool over was making him edgy.

She passed him a menu and shoved off to fill more cups.

"Now get this," Benedict whispered. "Next time you're late, the deal's off. I call the shots, and if you don't like them, you know what you can do about it. Understood?" This was all said through lips that barely moved, staring into his coffee cup.

John thought about telling him to fuck off, but he'd been told you didn't tell the guy to fuck off. Benedict was opaque, a man of few words, a planner, a nitpicker, a detail guy . . . and when the plan wasn't followed, a very bad man with a dangerous temper. So John shrugged (the way he'd seen Tony do it on *The Sopranos*).

"Got a name?" John asked, into the mirror.

"Benedict. You're John. Our employer's name is Urban. From now on, those are the only names we use. I don't know your real name and I don't want to. And you don't know anything about me. We've got this job, John, and then after, nothing. After, if we run into each other on the Vail ski slopes—not saying I ski in Vail; that's a for instance—don't even look my way. Understood?"

John hesitated. It was a turning point. Continue, or get out. Everything in him screamed, "Turn and leave and don't look back." But he was in too deep.

So he just shrugged, Tony-like.

After that first day, John was punctual. And he was careful about everything else, too; the gray-green camo khakis, the hat, the cheap digital watch . . . everything.

Like now.

John popped the trunk and they got out of the rental car and walked around to retrieve their tools.

The car was a nondescript rental, nothing that would draw attention—part of the reason John had been ordered to choose it. He'd also been ordered to remove the trunk light, so it wouldn't flash when the trunk was opened. The guy thought of everything.

John guessed he should have felt happy about it, but all he wanted was to be done.

In the dark trunk, there was a small, zippered travel kit along one side. John picked it up, reached around, and tucked it into the back of his pants. Then he hefted out a 20-pound sandbag and the oddly fashioned pair of jaws. The jaws were bound shut with a bungee cord, the substantial fangs carefully fitted, as though they were still embedded in the large cat's skull. Benedict leaned in and pulled out four footpads. The large feet were attached to the ends of cedar poles using a spring-loaded industrial hinge. The poles could be easily swung and carried. The sharp claws extended stiletto-like out of the pads. The one time they'd tested the claws, Benedict had swung them across the leather face of a punching bag. The hinges sprang out like switchblades, leaving four evenly spaced, deep lacerations. Perfect.

Awkwardly, John positioned the sandbag so he could push the Indiglo on his cheap wristwatch. 6:12.

Benedict did the same. "Let's hustle," he said.

They turned and started off through the dark, walking along the dirt road beside the railroad tracks. They walked in silence, thinking about what must be done. The eastern light was hardly a trace, but it would come on fast. They hurried 50 yards to the minimum-maintenance road with a rusted gate. There was a shot-up NO TRESPASSING, PRIVATE PROPERTY sign wired across the bars. There was a small path around the right side of the gate and they stepped around the post, quickening their pace.

"Keep an eye out," John said.

"Just keep your eyes on the prize," Benedict said.

Like most of his partner's comments, it ticked John off. But he shut up and kept walking through the dark and told himself, *In 2 hours, I'll be someplace else and Pope Benedict'll be gone.*

It took less than 2 minutes for Jack to rocket down Chester Drive. At Highway 13 he pedaled easily across the blacktop, biked 50 yards up the shoulder, and turned onto the frontage road.

He was still a mile from the plant and a little farther to the minimum-maintenance road. He could see the faintest start of light in the eastern sky, barely a shadow. He liked hitting the river bottom in that special half-light of dawn. Judging from what he saw off the horizon, he was right on schedule.

Jack pedaled easy during this part of his morning, saving himself for the hard exercise of the river bottom. He had paid Mountain Cross Bikes to build several private bike trails down by the river. The trails wound through McGregor Industries' low-hung trees and up and down the small ravines leading into the river. Once you entered them, staying on your bike on the trail required unwavering concentration. If you weren't totally focused, you could end up facedown in the dirt or with your torso wrapped around a tree trunk. It was the kind of challenge Jack liked because it kept him feeling alert and alive.

But here, along the quiet, flat dirt road, he could ease up and contemplate his day.

It had been an intense six months for McGregor Industries. In less than two weeks, his sale to Garkill United would be final and he'd have a lot more time for mountain biking. And just about anything else he'd postponed because of work, which was plenty. Best of all, the sale of his company was on his terms. He was getting out from under a business that had occupied 60-plus hours a week for almost 30 years. And Jack wasn't looking back. First up: a round-the-world trip he'd been holding so close to his vest not even Carla knew about it. They were going to become reacquainted in some of the finest hotels and biggest beds across five continents.

Jack kept his bike centered on the poorly lit gravel road. The insects chirruped in the dark. The frontage road was bordered on two sides by heavy autumn bush and occasional trees. You never knew what critters might scamper out of the weeds—could be another skunk or a deer, so it was best to keep to the road's center.

Only five insiders knew about the company's pending sale, and none of them liked it. CFO Spencer Higgins and Treasurer Phil Traub had to know. No way around it. Jack had needed their help. They would both benefit from the sale, Spencer more than Phil.

Madeline Baxter, the company's vice president of human resources, had to know. Maddy had been around since Jack was a kid. He suspected she had been his father's plaything, though he was only guessing. Jack kept her around because it had been a promise to his father. But once he was out from under the business, she'd have to fend for herself, and Jack was pretty sure Garkill would cut her loose.

A year ago, Jack asked Spencer to give Susan Connelly a better job title and more money.

Most people knew Jack had a problem with women. Sometimes he made bad choices and worse passes, and when Susan threatened a lawsuit, he'd reached out to Spence and told him to promote her. You could do that kind of thing when you owned the company.

Spence made the long-haired blonde a financial analyst. She was good with numbers. After Spence requested several out-of-season profit-and-loss statements, Susan figured out the pending sale and had to be brought in on it.

The only other person who knew about the transaction was Angie Sweet, assistant treasurer under Traub. Like Susan, she discovered the pending sale because of her acumen with numbers. When there was a lot of excited financial work out of season, she made a rare visit to Jack's office and confronted him.

You had to admire Angie. If she wanted something, she pursued it. Jack misread her ambition and made a play for her in the corporate boardroom. Angie let him know less discreet women could use that kind of thing to file a lawsuit or make a stink. Jack let her know it would be her word against his. But to placate her, he'd brought her into the fold, with assurances she would benefit like the others from the sale. Not much, really. But enough to purchase cooperation and silence.

Business.

If Carla knew about Jack's indiscretions, she was too savvy to say anything. On the other hand, Jack had been lucky: in the instances he was fortunate enough to find a willing partner, and eventually needed to end things, he'd never had to deal with troubled tears, incriminations, or finger-pointing. And especially not with confessions to a spouse, a boyfriend, or his own wife.

The truth was, Carla had all the right curves in the best places, and even after seven years of marriage she still set his limbs on fire. That was why they were going to celebrate her 38th birthday in Bali. It seemed a fitting place for the woman who had agreed to be his permanent concubine.

Jack kept pedaling easy.

None of the five liked the sale because they all feared the repercussions, and the only one making serious cash on the transaction was Jack. Spencer, Phil, and Maddy would all lose their jobs once Garkill took over. Angie and Susan were both too good-looking, too young, and too competent to do anything but land on their feet. But they'd no longer be thinking they were the heirs apparent to becoming officers of the company. Besides, Garkill wasn't interested in the business end of the operation. It was clear that what they wanted was McGregor's storage capacity and distribution network, particularly down on the river.

He couldn't blame the five for not liking it. He'd tried to be sympathetic, though it wasn't his nature. Two of them would make good money from the sale. Not enough to carry them into retirement, but certainly enough to tide them over. Maddy was old enough she might retire. He had no idea how she'd managed her money, and frankly he didn't care. For an HR vice president, she'd done what was expected: smiled and forced objectionable policies onto a disgruntled workforce. And whenever the occasional employee with a backbone made a ruckus, she had a knack for cutting them loose.

He reached the intersection and turned onto the minimum-maintenance road. There was a gate up ahead. It was getting light enough to see the shot-up sign, but Jack had been around it so many times he dodged right along the worn rut, turned around the steel post, and kept pedaling.

"Hurry up," Benedict hissed.

"Just a minute." John stepped onto the tree limb, unsteady in the near-dark. Above him three huge oak branches stretched over the road.

"Give it to me," John said.

Benedict reached up to hand him the 20-pound sandbag. John took it and tried to get situated.

They knew their rider would be coming from the southeast, down the road they'd just hiked. There was a quarter-mile stretch before the rarely used ruts curved to the left, approaching the river. The road ran for another 200 yards before ending near the loading dock and river pier and the start of the mountain bike trail. The pier was remote and at this hour unoccupied and quiet.

Across the road, the land dropped to the wooded river bottom. If you pushed through the briar and maple trunks another 50 yards, you'd hit water. The late September foliage kept the river hidden, but they could smell the wet metallic odor and the faintest trace of rotting deer.

Once John was situated, he nodded. "Ready."

It was growing lighter. Benedict looked up and said, "Just make sure you hit him."

"Get down and stay out of sight," he answered, trying to make it sound like an order.

But they both knew Benedict was in charge.

Now that John was in the tree, he worried about everything that could go wrong. The rider could be too far over for a clean drop. If the bike was coming fast, timing the drop would be difficult. And what if he missed? The jerk was fit and muscular and his temper was legendary. There were two of them, so he felt confident they could finish the job—if it came to a stand-up fight. But his partner would have to be careful, coming in from behind. And it would be hard explaining unnatural contusions on the victim's body.

They had all discussed it. There could be no stand-up fight. Not with Jack McGregor.

He reminded himself the plan was a good one—they'd been over it a thousand times. He knew there was plenty of risk, but the reward was worth it. He watched Benedict move up the road another 20 or 30 feet before hustling across the narrow dirt rut and disappearing over the ravine edge.

Less than 2 hours, John thought, trying to focus beyond the bad part, when this would be behind him. But it faded like a whisper. Because now he was on edge, nervous and watching . . . and trying to think about nothing.

Now they were both in position.

Now they waited.

Jack came around the bend and was startled by a flock of grackles. They rose squawking from the tree edge. The birds were starting to gather. The overhead geese were beginning to assemble for their southern migrations. As Jack came around the bend, the dawn was light enough to discern the pier's creosote pylons, more than 200 yards distant. He was still mulling his morning and his day, which was going to get busy with one meeting after another. He wouldn't be home until after 7 tonight, so he reminded himself to enjoy the ride.

The start of his mountain bike trail was just this side of the pier. From the loading dock it turned right, into the trees, dropping fast to the river bottom before making a snakelike oxbow through the woods.

He pedaled easy, trying to prepare himself for that first precipitous drop to the river, 15 feet straight down, when his stomach lifted and the air hung in his chest. He approached the huge oak and for the faintest second, in the half-light of dawn, he felt something out of place, something wrong about the morning . . . something.

Then he was hit hard on the back of his neck and shoulder. He veered and started to go down, and for one startled moment, dropping, he wondered what the hell hit him. The road seemed to rise up and smack his head like an anvil.

Then the world turned black.

But only for a few seconds.

The ground twirled like a whirligig and he started rising out of vertigo, suddenly nauseous. He couldn't move. He thought he might throw up, tasted bile and black coffee, but didn't retch. The side of his face was pressed against gritty earth. His eyesight was starting to clear and he saw something that didn't make sense. He watched a man climbing sideways down a tree. He blinked, still coming around. He blinked again and realized it was the big oak almost 15 feet behind him. Then he remembered where he was and what happened, but he was still unclear about what hit him, and he was having trouble getting up.

The figure dropped to the ground and bent to retrieve a bag. The bag appeared heavy as the man labored with it. And then Jack realized if he wanted to live, he'd better get up. Fast.

The man was as startled to see Jack rise as Jack was to manage it. The fit CEO caused the killer to pause, for just one second, uncertain, long enough for Jack's vision to clear and his head to shake off the blow, and he eyed the man in front of him holding the 20-pound sandbag.

"You!" Jack managed, recognizing him.

Jack wasn't going to wait for the man to speak. He was going to teach the man a lesson. He'd spend a little time getting him to talk, provided he could check his rage long enough to keep from killing him. He took one step forward, like a fighter, raising his fists.

And that was the last thing he remembered.

"Good thing he didn't hear you," John said, coming forward.

"Shut up! He's still alive, you idiot. Get the jaws. Let's finish it."

CHAPTER TWO

When Sam Rivers, special agent for the U.S. Fish & Wildlife Service (USFW), stepped down from the witness stand, the defendant, Angus Moon, tensed his manacled wrists and ankles. In retrospect, the only one who noticed the convicted murderer's edginess was Gray, the wolf–dog hybrid Sam had rescued from Moon's illegal breeding operation.

Sam wasn't testifying about Moon's operation. It was an extradition hearing. The crime Sam helped solve seven months earlier, up on the Iron Range, helped the Canadian Royal Mounted Police solve a 2005 double homicide in the Quetico woods. The Canadian crime had been stale until Angus's DNA fingered him as the executioner. Today, Sam's testimony was sending Moon to the bottom of a Canadian prison cell for the rest of his life.

But Sam should have known Moon would not go easily into his dark night.

For the entire 10 minutes Sam was on the stand, Moon's fiery gaze focused on him. Sam appreciated the tension.

On his return to the table, Sam answered his gaze with a look that said, *You deserve lethal injection, but we will settle for a 9-by-6 cage.* And that's what must have triggered him (though you never knew with Moon).

When Sam neared the defendant's table, he turned to Gray, tucked beside fellow USFW agent Mac McCollum, who held Gray's leash. Sam watched the big hybrid grow suddenly tense. And then the leash flew out of Mac's hand as though it was some kind of magician's trick.

Sam turned and glimpsed Moon halfway over the table, his cuffed hands sailing straight for him. Sam dodged left, too late. The woodsman caught his shirt, raging like a rabid wolverine, all guttural sound, not a clear word in it.

Sam twisted as he went down, spinning Moon, though he still held on. Then Sam hit the floor, hard, shirt buttons popping like firecrackers. The force of his twist flung Moon to the side and tore one of his hands loose. Sam rolled and kicked and heard the air blow out of Moon like a bellows. Then Gray was on top of Moon, all tooth and claw. Moon rolled, covering himself with his arms, protecting his head and neck, howling beneath Gray's lupine fury.

In the background, the judge was hammering, "Bailiff, bailiff, bailiff!"

The bailiff stood near, uncertain how to break it up.

Sam was on his feet and for a split second Sam thought Gray deserved a little payback. Wolf dog breeding operations weren't illegal in Minnesota. Moon's had been closed because it was cruel and inhumane.

Finally, Sam reached in and grabbed the back of Gray's neck.

"Gray!"

He pulled, but Gray was in some other place, trying to free himself so he could finish what he'd started with Moon.

"Gray!"

When the bailiff finally saw the hybrid pause, he danced in quick and put a knee in Moon's back. But Moon was spent, his breathing ragged.

"You're a . . ." he wheezed from the floor, "dead man . . . Rivers!"

Mac sprang up beside the crowd and started to pull Sam back. Sam grabbed Gray's leash. Gray was still focused on Moon, hoping for another chance at revenge.

The judge was hammering her gavel. "Order, order . . ."

But the fight was over.

In the adrenaline aftermath, Sam turned to Mac and said, "Looks like Gray got some back."

Mac looked pale. So did the overweight prosecuting attorney Charlie Carter.

Moon was disappearing through a side door, cussing like a devil. His only legible words were "dead man, Rivers . . . and that dog too!"

And then the door made a sucking sound behind him, like the surface of the River Styx.

The courtroom settled into an uneasy calm.

His testimony finished, Judge Stalter told Sam Rivers he was free to take Gray out of her courtroom, so they could both get some air.

Charlie tried to read the judge's response, but she was opaque. He hoped Gray's fury hadn't damaged their hearing.

There were still some motions to address, but Moon wouldn't be listening.

The judge decided it was time to call a brief recess. She stood up, shaken, and returned to chambers.

Sam's shirt was torn and, after he'd settled down, Mac said, "One second I was holding on, and the next Gray ripped that leash right out of my hand like it was spring loaded." Mac was excited and still a little pale. "Sorry," he added.

"I'm just glad Gray got his chance," Sam said.

Now that the judge was gone, Charlie said, "I think we're OK. Moon started it, so I can't see how she can rule against us." Charlie was whiter than Mac, but excited too.

"Nobody likes a dog beater," Sam said.

Mac turned to Sam and said, "Your elbow's bleeding."

Sam turned his arm to examine it. It was a scratch, but oozing blood. He'd need to tend to it.

"I can finish up here," Mac said. "I'll call you when it's over."

"Sounds good," Sam said, for the first time feeling his elbow throb.

"That was a little more than I bargained for on a Monday morning. It's never dull with you, Rivers," Charlie said.

"It's good for your circulation, Charlie."

"I take pills for my circulation."

When Sam turned to leave, he noticed a reporter in the back of the room.

Diane Talbott had her notebook out, writing with fury. Diane was the *Vermilion Falls Gazette* reporter who had covered his work seven months earlier on the Range. She'd gotten a lot of mileage out of the story. Out of Sam, too.

She looked good.

CHAPTER THREE

On his way out of the courtroom, Sam, with Gray, paused in the aisle and Diane looked up from her writing. She wore a long-sleeved, fitted T-shirt with a latticework of tree saplings silk-screened across its front. Her salt-and-pepper hair was tied back into a long, thick braid. She smiled and set her notebook on the bench beside her. It was a favorable sign.

As she stood, Sam appreciated her familiar substance; it had been more than six months, but it was easy to recollect the intimate moments they'd shared. Diane was more than 10 years older than Sam, but she was fit and strong and, other than a few streaks of gray, showed no signs of aging. She wore blue jeans cuffed at the bottom and a pair of hot-pink Converse sneakers.

Sam wasn't sure what to think when he saw her because their parting had been abrupt. By rights, she could have been cold; he hoped she would be something else. When she approached, smiling, he was heartened. But then he noticed her eyes focused on Gray, whom she hadn't seen since he was 6 months old.

"Gray," she said. "You sweet, sweet, grown-up boy."

In spite of his recent encounter with Angus Moon, Gray's attitude suddenly shifted and his tail started wagging. For thousands of years, wolves learned to be skittish around humans. But for Diane, Gray was all malamute.

Diane bent down, rubbed Gray's cheeks, and put her face to the big hybrid's nose.

Gray whined.

"I believe you just gave me the title for my article," she said. To Gray, not Sam. "Dog Finds Justice in Courtroom."

Finally done smooching Gray, Diane stood, tempered her smile and extended her hand to Sam.

"I'd love to read it," Sam said. Diane's eyes flashed brown and green and her grip felt strong and good in his hand, but cool.

"That was some kind of courtroom drama," she said.

"That was Angus Moon."

"That was Sam Rivers," she said. "Did you say anything to piss him off?" She turned to retrieve her notebook.

Always the reporter, Sam thought. "I was *thinking* he deserved lethal injection. But I suspect it was my grin that triggered him."

"Gray was getting even," she reached down and patted the big head. The dog was still breathing from all the excitement, his tongue hanging out. "This guy looks magnificent."

Gray stood beside Sam, obedient, maybe even regal. He had an oversized head, pointy black ears, substantial incisors, peculiar bicolored eyes, and a white muzzle mask. He weighed 90 pounds and stood almost 36 inches at the shoulder, medium-sized for a large breed of canine. Gray was living proof you could survive the torture kennels of Angus Moon and live to fight and thrive another day.

"He never ceases to surprise me," Sam said.

"The service letting you keep him?"

"It's a provisional trial. Magdalen says if I can get him up to speed as a search and rescue dog it would help his status. But she knows there are plenty in the service who think a wolf–dog hybrid sends the wrong message."

"Carmine Salazar?"

Carmine Salazar was an influential USFW accountant who had moved in with Sam's ex-wife. Sam thought Carmine was trying to get rid of Sam, too, and thought the best way to do it was to suggest that his overattachment to a wolf dog was a sign of undercommitment to the service.

Sam looked at Diane and remembered he'd shared a lot back in February. "Especially the bean counter. I think he's behind some kind of effort to get Gray blacklisted before he can prove himself."

"It'd be a shame." She gave Gray's big head another rub and Gray's eyes squinted. "I've got to get to the bathroom before the judge returns," she said. She peered at the bloody elbow. "You should tend to that."

She reached over and touched his arm, holding it carefully and turning it.

Her touch felt good, but there was an ache where the skin was bloody.

"Looks manageable," she said.

"Maybe we should have lunch later?"

She thought about it. "That might work."

Then they turned and Sam and Gray followed Diane out of the courtroom. Sam told her he'd call her around noon and they could figure out where to meet.

Once outside the courthouse, Sam and Gray walked around to settle down. The sun was high and the day warming. There were few places where a second summer was more appreciated than in Minnesota, where all the residents knew snowfall and a deep freeze were only weeks away.

He turned on his phone, and once it found service there was a beep, a message from his boss, Kay Magdalen.

"Rivers. Call me. It's urgent."

Sam wondered if she'd already heard about the courtroom scene. While he appreciated Gray's assistance in the fight, some would use it as proof Gray was out of control. Magdalen had more contacts than the National Security Agency, but Sam couldn't imagine she already knew about the outburst.

There was only one way to find out. He speed-dialed her number and waited.

Now that he was done testifying, she'd want him back in Colorado, just when he was starting to enjoy the beautiful Minnesota weather . . . and was looking forward to lunch.

Magdalen answered on the second ring.

"Rivers," he said.

There was a pause. "Do I hear traffic?"

Plenty of cars and trucks were pulsing along Robert Street. "Yeah, traffic."

"I thought you were testifying?"

"I'm done."

"How did it go?"

"Angus Moon tried to get a piece of me."

"Really? What happened?"

Sam explained the woodsman's table leap and near success and how Sam subdued him by placing a boot in his diaphragm. He left out Gray's rabid assistance.

"Glad to hear you kicked his butt."

"Well, the bailiff helped a little," Sam said.

"When will it wrap up?"

"Moon should be heading north later today. Tomorrow at the latest. Mac's still tracking it and will keep us informed."

"Good," Magdalen said. "Something's come up that needs your attention. You need to head over to a place called Savage."

"Savage?"

"Savage, Minnesota. It's a town. Suburb south of the Twin Cities. Looks like southwest of Minneapolis."

"I vaguely remember the name. What's up?"

"A mountain lion just killed some guy."

"What?" Sam said. "A pet?"

"No. They think it's wild. Some guy was mountain biking this morning down near the Minnesota River Valley, in Savage, and a mountain lion picked him off."

"A wild mountain lion?" Sam repeated.

"That's what I said."

That was unexpected. "Have mountain lions suddenly gone on a rampage?"

Last September, Sam and Gray investigated a lion kill of livestock at Mable Swenson's cattle ranch, 2 hours outside of Denver. It was dusk and the lion, protecting its kill, appeared out of nowhere and might have killed Mable if Gray hadn't interceded.

"When it rains it pours," Magdalen said.

"That's bizarre," he said. "Something like that happened out West with a mountain biker. In the Santa Monica Mountains. But there are a lot more lions in California. They're almost unheard of in Minnesota."

"Is that mountain bike incident in your report about that lion out at Swenson's place?"

"A footnote."

"Fascinating," she said, without conviction.

"So what do you need?"

"We need you to go over and have a look. The sheriff called the Minnesota DNR, looking for an expert. Got hold of a guy by the name of . . . just a sec." Papers shuffled. "Tom Bennigan. But Bennigan told him Minnesota hasn't seen a lot of mountain lions. So the DNR called the local Fish & Wildlife office. The local office said the same thing; none of those Minnesotans have ever seen a lion. But they checked the service database and found your report. So they called us. They wanted to speak with someone with a little background, who would know how to hunt down this killer. When they found out you were in Minnesota, they wondered if they could borrow you."

Apart from being genuinely interested, this could also work in Sam's favor. He was sure to miss lunch with Diane, but he thought, given the circumstances, maybe dinner was a possibility.

"Give me the details," he said.

Magdalen told him Sheriff Russell Benson wanted someone who knew wildlife to help them catch this killer. The victim was some kind of corporate bigwig, and the sheriff knew it would get plenty of publicity. And that would bring out the crazies. People with guns who hoped to shoot the man-killer. And others who would feel threatened and start calling local law enforcement, the DNR, and probably their congressman, looking for protection.

"Savage," Sam said, noting the address. "I think that's west of here."

"I guess. Along the Minnesota River Valley. Who in the hell names those Minnesota towns? Defiance? Savage?"

Until he was 17, Sam Rivers had lived in Defiance, Minnesota, the name of which prompted some ribbing from his boss.

"Norwegian bachelor farmers," Sam said.

"They had some kind of sense of humor."

"It was probably akvavit-induced," Sam said.

Magdalen also gave him the number for DNR Conservation Officer Bennigan, Chief Deputy Leif Anders, and Deputy Ole Sorenson. Sam could bring Mac up to speed when he was done in the courtroom, provided the sheriff would be open to more assistance.

On the drive to Savage, Sam tried to recall everything he could about his most recent encounter with a cougar. Mable Swenson had reported the predation of one of her calves and needed Sam to review and bless the kill, so she could file with the Department of Agriculture for reimbursement.

Sam and Mable had hiked with Gray out two dirt ruts that bent around Mable's barn. Mable cradled a lightweight Remington 700 AWR .30-06 with a scope, and she knew how to use it. She was a small woman, wearing worn jeans and a work shirt. There was a pack of Marlboro reds in her breast pocket. It was early September, still plenty hot around dusk. Mable had sweat spots under both arms and dirt on her jeans. She wore a tattered straw cowboy hat over scraggly shoulder-length gray-brown hair. A pair of weathered black cowboy boots completed her ensemble, like a fashion statement for the working, undersized cowgirl market.

There was a gulch a quarter mile back that cut through her property in a jagged north–south diagonal.

"It's out there." She pointed in the distance to where a huge cottonwood grew near an outcrop of rock.

Sam and Gray followed her through the cattle-grazed field.

It had been a dry summer. The grass was thin and crackly. Wisps of dust kicked up around their feet. Gray walked quietly beside them, scanning and sniffing the terrain.

"For a young one, he's damn quiet," Mable said.

"He doesn't say much," Sam agreed. "But when he does, he's serious."

Black Angus cattle grazed off to the right. Gray looked up and followed them with his eyes, intent, but keeping his patient stride next to Sam.

As they neared the rocky outcrop, Sam peered over the huge, rounded boulders that formed the near edge of the gulch. Just beyond and to the left of it, the branches of the cottonwood towered over the gulch, its canopy stretching above the big rocks.

"Cougars get a little possessive about their kills, Mable. Particularly at dawn and dusk, when they return to feed."

"This one killed yesterday at dusk, I think," Mable said. "Looked like it leaped down from those rocks, broke the calf's neck, and then dragged it to the bottom of the gulch to feed."

"Killed and fed last night, and you found it this morning?"

"That's right."

"Did you find anything other than tracks?"

"Just the tracks. You'll see. And what's left of the calf. It ate most of its insides—heart, lungs, some gore."

"Good. Let's be quiet. Maybe we should split up and take both sides of that outcrop."

"Suits me."

"You head left. Gray and I can turn around the right side. If you see something, stay still."

"If I see something, it's dead."

Sam knew she had the right. "Just make sure you know where you're aiming."

"Damn straight."

Sam hated to see a magnificent animal shot, but if it was killing livestock, there were only two alternatives: capture it alive or kill it. And at this point, even Sam Rivers wasn't going to lasso a cougar. They were lions, and they were accomplished, aggressive killers. Unlike their African cousins, cougars didn't gather in prides and share in the hunt. Neither did they share their kills. After cougars grew old enough to leave their mothers, they lived a solitary life, only coming together to mate. They were one of North America's most lethal predators. "Did you know you can scare off a cougar by windmilling your arms and screaming?" Sam said.

"Did you know you can stop one with a bullet?"

"I'm just saying they're easy enough to scare away," Sam said. "They're not like grizzlies."

"My daddy taught me how to shoot before I could read. Taught me anything pestering our cows gotta be stopped."

Mable's perspective was typical of ranchers. Sam suspected if it were his livestock being killed, he might feel the same way.

"We'll meet at the bottom," Sam said, starting to veer toward the right side of the outcrop.

"At the bottom."

They split apart and started walking in opposite tangents. The rise of rock ran along the gulch edge for 40 yards. The highest boulder climbed to more than 15 feet, but there were plenty of different-sized rocks marking the cliff face with dark crevices. In the dusk, the tan-colored stone was a beautiful yellow-gold. The crevice shadows were accentuated and growing darker. Sam scanned the boulders, but in the dusk light, the rocks were solid and still.

Sam and Gray made a wide arc, starting to circle the right side. Mable walked to the left. As they approached either end of the ridge, they turned and signaled to each other through the waning light, then disappeared around the outcrop.

Picking his way along the rock edge, Gray suddenly appeared edgy, tense, at full alert—as though he smelled something. The only thing Sam's dull nose detected was a whiff of carrion. In the day's heat, the calf carcass had decomposed, sending an acrid odor out of the gulch. Sam peered down into the ravine and spotted the remains tucked into a shallow grave under a creosote bush. Two ravens were pecking at a protruding leg. The black birds must have heard his approach. They paused and cocked their heads, peering at the intruders.

The ravine's sides weren't more than 10 or 15 feet, gradual and covered with sparse bunches of mountain mahogany and scrub oak. Sam paused and brought Gray to heel, waiting for Mable to appear along the other side. As soon as the ravens saw the big hybrid, they rose squawking into the dusk light.

Sam turned to watch them, then turned to look for Mable.

Then he saw it.

On the far end of rocks, there was one large boulder. Near the top, Sam glimpsed something peculiar. It had too much symmetry to be part of the boulder wall. It was the outline of a feline head. With sickening comprehension, his vision assimilated two pointy ear spikes and brown fur. The head was still, intent and focused— Sam guessed on Mable. The head remained watching, while the rest of the animal's body coiled tight as a spring.

It all happened in less than an instant: the sudden realization that it was a lion and was probably getting ready to leap on the unsuspecting Mable, and his scream.

"Mable!"

Then a dark blur shot away from Sam's side. Sam watched in horror as a denim mound toppled into the ravine. Gray's shape fired along the gulch edge like a rocket, closing the distance between him and Mable's tumbling body. Sam saw Mable's rifle tumble into scrub oak. The cougar materialized out of rock. It must have leaped and either knocked Mable to the ground, or Mable tripped and fell at the moment the lion was ready to pounce. The diminutive woman was sliding headfirst down the hillside. The lion paused at the edge, recognizing vulnerability, beginning to recoil, getting ready for another leap, this one lethal.

And then Gray hit it broadside. There was a tumble of fur and howling and a bone-clattering death growl. The cougar let out its own curdling scream.

The big cat leaped out of the brawl like something fired out of a cannon. It took two steps before springing into the lower branches of the cottonwood. And then Gray started baying.

The mountain lion, 10 feet aboveground and in the safety of the tree branches, scooted up a few more branches, curled around, turned, pushed one big paw out of the leaves, made a quick swipe into the empty air, growled once more, spit a little anger, and then grew still, watching Gray intently. Gray turned, bayed, and turned again to get another look before finally settling down and focusing on the big cat.

By the time Sam reached the tree, the cat realized its predicament. It was outnumbered. It moved a little higher into the branches, trying to conceal itself, focused on the business below. Sam retrieved Mable's gun from the scrub oak bush. Mable managed to climb to the top of the gulch at the same time Sam arrived with her rifle.

"Goddamnit . . . goddamnit!" She was sputtering and out of breath, but otherwise looked OK. A little shaken.

Sam stared at her, looking for damage. He still didn't know if she'd tripped, or if the big cat had knocked her down. Now she was breathing hard. It was a lot of excitement. Mable Swenson's face was tomato red, and once she collected herself, Sam knew, she'd be ready to tear something apart with those calloused hands.

"You OK?"

"I'm gonna kill that motherfucker!"

She was OK. "No, you're not," said Sam.

"Fuck if I'm not."

Sam whistled Gray into a sit. The hybrid backed off and came to heel but never took his bicolored eyes off the creature he'd chased up a tree.

Before Mable had a chance to turn ballistic, Sam opened the Remington's bolt and checked to see it held a cartridge and was still operational. Other than a little dust, the rifle appeared unscathed. He snapped it shut, flicked off the safety, and raised the rifle to his shoulder, steadying it in the dusk light. He peered down the scope's magnification, scanning to the right, then to the left, until he found a patch of brown fur. Then he moved carefully up the animal's flank until he was staring at its eyes. The cat peered back out of two black pupils set in a pool of iridescent gold and green, startling and beautiful.

"Sorry," Sam said. Then he moved down to the animal's heart and fired.

The Colorado cougar fell out of that cottonwood like a bag of hammers. Gray was on it, but Sam quickly pulled Gray off. Sam hated killing such a magnificent animal, but it had killed livestock and attacked Mable, so he didn't have a choice.

As Sam drove toward Savage, he considered how bizarre it was to encounter a mountain lion–human predation in this state, where there were very few of the big cats. Colorado's lion population was around 5,000, sizable enough to support a hunting season. But Colorado had only one recorded lion–human predation, and a few minor encounters, like Mable's. Still, if the mountain lion was too old or enfeebled to hunt its usual prey—in Minnesota, white-tailed deer—it might search for easier quarry. But a man on a mountain bike?

There *had* been an incident involving a mountain bike on a trail in the Santa Monica Mountains, outside Los Angeles. But it was unclear if it was actually predation. The man had a heart condition and some investigators wondered if he died of a blown ticker before the big cat found him. Mountain lions could also be opportunistic feeders.

On the other hand, a mountain bike racing through a big cat's territory could be mistaken for a running deer. Lions were also territorial. The cat could have lashed out at what it considered an intruder.

Regardless, in the Santa Monica Mountains, a man had been downed on a mountain bike and partially eaten. And then, within 24 hours, a female mountain biker near the same location was attacked and was being dragged by her helmet into some scrub oak when her friends caught up with her and beat the lion off.

In the wild, mountain lions were nocturnal and incredibly reclusive. But near urban areas, their behavior could be unpredictable. A couple years ago, Sam had read David Baron's *The Beast in the Garden*. It was ostensibly about an Idaho Springs, Colorado, high school senior who was attacked, killed, and partially eaten by a mountain lion while jogging in the foothills at the edge of town. But it also discussed incidents that Boulder, Colorado, residents had been having in the days and weeks leading up to the high schooler's death. When the deer began frequenting Boulder backyards, mountain lion behavior changed. The lions became emboldened and there had been some scrapes between people and the dangerous cats. And then the jogger in Idaho Springs had been attacked and killed.

Like the predation to which he now drove, it reminded Sam that regardless of how civilized and settled we had made America, once you stepped off the grid into places where predators still roamed, you had better cultivate a wary eye. And no place was as dangerous as the wild–urban interface, that zone where people enjoyed the wilderness but were still close enough to civilization to be lulled into a false sense of safety and security. Or worse, they were so firmly planted in the civilized world that the idea of a wild predator exercising its position on the food chain was beyond imagination.

Sam was glad Gray, with a proven mountain lion nose, was along for the ride.

He stopped once to get gas and change. Then he called Diane. When he got her voice mail, he said, "I'm afraid lunch is off, but I'm hoping you're free for dinner. I think it might be worth your while." He paused, suddenly realizing she might take that the wrong way, and added, "I'm working on a bizarre emergency I know you'll want to cover. I'll call you as soon as I can. Dinner's on me."

He hoped that was recovery enough. He also wondered, briefly, if dinner might lead to something more, but he wasn't sure he was ready for it. Not yet.

Almost 14 months earlier, Sam's seven-year marriage to Maggie Caldrot ended in divorce—her decision, not his. Three months after the papers were signed, he'd still hoped for reconciliation.

Then he heard Maggie had moved in with that weasel Carmine Salazar, and it finally put a stake through his heart.

Last February, Sam was called back to his boyhood home on northern Minnesota's Iron Range, where his work investigating a wolf kill of livestock had brought him face-to-face with his estranged father, who he'd thought was dead, and his father's lawless friends, including Angus Moon. The truth was, recovering his childhood and putting Moon and the others behind bars had helped Sam regain his emotional center. He and Diane had paired up to investigate what happened on the Range. But that was months ago.

They'd had their moment, and it had passed. And then he'd had to return to the Denver office.

Sam had no experience with reunions with old girlfriends. So he tried to put it out of his mind. But it was hard not thinking about Diane, who had on more than one occasion stood in front of him wearing only woolen socks.

CHAPTER FOUR

Nearing Savage, Sam noticed the political signs. It was an election year. There were mostly names he didn't recognize, but as soon as he crossed Interstate 35W, he noticed the sheriff's signs.

REELECT RUSTY BENSON

SCOTT COUNTY SHERIFF

Keeping Scott County Safe for 20 Years

(Paid for by the Committee to Reelect Russell Benson for Sheriff)

Interestingly, there were almost as many "Bob Lawson for Scott County Sheriff" signs. Lawson's campaign slogan was "Time for a Change."

It was tough to unseat an incumbent, particularly in a sheriff's race. But judging from the number of Lawson signs, maybe the sheriff was facing some stiff competition.

Sam kept heading south on 13 until he found the frontage road, turned onto it, and noticed a covey of official cars and a big white-and-blue emergency vehicle up ahead. There was a black-and-white Savage police car, two Scott County sheriff's cruisers, and a green DNR truck. He counted five officers and what looked like two ambulance workers in a confab cluster, probably talking about the craziness of a prominent local businessman being killed by a cougar. The sheriff's car was blocking a minimum-maintenance road. The rear doors of the ambulance were open, with a collapsed gurney inside. On the gurney, Sam saw a body covered with a white sheet.

If that was the victim, they had already messed with the kill scene. And if they wanted to advertise the killing, they were doing a good job with that covey of police cars and the ambulance and the flashing lights. The media wouldn't be far behind.

From the front seat, Gray stared fixedly at the commotion.

"Better put on your game face, buddy."

Gray turned at the words, then looked back to consider the scene, intense and interested.

Sam pulled to the side of the road and stepped out of his jeep. The huddling heads turned and looked, and a boyish deputy peeled away and started walking toward Sam. Judging from his face, he appeared to be in his late 20s. He was thin, small, and had short-cropped brown hair. There was something familiar about him, but Sam couldn't place it.

"Can I help you?"

"Sam Rivers."

The deputy didn't recognize the name. After the incident with Angus Moon back at the courthouse, Sam had changed out of his uniform. And he was in his own vehicle, a Jeep Wrangler, not a USFW truck.

"Special agent with Fish & Wildlife," Sam said.

The deputy's eyes sparked and he extended his hand. "Ole Sorenson," he said, a little shy. "You're the cougar hunter?"

"I've hunted some," Sam said.

Sorenson glanced at the dog in Sam's front seat, then back at Sam. The officer had intense gray eyes. His hair looked like it had been shaved with number 3 poodle clippers. He had large ears and an aquiline nose, and was lean as a fitness instructor.

"Then you know a lot more than anyone around here. Most of us have never seen a cougar, except in a zoo. Including the DNR and your local Fish & Wildlife guys."

"Mountain lions are rare in Minnesota, but not unheard of."

"Got some ID?" the deputy asked.

Sam opened his wallet and Sorenson examined his badge.

"Then we have a rare one causing problems," Sorenson said. "The sheriff's crossing his T's. He called up the DNR. They sent over a conservation officer, ah . . ." He reached around and pulled out a small tablet, glancing at it. "The CO is Tom Bennigan. The sheriff also called the Minnesota Bureau of Criminal Apprehension, who sent over some crime scene techs with Lieutenant Cole. Everyone's already checked it out. But the sheriff wanted someone who at least knew something about cougars and would know how to catch one. It's hard to believe in this day and age people can still get killed by a wild animal."

"It's uncommon, but it happens. Sharks, snakes, bears, mountain lion . . . It's good to remember we share the planet with some efficient predators."

"I guess. I've just never seen anything like it."

"It's definitely unusual, particularly near a populated area. Mountain lions usually have the good sense to keep their distance, at least from humans."

"Is that what they call them out West? Mountain lions?"

"Generally. But they go by a lot of names. Cougar, puma, panther, catamount, mountain lion."

The deputy nodded. "Well, it happened about a quarter mile down this road." Sorenson indicated the two dirt tracks blocked by one of the sheriff's cruisers. "It starts to get pretty wild down there. We can hike it."

"No one's driven it?"

"Nothing but a gurney. The gate's locked and the road's too narrow and rough for our patrol cars, or the ambulance."

Sam glanced at the back of the emergency vehicle. "Is that the victim?"

"That's him. Jack McGregor."

"Shouldn't have moved him."

The deputy looked up. Sam thought he blushed.

"I guess not," Sorenson said. "But he's been dead for a while and the crime scene crew is finished, and the sheriff and chief and the DNR guy all thought it was best to get the victim off the ground before any media could get in and take a photo. The sheriff's a little worried about the public's reaction and he still needs to notify the victim's wife." The deputy's face and neck were definitely red.

"Uh-huh," Sam said. "It would have been good to see the intact scene. Did you take photos?"

"Yes," the deputy nodded. "Lots of pictures."

"Where's the sheriff?"

"He's still down there. It's a hike and he didn't want to make it twice."

"The DNR guy with him?"

Sorenson nodded. "And Marlin Coots, the night watchman who found the body. And Chief Deputy Anders. They're all down there. Once we heard an expert was on the way, they decided to wait."

The fall day was turning hotter, but not too hot. You could not order a better late September day in Minnesota.

"Can you radio your boss?" Sam asked. "Tell him it'll be a little bit. First I want to look at the victim. And I want to make a slow walk of that road. Probably another half hour or so."

Sorenson's face appeared worried, but he nodded and said, "Sure." Then he stepped across the road while he reached up to his hand radio. He clicked it once. "Sheriff, you there? Over."

There was a pause, then, "Course I'm here. Where the hell else would I be? Where's the cougar guy? It's getting hot."

"Uh, just got here," Sorenson turned away, talking low. "He's going to have a look at McGregor. Then we'll be down. Over."

"What for? Just tell him to come down."

"I need to examine his wounds," Sam called over to the deputy.

"He wants to take a look at the wounds. Over."

"Oh, for Christ's sake. We need him to hunt the animal, not examine the corpse. Just tell him to get his butt down here."

Sorenson's flush deepened. "Ah, OK."

"We're burnin' daylight," the sheriff said.

Sorenson hesitated, then said, "We'll be right down. Over and out."

You never knew about county sheriffs, Sam thought. Sometimes they made excellent partners, like Dean Stoddard, the Vermilion County sheriff who helped him solve the crimes up north seven months earlier. But some, particularly those who had been sheriffs so long their judgment was seldom questioned, could be autocratic, or even despotic. Others were as crooked as a $3 bill or as prickly as a Joshua tree. Or both.

"The best way to catch a predator is to study what it left behind," Sam said, ignoring the sheriff's comment and the red-faced deputy. "If you know what it does when it hunts, you know what it will do."

Sorenson just nodded.

Sam walked over to the ambulance and pulled down the gurney sheet. The victim's face was bloodless and cold, with a waxy pallor and no spark in the half-closed eyes. His black hair was long enough to have a side part, with a little gray splintering his temples. The skin on the left side of his neck was torn and soaked in congealed blood. Judging from the position and size of the wound, Sam guessed the man's carotid artery had been severed.

It wasn't the first time Sam had examined a corpse. The death mask almost always summoned a strange complex of emotions. Sam felt empathy for the victim and his relatives and friends, and a kind of grim humility. Sam was still alive and able to observe death with all his senses, as though a curtain had been drawn and for a moment he was given a glimpse into something increasingly rare in modern life: Few people ever saw the stark reality of a dead body, particularly of someone whose life ended early from violent circumstance. These tragedies were whisked away and cared for by professionals not associated with the family. Then they were turned into ashes, or carefully dressed up and made up, all in an effort to minimize death.

A life cut short from such a terrible encounter demanded Sam's humble reverence and attention.

The victim wore a bright-yellow biking shirt and black biking shorts. The back and side of the shirt were soaked in blood. There was dried blood in the wound and down the side of the victim's neck, under which Sam could see a little bruising on the top back of his left shoulder.

Sam pulled the sheet all the way down. The body had the strange stiffness of a person who had been dead for at least 4 hours.

Sam remembered the mountain lion back at Mable Swenson's place. Once he was certain the big cat was dead, he had examined it, lifting its rear leg, checking its sex. Male. Its paw lifted and dropped as though death had brought on absolute relaxation. The animal had been transformed from a tapered length of coiled sinew and muscle to wobbly Jell-O wrapped in brown fur.

The victim in front of him had been dead long enough that his muscles and limbs were rigid and inflexible. Rigor mortis. He appeared to be about 50 and, apart from an extra inch or two around his middle (most men his age had more), looked strong, fit, and healthy.

But now he was dead.

Remembering the mountain bike kill in the Santa Monica Mountains and the suspicion it could have been a bad ticker, Sam guessed heart problems had nothing to do with this man's demise, though you could never be certain. The autopsy would verify the tenor of the man's heart, or at least the quality of its muscle.

The cycling clothes were expensive, including a pair of high-end, specialized white-and-black biking shoes. Sam noticed the Cannondale logo on the clothing. He remembered Magdalen saying he was a bigwig.

"Who is he?" Sam said.

"Jack McGregor," Sorenson said.

"My boss mentioned he was someone notable."

"He owns McGregor Industries. That includes all this land on either side of this road, a lot of land down by the river, and that potash and fertilizer distribution facility just over the ridge."

Sam thought about it. "Where's his bike?"

Sorenson paused. "Still down there, I think."

"Good," Sam nodded. The two ambulance workers were standing nearby. "Can you guys help me flip him?"

They looked at Sorenson and the deputy nodded.

The blood across much of the victim's back was sticky. There were puncture wounds through the top of the shirt and around the left side of the neck where a bite had made wide, tearing holes that had bubbled blood until it coagulated. The bite was consistent with a cougar's mouth structure. Mountain lions have four long canine teeth embedded in lower and upper jaws that can open to an angle of nearly 120 degrees. The jaws were wide and strong enough to easily hold or even crush a prey's neck or head. Near the back of the jaw, they have razor-sharp carnassials. Sam thought he remembered mountain lions had 28 teeth, all well designed for the purpose of catching, tearing, killing, and eating.

It appeared one of the fangs severed the man's carotid artery. Sam guessed he'd bled out in a matter of minutes. There was a nasty bruise along the left side of the neck that stretched across the top of his shoulder. So the blood had been flowing long enough to create a bruise, which meant maybe he was hit first and knocked off his bike?

Some skin was torn along the base of the skull and below it. There was a serious scrape on his right shoulder with some dirt and grit still embedded in the yellow nylon. The real damage was beneath the skin, to the neck, which appeared to be broken. The slight twist and the puncture wounds were real enough. The big animal, if that's what did this, got lucky with the carotid artery.

Sam had never seen a human killed by a mountain lion. He'd seen pictures of wounds from survivors. And from what he recalled, these wounds were plausible. There was a rake of claws along McGregor's back and claw marks along either side of his arms, on the outside and back, as though the big cat grabbed McGregor with its forearms while biting into his neck. The lacerations hadn't bled much. All the blood had come from the carotid.

He'd have to wait for the coroner, but maybe the cat's jaw snapped the man's neck while severing his artery, and then after he bled out, the mountain lion made the scratches? Sam wondered about it.

Down below, there was a clean incision in the victim's bike shorts, four evenly spaced slices that cut deep into skin and muscle. Sam guessed the cat's rear claws easily parted the high-grade spandex while making several deep cuts into McGregor's right and left hip muscles. Again, he noticed the wounds seeped blood, but not much. Judging from the location of the wounds, it appeared the animal dropped onto McGregor or attacked him from behind.

The fang and claw marks appeared real enough, but there was something bothering Sam.

In the cases of the Colorado jogger and the California biker, who were each apparently attacked and killed, both had been fed upon. It was important to remember these were wild animals and the reasons they killed were pretty simple. In each of those mountain lion kills, the humans' bellies had been slit open, almost as though the incision was made using a surgeon's scalpel. In both instances, the lions made the cuts to open the chest and stomach cavities, to feed on the heart, lungs, and internal organs.

An interesting behavioral anatomical characteristic of predatory cats was how careful they were with their claws. Mountain lion claws were like incredibly sharp scalpels, but they were only extended to fight, to kill, to cut up their victims and feed, or to mark territory. All cats were similar in this regard; when they were not using their claws for one of these limited uses, they retracted them. Even house cats.

The marks on McGregor were only kill marks. It didn't appear as though the big cat ate anything. Apparently, McGregor had been killed and left. And from what Sam knew about lion kills, that was unusual. Unless someone had scared the cat off before it could feed.

"Who found him?"

"Marlin Coots, the night watchman."

"When was it?"

"Marlin makes his morning walk of the perimeter around 8. That's when he found him."

Mountain lions typically hunted during transition points of the day—sunset or sunrise. If this happened around sunrise, it would have put the kill a little after 6, almost 2 hours before he was found.

"Would there be anyone else down there around dawn?"

"The night watchman doesn't think so. He says there's a loading dock near the place where the victim was found, but the dock workers don't start until 9."

If the man was attacked at dawn, as gruesome as it was to consider, a cougar would have fed. Especially if the kill site was secluded and quiet. It was another anomaly that made Sam wonder.

"So did the watchman . . ." Sam paused. "Did Marlin Coots see the mountain lion?"

"He'd seen it, but not this morning."

"He'd seen it before?"

"About three weeks ago, he photographed it, right down near where McGregor was attacked. It was in all the papers and on TV."

Sam thought about it. "Did he see anything else?"

"Nothing. No cougar. Nothing but McGregor lying dead and bloodied beside his toppled bike. And some tracks, hair, stuff like that."

"Tracks and fur?"

"Yes, there's some tracks. And the BCA—the crime scene guys—took some fur."

"You kept the fur?"

Sorenson nodded. "Those guys did. They put it in a baggie. They're going to test it."

"Good." Sam looked at the two ambulance workers. "You can turn him back over and cover him," he said.

He turned back to Sorenson. "Let's walk that road and have a look."

CHAPTER FIVE

The shy deputy nodded. He hadn't known what to expect from the USFW cougar expert, but the man was being thorough.

Sam returned to his jeep and opened the passenger door. Gray stepped down and walked a few paces to the edge of the weeds. He sniffed, lifted his leg, and left his calling card, at least in the canine world.

"That's a big dog," Sorenson said.

"He's still a youngster, but getting there."

Gray looked up and gave Sorenson a shy sniff.

"Looks like a wolf." Sorenson reached down very slowly and took one easy step forward. Gray bent his head and considered the deputy warily.

"He's a hybrid," Sam explained. "Half Arctic wolf, half malamute."

Gray sensed nothing untoward in the slight man and eased.

"He's a working dog. Or at least I'm training him to be one. Sit, Gray."

Gray sat and stayed while Sam reached in and pulled a shoulder bag out of his jeep. "Heel," he said. Gray eased up and came alongside Sam. Sorenson nodded to the gaggle of officers who turned and watched the USFW agent and the big hybrid walking toward the road. One of them nodded, but it wasn't warm. Two others considered Gray with a cautious expression. Lawmen could be as territorial as wolves.

The three of them turned around the blocking patrol cruiser and came to the shot-up NO TRESPASSING, PRIVATE PROPERTY sign. The gate was heavy-gauge iron, padlocked with a rusted chain. The lock hadn't been opened in a while. There was an easy dip in the path around one side. Sam noticed a lot of dirt bike tire tracks—thick tires with big treads. He paused for a moment and knelt to examine them. They appeared to be from the same bike. There were also boot prints in the dust. Gray stopped behind Sam, and Sam told him to stay. Sorenson was ahead, already turning up the lane.

"These bike tire tracks," Sam said, calling ahead. "These all from McGregor?"

Sorenson stopped and turned. "I guess. Marlin Coots said McGregor comes down here almost every morning to ride through the river-bottom woods. Used to, anyway."

"What about the boot tracks?"

Sorenson looked quizzical and came back a short ways to consider the tracks, apparently for the first time. "Probably Marlin's, but could be the sheriff's, the chief deputy's, emergency workers who brought down the gurney, the crime scene guys. Maybe the CO," he said, looking up. "We've had a lot of traffic here."

"It's a regular convention."

"I guess."

"Anyone photograph them?"

The deputy shook his head. "I don't think so. All the pictures were taken down at the site where the accident happened."

Sam set down his shoulder bag and pulled out his digital SLR with the 200 mm micro lens. The camera's body with its oversized lens was big and heavy, but it captured everything within range.

Sorenson paused, considering Sam. He watched him focus and snap, focus and snap again. If the sheriff knew the cougar hunter was wasting time taking pictures of boot prints, he'd blow a gasket.

Sam could feel the deputy's attention. He glanced up, and Sorenson met his gaze.

"I see seven, maybe nine different prints here," Sam said. "Maybe more."

Sorenson looked again and shrugged. "I guess," he said. "Marlin says people come down this road once in a while. Does this have something to do with the cougar hunt?"

"What kind of people?" Sam asked.

"Bird-watchers. Duck or grouse hunters looking for easy access to the river. People scouting good locations for deer hunting stands."

"What about the NO TRESPASSING sign?"

Sorenson glanced over. "People aren't supposed to come down here. And people aren't supposed to pass beyond this gate. But they do. Particularly, Marlin says, since they spotted the cougar down here earlier this month. Prowling its deer kill."

"When was that?"

Sorenson thought for a minute. "Earlier in the month. Can't remember exactly. Marlin could tell you. Do you think the cougar came all the way out here?"

Sam stood up from his kneel, called Gray out of his sit, and they both joined Sorenson on the road. He kept the camera out, strapped around his neck. "I doubt it, but you never know."

Again, Sam thought, a lion sighting in the vicinity prior to this morning's tragedy confirmed the recent existence of an apex predator. And it had killed a deer. That could mean it was protecting its meal. But three weeks, if it was in early September, was a long time to be feeding off a kill. He'd have to ask Marlin about it and see his photos. And he'd have to check out that deer carcass, if there was anything left.

The two dirt tracks stretched straight 200 yards, fading into a gradual left turn. Sam glanced up and peered at the country. To the right it was flat, open, and covered with late fall brush and just a few trees, some of them dead, probably from occasional flooding. Beyond the open country stood a line of trees in the distance— what appeared to be a mix of box elders, maples, and cottonwoods. The river's edge, Sam guessed. Down the left side of the maintenance road there was a 50-foot ridge rising out of a wide canal. The canal was man-made, probably flood control, but that was a long time ago. Now the surface of the water was 40 feet across and wild, with occasional lily pads and cattails skirting its edge. Up off the rise, he could see a long, steady peak of what must have been a pile of potash or fertilizer or both.

The air was redolent with the pungent smell of witch hazel and the slightly fetid, iron scent of the water beneath it. Red-winged blackbirds twilled from the cattails, and Sam watched a pair of wood ducks rise off the canal water and whistle over the pasture grass, winging toward the river.

He reached up with the camera, focused down the long road, and snapped one last photo before returning the camera to his shoulder bag.

Gray sniffed around the area. Sam thought he paused over something, but it was probably the unusual smells of Minnesota. The dog was used to Colorado and the West, though maybe Gray remembered some of his homeland, since his first few months were spent in northern Minnesota, in Angus Moon's hell kennel.

There'd been a lot of foot traffic down this road. And there were gurney tracks in the ruts.

Sam glanced up again to take it all in. It was a beautiful day in beautiful wild country.

But not for Jack McGregor.

"So what do you know about McGregor and his company?" Sam asked Sorenson.

While they covered the 200 yards and made the gradual turn toward the loading dock, Sorenson told him about McGregor Industries, and what he knew about Jack McGregor, a prominent Savage citizen. It wasn't much. Sheriff Benson and Chief Anders knew more, Sorenson said, because McGregor and his wife were active. Not exactly in local politics, but in chamber of commerce stuff. McGregor participated in organizations and efforts that were good for business. Mrs. McGregor did occasional charity work. Chief Anders had done some private security stuff for McGregor events, so he'd gotten to know them a little better. Sorenson explained to Sam about the white-tailed deer kill found earlier in the month, Marlin Coots and his triggered night photographs, how the papers and local media ran with it, and now this.

"So the body was close to the deer kill?"

"Almost directly above it. The deer kill was in the bottom of a ravine. I can show you when we get up there."

They made the wide turn, and up ahead Sam saw a huge oak rising from under the hill. The two road ruts continued straight. Across from the oak tree, the edge of the road dropped into river-bottom woods. There were four people waiting up ahead, three sitting on a log in the shade, and one leaning against the big oak. All of them were watching the two men and Gray approach.

Mountain lions could only eat so much in one sitting. Like many predators, they would kill, gorge, and then try to conceal what was left. They often returned one or two days later to feed again. Meanwhile, they'd keep an eye on the source of their next meal. But not for three weeks, unless the big cat was old or infirm. And if it was being driven by hunger, why hadn't it fed on McGregor?

The walk in the growing heat of the day made both men damp with perspiration. Gray walked beside them, occasionally sniffing and examining the trail, the rise of bush to the left and the ravine to the right leading to thick woods and the river beyond. As they neared the oak, the three men stood up off the log and waited. There was a perimeter of yellow tape wrapped around a large rectangle, just beyond where the men stood. A white mountain bike was leaning against the oak.

Two of the men wore tan khakis. The man beside them wore forest-green khakis. The DNR guy, Sam guessed. The two tan khakis were the sheriff and the chief. The man against the tree was big and rangy and wore gray and dark blue. Marlin Coots, Sam guessed.

One of the tan khakis had a thick mane of red hair and a big handlebar mustache. He was short, like Sorenson. But his belly pushed out the lower buttons on his shirt, taut as a belted watermelon. The black gun holster was comically askew, probably from the walk, or from sitting on that log. The chief or the sheriff? Sam wasn't sure, but he guessed the sheriff, given the man's age and the way he stepped in front of the others.

The other officer was tall and slim, with a good build. He had a military buzz cut. He looked to be about Sam's age, maybe a little younger.

The DNR guy was the same height as the sheriff, but young and fit. He wore his hair long and parted on the side, and was just a kid.

As they approached, Sam watched Marlin push off of the tree. He had a name tag and an insignia across his breast pocket.

The sheriff stepped forward, a little red-faced now. He looked irritated.

Sam ordered Gray into a sit.

The sheriff shook Sam's hand, considering him. "Sheriff Russell Benson," he said. "People call me Rusty."

"Sam Rivers."

The sheriff introduced Sam to Deputy Chief Leif Anders and DNR Conservation Officer Tom Bennigan. Then he turned slightly and said, "And this here is Marlin Coots, the man who found Jack McGregor."

Marlin greeted Sam by raising one big, awkward hand in the air. The name tag over his breast pocket said MCGREGOR INDUSTRIES. He had a large head and a flat face with big eyes.

The sheriff had sweat marks spreading under his arms and his brow was shiny. Marlin, DNR officer Bennigan, and Chief Anders all appeared unfazed by the heat or the hike.

"So the local DNR and your Fish & Wildlife don't know squat about cougars, at least in Minnesota," the sheriff started, a remark that caused the younger Bennigan to frown.

All the men in turn considered Gray, who remained obedient, but watchful.

"They're rare in Minnesota," Sam said.

"That's what I'm hearing. Officer Bennigan and Marlin have been filling me in. This one's been here awhile."

"So I heard." Sam looked at Marlin, but the big man just stared.

"You from Colorado?" the sheriff asked.

"Yes. Out of the Denver office. I was in town testifying at an extradition hearing."

"An extradition hearing? Someone smuggling bird feathers?" The sheriff snorted.

Everybody grinned. Sam smiled too, but said, "Angus Moon was wanted on two counts of murder in the Ontario woods."

"Was he a Canuck?"

"Dual citizenship."

"A goddamn Canuck. It figures."

"I don't think Angus Moon swore allegiance to anything."

The sheriff considered the comment, but said, "You service guys don't believe in uniforms? You check his ID?" he asked Sorenson.

"Yessir."

The sheriff turned and reconsidered the agent and his dog. "So I hope you have more experience with cougars than your colleagues."

Sam gave him the CliffsNotes. He'd authored the *Rocky Mountain Cougar Report*. The cats were more plentiful in Colorado, with frequent sightings and occasional livestock and pet kills. He didn't mention the human predations. There was a hunting season in Colorado. He told them about Mable Swenson's place and the animal he'd shot.

"Well, I hope you brought your weapon because it appears there's another killer on the loose."

Sam nodded. "I see that."

The sheriff paused. "Here's the deal, bud. The crime scene guys have already been here and left. Got plenty of evidence and took plenty of photos. Now I'm no expert on wild animals, which is why we called you in. But I can read a scene easy enough. This one looks like some crazy cat got the better of Jack McGregor. I don't know why. I don't know if it was sick or hurt or it was just plain bad luck. I know it's ugly and I know it's tragic and I know the family. So all I'm looking for here is for you to find this cat and kill it. Sooner the better. Because I still need to notify the man's wife and his business associates and then the damn media. And I can tell you after the news picks it up, it's going to be all we can do to keep the gun-toting crazies out of the woods, trying to join you in your hunt for this hellcat."

The sheriff paused.

Sam could tell Benson was used to the stage and appreciated quick, law-and-order decisions.

"Maybe you should mention to the news organizations that mountain lions are a protected species in Minnesota and only authorized personnel will be allowed to hunt the animal," Sam said.

The sheriff was startled, briefly. "Now that's just the kind of thing I wouldn't mention. If *your* relative was just killed by a wild animal, you think people want to hear a branch of the US government is protecting it?"

Sam shrugged. "Just thought it might help you keep the crazies out of the woods."

"I appreciate your input, counselor," the sheriff said, but there was nothing appreciative about it. "Now me and the boys have been talking about it and we think the best thing is to hunt this cat down right off, find it and kill it by the ten o'clock news."

Sam nodded again. The sheriff looked at Gray, who was sitting behind Sam Rivers, occasionally sniffing the interesting air.

"He a cougar hunter?"

"Not exactly, though he could definitely pick up the cat's scent. He's in training to be a service dog."

"Training? We need experienced hunters, not trainees."

"I shot a cougar last September," Sam reminded him. "Gray tracked and treed it before it had a chance to attack a woman.

I suspect right now that's more experience than anyone in Minnesota."

The sheriff considered the comment. "So he can track him?"

"Gray can track anything, if he has a proper scent."

"That what you do in Colorado? Run them down with dogs?"

"I don't. But a lot of hunters take that approach. Others use calls."

"Calls? What kind of calls?"

"Usually distress calls. Like a dying rabbit. But it works better out West, where it's more open. Here, the tree cover would restrict how far the sound traveled."

"So Officer Bennigan here says he knows a guy with coon dogs, so maybe that's where we start. You fellas and your dogs can run this cat down so we can let the Busy Betties know there's nothing to be scared of and it's safe to come out of their Savage homes."

"We can help," Bennigan offered. "I can phone my guy."

The young conservation officer appeared excited by the prospect. And Sam knew if it was a mountain lion, it would probably be nearby. Mountain lions were mostly nocturnal, so even if it had a 3- or 4-hour head start, it shouldn't be far off. But so far, he hadn't seen enough to determine *what* happened here. And in these river-bottom woods, coon dogs would find plenty of raccoons, which could distract them from the lion's trail. The only animal that had smelled a mountain lion was sitting quietly behind him. But Sam had no idea how Gray would react on a hunt with a bunch of coon dogs, particularly running through dense woods after dark, if it took that long to find the animal.

Sam needed time to look around and think.

"OK," Sam nodded to Bennigan. "Tell the guy to get down here with his dogs. The sooner the better. If it's a mountain lion—cougar—it shouldn't have gone far."

The sheriff's eyes grew quizzical. "*If* it was a cougar?"

Sam looked at him, but didn't say anything.

"What in the hell do you think it was, the Boggy Creek Monster?" asked the sheriff.

The other men grinned, but the sheriff didn't.

And neither did Sam.

"Marlin here's got pictures of the cat, taken less than three weeks ago. And like I said, I'm no expert, but it sure looks like a cougar. That right, Marlin?"

Marlin nodded.

"Earlier this month there was a confirmed cougar sighting and a deer kill right down in that ravine," Bennigan pointed.

Sam glanced at Bennigan, but was thinking he didn't care for the sheriff. The red-haired hothead wouldn't be the first local lawman he'd disliked. He ignored him and asked Bennigan, "Anything left of the carcass?"

Bennigan and Marlin both nodded and pointed back behind him across the road. "Bones and hide, mostly," Bennigan said. "It's pretty picked over."

"Right down in that ravine." The sheriff's arm pumped twice for effect. "Probably less than 50 feet from where this victim was killed."

"I'll have a look at it," Sam said. Then he turned to the sheriff. "After I take a look at the rest of the scene."

"This scene's been examined enough. We know what happened here. Now we need to find the animal and kill it."

"When you're hunting predators, the best predictor of what they'll do is what they've done. This one's killed twice, right where we're standing. So I'm going to spend a little time getting to know it before I run off into the woods with a bunch of dogs and a loaded weapon. You OK with that?"

The sheriff took a step closer to Sam, not backing down, and said, "This is what I want: that goddamn cat dead by the ten o'clock news. I don't give a rat's ass what you do to get it done, as long as it happens. Poison it with pork chops, if you have to. Just get it done."

Sam returned the sheriff's stare and thought of a couple comments, but finally said, "Your deputy mentioned they'd found some fur?"

"The BCA guys took it," the sheriff said.

After staring hard at Sam for another 10 seconds the sheriff finally said, "You can spend the next 10 days looking over this tragic accident, and I know in the end what you'll find. A wild cat came out of the woods and killed Jack McGregor. Now that's what I'll be telling his widow and his employees and the media, who I suspect will be down here by the time we get back to the cars, nosing around like a pack of jackals, wanting to know what in the hell's happening."

The sheriff stared at Sam and paused to give him a chance to respond.

"OK," Sam said.

"Good." Then he added, "I don't know what it's like in Colorado, but over here we don't waste time looking over what we already know. If it walks like a duck and quacks like a duck, it's a fuckin' duck. Just kill the fuckin' duck."

Sam knew if he pointed out some of the anomalies he'd already found, it would turn the sheriff's face as red as his hair. He briefly considered it, just to watch the fireworks. But instead, he said, "Like I said, Sheriff, the best way to catch a killer is to examine what it's done and then follow the trail it left behind."

The sheriff stared at Sam. "You do what you gotta do," he said, irritated. Then he looked at his deputy chief.

"So here's what I'm going to tell people. We have some 'expert hunters' tracking the animal, and we need to keep the vigilantes out of the woods. I'm going back to the car and make my calls, which I'm not exactly looking forward to. That work for you, Sherlock?"

Sam appreciated the difficulty of letting the man's widow know, and his colleagues and employees, and especially the media. But he couldn't, and wouldn't, do anything until he had a chance to examine everything. For now, he just nodded. But he thought a cuff upside the sheriff's head might knock some manners into him. Tick him off, too.

"Great," the sheriff said.

Before the sheriff could turn more flushed than he already was, Bennigan said, "I think we can be in the woods with dogs by late afternoon. Maybe earlier. We'll get him," he assured.

Sam nodded. "If it's a cougar, we should be able to find it pretty fast."

There it was again, Rusty thought. *If.* This cougar expert was pissing him off, but he didn't have time to deal with him. He wasn't looking forward to his visit with Carla McGregor. But while he had waited for Sam Rivers, he'd considered the situation. He *was* looking forward to the media, particularly if tomorrow morning his comments were backed up with a dead cat. This'd be good for his campaign, and there wasn't anything his opponent, ex-deputy Bob Lawson, could do about it.

"Just get the SOB," the sheriff said. Then he turned and nodded to Sorenson and Anders, wanting them to walk with him. The sheriff was careful to give Gray a wide berth, stepping around the sitting hybrid, whose back hair bristled.

Twenty yards up the road, the three men stopped. The sheriff turned his back to Marlin, Sam, and Bennigan. The deputy and chief deputy listened to the sheriff's muffled comments. After a couple moments, the sheriff and chief deputy turned and kept walking up the road, while Sorenson started back.

Bennigan said, "I'll go call that hunter with the dogs. It'll be awhile. The guy's up in Coon Rapids."

"You do that," Sam said. "I'll look over this scene and the deer carcass, and Gray and I can try to pick up a scent. The sooner we get into those woods with some hounds, the sooner we can verify the sheriff's suspicions. How long you think it'll be?"

"Probably late afternoon," Bennigan said. He considered Gray. "That looks like one heck of an animal."

"He is," Sam said.

Bennigan took a too-fast step toward Gray, and the hybrid's eyes grew intense.

"He has to be introduced," Sam said. Then he brought Gray out of his sit and let him smell Bennigan's hand, then Marlin's.

"What's with the eyes?" Bennigan asked.

"It's just a pigment thing," Sam said. "Makes his eyes bicolored."

"What is he? Part German shepherd?"

"A wolf–dog hybrid. Malamute and Arctic wolf."

"I heard they can be . . ." Bennigan thought for a moment, "a little difficult. A little wild."

"That's true," Sam said. "But wild can be useful in the Wildlife Service. Sometimes we go to some pretty feral places."

Bennigan nodded. "I better get going," he said, turning to catch up with Sheriff Benson and Chief Anders.

Sorenson approached and Sam guessed he was going to have a minder, which was just fine with Sam. He could use a little help, and Sorenson was easier to work with than his boss. Maybe Sorenson could give him some information of his own, about the sheriff and his reelection bid and whether the bad manners he'd just experienced were typical or just campaign jitters. Sam also knew the deputy would be along to report back everything Sam said and did. That could be useful too, Sam thought.

Sam turned and considered Marlin, who looked away, a little shy. He thought about the night watchman's name. A big fish, and waterfowl. Easy to remember. Apparently, Marlin's parents loved the outdoors or had a sense of humor, or both.

"Let's have a look at this site," Sam said. "Then we can go down and examine that carcass."

CHAPTER SIX

The call came in at 11 a.m. Urban had been waiting for it.

"Yes?"

"It's done," Benedict said.

"Why haven't I heard anything?"

"Law enforcement. First a deputy. Then the sheriff. Then the BCA. Now some wildlife guy."

"Wildlife?"

"Arrived about an hour ago. He's an agent with the U.S. Fish & Wildlife Service out of Colorado."

"You mean he was in town?" Urban said.

"At some hearing over in St. Paul. I guess he knows something about cougars."

"Is this something to worry about?"

"No," Benedict said. "He's an animal guy. So what?"

"I don't like the unexpected," Urban said.

"He's a tree hugger. He'll see what they've all seen. Prints. Hair. Real cougar wounds."

"Got a name?"

"Rivers. Sam Rivers. He's got some kind of dog with him."

"What kind of dog?"

"A dog, I don't know. Some kind of German shepherd?"

"You don't like dogs."

"I hate dogs. But I don't have to get close to this one. And if he gets too close to me, he's a dead dog."

Urban wrote down Sam's name. "Anything else?"

"The sheriff just returned to his squad car. We should be hearing something soon. And with all these official cars, the news can't be far behind."

"It's taking longer than we thought."

"About what I'd expect when a wild animal kills a prominent citizen. I can always put in a call to Fox. That'd get the newsies down there."

Urban thought about it. "Might raise more questions."

"I was driving by, saw a lot of cop cars, thought someone at Fox would be interested," Benedict suggested.

"They'd have your number. Even though it's a throwaway, I still don't like it."

"Suits me."

There was a pause. "So what about John?"

"What about him?"

"Was he helpful?"

"I thought he was going to shit himself. But when the time came, he did what was necessary."

"Do we have to worry about him?"

"I don't have to worry about him. But if I were you, I'd be worried. He's going to want what he's been promised. Sooner rather than later. He wants it so bad he can hardly think straight."

"That's not what I'm worried about. It's what he'll do later, when things aren't going his way."

"John is your problem. I just need to know the money will be there, where and when it needs to be."

"But he's a loose cannon and we both know loose cannons can do crazy things."

Benedict laughed, but it was more like a muffled hiccup. "If it's any help, I got what we used. His prints are all over it."

Urban paused. "That wasn't the plan."

"The plan was to take care of it. And I will, when the time comes."

"When you get your money."

"When we're all free and clear."

But that wasn't the plan. Urban knew men like John. John was predictable. Benedict was different.

"What about *your* prints?"

"My prints aren't on it."

Benedict was smart. "So, insurance."

"Insurance for both of us, depending . . ."

"We won't need it."

"But we got it if we do," Benedict added. Then, "Like you said, when things stop going his way, hard telling what the little prick might do."

There was a long pause. Then, "All right. Just keep an eye out. Find out what you can about this Rivers guy. I don't want any surprises. But no more calls on this line unless it's serious. Use the email."

"OK," he said, and hung up.

Urban had no idea what a wildlife guy from Colorado was doing on the scene, but Benedict was probably right. The sheriff was being thorough, and that could be a good thing, provided they all saw it was a cougar. And why wouldn't they? The physical evidence was real.

Five minutes later, Urban was still contemplating the development when the phone's display lit up. John. And he'd used his personal cell. Urban considered ignoring it, but knew he would persist.

"Use the throwaway," Urban answered.

"Wait! It's dead. Must be the damn batteries or something."

"So replace the batteries or use the email."

"Wait, goddammit."

"The longer we're on, the more they can find."

"They're not gonna find anything. Even if they got my phone, they'd see a number at the other end that led nowhere."

"Don't be stupid."

"No one's going to find out." Then, "We don't need him. Cut him loose."

"There may still be . . . things to do."

"Like what? It's done. Whatever else comes up, I can handle."

"So why haven't we heard anything, John? Can you tell me that?"

"How should I know? It's the authorities and it's Jack McGregor. It'll hit the press like a firestorm."

"But why nothing yet? It's been 5 hours."

John shrugged. "That watchman probably didn't find him until after 8. Then he'd have to go back, call the cops, people would have to get down there and have a look. I bet they got a book about this kind of thing. A playbook. They're just following their playbook."

"A playbook about a CEO getting killed by a cougar?" Urban said.

"About a guy getting killed. It's their killing playbook. Anytime it happens, they open the book and follow it, chapter and verse."

Another pair of hands had been necessary, but Urban always considered John expendable. John was insurance, if it became necessary. But his overly simplistic logic had to be managed. Urban needed to shake him up.

"Does that playbook call for an agent from the U.S. Fish & Wildlife Service having a look? Because right now there's an agent from Colorado examining the scene. That in the playbook?"

"How do you know that?" John said.

"Because I'm keeping any eye out." Urban knew it would anger him.

"Benedict tell you that?"

There was a long pause, during which neither of them spoke.

Then John said, "I'm telling you that guy's dangerous. He's a control freak."

"He's useful."

"What the hell does that mean?" John had heard Urban say it before, about Benedict's usefulness. The first time he'd heard it, it got under his skin. Now that he guessed Urban was still using Benedict, relying on him instead of John, it both angered and unsettled him. "You better be careful. Because I'm telling you he's trouble. Benedict is a son of a bitch."

Before John could add anything else, Urban said, "Stick to the plan. Any other surprises, use email," and the phone went dead.

It took 5 minutes for the redness to fade out of John's face. By the time it did, he realized Urban was right, but it didn't help. His mood after he had taken his shower—when he was starting to feel good again, thinking about life after Benedict—had turned.

Just be cool, he told himself.

But he wasn't really feeling it.

CHAPTER SEVEN

"The sheriff's a little stressed," Sorenson said as the three men approached the yellow rectangle of tape.

"Yeah?" Sam said.

"It's the fall election. For the first time in two decades, he's got a tough race."

Sam briefly considered making a contribution to the opposing candidate's campaign. But he didn't give money to politicians and he wasn't going to let Rusty Benson ruin his perfect record.

"He's not normally like this," Sorenson added.

They came to the edge of the tape and Sam stopped.

Sorenson and Marlin came up to stand beside Sam. Marlin was a big man, slow and deliberate. He seemed shy or maybe thoughtful. Gray appeared unconcerned, or comfortable with Marlin.

Sam was still trying to figure out if Gray's reaction to a person was an accurate assessment of the person's character. In Sam's line of work, he occasionally dealt with bad people. When Gray encountered someone Sam considered to be of dubious character, Gray's back hair bristled, and he made a guttural growl. Sam wondered if the hybrid smelled evil. But Gray had been shy with Mac, and Mac was one of the good guys. Now his comfort with Marlin indicated . . . what? Sam guessed he'd have to wait until he got to know Marlin better before he figured out if Gray was a good judge of character.

"He's running against Bob Lawson, a deputy Sheriff Benson fired two years ago," Sorenson continued.

"OK," Sam answered, though it still didn't change his mind about the sheriff. "I appreciate the context. But frankly, I'm a whole lot more interested in figuring out what happened here than in the sheriff's reelection bid."

The deputy blushed. "Sure," he nodded.

Sam slipped off his shoulder bag and pulled out his camera. "Marlin, when did you photograph the cougar around that deer carcass?"

"September 2," Marlin said.

"September 2?" Sam repeated.

The big man nodded. His hands were dinner plates.

"Pretty good memory," Sam said.

"It was the Monday after payday," Marlin explained. "I had money for the camera and sensor."

"Digital?"

Marlin nodded.

"Still have the photos?"

He nodded.

"Good. I'd like to see them."

"OK. The papers only wanted the one. It's a pretty good shot. The others only show part of him, or are a little blurry."

"I remember," Sorenson said. "I saw it in the paper and on the news. You could tell it was a cougar."

"I'd still like to see them all," Sam said.

Marlin nodded.

"Can you guys just talk me through this?" Sam dipped under the yellow tape. "Probably best if I go in alone, since you've both seen it. But tell me what you think happened."

The rectangle of yellow tape started at the tree and ran 20 feet down the road before it ended in a 10-foot strip. Sorenson said Lieutenant Cole and the BCA guys thought McGregor was biking toward the loading dock, as he did most mornings, when he was attacked from behind. He was knocked to the ground, and that's where the animal bit into him, clawing his arms and back and severing his carotid artery, maybe breaking his neck.

Marlin and Sam stayed outside the tape, but Marlin pointed out where he'd found McGregor and where most of the blood had seeped into the ground, and where the cougar's paw prints were pressed into the dirt. The crime scene guys found a good tuft of fur stuck to a nearby thistle. Another 10 feet down the road was where Marlin had looked down onto the white-tailed deer.

Sam snapped photos and carefully stepped down the weed-covered center rut. He took photos of bike tire tracks, several boot prints, a place where it appeared some part of McGregor hit the ground hard—probably his cheek, Sam thought, remembering the grit he'd seen on the dead man's face. And then he took several photos of the paw prints, one front and one rear. Finally, he snapped a broad shot that caught the thistle plant in the background and the trees beyond.

Sam didn't say anything until he was done. Then he shouldered the camera and turned around from the place where McGregor had been felled. He peered down the road from the direction they'd come, lost in thought.

Gray sat in regal silence, attentive, his eyes on Sam, familiar with his process.

Sorenson and Marlin watched. After he didn't say anything for several seconds, continuing to stare, Sorenson said, "Do you want to . . ."

But before he could finish, Sam held up a silencing hand, as though he was trying to hear something and wanted absolute quiet.

After a few minutes peering down the road, Sam turned and looked out at the river-bottom woods, thinking, listening. There was an uncomfortable 3, maybe 4, minutes of silence during which Sam did nothing but stare.

It had always been this way with Sam on a kill site. It didn't matter if it involved a human being felled by a mountain lion or an owl swooping down on a field mouse. Ever since he was a boy, he'd been entranced by wild drama. Being a biologist, he knew there was a scientific explanation for his sudden absorption. When he saw the remnants of a life-and-death struggle, it struck Sam in some primitive, deep place in his brain, triggering an adrenaline rush as though he was a current participant in the past-tense battle. Sam had long ago figured out how to channel that rush into an enthralled, almost hypnotic fascination. It was . . . strange.

He was a biologist, and he could describe all the physiological aspects of the process. But the only explanation he could summon for why it happened to him was much more mysterious, something buried so far under consciousness it reached back to a time before memory. He suspected it involved a brutal father (for whom he still felt some vestige of inexplicable love) who tried to mold him into something he wasn't. And a mother who recognized his love for wild animals, but not the killing of them. His mother knew how he felt because she felt it too. But she had lacked the power necessary to support and nurture his love of wild places.

In a way, Sam's intense interest in life-and-death struggles was because he felt them in himself, trying to reconcile a father who sought to dominate the natural world with a mother who sought to live in harmony with it. The intensity of that emotional conflict sometimes drove him to the bottle or to just walk away, or both. The last time he'd grown uneasy, then unbearable, he was with Maggie. She'd pushed him to try to understand what he was feeling, to go to the source of it, to articulate it. But it was far too opaque and complicated. So he left. It was the easiest thing to do, for them both. He disappeared. Into the mountains. For two weeks. Alone.

That was the beginning of the end of his marriage, and he couldn't say he blamed her.

Since confronting his criminal father last February on the Iron Range, Sam thought he'd turned some corner, that recovering his childhood helped. But lately he'd felt that old familiar twinge of uneasiness, and maybe the sad realization that you don't recover from a childhood like that. You do your best to recognize it, try not to act out of it, and maybe even use it, as Sam did now.

Sam had listened to everything Sorenson and Marlin told him while he examined the scene, and then used it to deconstruct and then reconstruct what happened here, to the best of his abilities. It was a movie. An intense scene of life-and-death drama. What Sam now saw, as he paused to let his hypnotic absorption flow, startled him.

"The victim," Sam finally said, coming out of it. "McGregor. He biked down here a lot?"

"Every morning, when the weather was OK and he was in town," Marlin said.

"Anybody else ride with him? Or anyone else use the trails?"

"No," Marlin answered.

"Why not?"

"It was private. It was Mr. McGregor's private trail."

"Who knew he biked the trails?"

Marlin paused, thinking about it. "Everyone, I guess. A local magazine did an article about CEOs staying in shape, and there was a piece in there featuring Mr. McGregor and his mountain bike trails."

"I remember that," Sorenson said. "It was in *Minnesota Monthly*."

"All these footprints, Marlin," Sam said, indicating the treaded-over ground. "These were made after you found him?"

Marlin thought about it. "Yeah. Some are mine, I guess, from before. When I saw Mr. McGregor lying on the road."

"When was that?"

"A little after 8. I came down this road right after Cammy replaced me. She's the day watchman. Woman," he corrected himself.

"And you came from that direction?" Sam asked, looking down the road.

"Yeah."

"Did you see anyone else? Anybody nosing around, or a car parked up there?"

"No."

"Why do you come down here after your shift?"

"My shift's over at 8:30. My last duty is to come down here and check the perimeter, all the way to the loading docks."

Sam turned and looked up the road. He could see what looked like an opening and the start of some kind of dock facility 200 yards ahead. "That the dock up there?"

"Yeah."

"And the morning you found the deer carcass . . . September 2." Sam thought about it. "It was a Monday?"

Marlin nodded.

"And you found tracks below?"

"There was one right around the deer, but it got trampled over. I think there are still a couple prints in some runoff down below. In a dry creekbed."

Sam turned to consider him. Marlin was an amateur naturalist. Sam had met them all over the country, whenever he headed into wild places. They were out-of-the-mainstream types who made a living as truckers or tradesmen. But they were more interested in wilderness and what it contained and stood for than just about anything else. And they were matter-of-fact about it. Setting up a motion-activated camera to capture an image of a cougar wasn't typical behavior for a night watchman. And he seemed to have a natural respect and feel for Gray, letting the hybrid grow used to him, giving the animal comfortable space.

"Did you take any pictures of the tracks?" Sam asked.

"Yeah. The next day."

"And you thought they were mountain lion tracks then, before it was confirmed by the night photo?"

Marlin nodded.

"Why?"

Marlin had to think about it and Sam had to help him. But only a little.

The heel pad of a cat print had three rear lobes, and two in front. And it wasn't just cougars. Leopards, lions, bobcats, jaguars, even house cats. They were all different sizes, but their paws' symmetry was the same. With regard to tracks, a feline was a feline.

After Marlin finished describing the prints, Sam looked up. "I guess you know your tracks, Mr. Coots."

Marlin shrugged. "I guess."

"So when you examined the paw prints up here," Sam said, "did you think they were the same as the ones you found below?"

Marlin shrugged. "I guess."

"Take another look."

Marlin bent to look, and so did Sam.

The first track appeared to be the right rear foot. It had the characteristic four toes and the center pad. More often than not, you couldn't identify the bifurcated front lobe of a cat's center pad. This one was incredibly clear. And there were four stiletto claw points at the tips of each toe. That was wrong, Sam knew. Or at the very least, extremely rare, for a cat. Any cat.

When Marlin stood up, he paused. "I mean, we've never seen any cougars down here. Or any other kind of cat, for that matter. Bobcats or whatever. At least before this. I guess the cougar who killed the deer could have had a mate. You think this one could be a different one?"

"Doubtful. But the prints down in that creekbed. Did you see claw points at the tips of its toes?"

Marlin considered. Then he shook his head no. "I don't think so, but I have pictures."

Sam had already photographed these prints and knew if Marlin's photos were good, he'd be able to do a print analysis.

Finally, Sam looked at his companions and said, "Let's have a look at that deer carcass."

CHAPTER EIGHT

Sheriff Benson hated house calls, particularly when he had to deliver such awful news. The worst part of a sheriff's job was telling a family member someone close to them—a child, parent, or spouse—was dead. Telling mothers their child had died or children their mother had died was the worst of the worst. But receiving that kind of news about *any* family member inevitably resulted in some degree of shock, then terrible sorrow.

Over the years, at sheriff conferences, the best way to handle dreaded house calls was always a subject of conversation. But house calls usually happened after traffic accidents, not after a prominent citizen was murdered by a wild animal. The thought of it made the sheriff shudder.

It also reminded him of that damn cougar guy, Rivers. The sheriff reached down and radioed the office.

"Dispatch."

"Jim, get me Myrtle, would ya?"

"Will do, sheriff."

The sheriff waited.

"Myrtle," she said, coming onto the line.

"Can you call Lieutenant Cole over at the BCA and tell him we need a quick analysis of that fur sample taken from the McGregor Industries site?"

"I can do that."

"The minute they confirm it was a cougar I want to know about it."

"Will do," Myrtle said.

"Good," the sheriff said, and clicked off.

The evidence, which the sheriff knew would come back cougar, would give him the definitive proof he needed to cease the second-guessing by some wannabe nature-enforcement guy.

Sheriff Benson turned off Chester Drive into Wannamake Circle, knowing how he would tell Carla McGregor her husband had been attacked and killed by a cougar. The only way to deliver it was straight up, point-blank. Begin with a sober apology. Then lay it out in as few words as possible. But the thought of it never sat well with him, and in this instance it was worse because he had known both the victim and his stunning wife.

The McGregors recently donated $1,000 to his campaign. It had been last July, and it surprised the sheriff. There was an incident last spring in front of McGregor's facility—an ex-employee, drunk and disorderly, causing problems at the company's gate. Chief Deputy Anders handled the situation. Jack had personally called to thank the sheriff, and the sheriff said, "That's what we're here for, Mr. McGregor." Normally, that would have been the end of it.

Less than one month later, his committee received the donation. Arlene, his wife and secretary of the committee, fired off the
usual thank-you note with an invitation to a meet and greet at the
Dan Patch Coffee Depot in the center of Savage, never expecting
Jack would show up. But he and Mrs. McGregor surprised the hell
out of him a second time. They both stopped by for coffee and a
little chitchat with the sheriff and Chief Deputy Anders, and it
was hard not to remember them, cheerful and happy on the coffee
shop's patio.

Jack had presence and power and a CEO's confidence. And
Carla was . . . well . . . younger and about as damn perfect in
body and face as the women he'd seen in some of Arlene's fashion
magazines. The sheriff was trying to remember the conversation,
which wasn't much more than a handshake and a comment about
the coffee.

When wives were along, you had to be careful about mentioning money, in case the women didn't know about it. But Sheriff
Benson was so startled by the McGregors' visit he spoke before he
caught himself.

"We really appreciate your donation, Mr. McGregor."

Jack smiled. The man's teeth were solid as ivory pegs. And he
had a damn hard grip.

"Don't thank me," he laughed. "That was Carla's idea."

The sheriff looked surprised. He extended his hand to Carla.
"Well, thank you, Mrs. McGregor. We do appreciate it."

"You can call me Carla, Sheriff," she said, reaching to shake
his hand. She nodded and shook Anders's hand too.

"And I'm Jack," McGregor said. "And for the record, I thought it was a good idea. It was just our way of saying thank you for taking care of that trouble we had down at the plant."

"As I think I mentioned before," the sheriff said, "that's what we're here for."

And that was about all of it, the sheriff thought, driving his cruiser to the bottom of Wannamake Circle. He and Anders had both been commenting on Mrs. McGregor's beauty when Arlene asked, "What are you guys talking about?"

It was a rhetorical question. Arlene could see Carla McGregor attracted men's attention like a tractor beam.

"How great you look in that dress," the sheriff said, knowing she'd recently purchased it for this event.

"Uh-huh," she said, doubtful.

The sheriff had never been in this part of his district, where every house was a mansion and the security-system signs were ubiquitous. There were only five houses near the circle's bottom, all with spacious yards and impressive fronts. The McGregors' had a half-circle drive that turned in front of a pair of white pillars with a large glass lantern hanging from an eave above a paneled red door. The front was redbrick, two stories high with perfectly appointed windows and a three-stall garage. The sheriff wondered if they had kids, and then remembered Arlene told him about their wedding, which she'd read about five, maybe six years earlier in the *Savage Current*. Something about a local Savage scion marrying a model. Judging from the absence of accompanying children at the coffee shop meet and greet, he guessed they were childless. Hoped so, anyway. Staring into a toddler's eyes would make the news he had to deliver much more difficult.

The sheriff pulled into the McGregors' drive and parked his cruiser near the front door. He got out of the car and approached the house, hesitating for a second before pushing the front bell. A gong echoed through the house. Like a death knell, he thought. Then he heard footsteps and the door opened.

"Sheriff Benson," Carla said, surprised. She extended her hand. She wore a pair of tennis warm-ups. There was a TV on somewhere in the house, behind her and to the right. Probably the kitchen.

"Mrs. McGregor," he said, taking her hand.

She must have noticed something. When she took her hand away her face changed, and she said, "Carla. Call me Carla." Serious.

"There's been an accident," the sheriff said. Straight up and point-blank, he reminded himself.

Her face fell an octave. And then she said, "Come in, Sheriff. I don't know where my manners are." And she turned and left the door open.

"Down at Mr. McGregor's facility," the sheriff continued.

She turned. "What?" she said.

"Mr. McGregor had an accident."

"Jack?" she said.

"Jack," he paused. "I'm sorry."

"How bad?"

"I'm afraid . . ."

She stared at him for an uncomfortable few seconds. "What?" she asked.

"Jack was bicycling behind his plant early this morning and was attacked by a cougar." In all his years of law enforcement he'd never delivered such crazy bad news. It was surreal. "He was down that remote road behind the plant. Near those woods by the river."

"Is he OK?"

"I'm afraid not. The animal caught him in the neck and . . . I'm terribly sorry."

Her face suddenly paled. "He's . . . ?"

The sheriff recognized her question, though he knew she hadn't asked all of it because she was afraid of the answer.

"I'm afraid Jack is gone."

She was stunned. "What?" she finally said. "Are you sure?"

"It happened sometime this morning. A cougar attacked him and . . ."

She turned and started toward the TV sound. Then she stopped. Then, "I've got to . . ."

But she never finished her words.

A low sound came out of her throat, like a desperate animal.

"I'm sorry," the sheriff repeated.

"Jack?" she said, as though calling him. "Jack?"

She took two steps, stopped again, then disappeared down the hallway and returned with some tissues. She came back, a little stunned, uncertain. Disbelief was settling into her face.

There was no easy way with news like this, the sheriff knew. The best thing he could do was stay silent and offer whatever solace she was willing to accept.

"I can't believe . . ." She was shaking her head. There was a quiver in her voice. And a whine. "A cougar?"

It wasn't a question, but before he could say anything, she added, "I told him." Her tissue-filled fist came up to her mouth. Her eyes were wet. "I told him they'd seen a cougar down there. I told him to be careful. But he said it was crazy. The idea was crazy."

She turned and walked down the long hallway into a rear family room. The sheriff followed. The room had a large rear picture window that opened to a second-story view over trees. There was a small stretch of yard between the window and dense woods. Carla dropped onto the sofa, mute, clearly in shock. There was a TV across from her, but it was dark. From the TV in the kitchen, two women discussed cheddar cheese, and then one said something and they both laughed.

"If there's anything I can do," the sheriff offered.

Carla was staring at the low coffee table in front of her. But she didn't appear to be looking at anything. She was stunned.

After an awkward silent minute, the sheriff said, "Is there any family? Do you have a mother or a sister? Someone you can call? Or we can call for you?"

Carla kept staring. Then she seemed to hear him. And she laughed. "Sheriff, my mother . . ." Then she paused. "No. No one. Jack has a sister, but they aren't close."

"Maybe a friend?"

"Yes," she said. "I can call someone."

"And I'll need your permission to have Jack examined by the coroner. Whenever there's been an unusual accident, the coroner will have to examine him. It's just a formality."

"Of course."

"And I will need to make a statement to the media. And if it's OK with you, I'd like to speak with some of his employees, let them know what happened."

"Yes, of course," she said, barely audible. Her gaze remained fixed on the coffee table. Her eyes were red rimmed and teary. She brought the tissue to her face and dabbed. The white tissue was blackening with mascara. Her face was pale as frosted porcelain.

"The coroner's office will call you when they've finished."

She nodded, just once.

"Well then, Mrs. McGregor, I'd better be letting folks know." The sheriff shifted on his feet, getting ready to turn and leave.

"Yes," she said, vacantly.

As he turned, he heard her shift on the couch. He glanced back and saw her looking at him, her face still broken up. The sheriff suspected it would be a while before the red went out of her eyes. "Thank you, Sheriff," she paused. "I'll wait for the call."

"It shouldn't be long, Mrs. McGregor. Call your friend."

She nodded, dumbstruck.

The sheriff stepped down the hallway and let himself out.

He stopped on the front step and took a long breath. The worst of it was over.

Inside, Carla gathered herself. After she had put her awful early life behind her, Carla had become the kind of woman who knew what to do next—the right step, the proper action. But now she was in uncharted territory, a devastating landscape. She listened as the sheriff's cruiser started up and then turned out of the drive.

After a couple minutes, she dried her eyes and walked into the kitchen. She shut off the TV and the house fell silent. Then she picked up the phone.

"The Club," said a receptionist.

"Tennis," she said.

"Just a moment, please."

Another pleasant woman answered the phone, "Tennis."

"Could you please give Jared a message for me? This is Carla McGregor."

"Certainly, Mrs. McGregor."

"Can you please tell him I'm canceling my afternoon lesson?"

Carla heard shuffling papers on the other end of the line.

"Sure." There was a pause. "Here it is. Three o'clock. Did you want to reschedule? He fills up pretty fast."

"Not now. Can you just give him the message?"

"Will do, Mrs. McGregor."

She thanked the woman and hung up.

Then she checked her watch. It was 12:40. Solar noon was 12:48. She had time.

Carla descended the basement steps and entered the rear furnace room. The room was unfinished, with storage shelves filled with rarely used items: Christmas decorations, blow-up mattresses, snorkeling equipment. The wooden gaps between the studs were filled with insulation. Jack never visited here, which was why it was the perfect location for her divination tools.

She stepped to a side wall, reached in behind the insulation, and, in the recess, found her Pescia paper, charcoal, and the ancient leather pouch containing three octahedral dice.

Then she climbed the stairs back up to the kitchen, which at solar noon would have the most light.

It was 12:43. Five minutes.

She laid the paper on the black granite countertop and used the charcoal to draw a seven on the cream-colored paper. Then she drew a 7-inch-diameter circle around it. She opened the worn leather pouch and tumbled the dice into her palm like three dark stars.

She'd discovered the dice years ago, in an old curiosity shop in San Francisco's Haight. She'd been suicidal, crazy with what had been until then the worst year of her entire 18 years, none of which she wanted to remember. But you didn't forget a childhood like that. You never forgot.

The dice shook out of the pouch, comforting in her hand. The dice had always provided comfort.

"Those are cleromancy dice," the proprietor had explained. "You use them to divine the future. They were carved out of bone. Powerful magic."

Carla was skeptical but willing because if she could figure out how to foretell the future, she could figure out how to take more careful steps in life, particularly with regard to men.

Her past was strewn with abusive predators as far back as she could remember. And they were the worst kind—all of them in positions of trust. A father first, though she was too young to remember him well. Then the Catholic orphanage. Then the Father. Then she ran. But until she was 16, she hadn't been able to stay away for good . . . or keep away from the Father.

But at 18, she'd been two years on the run and now she was old enough. She no longer needed to look over her shoulder.

The dice had helped. She'd spent her 20s mastering their use. They weren't always right, but lately . . .

Carla centered herself and waited.

12:45.

Over the years, she had established her ritual, informed by ancient texts: the right time, the right objects, the special paper and charcoal, the 7-inch circle, the number, and the right frame of mind. You had to cultivate an inner stillness. In spite of today's tumult, she forced herself to be calm, grew centered. She knew she needed to be calm as a millpond, still as death.

Dawn, solar noon, and dusk—the three best times to throw the dice. She had missed the dawn toss, and she'd grown anxious for noon's approach because she wanted to see what the dice foretold. The dice were comfort. The dice were solace. Only when her life's events dictated the need, or she was searching for insight.

For the last month, they had been prophetic, remarkable, stunning in all aspects. She had been on a magical roll. Each of the specially carved dice had eight sides, containing the numbers one through seven, and on the eighth side, one die had a moon, one a sun, and one a star.

A throw that came up with all three celestial bodies was extremely rare.

But in the last four weeks, Carla had tossed the auspicious reckoning no less than four times.

And was today's tragedy—the utter devastation of it, the firestorm that would make a scorched earth of her current life— was that what the dice had foretold?

It was a sign. She knew it was a sign.

And her other throws were nearly as prescient.

12:47.

She quieted herself and waited.

Finally, in the still sunlight of solar noon, she carefully threw the three dice onto the 7-inch circle.

A six, a five, and a two.

Thirteen.

The worst sign. The one that suggested *misery* if she pursued her current course.

She had feared it.

Jack was gone. There would be the usual activity around the dead, particularly around someone so prominent. A cremation. She remembered it was what Jack wanted. She knew she could take care of it, of everything that was now required of her.

But now she wondered what else must be done.

CHAPTER NINE

Leaving Wannamake Circle, Rusty felt relieved. His conversation with Carla had gone about as well as he could have hoped. It was never easy to tell a loved one their husband, child, parent, friend was gone. They might have been fine over breakfast. A high schooler might have grumbled about having to take out the trash; a spouse on the way to the grocery might have said, "Hey, do we need anything else besides ketchup?" And then suddenly the drumbeat of ordinary life ceases with the stillness of a filled grave. There weren't going to be any more complaints about chores or questions about groceries.

He wondered how Carla had last said goodbye to her husband. He imagined she was probably still in bed when Jack left for his morning ride. She'd taken the news in the usual way, with disbelief, then shock, then tears. But she had at no point lost control. She'd done better than most, he thought.

At least there were no children.

These times always reminded Rusty to tell Arlene he loved her. He tried to remember what they'd spoken about the last time they'd exchanged words, but he couldn't recall when they'd last spoken, let alone what they had said. And that made Rusty shake his head. He and Arlene had been breaking bread so long that if he had said anything other than "I'll call if I'm going to be late"—anything like "I love you, Arlene"—she would have eyed him with suspicion and said, "What's that supposed to mean?"

At the top of Wannamake Circle, he called the office.

"Sheriff?" Myrtle said.

"How are the calls?"

"Someone's been listening to our channels again, and word's gotten out there's been some kind of accident. Either that, or they've seen the commotion down by the plant and wondered what the heck is going on."

"So who've we heard from?" the sheriff asked.

"We've had calls from MPR and the three local channels. Anders tells me a guy from MPR and one from the Fox News affiliate are on the scene. And both the *Star Tribune* and *Pioneer Press* have made calls. Fox News wonders if it's a chemical spill."

Just about everyone in the sheriff's office felt the media was a necessary evil, particularly in an election year. But if you weren't careful how you fed them, you could get your hand bit off.

"Can you set up a press conference and get the word out? And you better fill in any outlets that haven't caught on. Those *Sun Current* newspapers. Any radio stations you can think of."

"OK," Myrtle said. "What time?"

The sheriff checked the dashboard clock. His turn signal was still blinking. "Make it 1:30. Sooner the better."

"Will do, Sheriff."

"And can you call Anders and tell him to make sure Tom Bennigan from the DNR and that guy from Fish & Wildlife,

Rivers, are both at the conference? Bennigan's going to catch that cat. And if any technical questions come up about cougars, I want Sam Rivers there to answer them."

"OK, Sheriff."

"And we might as well invite whoever needs to be there from McGregor Industries. I suspect they know the gist of what happened, but we better get them the facts. Call their HR folks and find out who should be present. Tell them I'll want to debrief them after the conference."

Myrtle took it all down and let him know she'd take care of it.

After the sheriff hung up, he turned right onto Chester Drive. On the road's shoulder, he saw one of Lawson's signs.

BOB LAWSON FOR SCOTT COUNTY SHERIFF
Time for a Change

He reached down and clicked Myrtle back.

"Sheriff?"

"Can you call Arlene and tell her to have someone come up to the corner of Chester Drive and Wannamake Circle and put up a sign? Lawson's got one up here . . . looks out over the whole damn valley. These things are cropping up like toadstools."

Technically, it was illegal to use official time or staff on his campaign, but he and Myrtle went way back. They didn't like each other's politics, but they both wanted to keep their jobs. Besides, she'd call Arlene, who was heading up his committee to reelect.

"I got it, Sheriff," Myrtle said, and added it to her list.

"Tell her to bring a half dozen and spread them around."

After he hung up, he remembered about Arlene. His pants felt tight. Seemed like they were getting tighter every year. As soon as this election was over, he was going on a diet. *Shoot,* he thought. *She knows I love her.*

Then he turned and headed back to the office.

Sam, Sorenson, and Marlin had made it as far as the river's edge, and then turned around. On the way back to the carcass, Sam was explaining cougar habits to the deputy and Marlin.

Cougars marked territory. Some biologists believed the typical cougar staked out a 200-square-mile territory, which it traversed and hunted. And cougars were solitary, except when they were cubs or as adults when mating. They claimed open ground as their own and marked it with ground scrapes: a small, clear patch cougars pawed up with their hind legs and then sprayed with urine. If this was a cougar's territory, and a kill the cougar was still marking, Sam expected Gray would have found one of the pungent scrapes. It was a warning to other animals, especially other cougars—though Sam suspected this one was far enough afield, in Savage near the Twin Cities, that it didn't have to worry about competition, at least of the *Puma concolor* kind.

But after spending almost an hour reviewing the deer carcass and the area around it, including what was left of two prints down in a dried-up creekbed, Sam found no recent evidence of the animal.

"Marlin," Sam said, "it doesn't look to me like there's been a cougar around this kill since your night photos."

"You mean other than this morning?" Marlin asked.

Sam paused. "I mean nothing down here around the carcass. And other than the couple of tracks up on the road, I can't find any other physical sign the cat's been prowling this deer kill."

Marlin shook his big head. "I guess," he said. "I been down here every morning, or most of them, since I found the deer, and I haven't seen any cat sign."

"But the papers said they're hard to spot, that you almost never see them because they prowl at night," Sorenson said. "And this morning we know it attacked Jack McGregor."

"Maybe," Sam said. "But you'd think the cougar would stay down here in the woods and check out its old catch, rather than walking on a road. They are secretive and reclusive. They don't like being in the open, generally. Which is why we never see them. Other than your night photos, Marlin, did you ever really see the animal?"

"No."

"But we have the pictures," Sorenson argued. "And there are the tracks and hair and stuff up top. It must have finished one of those wide circuits, come back to check out its kill, and maybe heard McGregor?"

"Maybe," Sam said again, skeptical. "It's just interesting the cat didn't put in an appearance down here."

"How do you know it wasn't down here?" Sorenson said. "With all these weeds trampled down and the steep hillside, where would the cat leave a track?"

Sam turned to Marlin. "What do you think, Marlin?"

Marlin looked thoughtful, as though he'd never considered the question. "They found that hair up top on that thistle. There's thistle and blackberry vine all over this hill. Seems like the cat would have left some fur down here, too, if it had come this way."

"I agree," Sam said.

"Maybe it was headed down the road to get to its deer, taking the easiest route, and then heard or saw McGregor," Sorenson said.

"Then what?" Sam asked. "If it went to all the trouble to kill McGregor, why didn't it feed?"

The thought had never occurred to either of the other men, who now pondered the grisly prospect in silence. After a few moments, Sorenson said, "Maybe it got spooked."

"By what? By who?" Sam asked.

"Maybe a riverboat, or a plane?" Sorenson posited.

"Maybe," Sam said, looking toward the river, doubtful. Still, they had tracks, fur. And the wounds on McGregor's body were pretty definitive.

Sam made one more cursory glance over what was left of the deer, but found nothing. Then he summoned Gray and they started up out of the ravine.

So far, Gray had shown some promise in his Search and Rescue Technician (SARTECH) training. There were numerous levels and types covering everything from finding earthquake victims in fallen buildings to tracking people through remote wilderness to finding cadavers underwater to recovering avalanche victims under 20 feet of snow. The SARTECH I certification was the most difficult, qualifying Gray to track just about anything in both urban and wilderness settings, which was why Sam chose it for Gray.

But Sam had been protective of their training, not wanting to make it known until he was absolutely certain of Gray's abilities.

While he had no doubts about the hybrid's nose or instincts, Gray was young and easily distracted. His nose was so sensitive it was sometimes overwhelmed by the fabric of scents in front of him. It wasn't difficult to discern and follow the thread. But sometimes it was much less interesting than more colorful weaves.

The dog's nose had led to occasional mishaps, places where Gray had gone astray, interested in some other, usually organic scent, almost always an animal. On more than one occasion over the last month, he had been lured off the source of his scent to tree a raccoon or follow a leaping squirrel.

Once up top, Sam slipped Gray under the crime scene tape and had him smell the two cougar prints. He was curious what Gray would do once he sensed the ground where the cougar had walked.

Gray sniffed the prints. When he glanced up, Sam praised him. "Yeah, that's it. You smell that? That's it. Find, Gray. Find it. *Find.*"

Many types of dogs had hypersensitive noses, containing more than 220 million olfactory receptors (compared to an average of 5 million in humans). Those receptors enabled dogs to smell and track an object from a few remnant molecules. Humans required a veritable colony of cells before they smelled something rancid. A good scent dog could pick up the molecules of decay more than a mile away.

When people—convicts, for instance—escaped and ran through dense forest, pastures, or urban streets, they shed small skin cells, hairs, drops of perspiration, and other minute particles that contained their scent. It was that scent a good trailing dog followed.

Sam had told Gray to track the cougar from the odor he discerned in the cat's paw print.

Gray paused, put his nose in the air, then back down to the ground, then in the air and to the ground again. They were all the correct signs; Gray seemed to understand. He started down the inside length of yellow tape, with a kind of working dog's focus. He ducked under the far end, and began returning along the path they'd originally taken to get here.

"I guess he's ready to go back to your jeep," Sorenson said.

Marlin just watched.

So did Sam. It wasn't the direction he expected, but Sam trusted Gray's nose. "Maybe," Sam said, and started following.

By the time Sam, Sorenson, and Marlin had followed Gray all the way back to their cars, Sam wondered if Gray accidentally picked up the scent of one of the investigators instead of the cat. The area around the prints had plenty of carefully placed tracks, where investigators, Sam knew, would have stepped around the scene to examine it. But he remembered Gray had stuck his nose right into the print. And then he'd given Gray the command, so it puzzled Sam.

Sam assumed after a cougar had killed down by the river, it would have headed into the woods, not out to the highway. But here they were.

By the time they were all beyond the locked gate, Sorenson became preoccupied with the scene. There were more vehicles, a

Fox News affiliate van, and either a bystander or a reporter. Looked like a reporter, though the car was civilian.

Marlin kept an eye on Gray, curious about his progress. But quiet, too.

Once they passed the other side of the gate, Sam leashed Gray. Gray was confused, apparently still interested in tracking. Sam would let Gray continue, but only after they got through the traffic on the road, which was starting to confuse the hybrid.

Sam placed Gray in a sit, and Gray obediently, if anxiously, obeyed.

Sam, Sorenson, and Marlin were watching the approach of another TV van when Sorenson's radio beeped.

"Deputy Sorenson."

"It's Anders," said the chief deputy.

They could see him up ahead, intercepting the vans.

"Sheriff's holding a news conference at 1:30. He wants Bennigan and Rivers to be there, in case any questions come up about the hunt, or the cougar."

Sam overheard the call and nodded.

"I'll have to call Bennigan. But Rivers will be there."

After Sorenson placed the radio back on his shoulder patch, Sam turned to him and said, "So I'll have to let the sheriff know I have questions."

Complications, Sorenson thought. He knew the sheriff wouldn't like them. And because the sheriff wouldn't like them, Sorenson knew eventually the sheriff would become a pain in his ass. Chief Deputy Anders too. Crap rolled downhill.

"What kind of questions?"

"I guess, anomalies. Just a few minor details that don't exactly add up."

"I don't think the sheriff's going to be interested in hearing about anything other than the hunt."

"Then you better let him know that if he asks me any pointed questions—like 'Are you 100% certain it was a cougar?'—I'll have to answer truthfully."

Sorenson stared at him until he was certain Sam was serious. The sheriff's Boggy Creek Monster comment came to mind. It was the only humor he'd heard today. But he said, "Probably best if you wait until after the press conference to talk about any doubts." Sorenson reminded himself to try to be absent when Rivers voiced his concerns.

"I'll wait," Sam agreed. He just hoped the sheriff fielded most of the calls and the media didn't ask questions he might have a hard time addressing.

The Fox News van was parked near Sam's jeep. The other vehicles began to pull out. There were only three official vehicles left: two sheriff cruisers and one from the Savage police department. The TV van had just started its engine and was getting ready to pull out, had probably gotten word about the conference, Sam guessed.

A woman in the front seat watched the three men walking away from the rusted gate, Sam with the big hybrid on a leash. The woman's hair was long, black, and shiny. Beneath her crisp bangs she wore too much makeup. She looked more like a model than a journalist, Sam thought. Or a sorority coed. He watched her stare at Gray, then him. She had a question on her face, but didn't nod or wave, just turned forward to watch the road as the van pulled out.

"I've seen her on TV," Sorenson said.

"Me too," Marlin said.

"She any good?" Sam asked.

Both Sorenson and Marlin shrugged. "I guess," Sorenson said.

"She's got the look," Sam said.

The reporter made Sam think of Diane, who was about as different from the TV reporter as one could get and still be in the same profession. He'd call Diane when he got in his car, make sure she knew about the press conference.

Sorenson gave Sam directions to the office and then headed back to his cruiser.

With Sorenson out of earshot, Sam turned and said, "Marlin, I need to see those photos. The ones you shot earlier this month. Can you email me the digitals?"

Marlin paused. "The memory card got damaged before I could download them. But I had time to make prints. They're at home, though."

Sam knew his afternoon was already filling up. "How about if I stop by tomorrow morning, before you walk the perimeter?"

Marlin nodded. "I make my rounds at 8. Then it's quittin' time, generally."

"How about if I stop by around 7?"

"Sure," Marlin shrugged.

Marlin told him where the gate and guard's shack was located, and then turned and started back toward the plant.

Sam and Gray walked toward his jeep.

Gray was still onto something, periodically pulling at the leash, wanting to continue tracking up the road beyond the direct line to their jeep. He was trying to follow along the gravel road edge but was anxious about it; Sam could tell because he was having to pull Gray back toward the car. By now, Sam wondered if the paw prints had too little scent to follow, or if there were too many confusing cross scents. Or maybe Gray was following a BCA investigator's scent. Regardless, Sam was ready to let the effort go.

But Gray wasn't.

Chief Anders's cruiser was the last car to pass them. Sam gave a nod as he and Gray approached Sam's jeep. The chief drove another couple hundred yards down the frontage road and turned, rising to a set of railroad tracks. As soon as the chief's cruiser was over the distant rise, Sam let Gray off leash. Once he did, Gray shot over to the road's shoulder, nose to the ground, picking up scent. Sam followed Gray 50 yards ahead, to the side of the road, beside a thick stand of river maples, where the hybrid began turning in excited circles, the way he did when scent disappeared or he came to the end of whatever was making it.

Sam looked around, in the ditch and up in the maple branches, but he couldn't see anything. He could see fresh tire tracks in the gravel shoulder where a car had been parked. Recently. And Gray was definitely excited, waiting for his usual praise. If Gray had followed an investigator's scent out to the side of the road, the scent would end here, where the investigator got into a car and drove off. But why would an investigator park so far away from the opening to the maintenance road?

Regardless, Gray was awaiting his praise.

"OK, OK," Sam said. "Good boy. Good boy. That's the way," Sam said. Finally, it was the satisfying conclusion to their scent game, and Gray eased a little, ready to return to their jeep.

Sam's vehicle was parked near the railroad berm. The berm was covered with fall growth. Two narrow steel railroad tracks marked the top of the rise. More than 100 yards down the tracks, a pair of high-powered field glasses peered out from beneath a stand of scarlet sumac. Sam might have caught a glint from the large lenses, if he had looked in the right spot.

But Sam didn't look down the road. He got in the jeep and started toward the sheriff's office.

The binoculars came down and Chief Anders watched Sam drive and turn toward Highway 13, rising over the railroad tracks to the blacktopped highway. Then he looked away, thinking . . . about how he was going to take that goddamn dog off his scent. And the USFW agent, too, if he got too close.

On the way to the sheriff's office, Sam called Diane.

"How's the hearing?" Sam asked.

"There's more to an extradition hearing than I thought. I'm going to tape it, in case I can't sleep tonight."

"You still in the courtroom?"

"God no. That judge is a tyrant. My phone was almost confiscated. We recessed for lunch. I picked up your message," she said.

"I've got something you might find interesting," he said.

"Watching paint dry would be more interesting."

"There's been a cougar kill over in Savage," Sam said.

"Someone shot a cougar?"

"A cougar killed a man."

"What?! A cougar killed someone? In Savage? Was it a pet?"

"Could have been a pet. But it appears to have been wild."

"Wild? We don't have wild cougars in Minnesota. At least not many. And especially not down here in the Cities. You sure?"

Explaining it all to Diane would take time. "Looks like," Sam said. "And the guy who died was kind of prominent. He owned some big plant down on the Minnesota River. I'm heading over to the Scott County sheriff's office for a press conference."

"Wait a minute."

There was silence, followed by what sounded like shuffling paper.

"What time's the conference?"

"1:30."

"That's 45 minutes." She sounded concerned.

"I bet the *Vermilion Falls Gazette* would be interested."

"Everybody'll be interested. I'm coming. Just not sure I'll be there by press time."

"I'll save you a seat."

"So it was an accident? A wild cougar killed some guy?"

She was walking.

"You didn't hear this from me," Sam said. "It appears the guy was mountain biking down near the Minnesota River. It's pretty remote, but still a Twin Cities suburb."

"I know Savage. It's not that far out."

"There's plenty of wild country down by the river."

"Did you see it?"

"I saw where it happened."

"A cougar killed him?" It was hard for Diane to believe.

"Looks like it." Sam repeated. "Most of it, anyway."

"What do you mean?"

"There were a couple weird things about it."

"Like what?" Diane asked.

"Like the fact it was a cougar, for starters. Other . . . small things. I don't know."

"What other things?"

"I can't go into it right now because I'm still trying to figure it out myself. Besides, that's not for public consumption."

There was a pause, while Diane considered rephrasing her question.

"Do me a favor, Diane, and don't ask too many pointed questions at the press conference."

"I'm a reporter," Diane said.

"I know you're a reporter. Just do me a favor and don't ask too many questions and we can talk about it later."

There was another pause. "OK," she said. Then another question, "Who was it?"

"Guy by the name of Jack McGregor. He owns McGregor Industries. A big fertilizer and potash facility down off Highway 13. Or owned it, anyway. Act surprised when you hear his name."

"I'm on my way," she said, and hung up.

As Sam drove toward the sheriff's office, he started thinking about Diane. After the last time they'd slept together—February—he'd returned to Colorado and waited three weeks to call and tell her now was not the time in his life when he should become involved with anyone. He needed time to grieve. It had been too soon since his divorce and it didn't feel right. The call had been the correct one to make and he was pretty sure Diane agreed. But sexual politics were tricky, Sam knew. What he thought now was how little the intervening months had taught him, especially about sexual politics. He'd experimented, but not that much. He'd had Gray to raise and it was taking him longer than he thought it would to process his divorce. What he wondered, driving toward the sheriff's office, was whether there was still a spark. There had been much more than a spark. Last February, up on the Iron Range, from Sam's perspective, there had been a wildfire.

But not much had changed regarding Sam's status; he was still in a holding pattern. And he could feel the same issues that had ruined him for Maggie were still issues.

He remembered Kay Magdalen's advice about getting over a divorce; it was equal to the half-life of the marriage. In his case, that would be five years. Sam had only been divorced for one. By Magdalen's measure he still needed time to process.

But what he and Diane had shared was powerful mojo, at least of a physical kind. He couldn't imagine suggesting they enjoy each other's company for a couple days just while he was in town. It wasn't the right thing to do, given his status. So he tried to put the memory of Diane in bed out of his mind.

But it was like asking a genie to climb back into her bottle.

CHAPTER TEN

When Sam entered the sheriff's office, there were six media people waiting, easy to recognize. There was a young man and the woman Sam had seen in the van. They had $100 haircuts—the woman maybe $150—and they were well dressed. The man wore a casual sweater vest and a high-thread-count starched and pressed white shirt. Not a hair out of place. The woman wore a dark-blue business suit. Her hair fell across her shoulders like water. They were talking when Sam walked in. They briefly turned, considered him, recognized his $12 haircut with clothes to match, and went back to their conversation.

There was a long-legged woman in jeans with sharp features, frizzy hair, and a runner's lean features, probably mid-40s, and another guy with a plaid shirt, jeans, and a paunch. The woman had a purse and the man a "murse"—both weathered leather shoulder bags. The newspaper reporters appeared bored.

Two people had come to write, two to be on TV, Sam thought. And there were two cameramen with serious equipment.

Sorenson hustled Sam through the main waiting area into a cement-block conference room. Someone had moved a dictionary stand to the far end. There was still a dictionary on top of the stand, looking heavy, stately, and official. Sam guessed the dictionary stand was going to double as a podium. The room was cramped, but functional.

"Just wait a sec," Sorenson said. "The sheriff wants to have a short meeting before the conference gets started."

"Where's Bennigan?" Sam asked.

"I called him on the way over. He's on his way."

Sorenson left the room and Sam found a seat near the podium and sat down. Gray was back in the jeep, and Sam wondered if he'd cracked open the windows far enough. It was a warm afternoon, still beautiful, not a day to be in a cramped jeep in a parking lot, or a cement-block conference room talking to reporters. Sam was just about ready to get up and check on Gray when Sorenson ushered Bennigan into the room.

Bennigan nodded to Sam and Sam said, "How's the coon dog roundup?"

"My guy's going to meet us down at that gate around 5. You still in?"

"Sure," Sam said.

The idea of running through the woods in the dark behind a bunch of baying hounds sounded . . . well, interesting. Maybe even fun. But he wondered about Gray. More to the point, he wondered if their efforts would be successful. In the Minnesota River Valley, the dogs would come across plenty of coons, or raccoon signs, and he had doubts about whether coon hounds would pursue a cougar when so many of their preferred prey were around.

He also recalled Gray's curious effort. Gray was still young and, while he had demonstrated competence as a SARTECH dog, he'd likely missed the mark with his effort to track that cougar. And if Gray, who was at least familiar with the scent of *Puma concolor*, had missed it, Sam was doubtful coon dogs would have better luck.

The sheriff and Chief Anders entered the room.

"You men ready for a little show?" the sheriff asked.

The sheriff's gun hung properly at his side. He wore a crisp new shirt and he had combed his red mane. His big mustache shone with what Sam guessed might be mustache wax. A little sunburn made his nose appear bigger than usual. "Ready, Sheriff," Sam said.

"You look good, Sheriff," Bennigan said.

"Course I do," the sheriff said.

Bennigan and Sorenson smiled.

Then the sheriff started in. "I'll do the talking. We'll lay it out square, tell exactly what happened. You two are here," he glanced at Sam and Bennigan, "to answer questions about cougars and about the hunt. We don't want any cougar-killing wannabes heading into the river valley with guns, trying to bag this killer. We are going to hunt this animal down because it's our duty and we know how. Besides, I'll be sure and let everyone know hunting is illegal in that part of the valley. Plain and simple."

The sheriff paused.

Bennigan nodded. "Sounds good, Sheriff."

The conservation officer was nervous, Sam thought.

"You're the cougar expert, Agent Rivers," the sheriff said. "If any questions come up about cougars and their habits and whether this kind of thing has ever happened, I'll look to you to answer them."

"Sure," Sam said. Over the last 20 years, Sam had been interviewed on several occasions. He appreciated the process. Educating the public about wilderness and wildlife issues was part of his job.

The sheriff stared at him and paused. "We haven't had a chance to talk since you returned. You find anything I should know about?"

"Not exactly," Sam said.

The sheriff kept staring, considering Sam's response. "What the hell does that mean?"

"There's plenty of evidence it was a cougar kill, but I still have some questions," Sam said.

"What questions?" the sheriff said. "The claw marks, the bite marks, the prints, the fur. The earlier sighting. The BCA's investigation. What're the questions?"

"It's not just one thing," Sam said.

"Oh, for Christ's sake," the sheriff interrupted, blowing hard.

This was the start of the conversation Sorenson had wanted to avoid.

Sam could feel Bennigan's interest, and Sorenson squirm. Chief Deputy Anders stood to the side and behind the sheriff, by expression noncommittal. Sam couldn't tell what he thought, but he looked like a chain-of-command guy, probably ex-military.

Before the sheriff lost his composure, Sam said, "I'm just saying I'll have to take a closer look at the evidence."

"Now listen," the sheriff said. "That's where you're goddamn 180 degrees out of line. Your job is to find this cat and kill it. You and Fido. All we need you to do is your damn job. Let the BCA, who last I checked are experts in this kind of thing, finish their investigation. They have questions about cougars, they'll get back to you. Meanwhile, I need you, Agent Rivers, focused 100% on bagging this animal. Tonight. That clear?"

Sam paused, but finally said, "Crystal," low and serious.

"Well, that's just perfect because, for our friends in the press, this needs to be an open-and-shut case. A cougar came out of the woods and killed Jack McGregor. It's what the crime scene boys found. It's what me and officers Anders, Sorenson, and Bennigan found. And it's what the media is going to hear."

Sam stared at the blustery sheriff. "I agree. We give the press the most plausible story, no doubts expressed."

The sheriff kept staring. "Good," he said.

"But when the BCA finishes its draft report, I'd like to review it," Sam said. If this was going to be a pissing contest, he'd better mark some territory.

"Agent Rivers, once the professionals finish their report, we can talk. Until then, I want you and Officer Bennigan to catch the cat. That's all you got to do. Just get the damn cat. Easy enough to follow?"

The sheriff glanced at Chief Deputy Anders and Deputy Sorenson to let them know they'd talk about this later. They knew what it meant; one or both of them would be shadowing Sam Rivers like a North Korean minder.

Sam caught it, too, but just nodded.

When the media was finally ushered into the room, there were three TV crews. Three camera people started setting up tripods. The two newspaper reporters came in and sat down at the table, starting to pull out their notebooks. They were joined by a fresh-looking kid, probably 21 or 22, with glasses and a large Minnesota Public Radio tag. And, finally, Diane entered the room, right before the sheriff glanced at his watch.

A handful of the sheriff's staff were also present, including an older woman with what looked like blue-gray hair. It sat on top of her head like clumps of steel wool. But everyone, including the sheriff, deferred to her. Myrtle. When Myrtle came in, she was followed by two men in business suits with ties and an older woman in a navy-blue corporate outfit. They sat in the empty chairs at the far end of the room.

McGregor employees, Sam guessed. The woman looked about as old as Myrtle, only well dressed in a conservative blue suit with an off-white silk blouse and a big red bow tie. The men appeared to be in their 40s, one with thinning blond hair and tortoiseshell glasses, the other with black hair starting to show gray. The dark-haired one looked serious. The light-haired guy looked country club, Sam thought. The older woman looked wizened and hard, as though the corporate life had taken its toll. If Sam had to guess, he'd say the woman was in charge.

Once the red video camera lights came on, the sheriff cleared his throat, introduced himself, thanked everyone for coming, and started in on his rehearsed comments.

He'd done this before, Sam thought. Sheriff Benson was sober and serious, explaining about Jack McGregor and his tragic accident.

The reporters and cameras soaked it up like crime scene cleaners sponging blood. The sheriff appeared official and in command. Exactly, Sam guessed, how he wanted to look in an election year.

Diane waited until the sheriff was finished with his prepared statement and then interrupted with the room's first question. "Has anything like this ever happened before in Minnesota?"

The sheriff glanced at Sam, then said, "Not on my watch and not that I'm aware of. But if you have any questions about cougars, we have a cougar expert on loan to us from the U.S. Fish & Wildlife Service." Then he turned to Sam and said, "Agent Rivers?"

"There *have* been recent cougar predations involving people, but not in Minnesota," Sam explained, starting in like the Nature channel. During his comments he glanced around the room at the other reporters, and their cameras, giving equal time to each. He enumerated the Colorado and California incidents. "There have also been plenty of close encounters that didn't end in death," he concluded.

"But aren't there a lot more cougars in Colorado and California?" Diane asked.

"We estimate the Colorado and California populations to be around 5,000 each," Sam said.

"So they're rare in Minnesota?" asked the reporter with bangs.

"Very rare," Sam said. "I'm guessing over the last century there have been less than 50 sightings. And, to the best of my knowledge, no one has ever found any breeding animals or permanent residents here. The few occurrences verified by camera or biological evidence are most likely from wandering individuals from out West."

The TV reporter followed up with a question about the difference between a mountain lion and a cougar. Sam explained that mountain lion, cougar, puma, panther, catamount: "They're all different names for the same animal. Out West most people refer to them as mountain lions. In other parts of the country, cougars, and in others, pumas or panthers. But it's the same animal."

"They're seldom seen in Minnesota and yet one of them kills a man?" asked the sharp-featured newspaper reporter.

"It's very unusual, but it happens," Sam said. "A cougar's primary food source is deer. They'll migrate to wherever they can find them. And since deer aren't usually hunted in urban areas, their urban populations are growing. The cougar follow the deer."

"What's the chance anyone else could be killed by a cougar?" asked the other newspaper reporter.

"About as likely as getting struck by lightning twice in the same place," Sam suggested. Then he explained that it must have been an incredibly unfortuitous series of events that brought man and cougar together and ended like this, in regrettable tragedy.

"You think this was the same cougar we heard about earlier this month?" the woman TV reporter asked.

"That seems likely," Sam said. There was a lot he didn't know, but he agreed with the sheriff on this point; the media didn't need to hear his suspicions or talk of anomalies. "All signs suggest it. Cougars are territorial. They stake out a 100- or 200-square-mile region and they patrol it. It's entirely likely the one seen earlier this month was making his usual rounds when Jack McGregor stumbled across his path."

There were a few more questions about what they were going to do about it. Sam was getting more airtime than the sheriff, which is why he figured the sheriff introduced DNR Conservation Officer Bennigan, the local boy who spoke nervously about their use of coon dogs and their sundown hunt. The cameras liked the local boy. They drummed up some softball questions and let him hit them out of the room.

Were cougars easy to hunt?

What was the process?

Was it legal to hunt in the Minnesota River Valley, in Savage?

The young CO with short-cropped hair and the green DNR uniform would look good on TV—exactly what the local ratings wanted.

The sheriff interjected a few more comments, reminding the press to please be sure to let their readers, viewers, and listeners know it would be better for folks to stay out of the wilder sections of the Minnesota River Valley. He drew out the explanation with some detailed references to the places people should avoid. He assured everyone he expected to find the cougar within the next 48 hours. And he most assuredly let them know he was in control.

"Thanks for coming," he concluded, with a politician's gracious smile.

When it was over, Sorenson escorted the media out of the conference room. Diane glanced at Sam and gave a quick upward nod, which Sam took to mean he should call her later. The three McGregor employees were asked to stay, along with Sam and Chief Deputy Anders.

CHAPTER ELEVEN

Bennigan leaned over to Sam and said, "I've got to run some errands before meeting this guy down at the gate." He glanced at Sam's light gear and said, "It could get chilly tonight, this time of year."

"I remember," Sam said.

They exchanged cell numbers, and Sam told him he'd be at the gate by 5 p.m.

The sheriff turned his back to the others seated in the room, leaned down to Sam, and said, "I want you here, Agent Rivers, in case these McGregor folks have any more questions about cougars. But keep it to cougars. Understood?"

Sam nodded.

The sheriff had been satisfied with the conference, thought it would show well on the evening news and be good for his reelection campaign. But he was still being officious, particularly in front of prospective voters and possible friends of Jack McGregor's, who with luck might become campaign contributors. The sheriff also didn't want Sam to share any of his doubts. If he mentioned a word about anything questionable, the sheriff would cut him off faster than a duck's head on a butcher block.

The three McGregor Industries employees were stunned by the news but looked more worried than saddened. On more than one occasion during the press debriefing, Sam watched them exchange anxious glances. Now he was looking forward to hearing from them.

There was Phil Traub, the company's blond-haired treasurer; Spencer Higgins, the dark-haired, pinch-faced CFO; and Madeline Baxter, vice president of human resources.

Maddy was the first to speak, but not to the sheriff. She turned to Spencer and said, "So what in the hell does this do to our deal?"

Before he could answer, Phil said, "Maddy. Jack is dead."

She peered over at Phil and thought about saying something, then thought better of it.

Sam recognized a nasty flash in her eyes.

She turned back to the CFO. "Spence?"

Spencer turned to her and said, "The deal's too far along to quit now. It's full steam ahead, Jack or no Jack."

"What deal?" the sheriff asked.

Spencer turned to the sheriff and then to Sam and the chief deputy. "Can I speak in confidence?" he said.

The sheriff nodded. "Course. We all know what's said in this room stays in this room."

"This is highly confidential, but Jack had entered into an agreement to sell McGregor Industries to Garkill United."

"That big company down off Hennepin?" the sheriff asked.

"That's their Minnesota office," answered Spencer. "Their headquarters is in Chicago, but they're all over the world. An agricultural conglomerate."

Sam knew them. You couldn't work in the wild and not know about Garkill. They were huge and viewed terra firma through a prism largely colored by dollars and cents. They had buckets and buckets of money. They had grain trucks and elevators full of it. But they were smart about not pushing the environmental laws, unless it was in a country where they had enough clout to pull it off.

"When is the sale going to happen?" Sam asked.

"Less than two weeks," Spencer said. His pinched face looked even more worried.

"Any way we can stop it?" Maddy asked. Her face was worn leather. At one time, she might have been beautiful. Now she looked mean.

"Not at this point," Spencer said.

"This is moving forward," Phil added. Apparently, he was over Jack's death. "We've gone too far and have taken too many steps."

Maddy was still looking at Spencer, the CFO.

"Besides," Phil added, "Jack would have wanted it."

"Like you said, Phil, Jack is dead," Maddy said.

"That doesn't mean we shouldn't carry out his wishes," Phil said.

Maddy looked at them both. Then she glanced at the sheriff, Sam, and Chief Anders, considering. "This sale is benefiting some of us more than others."

"I don't think this is the right time or place for this conversation," Spencer said.

Phil appeared offended and ignored Spencer, turning to Maddy and declaring, "Jack took care of us."

"He took care of you," Maddy said. "And Spence. He tossed me a bone. And what do you think is going to happen when Garkill takes over?" She didn't wait for her colleagues to answer. "There's going to be a bloodbath at McGregor."

Spencer turned to her and said, "None of us liked it and none of us wanted it. And for the record, the deal's good for me and Phil, but we won't be retiring. Not that it matters. The deal's too far along now to turn back. Garkill has every legal right to finalize the transaction, and I'm sure that's what they'll do."

"I appreciate your concerns," the sheriff said. "But right now, we have a more pressing issue. You need to let your employees know about Mr. McGregor's death. Preferably before the five o'clock news."

Maddy looked at him. "As soon as I get back to the office, I'll draft an email and letter and get the word out. You think you'll get this cougar tonight, Sheriff?"

The sheriff turned to Sam. "Agent Rivers?"

"We're going into the woods with dogs later today. With any luck, we should pick up the cougar's trail. They don't usually stray far after sunup, so it shouldn't take long to find it."

"We'll know for sure in the morning," the sheriff added.

"Then I'll mention the hunt because some of our workers will be worried about that cougar on the loose. Particularly our employees who work the dock and the back lot. These hunters will be careful?"

"Of course," Sam said.

"Because we have people back there."

"Just tell them to stay close to the dock and loading facility," the sheriff said.

"I don't think anyone will be straying into those woods," Maddy said.

"I don't think anyone has anything to worry about," Sam said. "Just make sure your communication to employees includes our contact information."

"Good idea," the sheriff said, and gave Maddy his phone number and Chief Anders's.

Sam did the same and said, "If anyone sees any sign of that cougar, we want to know about it. And make sure you mention it can be any kind of sign. Tracks, a tuft of fur on a branch, deer kill, scat, anything."

"Scat?" Spencer asked.

"Feces," Sam said.

"Oh," Spencer said.

"I'll mention it," said Maddy.

They all sat for a minute in silence, contemplating cat feces.

"How many people know about the sale of McGregor Industries?" Sam asked.

"We've held it pretty close to the vest," Spencer said. "Apart from us three, there's Susan Connelly in my office and Angie Sweet in Phil's. They're both financial analysts."

Sam thought he saw another flash across Maddy's face. But this one wasn't nasty; it was knowing. Then she looked away.

"Just the five of you?" Sam asked.

"Nobody else knows anything. Except Jack's wife."

"I don't think this is any of our business," the sheriff said.

"And these financial analysts wouldn't say anything?" Sam asked.

"They both signed NDAs," Spencer said. "Nondisclosure agreements. Besides, they both benefit from the sale, and if it was found out they'd shared it with anyone prior to the announcement, they wouldn't get a dime."

"Did you all sign NDAs?" Sam asked. He could feel heat from the sheriff's countenance, which had suddenly turned toward him.

"Yes," Phil answered. "Jack was adamant about it."

Apart from Phil's feigned sorrow over the accident, there didn't appear to be much sadness over Jack's passing. Sam guessed the man hadn't inspired love or admiration. But had he inspired enough anger to incite someone to . . . to what? Somehow kill him with a cougar?

But there was motive.

"Well, thank you for coming," the sheriff said, putting his hands on the table and starting to shift in his chair.

"Just one more clarification," Sam interrupted. "So the five of you know, and none of you were particularly excited about the sale?"

Phil shrugged. Spencer looked at Maddy with eyes that repeated "not the time or place." Maddy turned to Spencer and said, "Jack was walking away with $52 million and change. We were getting a handshake and chump change."

"Maddy," Spencer said. It was shaming, but the shame rolled off Maddy like water off a wood duck. She was angry and knew that once Garkill took over she was going down.

That kind of disillusion could be useful, Sam thought.

"If others at the plant knew about it—other employees— would they have wanted it stopped?" Sam asked.

"The white-collar guys would have," Maddy said. "Most of them will lose their jobs. Not that they could do a goddamn thing about it," she said, point-blank. "But nobody else knows. Why?"

"It was a tragic accident," the sheriff interceded. He didn't look at Sam. "We're just trying to understand the whole situation, from a media perspective."

Sam watched the three, but he wasn't sure they were buying "media perspective."

What Sam saw were three corporate executives he guessed were adept at killing on the corporate floor, but in business boardrooms and backroom deals, not with their hands.

Still, if anyone else knew about the pending sale and wanted to fight it, then clearly there was reason to have Jack McGregor gone. But the timing wasn't right, given the near conclusion of the sale. At this point, it would have been about getting revenge rather than trying to stop it. And the fact was, all signs still pointed to a cougar. Or at least most of them. And DNA tests were definitive. They would know for certain when the hair samples were analyzed.

"So I presume Mrs. McGregor is going to be a very rich woman?" Sam asked.

This time the sheriff had had enough. "Agent Rivers, that's really none of our business."

Phil, Spencer, and Maddy exchanged glances. Then Maddy shrugged, ignoring the sheriff's comment. "Jack didn't really share his personal life with us. But my guess is, she'll get $50 million, less taxes. But you'd have to ask Carla."

Sam knew he would. Fifty million was a lot more than chump change.

The sheriff was thinking he was going to have a come-to-Jesus meeting with Agent Rivers, once they were finished here. And he was going to have Anders or Sorenson be the wannabe detective's permanent companion. But all he said was, "Again, we really appreciate you coming down to speak with us. I'm very sorry for your loss." He finally finished and stood, before Sam could ask any more questions.

The three thanked the sheriff, more because it was the appropriate gesture than out of sincerity, and stood up to leave.

Maddy said she'd send out an email and letter as soon as she got back to the office, so employees would find out before they saw it on the evening news or on newspaper websites. She would include the contact information for everyone. And she wanted to be informed about the cougar hunt, just as soon as the animal had been killed, so she could let McGregor's employees know.

"Of course," the sheriff agreed.

"When were the other employees going to hear about the sale?" Sam asked.

"Day of," Maddy said. "And not a moment sooner."

"Jack didn't want anyone to know about the deal until the ink was dry," Spencer said.

The sheriff finally ushered them out the door and said, "We'll let you know about the cougar hunt first thing in the morning."

After the sheriff said his goodbyes and the McGregor executives were gone, he closed the conference room door and turned to Sam.

The quiet chief deputy seemed to step back, not wanting to be spattered by the bloodshed.

"I'm not sure what that little circus was about, but you need to leave the goddamn questions to the professionals," the sheriff said. His mood had shifted from a pleasant second-summer day to a winter squall. And he was just getting started.

"*You* ask questions that pertain to wildlife and hunting and cougars." He jabbed a sausagelike finger at Sam. "And you only answer questions about those topics. Otherwise, you keep your mouth shut. You understand?"

Sam knew he'd been out of line. But there were still some serious unanswered questions about the kill. And the pending sale of McGregor Industries only muddied the already turbid waters. He knew the proper response to Sheriff Rusty Benson involved contrition, but it was hard for Sam to summon an apology. "Sheriff . . ." he started.

"Have you ever seen anyone dead before? I mean a human?" continued the sheriff.

"More than I'd like," Sam answered.

"Well, I've seen plenty. And so have the state crime scene guys. So just leave the goddamn analysis to us."

"Mrs. McGregor is going to be a very wealthy woman."

"Oh, for Christ's sake," the sheriff said. "She's also one of the prettiest women west of the Mississippi. And one of the nicest. Carla McGregor . . ." He didn't finish. "What the hell are you thinking?" he asked, his face turning crimson.

This is what Sorenson had wanted to avoid: Sam's out-of-line comments in front of the sheriff, ignoring the line of command. They were like whacking a beehive with a blunt stick.

"You think someone was pissed off about the sale of McGregor enough to hire a goddamn cougar to waltz down that road and kill Jack McGregor?!" the sheriff said. "What's the going rate for a trained cougar assassin, Agent Rivers?"

Sam knew it sounded crazy—like something out of *Hound of the Baskervilles*. But he wasn't going to give the sheriff any satisfaction because the weeds were filled with just as much motive as cougar signs.

"Do you know what we do in law enforcement, Agent Rivers? We follow the evidence. And personally, I like it when the evidence is so goddamn obvious it makes our jobs easy. We have a sighting. Then prints, fur. And something just like this happened out West. Man on a mountain bike downed by a cougar. And you still suspect the Boggy Creek Monster?!"

"I'm just trying to understand the big picture," Sam said.

The sheriff's face grew a shade redder. "Is that so, Agent Rivers? Well, I'm *so* glad our colleague from Fish & Wildlife is along to help us *understand the big picture*. Now once that big picture comes into focus, you think you can do us a favor and catch the goddamn animal that did this?"

"That's what I plan on doing," Sam said.

The sheriff was too angry to recognize the ambiguity of the question or Sam's response.

"You can go now, Agent Rivers." He said it like a face slap.

The sheriff, smoldering, turned to his chief deputy so that his back was facing Sam.

Sam was being shunned. He considered some suitable responses, but knew leaving was the correct one. He turned and walked out of the room.

Less than a minute later, Sam was walking across the parking lot to his jeep when Chief Deputy Anders came up behind him.

"You need a hotel recommendation, Agent Rivers?" Anders asked. Sam guessed Anders had just received his new orders from the sheriff: keep tabs on Sam Rivers.

They talked briefly. Chief Deputy Anders was a man of few words. During the entire meeting, he hadn't made a single comment and had kept his presence low-key. The chief deputy recommended the Quality Inn down on Highway 13, not far from McGregor Industries. It was a two-star motel, but the price was right and it was dog-friendly. "Got a pool too," the chief deputy said, which for him was color commentary.

The chief deputy told Sam he'd help him with whatever else he needed, so long as they kept to Sheriff Benson's guidelines. When the chief talked about the guidelines, he was serious, so Sam just nodded. But Sam knew he would only follow the sheriff's directives as long as they didn't interfere with him interviewing whoever he wanted. And he would ask whatever he pleased. But he'd been forewarned; his questions would have to be asked out of earshot of the chief deputy and everyone else at the sheriff's office.

Sam was going to check into the hotel, change into some hunting gear, and meet Bennigan and the coonhound hunter down at the McGregor back road gate by 5. "You coming?" he asked. It would be fine to have the chief deputy along on the hunt, where Sam wouldn't be asking pointed questions of anyone, except maybe raccoons. And it would show the sheriff he was cooperating.

"I can't make it tonight. But Deputy Sorenson will be there."

"OK. Can you let him know? The gate at 5?" The crowd would make for more commotion in the woods, and that could be a good thing. Cougars didn't like crowds, dogs, or people.

The idea of running through dark woods in search of a man-killer intrigued Sam. But he had no illusions about what they would be doing if they found the cougar. They would be shooting a magnificent apex predator that was protected in Minnesota. Sam would have no choice. If the animal had attacked and killed a man this close to a major metropolitan area, there was little doubt it would come in contact with others. It would need to be stopped.

He recalled shooting the cougar out of the cottonwood tree on the Swensons' cattle ranch. It had been difficult, but necessary. But it was hard to take down such a beautiful creature in the prime of its life.

Sam drove down Highway 13 and booked a room at the Quality Inn. Definitely two stars, but for $56 a night, they let him keep his massive dog. Once in his room, he phoned Diane.

"I know I owe you dinner," he said. "But I don't think it's going to happen tonight."

She didn't sound disappointed, which would have disappointed Sam if he wasn't looking forward to this evening's entertainment.

But Diane didn't hesitate about the questions. He answered what he could, but mentioned only a few of his doubts. He told her they were all heading into the woods with dogs.

"Is this a law enforcement gig, or can anyone join? Might be an interesting angle to the story."

Sam thought about it but didn't think the sheriff would play along. He'd be too worried Sam would talk about his doubts and they'd get into the press and then the sheriff would have to address them. Sheriff Benson wanted a law-and-order conclusion to this incident. Preferably tonight.

If the sheriff knew he and Diane Talbott, a reporter, were friends and that he'd invited her into the woods with them, he'd turn apoplectic. Sam briefly considered inviting her, just to see the sheriff's reaction, but since he wouldn't be near enough to see the fireworks, it wasn't worth it.

"You can ask, but I don't think it'll go anywhere," Sam said.

Diane thought about it, but realized she needed more research and writing time and decided against it.

"I'm at a Travelodge in Burnsville," she said. "About a mile north of McGregor Industries on Highway 13. I'll be up late, researching cougars and working on this story. If you bag the animal anytime tonight, call me."

Sam listened for nuance in her invitation. But all he heard was reporter. "Sure," he said. "I'll call."

There was a pause before Diane added, "Just call me regardless. I'll want to hear about it."

"OK," he said. But the part of him listening for nuance thought . . . *maybe*.

CHAPTER TWELVE

A little before 5 p.m., Sam rolled up to the road's entrance with Gray. He was early and still alone. It was nearly 4 in Denver. He pulled out his phone and called his boss, Kay Magdalen.

"Magdalen," she answered.

"Hey," Sam said. "Just wanted to give you an update."

"First, let me hear your side of the story," she said, in a tone that didn't sound good.

"What?"

"A short while ago, I got a call from Sheriff Russell Benson, who asked some very pointed questions. About you."

"Like what?"

"Like what did I think about your qualifications, for starters? Like did I think you were a good agent, a team player?"

"What did you tell him?"

"What do you think?"

Sam knew he could sometimes be taciturn, sometimes verbose, and at other times, like now, recalcitrant. But it was always because of the case. In spite of the sheriff's comment, Sam followed the evidence, regardless of where it led.

"I guess you told him you hired me because you believed I could do the job."

"I told him you were the best investigator in the service, that you had plenty of field experience, and while sometimes your methods were unorthodox, you always seemed to find your way to a satisfactory conclusion."

"Uh," Sam said, "you've never told me that."

There was a pause. "Rivers . . ." She was irritated.

"So what did Benson say?"

"The sheriff wondered if we had any other agents nearby with lion-hunting experience. No offense."

"None taken."

"I mean, that's what he said, 'no offense.'"

"None taken."

"Rivers," Magdalen repeated. "Can you just try not to piss off the local constabulary? Just for a day or so? The sheriff would have pulled you off the case if you didn't have a boss who watched your back, and if he had anyone else to turn to who knows how to hunt down a mountain lion."

"Cougar," Sam said. "Out here they call them cougars."

She snorted. "Figures."

They talked awhile longer, during which Sam said he was waiting in his jeep right now, with Gray, and they were going into the woods with more hounds to try to track down the animal. That seemed to placate Magdalen, but Sam reminded himself to be more circumspect around the sheriff, even if the situation begged for pushback or counterpoint. And if he had serious doubts about what happened here, and some of the mountain lion kill's irregularities, he was going to have to keep them to himself, at least until he gathered something more concrete than nuanced suspicion. He was looking forward to the results of the DNA tests of those hair samples. DNA was definitive.

Magdalen had his back, but even her patience had limits.

After signing off, Sam watched Bennigan pull up by Sam's jeep and park. Then Sam heard a car approaching from the rear. He glanced at his watch and saw it was five o'clock. In his rearview mirror, he watched Sorenson approaching in his cruiser.

Sam turned to Gray and said, "I want you to behave yourself with those coonhounds."

Gray considered Sam's words, staring at him with those bicolored eyes, one wolf yellow, the other malamute blue. Sometimes it was a little unnerving. Not only the eyes, but the way Gray seemed to understand.

Sam recalled a comic he'd read once, in which a dog owner was talking to his canine. The caption under the owner read: "What the owner says." The speech bubble above the man read: ". . . and after I gave you that morning treat you shouldn't have jumped up on me. The next time I give you a treat, you better not jump, or no more treats, and . . ."

The caption under the dog read: "What the dog hears." The speech bubble read: ". . . blah blah blah blah treat blah blah blah blah treat blah blah blah blah blah treats . . ."

Sam figured it was the same with Gray. But sometimes the hybrid gave him a look that seemed to say otherwise.

Bennigan got out of his truck and approached. Sam did the same, telling Gray he'd be right back.

Sam was dressed in camo-patterned khakis and wore a tan vest over a green mock turtleneck. Bennigan had on his standard-issue green-and-khaki CO uniform, a .40-caliber Glock holstered at his waist.

It was still warm out, the temperature near 80 degrees but starting to drop.

"Where's the coon hunter?" Sam asked.

"He's about 2 minutes out."

Sorenson pulled up behind Sam's jeep. He was uniformed, like Bennigan, and also had what appeared to be a holstered Glock at his waist. Sam's 9-millimeter was squirreled away in a locked gun safe inside his glove compartment. He was happy to leave it there, given the already ample weaponry of his three colleagues. The Glocks would be enough to drop a cougar out of a tree. And from what he remembered, DNR COs were also issued a 12-gauge shotgun, which Sam guessed Bennigan might bring along. And then there was the coon hunter, who was certain to be carrying.

Sorenson had swapped out his standard-issue shoes for hiking boots. He appeared skinny and tense.

"Deputy," Sam nodded.

Sorenson nodded back. "Think we'll find it?"

"The cougar?" Sam said.

Sorenson nodded, worried.

"Between Gray and these coon dogs, we stand a pretty good chance."

"How far can a cougar go in a day?"

"Miles and miles, but that's not their habit," Sam said. "After the sun rises, they typically find somewhere to bed down. They're nocturnal hunters."

They thought about a cougar hunting in the dark. Sam thought Deputy Sorenson was concerned. Maybe a little afraid. Sam looked at Bennigan and said, "Do you have those antler hats? We always wear antler hats in Colorado. It's like bait to a lion."

Bennigan had also sensed Sorenson's anxiety and decided to play along.

"Yup. Got the deer scent too."

"Perfect. What we need is for someone to be in the lead and wear the horns and the scent, draw the lion in close."

"Someone lean, fit? Somebody who looks like he could run?" Bennigan turned and gave Deputy Sorenson the once-over.

"That's it," Sam said, also considering Sorenson. "Deputy?"

"I'm just following here," Sorenson said, clearing his throat. He was doubtful they were serious, but he knew nothing about coon hunting and less about hunting cougar.

"We got your back," Sam said. "Besides, first they leap onto their prey and knock them down. Then they go in for the kill. We see a mountain lion attack and try and break your neck with its jaw, we come running."

"That's not funny," Sorenson said.

Sam looked at Bennigan and smiled.

Bennigan started laughing. "I thought it was funny."

While they waited, they talked briefly about the perfect day and the way it was going to morph into a perfect night, and Sam said, "I hope, if that cougar's out there, he didn't run far."

"I'm hoping this guy's dogs'll find him," Bennigan said.

Sam considered the young CO. They were headed out on a search-and-destroy mission, and even though it was in Savage, an outlying suburb of the Twin Cities, he knew missions like this could take on a life of their own.

When he was first starting in the USFW, Sam had done some remote patrolling in the Colorado Mountains during elk season. More than once, he'd come upon encampments of four to five hunters. Normally, they were cordial and polite and pulled out their licenses, no questions asked. But there were rare groups with one or two who acted differently, knowing the lone officer was outnumbered and this was maybe one of their few chances to give officialdom a piece of their mind. He recalled one group of hunters who had a kind of *Deliverance* vibe.

There was only one way to deal with men like that: look them in the eye and remain firm and hypervigilant, in case things turned ugly. Whenever he recollected the instinctual threat he'd sensed, far away from anything civilized, he still felt an unmistakable fear factor. At the time, he was young. Today, he might handle it the same way, but fear would be replaced with a cool certainty in his perspective. Regardless, nothing ever happened, but sometimes it had gotten dicey.

Almost everyone in this group was from law enforcement, so he expected the hunt would be well organized and smooth, if such a thing was possible when running with hounds at dusk through river-bottom woods.

And then the quiet afternoon was broken by the sound of thudding music and a truck engine.

"I'm guessing that's my guy," Bennigan said.

"Who is he?"

"Jake Massey, a hunter I busted in early September. He was running dogs on park land. It was on the border. Public land on one side, park on the other, and he crossed the line. I gave him a warning, so he owes me."

The cacophony rose over the berm and a camo-patterned Ford pickup truck—its low fenders showing rust—turned into view, towing a trailer with a mud-spattered four-wheeler on top of it.

Sam, Sorenson, and Bennigan watched the truck and trailer turn onto the road and drive toward them. As it grew closer, the Allman Brothers' "Ramblin' Man" filled the warm September air.

"He likes to make an entrance," Sam said.

"He's a little rough around the edges, but he's got dogs," Bennigan said.

So had Angus Moon, Sam remembered.

Jake pulled to the side of the road, parked his truck, and killed the engine. The sudden silence was replaced by a chorus of what appeared to be four hounds, barking from their kennels in the truck's flatbed, guessing freedom and fun were near at hand.

Sam turned to Gray and saw the hybrid focused on the barking dogs, or at least their sound. Gray looked at Sam, curious. Then back at the dogs.

Jake got out of the cab and waited while Bennigan approached. He was big and rangy and appeared to be in his early 20s. A brooding belly pushed out beneath his dingy khaki-colored shirt. The rest of him was dressed head to toe in orange camo. He wore a vest, but it was wide open, and his five-day blonde stubble reached down his neck to the top of his T-shirt. His eyes were covered by a pair of wraparound sunglasses and his hair fell over his ears in unruly spikes.

"Hey, Jake," Bennigan said.

They shook hands, but it was tentative, and Jake glanced quickly at Sam and Sorenson. "Who're your friends?" he asked, suspicious.

Over the cacophony of dogs, Bennigan introduced them.

Sam's gut told him Jake had skirted a lot more borders than the one CO Bennigan had caught him violating. When Bennigan introduced Sam as an agent with U.S. Fish & Wildlife, the big man stared, whatever he was thinking concealed under his sunglasses.

"How come we need so much law to catch a cat?" Jake asked. "Especially Fish & Wildlife?"

"Agent Rivers is the only one here who knows anything about cougars," Bennigan said. "And Officer Sorenson is from the sheriff's office. I think I mentioned the cougar killed a guy?"

Jake nodded. The dogs were still making a ruckus in the back of the truck. The coon hunter turned and slapped an open palm against the truck, and the dogs stopped. "This is a straight-out hunt, right?" Jake said. "You're not expectin' to catch it alive, are you?"

"No," Sam said. "Track it, tree it, and shoot it."

There was suspicion in the big man's demeanor that made Sam think he should do a little official research on Jake Massey when he got the chance.

"The trail starts down this road," Bennigan said. "Where the guy was killed. Your dogs ready for a hunt?"

"They were born ready," Jake said. He walked over and examined the rusted chain and padlock fastening the gate in place. "Might have to cut this to get my four-wheel onto that road."

"Oh," Deputy Sorenson said. "I got a key from Marlin earlier." The deputy stepped forward and used his key to open the lock and part the chains.

Jake led them all back to his truck. The dogs were whining. He asked Sam and Deputy Sorenson to get the four-wheeler off the flatbed, while he and Bennigan started fetching the dogs from their kennels.

Jake and Bennigan pulled four dogs, one by one, out of their kennels. They were all 40–50 pounds, with big blotches of black, white, and brown. As they came out of their kennels, they could hardly contain themselves.

"What kind are they?" Sam asked.

"Treeing Walker coonhounds," Jake said. "Mostly."

"There's going to be lots of coons in those woods, but only one cougar," Sam said. "Can they find and hold a scent?"

Jake glanced up, wondering if it was an insult. "They've never smelled cougar. But they'll find it and hold it, if it's strong enough, you bet."

As each hound was brought down, Jake collared it with an expensive-looking orange glow strap and 6-inch antennas. Sam asked about the collars and Jake said, "They're Garmin DC 50 GPS dog trackers."

They had steel cable antennas and a 4-hour battery life, Jake explained. He tracked them on his Garmin Astro 320 handheld. "I'll never lose a dog in the woods."

Sam wondered how, if Jake had been using sophisticated GPS tracking equipment when he was caught on park land by CO Bennigan, he could have strayed so far afield. But he thought he knew the answer.

When Jake was finished explaining his dog-tracking equipment, he opened his cab, reached in behind his seat, and retrieved a long rifle case. He unzipped the case and pulled out what appeared to be a Marlin 336C. Sam recognized the weapon because he'd seen other elk and deer hunters use it.

"That's a lot of weapon for a raccoon," Sam said.

Jake looked at him and said, "But not for a cougar." He tossed the rifle case back into his cab, leaned the rifle against the truck, and reached back in to pull out a holster and pistol. "This is what I use for coons." After Sam saw it, Jake returned it to the truck's back seat, covering it with oily rags.

Bennigan and Sorenson each held a pair of hounds that were straining to follow the four-wheeler. The dogs knew that Jake and the four-wheeler led to the main attraction.

Sam turned and walked over to his jeep. He opened the door and let Gray come down off the seat. Gray immediately started toward the coonhounds, the hair on his spine rising.

"Gray," Sam said, which brought the hybrid to a stop.

As soon as the coonhounds caught sight of Gray, they turned toward him, ready to rumble. The hair rose a little higher on the back of Gray's spine.

"What the hell you plannin' on doing with that dog?" Jake asked.

"Hunt a cougar."

"My dogs'll find the cougar."

Sam had worked hard to socialize Gray to other dogs. He'd taken him to public dog parks in and around Denver since he was just a pup. But Gray was a loner. He never started a fight, but if some uncontrolled cur started one, he quickly let them know the pecking order. But he'd never been friendly with his dog cousins. He'd always been tolerant but standoffish. And it appeared as though he was going to be that way tonight.

"Gray won't mess with them, unless they start something," Sam said.

"What is he?"

"A wolf–dog hybrid."

"These here are designer dogs, special bred for what we're about tonight. Maybe you should leave that . . ." he paused, looking for the right word, "mix in your jeep, where he won't do any harm."

Sam didn't want to get into a pissing contest. But he wasn't going to leave Gray in the jeep.

"This *mix* is the only one here who's ever smelled a cougar. Last September he faced one down and saved a woman from getting attacked. I'd stake this animal's scenting instincts and capabilities against your designer dogs any day of the week because part of this *mix* springs from hunters who have been around for thousands of years and survived by killing what they ate. That's designer. Gray won't bother your hounds, unless they start something."

Sam wouldn't start anything either, he wanted to add. But he figured Jake was getting the message.

Jake shrugged. "Once Harley and his gang get onto a scent, they don't look or stop at nothin'."

"That'll work," Sam said.

Sam didn't have a radio collar for Gray because he knew he wouldn't need one. Gray would follow his own nose. And like a good pack member, the hybrid would make sure he always knew Sam's location.

They made their way slowly and carefully down the maintenance road, Jake taking the lead in the four-wheeler, followed by Bennigan with two dogs and Sorenson with two others, all of them straining at their leashes to follow Jake. Sam and Gray took up the rear.

Two hundred yards down the frontage road Chief Deputy Leif Anders peered out of the sumac thicket, watching the group of hunters get ready in the still evening air.

More dogs. He hated them. Perhaps more to the point, they hated him.

The chief had been on the sheriff's staff less than a year. He was a decorated soldier and a war hero, having won the Bronze Star in a firefight in Iraq seven years earlier. After Iraq, he'd re-upped for duty in Afghanistan, in the crazy Helmand province, where he had expected (and hoped) to die. And then a miracle, of sorts, when he not only survived but found out who and what he really was.

After 20 years, he got out, a double-dipper eligible for his pension at the age of 38.

Anders had always been a loner, which made him well suited for the military police. He didn't have friends and he didn't really need them. In the service, he'd been called Ice. And though he hadn't shared that detail with anyone in the sheriff's office, it was only a matter of time before his deputies had started calling him the Iceman, though no one did it in front of him. Anders had taken the job as chief deputy because he had the background, training, and personality for it. Like most people, the sheriff had been impressed with his credentials, particularly the Bronze Star. Which was just fine with Anders. Because the chief deputy's job was a good, safe, inside place to look for opportunities. Anders had plans. And those plans required money.

Anders watched the men and dogs gather at the road's entry. He'd noticed Jake make his entrance. He watched what appeared to be rancor flare between the coonhound hunter and Rivers. As soon as they were around the corner, starting down the road, he stepped out of the sumac patch and hurried toward Rivers's jeep. He didn't know what he was searching for, but he knew he had to look.

At first, Anders had considered Rivers just another annoyance, someone to put up with, as he did so many others. But then he'd watched him with the sheriff. He'd heard him express the one thing Anders and the sheriff did not want to hear: doubt.

About the cougar kill and the way it had unfolded and what it had done to Jack McGregor. Anders had supported and relied on the sheriff's perspective. It was the quick, law-and-order decision, the right one to make.

Rivers continued to suggest a perspective he would not relinquish, even in the face of Sheriff Benson's obvious and pointed irritations. And that's when Anders suggested they should keep a careful eye on Rivers, just to make sure he didn't cause problems.

The sheriff agreed.

After watching Rivers at the kill site, at the press conference, in the meeting with the McGregor executives, and now with this coonhound hunter, Anders recognized Rivers as someone who had a problem following orders. It appeared the special agent might be more than an annoyance. He might be someone Anders needed to deal with.

And he had a dog. Maybe more than a dog.

After getting Rivers settled in the Quality Inn, Anders spent some time researching the agent. He didn't like what he found. Seven months earlier, Rivers had uncovered murder and insurance fraud in the frigid north. And there were other stories, too, including one from the *Denver Post* referring to Rivers as the predator's predator. The article recounted a case he'd worked on in the Everglades, involving endangered Key deer.

Rare Florida deer were being annihilated from a section of the Florida Keys. Their total disappearance from an island they'd previously inhabited was suspicious. Rivers investigated, and after some digging and a few lucky breaks, he discovered a small group of developers who believed concern for the Key deer, which the

USFW estimated to number around 800 animals, was negatively impacting their development plans. They'd hired a South Florida hunter to rid the proposed development site of any trace of the small, endangered deer. And they would have succeeded, if the hunter hadn't begun selling Key deer skins, hooves, horns, and venison on the black market.

There was a picture of Rivers's 6'2" frame standing in front of the South Florida bulldozer he had single-handedly idled. His square shoulders and 195 pounds looked small in front of the huge shovel blade. But his greasy black hair, disheveled undercover clothes, and four-day facial growth made him look like the swamp rats he'd hunted. The article recounted how before it was all over, Sam Rivers had had to fight his way out of a backwoods bar.

Rivers's jeep was locked. Anders took out a deflated, thumb-sized bladder and inserted it between the top of the door and the frame. Once it was secure, he slowly inflated it until he'd made a half-inch opening. He'd cut and molded hanger wire into a foot-long wand with a rounded end. In the service, he had opened locked cars and trucks often enough and had become proficient at the process. After inserting the wand through the opening, he used the rounded end to press down on the automatic lock, which made a satisfying pop in the dusk light.

It was a hurried search. The car reeked of dog. He hated the smell almost as much as the animals that created it. But he was careful and quick, rifling through the front and back, and finally opening the glove compartment. A gun case, locked. Anders knew gun cases. He recognized the brand and knew how to open it but didn't have the proper tools. The gun case and whatever it held might be useful. There wasn't much in Rivers's jeep. But maybe there'd been enough.

Anders carefully locked and closed the door. Then he turned and started over to Jake Massey's truck.

At the kill site, Jake had instructed his dogs exactly the way Sam had instructed Gray earlier in the day. He brought each of the hounds up to the print and had them stick their noses into the footpad. Jake gave them the commands to let them know they should follow it. Then he unleashed them and they were off.

Their tails wagged and worried, and they zigged and zagged over the maintenance road and down into the edge of the ravine, and then finally Harley started barking and flew by Gray, returning down the road the way they'd come.

Sam took Gray out of his sit and said, "Go," which was all the big hybrid needed. He took off in gangly pursuit of the pack of treeing Walker coonhounds.

Jake worked to turn his four-wheeler around on the road and was out after them, and in about 60 seconds Jake and the dogs were around the bend and Sam, Sorenson, and Bennigan were hurrying to keep up.

"This seem right to you, Agent Rivers?" Sorenson asked.

"That's exactly what Gray did this morning. I thought Gray was following some kind of mistaken scent, but now I wonder."

Back at the vehicles, Anders had just finished searching Massey's truck. He found the .22-caliber pistol, something else that might be useful, depending. And in the glove compartment he found a small baggie of marijuana and three joints.

Hmm, he thought.

Then he locked and closed the truck.

When he stuck his head out, he could hear the barking dogs. But instead of moving away, they seemed to be getting closer. He listened, to be sure, and realized almost before it was too late that the dogs and the four-wheeler were piling down the minimum-maintenance road back toward him.

Anders turned, hustled across the road and up over the berm to the other side, crouching low in the bramble just as the dogs and Massey's four-wheeler blew out of the road's entrance.

Anders stayed low and hurried back toward his car.

It took Sam, Sorenson, and Bennigan about 5 minutes to return. On the side of the road, 40 yards beyond Jake's truck, the hounds were baying and worrying over the same place Gray had found that morning. Gray was sniffing and worrying over the space with the rest of the hounds, but remained mute.

"Damn strange," Jake said when they approached.

Bennigan and Jake started leashing the baying hounds.

"Here's where it ends," he added.

"What do you make of it?" Sam asked.

"I wonder if they picked up the wrong scent? I wonder if somebody's boots got mixed up with that cougar scent and they followed it back out here?"

"I thought the same thing."

"Cuz it looks like someone was parked here," Jake said, staring down at deep tire tracks along the road's shoulder.

Sam nodded. "Yup."

"There any other prints or fur or something else, back down by where it happened?" Jake asked. "Something else we might be able to use to get a bead on?"

Sam thought about it. "Let's head down into that ravine. There were some prints in a dry creekbed about 40 yards from that deer carcass. They're about three weeks old, but maybe we can pick up something from those."

"Worth a try," Jake said.

They turned the four-wheeler and dogs around and started back down the road.

For the next 4 hours, men and dogs picked their way south through a wild section of Minnesota River Valley. The dogs smelled the old prints in the creekbed and seemed to pick up a trace, growing excited and then agitated in the dusk light, until Jake let them off leash and they disappeared upriver, baying through the river-bottom woods. The men and Gray pursued, struggling though the woods until it grew dark and they had to don their headlights. For a time, the sound of the dogs grew more faint. But after 10 minutes, nothing. They were only blips on Jack's screen.

Gray was keen on following the hounds. But unlike Jack's dogs, Gray wasn't collared. And if the hounds succeeded in running down the cougar, they wouldn't need the big hybrid to chase it up a tree. Sam had to constantly remind Gray to stay near, a directive he accepted, reluctantly.

Finally, after more than 3 hours, Jake recognized the moment when he would have to start bringing them back. The collars had a 4-hour battery life, conservatively, so it was time to use his Garmin Astro 320 handheld to send a signal to his dogs. When the men finally caught up to them, they were baying around a huge maple. There were four young raccoons 60 feet overhead, keeping the dogs occupied.

By the time they had returned to their cars, kenneled the dogs, and loaded the four-wheeler back on Jake's flatbed, it was well after 10. CO Bennigan had taken out some maps and when he examined them, he noticed how the river narrowed near Shakopee. Judging from the light pollution, they hadn't been far from the next town down. Beyond Shakopee, the country widened out again into wilder river valley than the area around McGregor's facility. Not much farther was the Savannah Swamp, a large primitive regional park. Other than a couple of trails, it was a remote section of 1,000 acres of woods.

"If I was a cougar, that's where I'd hole up," Bennigan said. "That place doesn't get a lot of visitors. The few it does get come in winter for cross-country skiing. During the spring and early summer, it's a mosquito-infested swamp. And there's no agriculture and lots of deer. And poachers, come to think of it. This year we've gotten four reports about out-of-season hunters with guns. Found some gut piles too."

"Sounds like my kind of place," Jake said.

"Go ahead and try. I'll bust your butt just like I did up north," Bennigan said.

"First you gotta find me." Jake grinned.

Under the beam of their headlamps, Sam and Jake studied the map and came to the same conclusion. They all figured they would check out the swamp tomorrow and see if they could pick up anything. They all agreed the dogs, including Gray, had been onto something, and they were keen to head into the woods again tomorrow.

"Keep me posted," Sam said. He had to meet Marlin in the morning, and he wasn't sure how long it was going to take. And then he had some people he wanted to see. But first he would need to lose his tail, Deputy Sorenson. "I've got to finish testifying at that extradition hearing tomorrow. I'll meet up with you guys later in the day?"

"Sounds good," Bennigan said.

Jake Massey thought so too. He said he needed to get back to Coon Rapids, but was up for having a beer.

"Think I'll pass," Sam said.

Sorenson, too.

"I could use a brew," Bennigan said.

Deputy Sorenson said goodnight. Sam told him he'd call him in the morning, maybe they could grab some coffee before he headed to St. Paul. But it probably wouldn't be until after 8:30 or so, which was fine with the deputy.

On the way home Sam speed-dialed Diane.

He and Gray were dog-tired, no pun intended, and were ready for a good bed and shut-eye.

Diane picked up on the first ring. "What did you find?"

"Nothing. Raccoons. But I think those dogs were onto something."

"The cougar?"

"I think so, but it was odd." Sam explained about the dogs first running out to the road's shoulder, and then their subsequent run through the woods and the treed raccoons.

"What about Gray?"

"He didn't know what to make of it. I think he thought his coonhound cousins were crazy, running through the woods, making a constant racket until they finally treed a raccoon, and then jumping and baying around that tree. When we got there, he was standing off to the side, gazing at them, doing everything but using his front paw to scratch his head."

Diane laughed and there was a sudden ease that came across the line. They talked awhile longer, mostly about the case but also about Moon's extradition. She'd hurried through her coverage of Moon's hearing, which wasn't over, and filed the piece with her editor up north. She'd spent most of the day on McGregor's murder and had finally followed Moon's story with McGregor's, which would appear in tomorrow morning's *Vermilion Falls Gazette*. The *Chicago Tribune* was also interested in the story. She wanted to write a follow-up on cougars, particularly cougar predations. In the morning, before heading back to Moon's extradition, she was going to spend time researching cougars and starting her article.

"You'd think after this day I'd be dead tired, but I'm still a little wired," Diane said.

"Maybe you need a drink?" Sam suggested.

The day had started early, and he and Gray had been running since before their courtroom drama, which was the first adrenaline rush in a day that had held a few. It was the reason he'd decided not to go out with the younger Bennigan and Jake. But now, with Diane, *maybe* surfaced in the back of his thoughts like a cork.

There was a pause, during which Sam wondered if he'd sounded too suggestive.

"Rivers," Diane finally said. Then another long pause.

"What?" Sam said, trying to sound innocent. But he wasn't, and he knew it.

"Maybe I *could* use a drink," she said. But before Sam could suggest anything, she added, "Maybe I could use more than that. But for now, I'm hanging up."

Then the line went dead.

Sam was stopped at the T intersection on Highway 13. He was thinking about what they'd both managed to say without saying it.

One turn was toward the Quality Inn. The other, toward Diane.

He sat there, thinking. Then he looked at Gray.

"Eh," Sam said. "I'm too old and tired and mixed up for this crap." But he knew he wasn't.

He turned toward the Quality Inn.

CHAPTER THIRTEEN

John needed to drive. At first, when he got in his car, it was going to be aimless. *Just a drive in the dark,* he told himself. *I am in the dark and maybe following my headlights around for a while will give me some inspiration.*

But it didn't. All it did was make him think about Urban. He knew her real name. But since this new business started, she'd made him use Urban.

"From now on I always want you to call me Urban," she'd said. "I like using different names. Different names mean different people. And different people can do things they wouldn't ordinarily do."

It wasn't the first time he had been propositioned in an offbeat way, but it had been strange and surprising and different from all the other times. Because Urban was different. He'd had his eye on her for quite a while and he didn't try to hide it. It was the way he was. Smarmy.

But now he was in trouble, riding through the southern Twin Cities. He looked up and noticed he was driving down 169, crossing the river, heading south. Not a surprise.

Urban had broken his serve. That's what he thought. For his entire life, tennis had been his natural game. Tennis was how he made his living, such as it was. Until Urban, he hadn't thought about his future. He'd thought about the next good time.

Several months earlier, John recognized that moment when a woman knows she is being considered in a particular kind of way. She'd caught him on more than a couple occasions giving her the wandering once-over. And eventually they'd started playing. Together. They had slipped easily into what was comfortable for him. He knew the territory. At first, she seemed to enjoy being played. They flirted. And then gradually something else happened that was unlike the others. He couldn't tell where it was going and then he didn't want it to end.

And then she told him about Urban.

Urban was a different person.

Urban could do things.

And so they did.

Once across the river John turned on 13, heading north.

She was a drug. That's what he thought. She made him do things. He'd never been this way. He'd always had the upper hand. He'd always had his serve. Now . . . nothing. Now he just waited for the next good fix.

They'd had a handful of encounters. He knew before the first one they were going to be something. He'd kept a library of taped encounters. Video, when it was at his house. Just audio, when it was somewhere else. He'd been surreptitious about it, and afterward, when he listened or watched, it was exciting. It wasn't like one of those movies you pay for down in those shops off Hennepin.

These were recordings of his special moments and they reminded him of . . . what? What was the word?

Prowess, he thought. They reminded him he was powerful.

And when he listened to them, they were exciting.

Which is why he recorded her, at first. He wanted to be reminded of his prowess.

Urban had struck him unlike any other. Urban had cast a spell. Urban was a drug, and he was addicted.

He turned on Judicial Road and, after 5 minutes of driving, entered the CVS parking lot. He looked around. At this hour there were five cars but no one in the lot. He walked out to Judicial Road and started up the other side.

It was late and there was little or no traffic. The insects were trilling in the dark. John walked along the edge of Judicial Road, searching for the right place to turn into the black woods. It wasn't his first time; he knew where a gap in the foliage gave way to the small-game trail that would take him where he needed to go. But it was his first time coming unbidden. And now he came because he needed to . . . he needed to know.

It was dangerous. But the morning's call had unsettled him, and now he thought there was only one way to shake it. Not through work, not through a late dinner or the news accounts of the bizarre death of the multimillionaire, Jack McGregor, slain by a cougar in the Minnesota River Valley. The coverage had been sensational and perfect. The cougar was first spotted three weeks earlier, in almost the exact location where the attack occurred. It was bizarre and terrible, and until the animal was captured and killed, it was prudent to stay out of the woods.

John watched the coverage on channel 11. Sheriff Benson related the basic facts. Then the wildlife guy shared some facts about cougars, including speculation that the cyclist could have been mistaken for a running deer. And then a DNR conservation officer talked about what they were doing to catch the animal and reiterated that people should stay out of the woods.

The coverage reminded John to tell Urban, tomorrow, that Benedict should hit the road. They no longer needed him.

John heard the car before he saw its headlights. He side-stepped into the tree edge and waited.

The car rushed by in a flash. He watched the red taillights fade and waited for the insects to resume their calling. Then he stepped out of the branches and kept walking along the shoulder of the dark road. He was careful to keep out of sight. If anyone did see him, they would think he was a neighbor out for a late-night walk.

But it was better to be invisible.

After Jack McGregor, John had worried about being able to sleep. He'd called in to work to tell them he'd be late. And then well after dawn, he'd soaped down hard in a hot shower, and when his head hit his pillow, he'd settled comfortably into oblivion, at least until the sun was high off the horizon. There had been too much preparation, and finally, when it was all done and finished, he was exhausted. And so, he rested, peaceful as a king on his throne bed.

Then, leaving for work, he'd made the call. He knew he shouldn't, but he had to let Urban know it was good; they were good to let Benedict go. He'd done what was necessary and now it was finished. Cut him loose.

And then Urban told him how Benedict could still be useful and how he'd spotted the wildlife guy, and that's when the seed was planted. That's when the green-eyed jealousy began to grow. John hadn't been able to shake it. He could tell Urban was pissed. The hang up was message enough. But throughout the day, the more he tried to recall their conversations about Benedict, the more doubtful he became. Was it just him who had been adamant about getting rid of Benedict? John couldn't remember a single instance in which Urban had said, definitively, that Benedict had a shelf life. And the more he thought about it, the more he hated Urban's failure to share the full plan. Urban was being coy.

And that's what gnawed at him; that's what fertilized the seed of doubt and made it grow. Doubt grew quickly into suspicion. Mistrust made sleep hopeless. So he got in his car and started driving through the dark.

In the kitchen, Urban pulled down the bottle. The first day was nearly finished. It was almost midnight. The first part was done, and in spite of Urban's premonitions, nothing untoward had occurred. So she would have a drink. A glass of red. To celebrate.

John came to the patch of blackberry bramble, saw the bushy tree branches beyond it, and stepped again into the black wood.

He entered far enough to conceal himself, waiting for his eyes to grow accustomed to the deeper shade of darkness. There was an opening on the other side of the heavy brush, a small empty place in the woods that marked the start of the game trail.

A pickup truck approached along Judicial Road. He watched the headlights flash through dense branches and illuminate the shadows, revealing the small-game trail ahead.

The insects grew silent as the truck swept by.

It was another warm night. He waited for the bugs' chirruping return. Then he turned out of the empty place and started along the trail.

After a few minutes of walking, the lights glimmered through the trees. He recognized the back side of the houses—her house and the one next to it. He approached carefully, soundless. Through the rear windows he could see into partially lit rooms. He peered through the leaves at the neighbor's open second-story window. A late-night channel flickered. The neighbor always had her set turned full blast.

When he glanced to the back of Urban's house, he saw her. Just her head, tilted back, with a wineglass to her lips. He waited and watched.

He didn't have a plan. He'd just wanted to check, to make sure she was there and alone. Because if Benedict, or someone else, had been there, he would have . . . *what?* he wondered. He didn't know what he would have done.

Something.

What he knew was . . . Urban was a drug. She was a spell caster.

He waited and watched as she finished her glass of wine and finally left the kitchen, turning off the light. He waited through her imagined rise up the stairs. He saw the light come on in the curtained bedroom. He waited, imagining her disrobing. He wanted her. He wanted her more than anything he could remember. John ached in the darkness.

Finally, the light went out of the upstairs room and he stepped back, trying to get hold of himself. What did he think watching her from behind the house was going to do? Make him feel whole again? Calm his riled waters? Ease him, so he could step back into the black woods and fade into the dark night?

He did fade into the woods and the night, but not with ease.

PART II

September 24

CHAPTER FOURTEEN

There was a guard station next to the front gate. The entire front compound of McGregor Industries was surrounded by 10-foot-high chain-link fencing and an overhead tri-string of barbed wire. As Sam approached, he peered beyond the gate and saw a variety of parked cars, heavy equipment, and a backlot building that seemed to go on forever. The place was big. And protected.

By the time Sam approached the gate, the morning light was well off the horizon and beaming through another clear fall day. It was pleasant and satisfying, and both Sam and Gray were happy to be out in it. Marlin Coots had apparently seen Sam's approach and was in the doorway to the small guard house, pointing Sam toward an empty parking spot behind the structure. Then he stood in the early morning sunlight, waiting.

Gray remained in the car. Sam cracked the windows, got out of his jeep, and walked over to the guard house.

"Another perfect morning," Sam said.

"It is," Marlin nodded.

Sam sensed intelligence in the reclusive night watchman, at least enough to make him overqualified for his current position. For starters, Marlin knew the wild. Anyone who could read a cat paw print and know the difference, and know it was a very rare cougar and that all cat prints were basically alike, at least in structure, had spent some time in the wild. Particularly reading animal tracks. And that was not a skill commonly practiced in today's world.

The guard house was small. There was a drive-up window, a small table, a rack with keys and some tools, and two chairs. On top of the table were some papers, parts of a newspaper, and several photos. There was a small black-and-red day pack sitting on the floor in the corner. The photos were what Sam had come to see: the pictures of the cougar kill from three weeks earlier. But he'd also been curious about Marlin.

Marlin pointed out the photos and identified the one the papers used. It held the clearest image of the big cat. No doubt about it: *Puma concolor*. A cougar. This one apparently in Minnesota's backyard. It appeared healthy and magnificent and stared into the camera with feline wariness.

There was a deck of other photos, many of them showing glimpses of the big cat—a shoulder and the back of its head or hind quarters. And then Sam noticed a half dozen near the bottom of the pile, close-ups of three or four paw prints in creek mud.

"You took these the same day?"

"Yeah," Marlin nodded. "When I saw the camera had taken some shots, I hunted for more signs. Found those tracks in the creekbed, the ones I showed you yesterday."

"Can I borrow this one?" Sam asked, holding up the clearest image of the cat.

"Sure. You can have it. I mean, I scanned it, if you want the digital image."

"You learned this stuff from your dad?"

"Dad taught me about motion sensors and developing film. He was old school. The scanning and digital imaging I picked up on my own. It's easier to store and work with the images."

Marlin was full of surprises. "If you can email it to me, that'd be great. Can you also email it to a friend of mine, Diane Talbott?"

Marlin nodded. "Sure. Just give me the addresses."

"She wants to run the photo with an article she's writing. That OK?"

"Sure," Marlin said. "All the papers used it, earlier this month."

"She's probably going to run it in her paper, the *Vermilion Falls Gazette,* a small paper up on the Range. But also probably the *Chicago Tribune.* Does she owe you anything for it?"

"Nah," Marlin said, as though the idea was ridiculous. "No one paid me. I thought people should have a chance to see it. I was happy they ran it."

It was a simple, good answer. "And can you email me these photos of the paw prints? I've got some from yesterday and I'd like to compare them. Right off, I notice these don't show any claw points."

"Sure," Marlin said.

Sam thought about it. "In fact, Marlin, I'm wondering if you can give me a hand. I'll email you the photos I took yesterday, of the prints. Maybe you can take a look at them and compare them to these? I'd like another pair of eyes. Particularly from someone who knows a cougar print from a coyote."

Marlin nodded and blushed a little. He was happy to help and appreciated being asked. "You think they're different?"

"I can't be sure until I take a closer look. But it would be good to get a second opinion."

"Sure," Marlin said.

"Have you seen the papers this morning?" Sam asked.

Marlin shook his head. "I was going to pick one up when I left."

"Me too," Sam said. He reminded himself to buy both local papers. He'd like to read what they said about McGregor's death. Sam also missed last night's TV news coverage, given his late-night hunt in the woods. "Did you watch the news?"

Marlin shook his head no. "I'm usually asleep for the news."

"Have you seen anyone nosing around?"

"No one. It's been quiet, like normal. Cammy should be here any minute. Then I'll make my rounds, like I did yesterday."

"Mind if Gray and I tag along?"

"Sure. I mean, that'd be fine."

On cue, Cammy, the day watchwoman, drove up in a battered Subaru. She was a stout, gruff woman, probably in her early 30s, dressed in a gray uniform with her name tag over her left breast—CAMMY—and a MCGREGOR INDUSTRIES patch on her right breast pocket. She wore her hair in a crew cut.

She and Marlin greeted each other. Marlin told her it'd been a quiet night and she nodded. Marlin introduced her to Sam. Then Marlin reached down, shouldered his day pack, and he and Sam walked over to Sam's jeep for Gray. Gray stepped down to the blacktop, happy to be out in the day.

The morning *was* beautiful. They talked sporadically as they retraced the minimum-maintenance road, patrolling McGregor

Industries' perimeter. Marlin was interested in Gray. He asked some questions about how the dog was bred, and how he'd come into Sam's hands.

After Sam told him the story, Marlin said, "I read about some of that yesterday, after I got home."

"You read about it?"

"It was in that newspaper you mentioned. The one up north. And there were three or four stories in the *Star Tribune*. One of them mentioned the dogs."

"From last February?"

Marlin nodded.

"You checking up on me, Marlin?" Sam asked.

Marlin blushed and said, "No, I was just curious. Someone said you were a wolf expert and you broke up that ring last February, up north. I remember when that hit the news."

Sam smiled. But he was surprised, imagining Marlin going home yesterday, much later than usual, and searching the internet. From what he could tell, no one in the sheriff's office had inquired about his past.

While they walked, Sam explained how Gray was still in training and how the service wasn't sure they'd use him, but that Gray would always have a good home with him.

Gray walked beside Sam, occasionally checking to make sure his gait was in line with Sam's. Gray appeared entirely comfortable with Marlin, and he liked walking down the road with the two men in the clear September morning.

"How do you like working here?" Sam asked.

"It's an OK job."

"Just a job?"

"I guess."

"How long you worked here?"

"Almost 20 years."

"So what did you think of Jack McGregor?" Sam asked.

"He was always nice to me."

"Was he like that with everyone?"

Marlin paused. "Not exactly."

They walked another 10 yards before Sam asked, "What do you mean?"

He shrugged. "I've heard others say things. You hear things . . . see things, on this job." He was quiet for a minute before he added, "My dad told me it's not good to say bad things about people who have passed. And Mr. McGregor was always nice to me. His dad knew my dad."

"Your dad worked here too?"

"He was out on the back lot. Drove a truck."

"Did your dad get you the job?"

"No. But it made a difference that Mr. McGregor knew my dad and knew how hard he worked."

"Your dad had a good reputation?"

Marlin nodded.

"What about Mr. McGregor? How was his reputation?"

Marlin looked off toward the distant trees marking the river's edge. "So-so."

"Was he tough on his workers?"

Marlin shrugged. "Not exactly."

"Was he a head buster, Marlin?"

That made Marlin look. "You mean, did he yell at people?"

"Yeah. Something like that. Did he crack the whip? Make people work like dogs?"

"Not exactly. But they've been working pretty hard the last *few* months."

Sam thought about it. "Was there anything else about Jack McGregor besides hard work?"

Marlin turned and looked at Sam.

"You going to make me keep guessing, Marlin?"

The man had big eyes that stared at Sam like a pair of high beams. Marlin was looking for something, gazing intently and not hiding it. Sam felt like he was being summed up.

"Not exactly," Marlin finally said.

Sam smiled.

They walked a few more paces before Marlin said, "I'll show you, when we get back to the shack."

They kept walking down the road, enjoying the morning. Marlin was a big man, but not a big conversationalist.

There was still yellow crime scene tape around the tree and section of road where McGregor was attacked. Marlin and Sam were reverential as they passed the scene, remembering what had transpired a little more than 24 hours earlier. They passed it and walked 200 more yards to the loading docks on the Minnesota River. The morning was cool but warming up. Three workers were just arriving and looked up from a dock shack. One of them waved, and Marlin waved back. Then Marlin and Sam turned and started back the way they'd come.

At the guard shack, Cammy was waiting outside the door, next to the window, enjoying the morning sun.

"We're not gonna have this much longer," she said.

"Nope," Marlin said. "You want to make your rounds?"

"Yup," she said, and then she glanced down at Gray and said, "That's a big friggin' dog." She didn't move to pet him.

"He is," Sam agreed.

"What kind?"

"He's a wolf–dog hybrid."

"No shit? Half wolf?"

Cammy looked at the dog's eyes, one blue, one yellow. "What's with the eyes? One of them blind?"

"No," Sam said. "One of them lacks pigment, is all."

Cammy considered it, then pushed off the guard shack wall and started walking toward the backlot.

Marlin turned to Sam and smiled. "After I walk the perimeter, Cammy checks the lot, the machine shed, and the other buildings."

He waited until Cammy was out of earshot and then said, "If you want to put Gray back in your jeep, I'll show you some photos."

After Gray was stowed, Sam returned and found Marlin rummaging in his day pack. He brought out a flat brown paper bag. He held it in his hand, turned to Sam and said, "Sometimes we have issues with the night cleaning staff. Nice people. For the most part, pretty hard workers. But sometimes, things come up."

"What kinds of things?"

"Over the last year, a microwave disappeared from a break room, some power tools out of the machine shed, and then a TV with a built-in DVD was stolen out of the executive conference room."

Marlin paused to let Sam absorb the gravity of the thefts.

"Is that abnormal?" Sam asked. "I mean, most businesses expect a little employee theft, don't they?"

"Not Mr. McGregor. He took it personally. It was the only time he ever yelled at me, though I'd heard him yell at others before. He wasn't a big yeller. But lately he seemed a little tense."

"What'd he say?"

Marlin paused. "I'm kind of head of security around here," he said. "The power tools and the microwave weren't so bad. But when the TV went missing out of the executive conference room, Mr. McGregor was pissed. He said, 'Marlin, you gotta figure this out. I don't care what you do, just make sure it stops.'"

"Did he call the police?"

Marlin shook his head. "I wanted to because I'm not exactly law enforcement trained. But Mr. McGregor said, 'I'm not going to get the locals involved because they'll just come in and start accusing people.'"

Sam thought about it.

"I think Mr. McGregor thought if the police got involved, some of his night staff would disappear," Marlin said.

Sam nodded. "So what did you do?"

"First I made sure we replaced the video DVD player with a new one, nicer."

"Bait?"

Marlin nodded. "Then I hid some cheap digital cameras around the place. With infrared triggers. Only I didn't tell anybody."

"McGregor didn't know?"

"Nobody knew. I didn't tell Cammy, anyone. And I hid them pretty well." He glanced out into the lot to make sure they were alone. There was a guy 50 yards away, crossing to his car. Otherwise, the lot was empty. It was still a half hour before shift end.

"So what did you find?"

"You can have these," Marlin said. "They were taken in the executive conference room a few months ago. After hours. I only made the one set from the images. Then I got scared and decided to erase the images."

Sam took the flat brown paper sack, curious.

"I like to take photos," Marlin explained. "I have a lot of wildlife shots. Now with digital it's pretty easy to set up a few cameras."

The man blushed about as red as you could get and still be considered healthy. It was the photos and his much-longer-than-normal statement. Marlin was uncomfortable, and he didn't want Sam to examine the photos here. But when Sam looked out the window, the lot was still empty. He flipped open the sack and took out a sheaf of 4-by-6 prints tucked into a ziplock bag. Through the plastic the top picture showed two people in the conference room. The image was a fuzzy black-and-white. Definitely a cheap camera. The resolution was poor and the light was too white. But he could see it was Jack McGregor. And a woman, leaning against an oversized conference table."

"Who's the woman?"

"That's Mrs. Sweet, a financial analyst. Now I think she's assistant treasurer. She works with Mr. Traub."

Traub was McGregor Industries' treasurer, Sam remembered. Sweet looked young. Nice figure. Long black hair. Sam remembered she was one of the five who knew about the sale of the company.

Sam pulled the sheaf of photos out of the ziplock bag. He quickly leafed through them and watched McGregor approach Sweet. They were talking. And then the photos changed, each one showing McGregor getting closer. They were stills, but you could feel the scene, when McGregor crossed some line. And suddenly his hands were on her—way out of line, judging by the progression of photos. The images were poor quality, but clear enough to sense Sweet had first been shocked and then had pushed away from him and fled.

In a courtroom the pictures would have supported a claim of harassment if not sexual assault. Sam guessed Sweet could have used them to name her settlement amount, no questions asked, provided she knew they existed.

Sam looked up and saw Cammy crossing the lot. "McGregor never knew about these?"

Marlin shook his head, emphatic. "God no," Marlin said. "After these, I took down the camera, at least in the conference room. Nobody knows about these. Except you, now."

"Did you ever see anything else?"

"You mean, with Mr. McGregor?"

"With McGregor. Or did you ever see who was ripping off the place?"

"Not yet," Marlin said.

"How long ago were these taken?"

"It was quite a while ago. Around early spring."

"What time of day?"

"I work the midnight-to-8 shift. The infrareds were timed to come on after the night cleaning staff finished their work, sometime after 9. So it had to be sometime after that, and before I made my rounds. So sometime between 9 and midnight. Over the last few months, Mr. McGregor was putting in a lot of late hours. Him and some of the other executives."

"So 9 to 12," Sam said.

Marlin nodded. "Had to happen then. There's something going on, because of the extra hours people are putting in. Not only Jack McGregor."

"Any idea what it is?" Sam asked.

Marlin shook his head no.

Sam asked if he could keep the photos.

Marlin shrugged. "Sure."

He returned the photos to the ziplock and brown paper sack and then folded it so he could slip them into his back pocket.

"I've heard things, like I said. But that was the first time I ever saw anything," Marlin said.

"I appreciate that, Marlin. Don't worry about it. You were only doing your job."

"If anyone sees those," Marlin said. "They'll probably wonder why I didn't come forward."

Marlin was worried and he felt bad. Sam could feel it. "No one from McGregor will ever see them. I'll make sure of it. At this point, it's just interesting background. What other things did you hear about Jack McGregor?"

Marlin shrugged. "He liked women. My dad said Mr. McGregor's dad liked women and then he told me his son, Jack, was . . . the way Dad said it was 'The acorn did not fall far from the tree.'"

"I guess," Sam said. He grinned a little, and Marlin grinned back.

Cammy was getting close. Sam nodded to Marlin and said, "OK. Let's just keep this between us. It's probably nothing, but I appreciate you sharing it."

Actually, it was plenty. But Sam didn't want the night watchman to worry.

Marlin nodded.

Then Cammy came into the shed and said, "God, it is one motherfuckin' beautiful day!"

CHAPTER FIFTEEN

O n his way out of McGregor Industries, Sam rummaged in his breast pocket for his iPhone. It was set on vibrate and when he looked at the screen, he saw one missed call. A local number, came in about 30 minutes ago. Probably Deputy Sorenson. He did a callback.

Sheriff Benson answered. When Sam identified himself, the sheriff sounded pleased.

"I got a call from Lieutenant Cole over at the BCA this morning," the sheriff said. "It's cougar hair all right."

Sam paused. He could feel the sheriff gloating over the phone. "That's good," Sam said. "It was the hair taken from the site?"

"Course it was. Where the hell else would we get cougar hair?"

Sam considered responding, but let it go. "That's great," he said.

"Isn't it?" the sheriff said.

"I mean, it's great for our accident, but also because the University of Colorado is always looking for mountain lion DNA, particularly those east of the Rockies, since they're rare. They've started an international mountain lion DNA database, cataloging all the DNA ever collected, which isn't much."

"Fascinating," the sheriff said, without conviction.

"You think the BCA would send the U a copy of the record?" A second opinion would be prudent, and they *were* building a database.

"Don't see why not. Myrtle can help ya," the sheriff said. "So I heard from Deputy Sorenson you struck out last night."

"That's right. But I think the dogs were onto something. We just ran out of time."

"Damn right they were onto something. You going out again this morning? With the dogs?"

"Can't this morning. Extradition hearing in St. Paul," Sam said, vaguely. "But we're thinking about meeting up later today, probably around 4 or 5 again. Down at the Savannah Swamp," Sam said.

"Thinking about? Rivers, there's a cougar out there and yesterday it killed someone, and if I had a nickel for every call I've received from the Busy Betties worrying about stepping into their backyards, I'd be rich. Rich!"

Sam paused, thinking of several things to say, all of which were inflammatory. "OK. We will be meeting at 4 or 5 to comb through the Savannah Swamp."

"Just get out into the woods and kill that thing," the sheriff said. Then he hung up.

Sam hated it when people with bad manners and big egos got the last word. But for now, he'd have to live with it.

Another call came in, the same area code and preface as the sheriff's number. Deputy Sorenson, Sam guessed.

"Sorenson?" Sam said.

"Where are you?"

"Turning onto Highway 13, looking for some coffee and breakfast before I have to head over to that extradition hearing," Sam said. He hoped the deputy wasn't in the Quality Inn parking lot.

There was a pause, during which Sam wondered if Sorenson knew he wasn't at the hotel. Technically, Sam was supposed to avoid McGregor Industries. And he didn't want to tell Sorenson the reason he'd visited, or what he'd found. He was considering a plausible excuse, when the deputy spoke.

"I could use a good cup of coffee," Sorenson said. "How about I meet you?"

"Sounds good to me. Got any recommendations? I need a good cup of coffee and maybe a bagel . . . egg sandwich . . . something simple and fast."

"Dan Patch Coffee Depot," Sorenson suggested. He told Sam how to get there. The place was about 5 minutes from the Quality Inn. The deputy would take a little longer, since he was coming from the sheriff's office. And that was fine with Sam, since he was coming from McGregor Industries.

The coffee shop was an old, converted train depot. There hadn't been a train for a long time. There were old photos of horses on the wall. While Sam waited for his egg sandwich, he sipped the local brew and read about Dan Patch, the name of a local harness racehorse. Apparently, he set several harness-racing records in the early 1900s, one in 1906 that he held more than three decades.

Sam picked up his food, and then found a newspaper and a corner table.

He laid out the *Star Tribune* and column one declared "CEO Killed by Cougar." The article said cougars were extremely rare in Minnesota and then referenced the fact that one had been seen in the area earlier in the month.

On the inside page, there was an interesting map indicating by shaded areas the number of Minnesota cougar sightings over the last 50 years, 90% of which were in the top quarter of the state. The remaining 10% were spread through the map's upper middle and lower middle areas. There had been no sightings in the state's bottom quarter.

The article quoted Sam: "Cougar attacks on people have been known to happen in Colorado, California, and elsewhere. And some have been deadly. It's good to remember we share the planet with some efficient predators."

The reporter conveniently left out the number of modern attacks ending in death: just two. It was more sensational to leave it vague.

There were several quotes from Sheriff Rusty Benson. The one Sam liked best was "The public has nothing to worry about because we have experts in the field right now tracking this animal, and if it's anywhere in Scott County, we'll find it. For the time being, it would be prudent for people to stay out of the wilder parts of the Minnesota River Valley, at least until we apprehend the animal."

Then the article said if you were attacked, you should yell and fight and kick—whatever you could do—because, unlike some animals that are further provoked by a target that fights back, cougars could be frightened off.

He was searching for the *St. Paul Pioneer Press* when Deputy Sorenson entered, nodded, and then went to the counter to order some coffee of his own.

"Best coffee in town," the deputy said, approaching Sam with a cup.

"It's good," Sam agreed.

"How'd you sleep?"

"Better than I expected."

"Glad to hear it. Quality Inn OK?"

"It was fine," Sam said. "Nothing special. Just about right for Gray and me." Sam searched the deputy's face for any inkling he knew where he'd spent his morning, but the deputy's expression was frank and open.

They talked briefly. Sam mentioned he had to be in St. Paul by 10, and that around 4 or 5, he planned on heading down to the Savannah Swamp but still hadn't settled on the exact time.

"Good. So the sheriff wanted me to remind you it was important we found and killed the cougar by the end of today," Sorenson said. He blushed a little, hearing how crazy it sounded.

"I can't see that's a problem, Deputy. We'll just call him up, find out where he lives, and go to his house and shoot him," Sam said, expressionless.

The deputy squirmed a little, turning more flushed. "I guess Bennigan has him convinced it'll happen today."

"I've met plenty of outfitters who make promises they can't keep," Sam said, taking a long sip of coffee. "Lots of outfitters will take people's money and promise them they'll bag a trophy that

doesn't exist or they can't find. I'm not saying the conservation officer is a liar, because he's a good guy. It really boils down to where
you fall on the spectrum between pessimism, realism, and opti-
mism. Bennigan must be an optimist, because we have no idea
where that cougar is, and only a hunch it might be in that swamp.
And if the sheriff was more of a realist, he might think about the
fact there's no one on this hunt or anywhere in the state that's ever
seen a cougar, let alone shot one."

Sam thought maybe the coffee was revving him up, because
he knew he could keep going.

But the deputy surprised him and said, "It's an election year.
The sheriff gets a little crazy in an election year. We're a little more
than a month out."

The deputy's cell phone went off; it was the opening guitar riff
from Jimi Hendrix's "Purple Haze." That was unexpected.

"Sorenson," he answered.

After a pause, he placed a hand over the phone and whispered,
"Bennigan."

Then he returned to the call. "The sheriff wanted me to follow
up. He forgot to ask if you needed anything."

Sam could hear some chatter, but not the words.

Sorenson nodded. "OK. OK. So when are you headed out?"

Sam raised a finger, indicating he had some questions of
his own.

After another pause, Sorenson said, "Sounds good. Sam Rivers
is here. He wants a word." Then Sorenson passed over the phone.

"So when?" Sam asked.

"Tell you the truth, I'm just getting up. Jake and I had a beer, and it tasted so good we had another." There was a pause. "Maybe one more after that."

"So you're not hustling to get down to that swamp?"

"Ah, no."

Sam checked his watch. It was close to 9. "So how about we meet down there around 4? I saw there was a central parking area with trails heading into the main part of the swamp."

"That'd work, I think. Massey lives up in Coon Rapids. He didn't get headed north last night until after midnight."

"So did you close down the bar?"

"Women," Bennigan said, vaguely.

"I thought you were supposed to be 100% focused on this cougar hunt. From what the sheriff's saying, you're going to get that cat today."

There was a pause. "Ah," Bennigan said. "I told him we'd probably get it. Or we should. Something like that. I don't think I was that definitive."

Sam grinned. "You don't remember what you said?"

"I left that message on his voice mail, last night," Bennigan said. "After a couple of beers."

"So it was alcohol talking?"

"Just three beers," Bennigan protested. There was a smile in his voice. "And maybe a couple of women."

"You mean you were trying to impress them?"

"Something like that."

Sam chuckled. Young guys, he thought. But judging from the way Jake Massey looked even before running through the woods last night, Sam questioned the judgment of their female friends. "I'll see you there at 4."

Sam and Sorenson talked over their coffee. Two or three Depot customers nodded to the deputy, one calling out, "Hey, Ole," as though he were in an episode of *The Andy Griffith Show.*

"Hey, Gus," Sorenson smiled.

Ole Sorenson was a good man to have out in the community, in uniform. He was a good representative of the office. Pleasant, nice, quiet, and with a demeanor that was a cross between an Eagle Scout and a member of the clergy. Plus, he appeared so healthy and fit his uniform was contoured to his frame like a deer-leather glove.

Sam asked about a nearby pet food outlet and the deputy told him about one just up Highway 13, in a strip mall near 35W. They talked briefly about the cougar kill. Sam asked about McGregor's family. There were no kids. There was a sister who lived in Ohio, but apparently they hadn't been close. That meant his wife was going to inherit a lot of dough, which, given what he'd just learned about McGregor, seemed somehow appropriate.

Then Sorenson said, "I didn't know Jack McGregor or his wife. But I saw them once. Right here at one of the sheriff's fund-raisers. McGregor seemed like a pretty nice guy. I was introduced. I remember he had a strong grip and a piercing eye. He was kind of an in-command guy."

"What about his wife?"

"Attractive," Sorenson said. "She was . . . really something. But she had a handshake like ice."

"Cold hands, warm heart," Sam suggested.

"I can't talk to that, but she seemed nice enough. I guess, maybe she was warm. Smiled nice, anyway."

"She was younger than McGregor?"

"Oh, yeah. At least a decade, I'd guess. I know it's cliché, but she looked like the kind of woman an older millionaire guy would be married to. Though McGregor looked pretty fit too."

"They live in town?"

"Just up the hill, off Wannamake Circle. I've patrolled up there," Sorenson said.

Then he leaned in and quietly added, "But pretty much just to see the homes. Theirs has a circular driveway," he said, as though it was the epitome of opulence.

"That in Savage?"

"Yeah," Sorenson nodded. "Just about 4 miles from here. They live in one of those new mansions, or big brick things anyway. There are only a handful of homes down in the bottom cul-de-sac, but they're all big. And they all have private security signs out front. On the couple occasions we've been down there, it was to follow up on a tripped sensor, but they were mistakes."

"What kind of mistakes?"

"Someone forgot to set it right. The McGregors have a neighbor, Winetraub I think her name is. Lives alone, and she's old, but still pretty spry. She's set off hers a couple times. I went on one of those calls and she offered us milk and cookies. I kind of had the feeling she intentionally set it off, just for some company."

"Expensive company. I think the homeowner gets charged when those are triggered by mistake."

"I think there's some kind of quota. Trip it once, OK. Trip it twice, you pay. But it's only expensive if you can't afford it."

Sam smiled.

"Other than mistaken triggers or sightseeing, we never need to go down there," Sorenson said. "But Chief Anders has been inside the McGregors' place."

"What for?"

"He met the McGregors here, maybe six months back. The day I did. He seemed to hit it off with them pretty good," he said. Then he leaned in. "Which is surprising, given the chief."

"What do you mean?"

"The chief isn't exactly full of warmth and personality."

"Can't say as I have a feel for him. I think I've heard him say about 10 words. And I'm not sure I liked them all."

"That's the chief," Sorenson said. "Some of us call him the Iceman."

Sam smiled.

They talked a little more and then walked out to their cars. On their way out, Sorenson turned to Sam and said, "Can you check in when you get out of that hearing? The chief wanted me to make sure." Then, realizing he probably shouldn't have said that last part, he added, "About the hunt—he wanted to make sure I met you guys down there."

"Will do," Sam said. But it wasn't about the hunt, and they both knew it.

Sam waited until the deputy pulled out of the lot. Then he started his jeep. Gray was glad to see him, and Sam said, "We're going into the woods again tonight. But first I need to check on a few things." The big hybrid looked out the windshield, content if not exactly happy. Sam had noticed this about Gray. He was one of the most intelligent dogs—animals, for that matter—Sam had ever known. But he was a worrier.

Sam tried to look up an address for the McGregors, but his app kept dropping. *Diane*, he thought, and called.

"What?" she said.

"Is that your friendliest greeting?" Sam said.

"I don't usually answer the phone when I'm on deadline. You should feel honored."

"I do," Sam said. "Can you do me a favor and look up an address? My map app keeps dropping."

"Am I your secretary, Rivers?"

"Nothing like her. You're a serious, independent, professional journalist. I'm just a friend reaching out to a friend for a little help."

There was a pause while Diane thought about it. "Whaddya want?"

"Carla McGregor."

"What about her?"

"I want to know where she lives and how to get there. I think the place is called Wannamake Circle."

Sam heard her clicking. "Here it is. 1617 Wannamake Circle."

"Can you get me the directions?"

She sighed. Sam knew he was pushing it. He heard her clicking again. While she waited for the map to come up, she said, "I've got to get going to that hearing. But guess what I found out?"

"What?"

"There have been two sightings of cougars in the last three years, including the one earlier this month behind McGregor Industries. The other one was up near Pine City."

"Sounds about right."

"That's what I thought. The only other cougar news I found in Minnesota was in a local crime report, up north, in Lake County."

"Crime report?"

"The Rushing River Lodge and Restaurant up on 61 reported the theft of a bear rug, a cougar wall mount, and a moose head, three weeks ago."

"Someone stole taxidermy?"

"And cash. They cleaned out the register."

"Sounds like an Iron Ranger."

"Yup. I've been to that restaurant. It's just south of Grand Marais, probably 20, 25 miles. It's one of those rustic places, with trophies hanging over rafters, on the walls, all over the place."

"Hard to figure out how they're going to fence stolen taxidermy."

"Craigslist, eBay. It's been done before. Or maybe they stole it for their own cabin collection," Diane suggested. "I remember a lynx wall mount at the place, in the main dining area. I remember the cougar skin because it was big. Big head snarling, paws stretched out across a wall. But it looked a little moth-eaten. The moose head was huge. Whoever took this stuff had a truck."

"Doesn't everyone in Lake County have a truck?"

"Hey, we don't have your mild Denver winters, where snowfall melts in 24 hours. We're rangers," Diane said. "We're tough people and we need tough vehicles."

"That sounds like a commercial."

"Just saying . . ."

"So they stole animal rugs and a moose head and cash?"

"Way up north," Diane said, as if that explained everything.

"Probably high school kids."

"I don't know," Diane said. "Last year two guys broke into a DNR storage facility in St. Paul. They were going for power tools but ended up hauling out a dozen confiscated deer mounts."

"How'd they get those out?"

"Flatbed trailer."

Sam started chuckling. "They did a heist with a flatbed?"

"It's better than that. First they broke in and went for the power tools. When they saw the confiscated deer trophies, they went back and got the flatbed. I guess it took them most of the night."

"I guess it's not a high-security place."

"A simple lock on a chain-link fence."

"No cameras?"

"Apparently no cameras and it's in an out-of-the-way St. Paul warehouse district."

"Did they ever find them?"

"In about two days. When they tried to sell the deer heads on Craigslist. One of the mounts was a 14 pointer."

Sam smiled. There was no accounting for the criminal mind. "Got those directions?"

Diane read them to him. "You paying the wife a visit?"

"Yup."

"You owe me, Rivers."

"Dinner wherever you want. I'll even buy you a drink."

"How can you buy me dinner if you're hunting a mountain lion in the Savannah Swamp?"

"Maybe we'll get lucky." As soon as he said it, he knew it didn't sound right.

She paused, then said, "Fortune favors those who deserve it."

CHAPTER SIXTEEN

Chief Deputy Anders had risen well before dawn and readied himself for his day. The chief was meticulous about his mornings, everything in its appointed place. Normally he would drink one cup of black coffee and head to the gym, work out for an hour, and then return home to get ready for work. But today was going to be different.

This morning he did not shave. He showered, had one cup of coffee, dry toast, and juice, and then returned to the bathroom to spend more time in front of the mirror. Anders had grown accustomed to transforming his appearance over the last month.

The first time he had discovered his connection with Urban had been four, maybe five months earlier. Urban was more guarded than he was. He didn't trust her, but recognized the connection, like ice crystals spreading across a picture window. Perhaps more importantly, he recognized that the connection might yield benefits. In retrospect, both of them did. So they cultivated whatever it was they saw in each other. Something hidden, cold, and feral. But not physical. Physical had never been part of it.

Anders pulled out a fake mustache and took more than 10 minutes to properly affix it to his upper lip. He was good at it, appreciating the dramatic change to his appearance. Anders began to disappear and become Benedict. He enjoyed the process and took the time to make the transformation convincing. Not only the hair and the unshaven face and the mustache, but the attitude. And the names. Benedict smiled remembering how he had told John about the names the first time they'd met. It was at the Black Angus truck stop down off 169, a place well out of town where he could be sure the disguise would go unnoticed and the venue was so remote he would never be recognized.

He'd worked on his demeanor. Cultivating the attitude of a cold-blooded killer had been, well, not difficult. He just needed to pump up the worst parts of his personality, the character traits he kept in check because it was the only way he knew to survive. But as Benedict, as Mr. Hyde, he could let them out.

The names, he thought, had been an inspiration.

John hadn't liked his name.

A few days in, after they'd figured out they could work together, John started in about it.

"I think I wanna be Clint. Not John. Just Clint. Like Eastwood," John said.

"Clint's a nobody," Benedict said. "You're John."

"Under the circumstances, I'm not comfortable with John. John's a john."

"John was a pope," Benedict snarled. "You don't have to like a pope's name. You respect them. They have power."

That actually made John feel a little better. "You talking about John Paul?"

"God no! Pope John XII. A medieval pope. Those popes had guts and knew how to use them."

"So Benedict isn't the recent Benedict?"

He laughed then, a short burst of desultory air that seemed to say *you stupid SOB,* which was what he'd been thinking. "Benedict IX. A real hell-raiser. Smart, too. The only pope to be pope three times."

"So who was Urban?"

"Urban XI. He liked to torture his cardinals, who both respected and feared him."

From the beginning, John wondered how Benedict knew Urban. But John knew better than to ask that. So instead he asked, "How do you know so much about popes?"

"Twelve years of Catholic education."

"You a Johnny? Or did you go to Benilde?" St. John's Prep and Benilde-St. Margaret's were two local Catholic high schools. But John was fishing. Benedict could tell John didn't think he was from around here.

So Benedict just looked at him, to let him know there shouldn't be any questions. "I was raised by nuns and priests. What I know about popes was earned the old-fashioned way. By the backs of their hands. Or fists."

None of it was true. He only wished he'd been raised by nuns and priests. They would have been better than the Arkansas home that had spawned and spurned him. Maybe being raised by clerics would have made him something other than what he'd learned he was in the Helmand province in Afghanistan. What he'd learned he was capable of. But he didn't really think about his childhood much anymore, or of what he'd become.

Now he just worked on perfecting his disguise. Now he was working his plan.

Finally, he put on his hat and glasses and went out to his nondescript black Chrysler 200. It was a used car, different from his work car. *All the better to blend in and disappear,* Benedict thought.

He took Highway 13 to the Quality Inn and parked in the far corner of the lot, where he could discreetly keep an eye on the front door. He didn't wait long. A little after 7, Sam Rivers emerged, leading the big dog. They wandered over to the edge of the lot where the blacktop opened onto a wide grass border and then weeds. The big dog lifted his leg and relieved himself.

Benedict watched Rivers and the dog get into his jeep and pull out of the lot, turning south on 13.

McGregor Industries, Benedict guessed. Sure enough, Rivers drove down the road about a mile and turned into their entrance.

Benedict drove by going 50. Glancing over, he saw Rivers's jeep pulling into a distant parking space.

Another mile down 13, Benedict found a place to turn around and headed back. Two hundred yards beyond McGregor's gate, he found the place where he had turned onto the frontage road the night before, when he'd kept a watchful eye on the hunters. If he was a betting man, which he wasn't, he'd wager Rivers was going to take another look down that road. He wasn't surprised to see Rivers and the dog accompany Marlin Coots as he walked back to the McGregor lot on his morning rounds. They were gone for a half hour.

Benedict returned to his car and waited for Rivers's car to emerge. At this hour of the morning, a steady stream of vehicles entered the McGregor turnoff. He wondered what was keeping the special agent.

Finally, after another half hour, Rivers emerged. Benedict watched the jeep reach the end of the drive and pause. Rivers made a call, talked with someone, hung up, and turned right onto Highway 13.

Benedict followed.

At the Coffee Depot, Benedict found another nondescript side street where he wouldn't be seen but could keep an eye on the Depot's entrance. After a few minutes he watched Deputy Sorenson enter the coffee shop. Then Benedict waited for nearly an hour, until Rivers and the deputy walked out, heading to their vehicles.

The sheriff had given Deputy Sorenson orders: keep tabs on Sam Rivers. Benedict appreciated seeing the dull deputy with the USFW agent. But he was glad when the deputy returned to his own car and pulled away, while Rivers went to his jeep and made another phone call.

Yesterday, he had been told Rivers would attend today's extradition hearing in St. Paul.

Now Benedict watched and waited.

Finally, when the jeep pulled out of the lot, Benedict slowly pulled away from the curb. He stuck with the jeep through three turns, increasingly agitated by Rivers's direction. When Rivers turned onto Wannamake Circle, Benedict sped by, reaching into his breast pocket, pulling out the throwaway, and pushing the speed dial he hoped would bring Urban onto the line.

CHAPTER SEVENTEEN

Emma Winetraub sat in her living room, perusing the morning paper, waiting for her show to come on. *In Minnesota* aired at 10:30. Emma, routine as a Swiss timepiece, would turn on the show and listen while she fixed herself a morning snack. She had more than an hour before her show began. Now she was just killing time.

Her husband, Clarence, who had made a fortune in the retail diamond trade, had been dead for seven years. It had taken her about six months to settle into her new routine. She rose around 6, sipped coffee with the sunrise, read the front page section of the *Star Tribune* (she saved the rest for later), turned on the *Today* show—at least for the first hour, while she made herself breakfast. Then she usually ran an errand, as she did today, picking up her blood pressure medication from the Savage CVS. Midmorning, she was back in the living room, finishing the paper and keeping an eye on the cul-de-sac.

Emma was the self-appointed neighborhood watchwoman. She was 80 years young, she liked to say, and though she was a little large around the back end and slightly bent over, she could still get around. She liked to sit in the front room in the morning, where she could keep an eye on the circle and finish the paper. In fact, she had hung her living room curtains so they were appointed for the job. There was a gauzy inner curtain that was pulled across the front picture window, sheer enough to be transparent, at least from the inside. From the outside, it was a taupe-colored wall. That meant Emma could see out but no one could see in; Emma preferred being the watcher, not the watched. Thick side curtains framed the window edges.

Whenever Emma saw something interesting—an unknown car coming into the cul-de-sac or a rare walker (Carla McGregor, her neighbor, was an early morning walker)—Emma would rise from her chair, step along the living room wall, and part one of the heavy side curtains to get a clear, unobstructed view. She knew no one would notice because when Clarence was alive, she had made him come into the cul-de-sac six or seven times, by car and on foot, from different angles, and tell her if she could be seen from outside, but he'd assured her he could see nothing.

Clarence had complained about her surveillance, but there wasn't much he didn't carp about, God rest his soul. She'd loved Clarence. It took Emma the first five years of marriage to grow accustomed to living with a sourpuss. By then, she had mastered the art of dodging bad moods, like watching the approach of a distant squall and knowing what would be required to weather it—only a hat, or full-on boots, rain pants, and a slicker. For 50 years, she had read Clarence's signs like an expert meteorologist. And then he died.

She still missed dodging his bad moods. But Emma wasn't one to hold on to sorrow or dwell in the past. There were too many interesting things in the world, like Sunday church services, bridge at the Club, and keeping watch over her neighbors. Emma had a gossip network as extensive as an Amazonian spider web. She was more than content to spend her days as the neighborhood overseer.

On very rare occasions, she would tune in for the fourth hour of *Today* at 10:30. Today she was thinking about it, perusing the paper's variety section—uninterested in Adele's appearance at First Avenue—when she heard a strange car enter the cul-de-sac. There were only five houses on the circle. For an 80-year-old, Emma had remarkable hearing, an ear attuned to the sounds of her neighbors' cars. This one was different. It had a high tire whine, maybe from a service truck. The rugged wheel slap made her glance up.

Emma watched a jeep slow as it approached the bottom of the hill. It entered the circle, paused, and then turned toward the McGregors' drive.

Wasn't this *interesting*, she thought. She rose from her seat and walked along the near wall, out of sight, to position herself at the curtains' edge.

The McGregors lived next door. Yesterday afternoon Emma had been in the kitchen when the sheriff's cruiser had entered the circle. She'd heard the strange car, come into the living room to see who it was, and watched the sheriff pull into their driveway.

That was odd, but not the strangest thing she'd seen happen at the McGregors'. On more than one occasion, a county deputy had actually visited Emma's house over an incorrectly triggered home security system. Emma had been embarrassed, but excited by the call and happy to know her system was operational. Maybe the McGregors' system had been triggered? But when she saw Sheriff Rusty Benson get out of the car, looking grim, she wondered.

She watched Carla let the sheriff in. He stayed for just 5 minutes and then left, still grim-faced.

Emma turned on the TV, just in case, but the noonday news was over. Then she turned on the radio and kept it low and in the background until the late afternoon, when the awful news about Jack McGregor was reported. She had a moment of panic, wondering if the woods behind her house were safe. But they stretched for only 50 yards before hitting Judicial Road. And though there was plenty of open country around Wannamake Circle, it was mostly farmland, broken up by ever-expanding housing developments. The idea that a cougar would come up from the river valley to prowl the narrow strip of woods behind her house was ludicrous, she finally decided (a sentiment that was confirmed when, later that day, she heard an expert on the news explain how cougars were rare in Minnesota and the risk to the public was low).

Then she wondered if she should go next door to offer solace. But the McGregors had never been friendly, particularly Carla. And she didn't really know the woman. It would be better, she thought, if she offered her condolences on one of the rare occasions they encountered each other on the street, or at the Club. But Emma thought she would wait a few days before taking the chance to run into Carla, given how terrible the news was.

Her third thought was about the McGregors. And again, Emma could not help herself. She wondered if Jack's end was God's will, given what she knew about both of them, Jack and

Carla. A lifetime of observation had given her a clear sense about God's wrath; eventually he punished those who deserved it. Eventually. It had seemed to her the McGregors had been cheating fate and were overdue for a little justice, though she wondered if God might have overdone it with Jack. Jack's end had been summoned by the Old Testament fire-and-brimstone God, not the merciful one. Jack had been a reasonable neighbor. Carla, on the other hand, kept to herself . . . mostly.

Once she was over the initial, terrible shock of Jack's sudden and bizarre death, Emma's phone started ringing. First Immogene. Then Betty, Mary, and Martha (of all people). They called in the late afternoon to ask if she'd heard the news. And Emma was only too happy (excited, really) to share what she knew.

Now she watched a young man pull into the McGregors' drive. There was a big dog in his front seat. Emma briefly wondered if it was one of Carla's *friends,* but then quickly discounted the idea. For starters, she knew Carla wasn't home because she'd heard her leave more than an hour earlier. Normally Carla left around 9 to work out at the Club, Emma knew. The McGregors belonged to her club, and on more than one occasion she had seen the young woman exercising on Tuesday mornings; she played tennis Monday and Thursday afternoons and exercised in the gym most other days. But Emma couldn't believe Carla would be exercising today.

She watched the man—tall, dark hair, angular—get out of his jeep and shut the door. And then she thought she recognized him. As he approached the McGregors' front door, she suddenly remembered. He had been on the news last night, with that nice sheriff. He was the expert who said something about cougars being rare and that the public shouldn't be worried. He'd been handsome on TV, she remembered. But he'd been sitting, and now she could see he was tall and the opposite of what they said TV did to people—made them appear larger than they were. This man, she remembered, was in some kind of law enforcement. Something official, but Emma couldn't recall.

And that's when Emma decided it was time to get her mail. Her mailbox sat at the end of her drive, just 30 feet from the McGregors' front door. And since Carla was gone, she wouldn't answer the door. Emma thought it was a priceless morning for fishing (what morning wasn't?), so she hurriedly glanced in a living room mirror, composing herself.

She walked slowly to the mailbox. She glanced over once, to see the young man waiting at the front door. Perhaps he had not heard her open and close her front door? At her mailbox she opened the small door, reached in to pull out her mail, and then closed it with enough force to send a metallic smack across the yard. Then she took a moment to examine her small stack of mail. She didn't really look at it, knowing it was all junk. Emma's mail usually went from her mailbox to the kitchen trash, unless it was one of those sales at Chico's. Satisfied she'd taken enough time to attract the man's attention, she turned and started back toward her front door, glancing up at just the right moment to catch the man's eye. When she noticed him looking at her, she offered a comment.

"I don't believe Carla's home," she called over to him. "I heard her leave about an hour ago."

Sam considered the short, wide older woman. Women, particularly older women, were almost always more talkative than their male counterparts. They were also observers of the social scene and on more than one occasion had been useful sources of information.

"Any idea when she'll return?" Sam asked.

Emma halted her feigned return to the house and considered the man with suspicion. "I'm not sure," she finally said. "Most mornings she goes to our club to exercise, but I would be surprised if she was there today. Can I ask your business?"

Sam crossed the McGregors' side yard and approached the white-haired woman. He remembered what Deputy Sorenson had told him. That she was older, lived alone, and had possibly triggered her security system just to see nice officers come visit. That kind of neighbor could have information.

"I'm sorry," Sam said. "My name's Sam Rivers." He extended his hand.

Emma took it, reservedly. "Mrs. Emma Winetraub," she said.

"I'm an officer with the U.S. Fish & Wildlife Service."

"Oh," she said.

"Were you aware of . . ."

"Oh yes," Emma said, with gravity. "You mean, Mr. McGregor?"

Sam nodded.

"Tragic. Just tragic," Emma added.

Sam was a student of human behavior. Growing up with an alcoholic father was fertile soil for cultivating the skills required to read moods. Emma's countenance didn't fully reflect her words. Her eyes didn't seem to *feel* Jack McGregor's death. Frankly, they were more inquisitive than concerned.

"It is. And rare," Sam said.

"Were you," Emma paused, "on TV yesterday, with that nice Sheriff Benson?"

Sam nodded. "Yes."

"So things like what happened to Jack have happened before?"

"I'm only aware of two contemporary incidents in the whole country when cougars attacked and killed people. One happened more than a decade ago, and the other a few years back. But those were in states where there are a lot more cougars. There have been plenty of scrapes, but what happened to Jack McGregor almost never happens. Particularly in an area not known for cougars."

"The idea that, in this day and age, in a place like Savage, an animal . . . *animal*," she said, "could come out of the woods and . . . Well, it's just barbaric."

"Yes, it is," Sam agreed. "Sometimes the wild can be a dangerous place. Even this close to civilization."

Emma had to ask. "You don't think that cougar would come up here?"

"Not a chance, Mrs. Winetraub. For starters, where Jack was attacked, it's all woods and river bottom, even though it's within the Savage city limits. There's a lot of cover down by the river, and a direct greenway to wilder places. To get up to your house, a cougar would need to cross a major highway and sneak through a mile of neighborhoods. And cougars aren't partial to humans or the places we live."

"So there's no chance?"

"You have nothing to worry about," Sam assured her. "So Mrs. McGregor normally exercises at a club most mornings?"

"Monday and Thursday afternoons she has tennis practice, and most other days she visits the Club gym. She is a *very fit* young woman."

"I see," Sam said. "Where's the club?"

"Over in Minnetonka Beach, on the lake," Emma said.

"What's the name of the club?"

"Just 'the Club.'"

"The Club," Sam repeated. "Is it far?"

"From here? About 45 minutes, if you avoid rush hours." Emma's eyes lowered, just barely, but enough to signal minor suspicion. "You never mentioned why you wanted to visit Carla," she said.

"I just wanted to let her know that if she had any questions, like you did, about cougars, or about what happened, I could answer them."

"Oh. Of course."

"How's she doing?" Sam asked.

"I haven't spoken with her," Emma said. "We are neighbors, and cordial, but not close. The McGregors pretty much keep . . . kept . . . to themselves."

"So you belong to the Club too?"

"I do. Clarence, my late husband, thought it was good for business. Now I've made friends there, so . . ."

"And Mrs. McGregor's a tennis player?"

"Yes. Pretty good, I understand. The tennis courts are near the grill, so I sometimes see her playing when I'm meeting friends for lunch. Or I see her practicing with Jared Sparks, one of the Club's pros."

Sam nodded.

"Jack was very fit too," she continued. "They were both regular exercisers. I often saw Jack leave in the morning, sometimes before dawn, to ride his bike."

"You must be an early riser."

"The early bird gets the worm, Mr. Rivers. You should know that," she smiled. "But I'm also old and don't sleep like I used to."

Sam smiled. He looked over at the McGregors' house. With its circular drive, well-tailored grounds, and expansive brick façade, wealth was apparent. "These are all very nice homes," he said.

"It's the covenants," Emma said. "All of the houses on Wannamake Circle must have three-car garages and a minimum value."

"I figured," Sam said. "Well kept and secure." He nodded toward the security-system sign in the McGregors' front yard.

"You can never be too careful, Mr. Rivers."

"I guess not," Sam smiled.

Emma liked Sam's smile. "Not that it did Jack much good."

"You can't ever see that kind of thing coming."

"You can't," Emma agreed. "But I don't think Jack was one to worry about security."

"Did he put in that security system for his wife?"

"Oh, no. That's another covenant. Everyone down here has to have a private security system."

"Any idea when she might be back?"

"Carla? If she went to the Club, she won't be back before early afternoon. Though I can't believe she would have gone to the Club today."

"I'd guess not."

"Truth is, Mr. Rivers, I don't know the McGregors well, though we've been neighbors since they were married, about seven years ago." Emma paused. "I know they were risk-takers."

"Risk-takers?"

"They were . . ." Emma paused, thinking. "They were very physical people."

"You mean they were active?" Sam asked.

"Compulsive exercisers. Both of them. Only Carla's quite a bit younger than Jack."

"Ten years?"

"At least," Emma said.

The way she raised her eyes told Sam she didn't necessarily approve of the age difference.

"So she exercised harder than her husband?" Sam said.

"Carla's a morning walker," Emma reported.

"She goes on morning walks and then she works out?"

"Very active," Emma said.

"I guess. Does she work?"

"Carla? She doesn't have to work."

"I suppose not."

"I shouldn't say anything, but I often wondered if the two of them were swingers."

"Swingers?"

"I'm usually here most of the day. Sometimes all day," Emma said. "In the cul-de-sac you can hear whenever someone comes into our circle. I've seen Jack come home for lunch. One time I was upstairs when he came home. I looked out the window and saw him drive in, open his garage door, and . . ." She paused again. "There was a woman lying down in his front seat."

"You mean not his wife?"

"Definitely not Carla. The woman in the front seat was a blonde. Carla's a brunette. They were there more than an hour, and then left the same way."

"You saw them leave?"

Emma paused. She had a wizened face and hunched shoulders, but plenty of energy. "I was reading a magazine and stayed by the window until I heard the garage door go up," she grinned. "When I heard the door, I looked out and there she was again, the blonde lying down in the front seat."

Sam knew surveillance wasn't easy. Sitting idly for more than 30 minutes caused the mind to wander. It was difficult to stay focused. But Emma stuck to the window and waited so she could watch her neighbor—more than an hour later—leave. The woman was a practiced observer.

"So do you think Mrs. McGregor knew about it?"

"I don't know. I've wondered about it because the truth is, Mr. Rivers, I've seen someone come out of the woods in the back." Emma waited for this detail to sink in. "It was pretty dark. He walked out of the trees and disappeared under the McGregors' second-story deck. I was going to call the police. But then I heard the lower sliding door open and then Carla's voice. And then they were gone."

"Gone into the house?"

"That's right."

"I'm guessing Jack wasn't home?"

"He's out of town a lot. I don't know if he was home or not that night."

"When did this happen?"

"I've seen a man over at the McGregors' house two times in the last six months. I've seen him leave twice and walk right into those woods behind our house. Both times before dawn, when I'm sure he thought the neighborhood was asleep. And I saw him come that once, in the dark. That was three weeks ago. But I could never get a very good look at him. It's too dark back there, where the lawn goes straight into the trees. But for money, Mr. Rivers, I'm guessing it was Jared Sparks."

"The tennis pro?"

She nodded. "One of the women at the Club, one of my card-playing friends, thinks they're intimate."

"Both times you saw someone out back, it was the same man?"

She paused. "He was wearing something dark. Maroon, maybe. Very dark but like warm-ups. Tennis warm-ups."

"You mean each time? The same thing?"

"Yes."

"And Mr. McGregor was never home?"

"I don't think so, Mr. Rivers. I don't think he knew about it. But I don't think Carla knew about Jack and his lunch dates. Maybe they gave each other permission?" Emma wondered, peering at Sam to see what he thought about it, the morality of it. She didn't wait for Sam to respond.

"But I'm old-fashioned," she added. "And I can't help but think what happened to Jack was God's way of telling us that kind of thing is wrong."

Sam didn't share Emma's perspective on divine justice. But he was willing to admit he didn't know. "Maybe," he shrugged.

But from Emma's reaction, he guessed she was looking for more than a shrug.

"From my perspective," Sam said, "that kind of behavior never leads to a good end." True enough, Sam thought, without bringing God into it. And it appeared as though his comments satisfied the informative Mrs. Winetraub.

CHAPTER EIGHTEEN

While Sam was speaking with Emma, Gray's eyes were fastened on him. When Sam returned to his jeep, Gray shifted from leg to leg and bobbed his head. Clearly, he was happy to have Sam back in the car. And he probably needed to stretch his legs and take a leak.

"OK, buddy," Sam said, scratching behind one of Gray's ears. "I'll find somewhere to let you stretch your legs, but only for a sec. I've got more people to see, and we've got to save ourselves for that swamp."

Gray squinted and his mouth fell open. As anxious as he usually was, he sometimes seemed to smile.

On the way over, Sam checked messages. There was one from fellow USFW agent Mac McCollum.

"Moon is done," Mac said. "He's headed north, later today. I hope the Canucks are happy. What's going on with that cougar thing? I saw you on the news last night. You looked like a Boy Scout. Sounded like one too. How about some help from a real professional? It's either that or catch up on overdue reports. And on a day like this, I'd rather be out in it. Call me."

Sam smiled. Mac dressed like a grandfather, talked like a truck driver, and knew a lot of people, both in and out of the service.

He was one of those guys with a natural ability to chitchat with just about anyone about anything, particularly if it meant he could avoid real work. Sam knew there were ways he could use Mac's skills, but he didn't think running through the Savannah Swamp was one of them. He'd have to think about it.

And unfortunately, Moon's extradition hearing was done. Now he'd have to worry about the sheriff's office. When they found out it was over, they'd wonder what he'd done with his day.

Since seeing Marlin's photos, he'd decided it would be good to pay Angie Sweet a visit, just to speak with her. And while he was there, he could speak to the only other person at McGregor who knew about the sale. Another young woman. He wondered if Jack had a reputation and suspected the women would know, especially Mrs. Sweet.

He dialed McGregor Industries and asked for Madeline Baxter.

She came on the line and said, "This is Maddy."

"Sam Rivers," Sam said.

"Agent Rivers?"

"Yes. Thanks for taking my call. I'm wondering if I can speak with the other two employees who know about the McGregor sale."

"Angie Sweet and Susan Connelly?" Maddy asked.

"That's right. Could you connect me, or help me set up interviews?"

There was a pause. "Do you have to speak with them today?"

"It'd probably be best. It's customary, with this kind of accident, to speak to close associates—you never know what might turn out to be helpful."

"The problem is, Agent Rivers, we're right in the middle of this thing." She paused. "Just a second."

Sam thought he heard her get up, cross the office, and close the door.

"Thing is, Susan and Angie are totally focused on crunching last-minute numbers and we don't want to pull them off it until they're done."

"When will they be done?"

"Probably not until the sale, or right before it."

"When's the sale?" Sam asked.

"It's supposed to happen Friday the eighth. We'll see," she said, doubtful.

"I just need to speak with them briefly. It won't take long. I'll be back in Denver by the eighth."

There was another long pause. "It was a tragic accident, Agent Rivers. A cougar. So what else do you, Angie, or Susan need to talk about? Because the last thing I need is for you to come in here and upset them."

In yesterday's meeting at the sheriff's office, he had the distinct impression Maddy wasn't happy about the sale. He thought she'd welcome the distraction. Now she seemed to be making sure nothing interfered with its progress. Was she protecting them? Or herself?

"It's protocol," Sam said. "If I return to Denver without having spoken with all the affected parties, my boss will crucify me."

"I see," Maddy said. "And I appreciate your concern, Agent Rivers. But that's really not *our* concern. I will call both of them and let them know the first chance they get, they should call you."

It didn't take an empath to know he wasn't going to hear from Sweet or Connelly, at least not before the eighth. Sam thanked Maddy, reminded her of his phone number, and hung up.

Much of what Sam had found at the kill site was troubling. But as he considered the possibilities, was it realistic to think someone had somehow used a cougar to have Jack killed? In *Hound of the Baskervilles*, a fierce dog was kept in a cage and trained to kill. But this wasn't Sherlock Holmes and it wasn't Baskerville Manor, and the idea that someone had trained a mountain lion to chase and kill was ludicrous, even for fiction. It was Sam Rivers in Savage, Minnesota, and there were no curses or legends he knew of. There was a prominent citizen who had been viciously killed in a frightening and bizarre manner. And there was plenty about it that didn't make sense.

And then there was the sheriff's office and the BCA. The sheriff was just waiting for the lion's corpse to close the case. And the BCA had the final proof everyone needed: DNA analysis of the fur.

A more sensible investigator, Sam reasoned, would stop fighting city hall and accept the evidence, even though there were still lots of questions. Sam's anomalies might be unanswered, but they led to nowhere, and nowhere was a lonely place.

Sam had done a lot of work with Tracy McDonald, head of USFW forensics in Ashland, Oregon. Tracy not only did forensic work for the service but also, through his adjunct work with the University of Colorado, cataloged DNA samples of several North American species, one of them cougar. Last year, Sam had provided his office with a sample from the cougar they'd killed out at Mable Swenson's place. Tracy wanted every sample he could get, preferably from different parts of the country, so they could build out a complete DNA picture of mountain lions.

And Tracy owed him a favor.

Sam had the forensics lab on speed dial, and it only took a few minutes to connect with Tracy. When Sam explained what had happened and what they'd done, Tracy said, "Get me a copy of those DNA results, would ya? We need as many as we can get. Right now, our database has less than 100 samples."

Sam said he'd see what he could do. "But tell me something—is it pretty definitive? I mean, could mountain lion DNA be confused with anything else?"

"Like what?"

"I have no idea."

There was a long pause. "If they came up with mountain lion DNA, they probably got it from one of the university labs. And they're all pretty good. If they say it's lion, it's gotta be lion."

"Not a house cat or something?"

Tracy laughed. "The cats are all pretty distinct. It would be next to impossible to make an incorrect classification. Even from a house cat."

"OK, thanks," Sam said, and hung up.

Why couldn't he just let it go?

It didn't sound like he was going to hear from Susan Connelly and Angie Sweet anytime soon, but he wasn't sure he needed to. Marlin had photos of one of them being accosted by Jack. And Emma Winetraub had seen another driven by Jack into his garage. Sam wasn't sure what he might find out, but if he discovered one of them was having an affair with Jack, it would only reinforce what he already knew. Jack was a player. And sometimes players had messy lives that could lead to serious conflict.

The sun was out, but it wasn't as strong and intense as July light. It was slanted, off the horizon a little farther south. But the temperature was warm.

Sam needed to find somewhere to walk and think. Whenever he had to do some serious thinking, it was best done either driving or hiking, and best if he had some kind of destination or trail from which he couldn't stray. One time, out in Colorado, he'd been investigating a case and got in his car and started driving. North, as it turned out. He just went out onto the nearest four-lane, put his car on cruise control, and watched the miles tick by. Before he knew it, he was in Wyoming.

But he'd figured something out.

Now he used his iPhone to find the nearest park and got lucky. A few miles down Judicial Road was Murphy-Hanrehan Park, and it looked huge, with plenty of trails.

Traversing the park was a perfect way for Sam to think, and he had a lot to consider. Jack McGregor was a millionaire player. Apparently, the Lothario did not fall far from the father's tree, Sam thought, remembering what Marlin had said about Jack's father. It sounded like Jack's wife was some kind of player too, at least from Mrs. Winetraub's perspective. And now she was a multimillionaire, or soon would be. Sam wondered if the two women he had wanted to meet this afternoon were also into extramarital affection. Mrs. Winetraub said she saw a blonde lying down in the car seat so she wouldn't be seen. And there was a guy in warm-ups who apparently visited Carla when Jack was out of town.

Hiking through dense September woods with Gray was a perfect venue for contemplating the details of McGregor's accident and everyone involved. There was a lot of color, and you could only see 10 or 20 feet in front of you. Then the path would make a turn and you'd come into an entirely different section of woods, and an entirely different perspective.

They came to a field edge and there was a small path that wound more than 100 yards down to a big, lily pad–bordered pond. Gray turned and glanced at Sam, and Sam said, "Go," and gave the hybrid a hand signal that let him know he could run. And that's what Gray did, in an all-out gallop to the pond's edge, where he turned around and ran back, just to make sure Sam was coming. Then he returned, again at a full gallop, and leaped into the pond. Gray loved water.

Almost an hour later, they ambled out of the woods. It was a longer hike than Sam had wanted, but he knew Gray was young enough he would recover in time for the hunt. They both wore a few burs, and Gray had a few twigs in his hair, up on his back. His legs were still wet from where he'd jumped into the pond. Both of them, dog and owner, were happy. Gray's tongue lolled out over his incisors, and there was a little white froth in the corners of his mouth. He panted with appreciation. Sam's recollection of sere yellow and scarlet leaves and the clear backwoods pond made him smile. If there had been trout rising to the pond's surface, it would have been metaphorically perfect, given what had occurred to Sam on his hike through the woods.

The lily pond had reminded him of one he'd seen in the Florida Keys. Sam almost never thought about old cases, except when something about them informed his current efforts. On the way back to the jeep, he recalled some of the details of the poached Key deer.

In that case he was stumped, until he'd followed an unlikely clue. The only clue left, as Sam remembered. He answered a local classified ad involving the sale of Key deer antlers. Technically, trafficking in endangered species parts was illegal, and policing that kind of commerce was part of USFW's mission.

Sam called the number, posing as a private citizen. A guy by the name of Jeff Gunn answered and confirmed he had genuine Key deer antlers for sale, and they agreed to meet.

In the end it was the antler ad that eventually led to three local developers who had hired Gunn to rid the island of deer.

Walking down to the pond had reminded Sam of one of his perspectives regarding investigations. When pursuing a line of inquiry, pay attention to random similarities, chance associations, or seemingly bizarre occurrences of anything related to the inquiry, however remote. It was like doing homework and making the extra effort you suspect will never make a difference in your grade, but you do it because you're genuinely interested. Sam had a special appreciation for the bizarre occurrence, particularly if it was related to the wild.

Which is when he remembered the stolen cougar pelt up north. Cougars weren't classified as endangered or threatened in Minnesota, but they were rare. Sam felt it was an agent's duty to investigate any issues involving rare species. And this one involved a cougar. That's when he thought of Mac McCollum.

When he and Gray returned to the jeep, Sam called Mac.

"How's Mark Trail?" Mac joked.

"Good. Gray and I just came out of the woods. We saw a pileated woodpecker and two wood ducks."

"I bet you just earned a merit badge."

"I'm wearing it proudly," Sam said.

"I don't doubt it," Mac chuckled.

"I was thinking you could help me with something. Something that would take some phone time. I need your in-state network."

"Sounds like it beats pushing a pen."

First, Sam wanted him to check on the theft at Rushing River Lodge. Maybe speak to the Lake County sheriff, see if they'd caught anyone yet. See if there was anything left of the cougar wall mount. If there was, he wanted him to send it to Tracy McDonald at forensics out in Oregon. Mac had his info.

Then Sam wanted Mac to call Lieutenant Cole at the BCA and have him send the DNA results to Tracy for his database. Also, if the BCA still had any fur, he wanted Cole to send that to Tracy as well.

Mac took it all down and said he'd be in touch. "I know the Lake County guys. They're a little territorial, but we've worked together before."

"If they still have anything, FedEx it."

Mac told Sam he'd give him an update by the end of the day.

The only connection to Sam's current line of inquiry was *cougar*. Otherwise, Mac's review of the crime had absolutely nothing whatsoever to do with his investigation. It was random and probably a waste of time, but sometimes—in the case of the Key deer, for instance—it became important. And if nothing else, it would provide Tracy with more DNA for his database.

CHAPTER NINETEEN

Jared Sparks could use natural gut strings to drive a tennis ball at speeds in excess of 90 miles per hour. And while his racket finesse earned him a position as a prestigious club tennis pro, his skills at attracting and retaining women eclipsed anything he could do with natural gut. Ever since the young man of ambiguous ancestry could remember, two things were true: he could swing a racket, and women liked the way he looked.

Those who didn't know about Jared's early life might have thought he was born under a blessed star. The truth was much darker. His parents were part of a splinter religious sect with roots in rural Iowa. After a couple of bad harvests, its members were searching for a scapegoat. Jared's mother, with an unknown past, was an easy target. Jared's parents escaped to the Twin Cities, but life outside the commune was more problematic and difficult than either of them had imagined. Jared's father fled back to Iowa, while his mother was eventually forced to place her son in foster care.

If it hadn't been for Jared's acumen at tennis and movie-star good looks, he might have been shuffled from one foster home to another until he finally ended up behind bars. But early on, a foster parent watched him swing a racket and was awestruck by his natural hand-eye coordination. The man adopted Jared the way a professional scout picks up a promising high school baseball player for the minors. Over the next 10 years, the kid proved he could play tennis. And his clear good looks played well to his foster father's friends, especially at the country club.

Jared hung around the family long enough to win the high school tennis state championship and earn a scholarship to Purdue. But academics had been as difficult as tennis was easy, and he flunked out his freshman year. Regardless, the boy's startling green eyes; thin, square-jawed face; and perfectly aligned physique, along with a kind of cultivated (it wasn't natural) affability helped him begin making a living as a tennis pro. It had taken him a decade to work his way up to a halcyon place like the Club. On the way, he'd refined both his tennis skills and his awareness of women, especially ones with money.

Jared was a narrow, calculating, mildly predatory, sociopathic, late 20-something, wringing whatever he could out of life for his own purposes. He was rootless, shaky, and unstable and had lately fallen under the influence of a woman more than 10 years his senior. Outwardly he was young, handsome, confident, and legendary in the sack—meaning he demonstrated more care about his partners' pleasure than his own, up to a point. And he'd had a lot of partners. Women helped assuage his personal demons, however briefly.

Several months ago, when a new affair had started, he considered his latest partner a sign of his personal maturation. She was beautiful, married, discreet, and had lots of money. But lately she sometimes left him feeling moody, mercurial, and unbalanced and—like himself—could be aloof, game playing, and devoted, all on the same night. He'd recognized the trigger points that in the past would have made him lash out or cut off. However, with Carla he had played his hand coolly and carefully at first. But something else was happening now. The entire affair had taken a twisted turn, and rather than get out, he'd stayed in. And now it was spinning out of his control. Jared realized that if Carla broke it off, it would be some kind of seismic event, and he wasn't certain what he would do to survive that kind of wreckage.

Jared was lying on his back on a mat behind court four's floor-to-ceiling curtain. Early afternoons at the Club, Jared sometimes had an hour-long break. He liked to find an out-of-the-way place on the courts, where the curtains hung against the wall. If you knew how to get in behind them, there was a 3-foot-wide crawl space with a cushioned floor that was just about perfect for sleeping off lunch or catching up after a sleepless night.

Now he lay in the dark, wondering about Carla. He knew he shouldn't, but he was beginning to think he should pay her another visit, after dark. Or maybe call her. He knew she'd think it was a bad idea. But Jared had a deft hand and—at least when it came to women like Carla McGregor—a steely determination. But right now, a forced meeting seemed like the wrong play.

Then he heard two women coming down the back walkway, talking. He couldn't hear what they were talking about, but as they approached, their voices became clear.

"Want to get a bite to eat?"

They entered court four, the sound of their steps accompanied by Monica Mills's proposal to get something to eat.

Jared knew them both. Monica was a 47-year-old, slightly chubby regular at Jared's Friday morning open practice. He'd seen the way she looked at him. She was like many of the Club women: middle-aged, without the need for a job, and with time on her hands and a husband out of town or permanently at the office. Jared had considered taking advantage, but she wasn't his type. Besides, he was busy with Carla.

Monica was with Melissa Pratt, known by everyone as Mel. She was around Monica's age, but she was fit, with surgically enhanced curves and an attitude that conveyed she thought she was the most beautiful woman in the room, despite the fact she was a little wrinkled around the eyes, the corners of her mouth turned down, and her hair was colored boot black. She was also a gossip. He stayed quiet because he wanted to hear what Mel would have to say. She could be a rich source of information about her friends and enemies at the Club.

He listened to the pair chatter while they stretched. Then he heard the unzipping of one of their racket covers. They kept talking, finally deciding to go straight to Crave after tennis. They were both hungry and knew they'd be starving after hitting the ball for an hour.

And then their conversation turned to Jack and Carla McGregor.

"Killed by a wild animal," Monica said. "It's awful."

"Definitely tragic. But unless I'm mistaken about Carla, she'll land on her feet," Mel said.

"Well, she certainly won't have to work for the rest of her life."

"She wasn't working before."

"Can you imagine? One day her husband's here, vibrant and alive. And the next day he's dead," Monica said.

"And his young wife, not yet 40, is a multimillionaire."

There was a pause, while they both took it in.

"What would you do?" Monica asked.

"I wouldn't worry about waiting for a sale at Nordstrom."

"I'd buy every damn shoe in the store," Monica said.

"I'd buy the damn store," Mel said.

They laughed.

"I don't think Carla's going to spend a lot of time mourning. She doesn't strike me as the type."

"Why do you say that? It's so tragic, so sudden."

"Because I knew Carla before she was Jack McGregor's wife." There was a drop in Mel's voice. "Frankly, she was a whore."

"I heard that. She's got the figure for it," Monica said.

"Mark my words," Mel said. "I bet it's a matter of weeks before we see her at dinner with someone."

"Really?" Monica said.

"Really."

They both paused again, thinking.

"I'm hungry," Monica said.

"So am I."

"Are you suggesting what I think you're suggesting?"

"What?" Monica asked, feigning innocence.

"Let's go."

"Why not? I'm starving."

Jared could hear the women return their rackets to their covers and zip them.

On the way out, Mel said, "Crave has a yellowtail jalapeño sashimi that is better than sex."

They laughed and kept walking.

Jared returned to thinking about Carla. The idea she might end up having dinner somewhere with anyone but himself, as Mel suggested, darkened his reverie. He needed to pay Carla a visit, after dark, tonight. First he'd check on her, then he'd see. Lately she'd been . . . cold . . . even before the death of her husband. It had been a while. Tonight, he was hoping for a little heat.

CHAPTER TWENTY

S am and Gray returned to the Quality Inn. Sam fired up his computer and took a minute to compare the photos of the paw prints to the first set from the deer kill and the other from around McGregor's body. The prints from the recent kill not only had claw points, but the feet appeared wider, somehow harder, as though the cat had stepped on the ground with more weight. Could it be the difference in soil? Sam wondered. The soil in the creekbed was probably damp or wet clay and sand, softer than the black, cindery soil on the road rut.

To Sam it looked like the two prints made were from different animals. But that was crazy. *Two* cats in the Minnesota River Valley? Mountain lions were solitary, unless . . . it could have been siblings from a recent litter, just about ready to start off on their own. But these prints, both sets, appeared to have been made by adults. It was another thing that didn't make sense.

Sam emailed Marlin Coots. "The prints I mentioned. Yours, and the ones from the site taken on Monday. What do you think?" He attached the images and hit send.

Sam's cell phone rang.

"Rivers."

"What are you up to?" Mac said.

"Just getting ready to go into the swamp. Me and Gray. With a conservation officer, some hunters, and some dogs."

"You have a knack for fun."

"I agree," Sam said, though he knew his aging colleague would never run into a swamp after dark.

Mac thanked Sam for saving him from desk work. Then he suggested next time he might find him something a little less taxing. But he'd made the calls and he'd been successful.

Sam and Diane were right about the Rushing River Lodge. Mac knew the undersheriff in Lake County and got the complete update from him. Several trophies had been stolen, including the cougar wall mount. And the moose, which blew everyone away because of its size.

"Had to have a truck. Or a flatbed," Mac said.

They'd also robbed the place. Took all the cash, though there wasn't much.

"Anything left of the cougar?"

"There was. It was an old mount. It had a tail, but some kids yanked on it, and it broke in two places. Both pieces are about 2 inches long. The proprietor held onto them because he was going to have a taxidermy outfit in Grand Marais come down and fix it, but he hasn't had the chance."

Mac had asked the proprietor to FedEx one of the tips out to the address Sam had given him—Tracy McDonald's—and the owner said he was going to Grand Marais that morning and would get it done. "Said if he made it soon enough, the tip would be in Ashland by late tonight or tomorrow morning."

"What about the other one? Can you have him send it to me? Just for safekeeping?" Sam gave him his address at the Quality Inn.

Mac said he'd take care of it, that the proprietor should be able to FedEx it to him this afternoon, when he sent out the other tail piece to Tracy.

Mac had also gotten in touch with Lieutenant Cole at the BCA, who had sent their info to USFW forensics in Ashland.

Sam told Mac he owed him.

"I appreciate more Sam Rivers credit in my expense account. But I can't find any place that will take it."

Sam and Gray were just about ready to head out the door when Sam's phone rang again.

"It's Sorenson. Where have you been?"

"In my room for a while, getting ready for our hunt."

"I mean earlier," Ole said.

"Ah," Sam said. "When?"

"Like after the Coffee Depot, when you said you were going to the extradition hearing."

"You following me, Ole?"

"Do I have to?"

"No."

There was a pause. Apparently, Sam had been caught and he wasn't sure of the right response, so he ignored the remark and plowed ahead.

"We sound like a married couple, Sorenson. But I missed the wedding and the honeymoon."

Another pause.

"I'll see you at the Savannah Swamp," Sam said.

"We'll talk then," Sorenson said, and hung up.

Sam never would have picked the deputy for a confrontational comment like that one, which made Sam wonder if the sheriff or the chief had been in the room listening. Probably, Sam guessed. He'd try to tease it out of him down at the swamp.

Meanwhile, it occurred to Sam that he was being followed. Or at least he had been this morning. How else would Sorenson have known he wasn't at that hearing? Sam wasn't used to being the one followed. It made him feel like prey, and he didn't like it.

Sam thought he'd better take care of seeing everyone he could while there was still time. If the sheriff or the chief found out about his visit to McGregor Industries this morning or his inquiries this afternoon, Sam guessed they'd pull him off the case. And if they got lucky finding that lion tonight, he was definitely heading back to Colorado. He decided to drive around a while. First, he would make sure he wasn't being tailed. If he wasn't, he had just enough time to pay a short visit to a widow.

CHAPTER TWENTY-ONE

When Sam drove into Wannamake Circle, he could have sworn he saw a crack in the curtains of Emma Winetraub's living room windows. After a second, the gap closed, as though a cat had moved along the curtain bottom. But Sam guessed the cat was Emma.

It made Sam smile. He was the indirect beneficiary of the nosy neighbor, if what she had told him was true. And he hadn't heard anything yet to suggest she'd made any of it up. Jack McGregor had some kind of drive.

Sam still needed to hear from forensics. Sam had asked the proficient Tracy McDonald for a fast-track analysis of the cougar tail tip as soon as it arrived, so he expected to get his results soon.

He pulled into the half-moon drive and then backed his jeep out, parking along the cul-de-sac curb so he wasn't blocking the McGregors' drive. Sam glanced up at Emma's windows as he cut the engine, but her gauzy curtains were opaque in the afternoon sunlight.

The weather was still stunning, with plenty of sun and higher-than-normal temperatures. But there was a hint of change in the air. It was going to be a perfect evening for hunting cougars.

Gray was sitting beside him in the front seat, admiring the sunlight. Sam scratched the hybrid's head and said, "I shouldn't be long. Meanwhile, try not to chew the dash."

Gray whined a little, as if to say, "Don't worry about it."

The McGregors' outer door was all glass and looked as though it had just been polished. Sam pressed the doorbell and heard a Big Ben gong. He thought he picked up the sound of a TV. It was a matter of seconds before Sam heard footfalls and the door opened.

"Yes?" Carla McGregor said.

Carla had perfect skin, hazel eyes, long black hair, and a body that appeared shapely and hard—even under red tennis warm-ups. *Hollywood looks,* Sam thought. She wore a sports bra beneath her half-zipped red top. And she was barefoot. The woman appeared fit, with a ramrod back and a piercing gaze.

"Mrs. McGregor?" Sam said.

"Yes?" she said. She didn't open the door.

"Sam Rivers. I'm from the U.S. Fish & Wildlife Service," he said.

"Oh," she paused. "What can I do for you?"

"I was wondering if I could speak with you. I'm part of the team investigating your late husband's . . . tragedy. I'm very sorry for your loss."

She hesitated, considering. "I'm not sure I can tell you anything more than what I've already told the sheriff."

"My line of inquiry is a little different," Sam said. "I know it must be difficult, Mrs. McGregor, but I was wondering if I could ask you some questions about Jack. Anytime there's an accident like this, Fish & Wildlife tries to understand everything that contributed to the tragedy. If there is something, anything we can do to prevent it from happening again, or to warn people about taking precautions, we want to know about it."

She appeared pained, maybe even a little shell-shocked.

Sam took out his wallet and showed her his USFW badge. She barely glanced at it, then reached down and opened the door. "OK," she said, not much more than a whisper. She looked at Sam and waited.

"It's probably better if I come in and sit down. I have a few questions to go over. Would that be OK?"

"OK," she said.

When she opened the door, Sam noticed her toenails were the same color as her warm-ups, fire-engine red.

Sam stepped into the entryway and paused to take off his boots. There was a TV on in the background, probably in the kitchen, he guessed.

The entryway was two stories, with an off-white ceramic tiled floor and a huge glass chandelier hanging from the ceiling.

The room had a couch along the right wall, directly in front of a TV that was off. There were two easy chairs marking either side of a huge flagstone fireplace. The stone rose two stories, thick, heavy, and beautiful.

Carla sat on the couch, with her legs tucked up beneath her.

Sam said, "I know it sounds odd, Mrs. McGregor, but whenever something like this happens, the service tries to identify anything that might have precipitated the attack. Any action, or even scent the victim might have been wearing."

"Scent?" Carla asked.

"Like aftershave, or cologne?"

"Not at that hour of the morning, Mr. . . ."

"Rivers. Just Sam. There was a similar accident that happened out West, in Southern California, outside of LA in the Santa Monica Mountains. A guy on a mountain bike was killed by a cougar."

"I think I heard about that," Carla said.

"When that happened, Southern California agents made a thorough investigation. Turns out the guy had a heart condition. There was some speculation that maybe his heart failed and then the cougar . . . well, the cougar took advantage of the situation."

"Wasn't there another attack close to the same time? Another biker?"

So she knew about the attack. "That's right," Sam said. "A woman. She was being dragged into some nearby brush by her helmet when her friends came onto the scene and beat the animal off."

"Was it the same cat?"

"Yes. The necropsy determined it was the same cat." Remnants of the cat's first victim were found in its stomach, details that hadn't been made public and that under the circumstances probably didn't need to be shared.

"So the first man . . . it wasn't his heart?"

"We don't know," Sam said. "Did Jack have a heart condition?"

"Jack had the heart of an ox. It wasn't his heart that killed him."

"And he always biked down by the river?"

"Almost always," she paused. "Every once in a while, he'd bike the hills around here, just for a change. But he loved that river woods trail. He had it built for himself."

"Did you ever bike it?"

"No." Then she turned and said, "I still can't quite believe it. That he's gone. He was such a force."

"I've heard that," Sam said. "I'm sorry for your loss."

"Thank you, Sam. I don't think Jack did anything different yesterday morning than what he did almost every morning, weather permitting. You know they had seen a cougar down there, very close to where he was attacked?"

"Yes. Jack knew about it?"

"Of course. It was in all the papers. And I told him to be careful. But he wasn't the kind of man to worry about that sort of thing."

"I see."

"Jack always went down there before work. Every once in a while, he'd get a late start and be down after sunup, but it's that time of year, Sam. The days are getting shorter. And Jack was an early riser."

"I see," Sam said.

"Jack always said the early bird got the buck."

"Buck?" Sam was thinking deer, given the context.

"The dollar," she explained.

"Oh."

"Jack worked hard."

"I understand he was on the verge of selling his business?"

She turned to look at him. "Is that part of your investigation?"

"Not really. When some McGregor officials were debriefed about the accident, one of them mentioned it."

"Madeline Baxter," Carla said.

"She was there."

"Yes, the business is being sold. Jack was looking forward to it." She looked down, contemplative.

"Sorry," Sam said.

"It was just," Carla started, "as you say, a tragic accident. I told him to be careful of that cougar."

"Had Jack been down there every morning since the cougar was first sighted?"

"Yes. I was in California when that other accident happened. I remember it. So I looked it up, thinking if a cougar was down behind the plant and roaming those woods, there was no reason it might not do that same thing."

"Actually, it's very rare."

"Wasn't there another case, in Colorado? A jogger?"

"Yes. In Idaho Springs. A high schooler was running behind his school, in the foothills, and was attacked and killed. But again, it's incredibly rare."

"I just thought," Carla started, "given that it happened, it could happen again. But Jack didn't think that way. He was fearless, actually."

"So yesterday morning," Sam said, "nothing unusual? Not a different kind of deodorant? Or eat anything odd?"

"You mean something that might attract a cougar?"

"I don't know. Like I said, we're just trying to make sure we understand everything that happened around the event."

She thought about it. "No," she said. "I don't think he did anything he didn't normally do. He got up, put on his biking clothes, and took off. He probably had some coffee." She looked off. "Yes, he made coffee, like he always did. So he probably had some, went to the bathroom, and then got on his bike and left."

She grew quiet and Sam thought she was going to tear up.

There wasn't much more Sam could go over about the details of yesterday morning. And his visit was only tangentially about the details. The USFW did wonder about wildlife attractants, but Sam didn't really expect to hear about anything unusual. It was really Carla he wanted to see. He wanted to take her measure, size her up, and get a feel for who she was and the depth of her sorrow.

On his way out of the house, he said, "Again, I'm sorry for your loss."

"Thank you, Sam."

He was polite and cordial. Carla was appropriately grief-stricken. But if he was taking her measure, it felt contrived.

When Sam returned to the jeep, he found Gray curled up on the front seat. The hybrid stirred, still subdued from their midday run. Sam got in and started the car. Then he turned to his animal companion and said, "Not sure I got anything out of that." Sam thought about the interview. "I bet you would have been charmed," he said. "Like everyone else."

Gray's tail gave a thump-thump.

After Sam walked out of her front door and it was shut behind him, Carla hurried up the stairs, down the hallway, and across the master bedroom to the curtained windows overlooking the drive.

She peered down from the window edge and watched Sam walk around his jeep. Then she saw the dog in the front seat.

Big, wolflike.

"Moon," she said, out loud. "And a star."

Her dawn dice roll had been snake eyes and a four. In the lexicon of dice divination, a six meant more bad news, particularly with snake eyes. Loss, probably of money, but it could be anything. And as she watched Sam pull away from her curb, she thought she saw the snake.

Two bad rolls, back-to-back. After so many favorable signs.

She knew it was inevitable. And she knew what to do about it. In addition to Jack's funeral plans, she had spent the day reckoning her accounts.

If bad winds blew, she was ready.

Urban fetched her throwaway phone and dialed Benedict.

"That agent was just here. Rivers," she said.

"I know. I've been tracking him."

"Do we need to do something about it?"

"Yes."

"Not . . ." she hesitated.

"We just need to slow him down, take him off the trail. He's heading into the woods tonight on another cougar hunt," Benedict said. "Maybe if something happened to that dog?"

"Do it," Urban said.

"Done."

"I've got your first installment," she said.

"Good. I'll be by tonight. I'm on patrol after 10. Call dispatch around 10:30; ask if they can send someone down. I'll be in the neighborhood. You heard something," Benedict suggested, a reasonable excuse. "Maybe somebody trying to break in, take advantage."

"Good," Urban said, and hung up.

CHAPTER TWENTY-TWO

Sam's visit with Carla caused him to roll into the Savannah Swamp parking area 15 minutes late. Sam wasn't sure what to expect, but the parking area was primitive and remote, maybe a mile off Highway 169. Part of the road getting there was bouncy and rough, and Sam was glad he had his jeep. When he pulled into the turf lot, Deputy Ole Sorenson, Jake Massey, and CO Tom Bennigan were all peering over a map spread across the hood of Jake's rusted-out Ford 150.

They glanced up when they saw the jeep enter, but quickly returned to the map. The coon dogs started baying as Sam approached. Jake turned and yelled "Hey" to the back of the truck, slapping the fender with a dull metallic thud, and the dogs stopped their howling, at least for the moment.

"Gentlemen," Sam said, as he approached.

"Who's he talking to?" Jake said, looking up at Officer Bennigan.

Bennigan turned and looked at Deputy Sorenson. "Must be Sorenson," he said.

Sorenson grinned, but just a little.

Sam remembered they had some business to settle. "Deputy," he said, nodding to Sorenson.

Sorenson nodded back, a little cool.

"What's the plan?" Sam said.

"We're gonna kill a cougar," Jake said. "I can feel it." He looked up, considering the wall of trees east of the lot.

A beautiful September sun, still pretty warm, was setting over the trees. There was a hint of something in the air, maybe a weather change to a more seasonable temperature. Sam had been so busy he hadn't listened to the weather, but it felt different.

"And we think we got a good plan to get it done," Jake added.

They looked again at the map, and Jake and Bennigan explained how they could divide the huge park area into three hunting zones. Jake would take two of his dogs into the part of the swamp nearest Shakopee, Bennigan would take the other two coonhounds into the center of the swamp, and Sam and Sorenson would take Gray into the southernmost region, the one that opened out onto river-bottom farmland, farther south.

"You guys ever been in the swamp?" Sam asked. "How swampy is it?"

"It's a swamp in the spring. This time of year, it's just river-bottom woods, some of it pretty dense. This whole area," he said, sweeping his hand over the broad region of the map with the river running along the eastern edge, "is perfect woodland, with a few dense spots. But it's pretty easy to navigate, and it has plenty of deer."

There were no other cars in the remote lot. "And it looks empty," Sam said. "At least of people."

"Gotta be swarming with critters," Jake said. "And I bet our cat's one of them."

The four men and the dogs readied themselves in the dusk light. Their gear looked a little beat up from the previous night's run through dark woods. But they were all excited to be heading into the swamp.

Sam wasn't a big hunter, but he loved exploring wild places and seeing what they contained. When he was a boy, the wilderness was his refuge. His father had a farm up on the Iron Range, outside of Defiance, where Sam spent much of his time. But the farmhouse was on the edge of a 100-mile wilderness that stretched all the way into Canada; it was not only Sam's playground, but his place of solace, his spiritual center, a region where he could escape from the old man's abuse and wrath and experience a kind of grace, however brief and fleeting. The wilderness had gotten him through, he often thought.

Gray was both excited and anxious. Seeing last night's canine acquaintances outfitted with the bizarre orange collars and those foot-long antennas caused his bicolored eyes to grow inquisitive.

"We've got pretty good reception," Sam said, looking at his iPhone. He'd pulled up the map for the area and could see the entire 1,000-acre wood in front of him. He'd triggered his GPS and would be able to track his route on the screen, keeping to the southern area of the swamp. Since Gray wasn't wearing a tracker, he'd need to keep him close.

"We're looking for any sign," Sam said. "If there's a cougar in there, we should find something. Tracks, fur, something."

"Maybe another dead deer," Jake said.

Sam nodded. "Let's see what the dogs pick up."

Jake said, "We got 4 hours, and I'm feelin' lucky." The dogs were straining at their leashes. "These guys are excited."

They started off in the dusk light. There was a perimeter path around the swamp, a rough cut through brambles. The hiking path made a large oval around the edge of the trees, and on the back side along the river.

"Those woods have to be loaded with raccoons," Sam said.

"It's something else," Jake said, vaguely.

Sam thought Gray, too, was acting a little squirrelly. "Good," was all he said, and then he and Sorenson turned south along the trail and started hiking along the rough-cut path.

Jake, Bennigan, and the dogs turned north. They'd all spend the next half hour hiking to the river. Once they were situated on the back side of their regions, they'd start filtering through the woods, making their way back to the lot and cars, seeing what they could turn up.

While it was still light, they made good time. Nothing like a hike through the beautiful dusk along a trail that borders September woods to clear the air, Sam thought.

"You were a little testy on the phone," Sam said.

Sorenson flushed a little. "You lied to me."

"Not exactly."

"You told me you were going to that hearing, but didn't."

"How do you know I didn't?"

"The chief chewed my ass about it. He said he saw you before we met at the Depot, and you were coming out of the McGregor plant. Said he hung around on some side street and watched you drive over to Wannamake Circle. You talking to Mrs. McGregor?"

"The chief followed me?"

"Said he saw you coming from the plant and had a feeling."

Sam didn't buy it. "You're right, Sorenson. I lied. But with the best intentions."

"Your best intentions almost got me fired."

"Was the chief listening to you when we were talking on the phone earlier?"

"The chief and the sheriff both. Neither of them happy. The chief disciplined me. There's no doubt he would have fired me, and the sheriff almost let him."

"Over this?"

Sorenson looked away. "The chief's a jerk. Nobody likes him. He's a cold taskmaster and he doesn't really seem to care about anyone or anything, far as I can tell. He's an Iceman."

"Why doesn't the sheriff get rid of him?"

"The guy's a decorated war veteran. He has a Bronze Star, for God's sake. And he was a sergeant in the military police. He knows law enforcement." They walked a few more paces in silence, thinking about Chief Anders's Bronze Star and résumé. "The sheriff says he needs a tough chief, to keep everyone in line. And he might have one, but nobody likes him."

"So why didn't the chief fire you?"

Ole was still smarting from the afternoon's chastisement. "The sheriff's sister is my mom," he said. "I don't know if that's a good thing, though. Ever since the chief started, I've been think-ing about getting out of law enforcement."

Sam bet Bob Lawson, Sheriff Rusty Benson's challenger, could make good use out of Benson's nepotism, if he hadn't already.

Probably in campaign ads. But Sam said, "My advice—not that you're looking for it, but I've been in that situation, with an intolerable boss, and I'm not exactly good with authority—is the landscape changes, Sorenson. It sometimes changes quickly. Switching jobs or careers because you can't get along with a boss isn't the right reason to do it. You make that kind of change because it's the right thing for you.

"I had a classics professor in community college," Sam continued. "Taught me more about law enforcement and investigations than any of my law instructors. He had a saying: *Illegitimi non carborundum*. I guess it roughly translates, 'Don't let the bastards grind you down.'"

Sorenson smiled.

"We can't let 'em do it," Sam said.

They walked awhile longer, making good time. They came to the river in the near-dark. In another quarter mile, they'd turn into the woods and start making their way back to the lot and cars.

While it was still light, Benedict found the gravel road bordering the south side of the swamp. He took it, driving more than a mile off 169, seeing no cars or traffic. It was a low-maintenance road that dead-ended at the river. Probably a path for fishermen or hikers. Or grouse hunters, he thought, considering his camo disguise.

He backtracked from the river and found a short turnoff where he parked his car and popped the trunk.

Benedict hadn't come back from Afghanistan with any gear. But a piece of equipment he learned to appreciate because it was perfect for a predator, was night-vision goggles. He'd scoured online catalogs and used-equipment sites and finally found an outlet selling used survivalist equipment out of Idaho. The store had a website. Like many who bought equipment from sites like these, Benedict had used his alias to acquire the goggles, paying for them with a temporary debit card.

Anonymous.

Now he placed the goggles in the inside panel of his hunting jacket. He took out his 12-gauge and his 9-millimeter and stuffed the pistol on the opposite side of his jacket pouch. He placed the small binoculars in an upper pouch. And then he bushwhacked back to a vantage point where he could watch the vehicles, hunters, and dogs gather.

By the time Sam Rivers arrived, Benedict was peering through the binoculars from the distant edge of woods. His disguise was good, but if Sorenson ever saw him up close, he might recognize him. But maybe not. The deputy was young and stupid, and if the sheriff wasn't his uncle, the chief deputy would have cut him, just to send a message.

But tonight, Benedict didn't plan on being spotted. Tonight, he was going to blend into darkness and bide his time. Until he could find the right place and the right moment. Then, with luck, he was going to hurt the dog or put him down. It would be better to hurt him. Then the animal's treatment would preoccupy Rivers and take him off their trail.

They would, of course, wonder who had fired the bullet and why. But the area was remote, not easily traversable, and known as a poacher's paradise. Twice in the last year, the sheriff's office had gotten calls. And though they had found all the signs of poachers, they'd never caught anyone. Because it was too remote and there were too many places to hide.

Tonight maybe a poacher, or a hunter trying to find that cougar, was going to see Sam Rivers's dog, mistake it for a wolf, and try to take it down. Then the shooter would bleed back into darkness the way he'd come.

Rivers was too smart not to wonder about it. But he'd be too busy taking care of his animal.

Benedict knew how to use the night-vision goggles, and with the men donning headlamps, he knew the goggles would make them light up through the trees like roman candles. The dog should be easy to find.

At dusk, the deputy, Rivers, and the dog started hiking the perimeter road, heading straight for him. Benedict retreated farther back into the trees. From a safe distance, he watched the three pass. At one point, briefly, the dog looked up and stared at him, maybe seeing a glint from the binoculars. He was close enough so that the high-powered lens revealed one dark-colored eye, one eye lighter. Benedict took the binoculars away from his eyes, in case that cur somehow sensed him. But the three kept walking down the rugged trail and were quickly out of sight.

More than an hour passed and it grew dark. But not for Benedict. The night-vision goggles picked up the trail of the men and dog as though their feet had been radioactive. He followed them to the back side of the trail, to where it ambled for a quarter mile along the river's edge. And then from a distance, he watched them enter the woods.

Benedict backtracked and bushwhacked, making his way to a point where he could sit, wait, and eventually see them pass in front of him. He was in position by a little after 8, waiting and watching in a low point of river-bottom maples. There was plenty of undergrowth, but none of it was high enough to impair his vision. And it was open enough so he could see 50 yards through the forest of huge, sporadic trunks.

Benedict heard the group before he saw them. They made plenty of noise through the dense undergrowth. When they came into view, he saw the dog out in front, its head barely visible above a thick pack of itchweed.

Benedict lifted the 9-millimeter. The gun was a cutting machine. If he really wanted to kill the dog, he'd have used the shotgun. But it was too much weapon for his purpose. Wound, not kill.

He was positioned well to the side, watching the three approach. He looked ahead and saw the narrow opening that would provide the best vantage for a clear shot. He watched and waited. Not long.

Gray was maybe 50 feet out in front. He stepped carefully through the dark, smelling the rich forest smells, occasionally checking his progress to make sure Sam and Sorenson followed and were not too far behind. But he liked being in front. It catered to his alpha instincts. He kept moving through the trees.

Thirty feet to the side, Benedict aimed carefully through the woods. One tree trunk, then 7, maybe 10 feet of open ground, and that's where he'd shoot him. *Only to wound,* Benedict reminded himself.

In the distance, Sam and Sorenson heard two baying hounds, followed by Jake's and Bennigan's voices farther off.

"They treed something," Sam said. Gray turned to look and then continued walking.

Something just 2 feet ahead was giving off a fetid odor. When Gray stepped closer it was definitely the smell of something rotten. The moment he bent his head, a shot rang out through the trees. It startled Gray, and in an instant he ducked low, and then another shot, just feet away, accompanied by another that hit high up on his back. It cut along the top of his hide and he yelped, lost his footing, and fell.

Sam heard it and in the shadowy distance of his light beam saw Gray fall. "Gray!" he yelled, running toward him. "Gray!"

Sorenson was behind him. He took two steps and went down, tripping over a tree root.

Then in the distance, to the north, they heard one rifle shot, followed only seconds later by another.

Sam reached Gray as three more shots, from a pistol, rang out and Sam heard the *zip-zip* of the bullets whizzing through brush and understory.

And then Sam was on Gray and Gray was up, peering at him. Sam yanked him to a tree, thinking the pistol cracks came from his right. He brought Gray in close, peering into darkness.

"It's a dog! Hold your fire! It's a dog!" Sam yelled.

But there was nothing. He couldn't see anything. He thought he heard someone moving through the trees, but if so, they were quiet as a wild animal.

Sorenson came up beside them, breathing heavily.

"Get down," Sam said, cutting Sorenson's legs out from under him, dropping him like a bag of hammers.

"Someone shot at Gray. We don't know who the hell is out there or what they're doing."

Sam looked at Gray with his lantern light, but Gray appeared to be OK. He examined the length of him and saw the sticky ooze on the top of Gray's flanks, in front of his tail.

"You're hit," Sam said. His headlamp revealed a scarlet mat on top of Gray's hair, but it wasn't bleeding badly.

Sorenson was on his knees, peering at it from the other side.

"He got grazed," Sam said. "Looks like it'll need some stitches."

Then he peered in the direction from which he thought the pistol had been fired.

"Who the hell was it?" Ole said.

"No idea. Probably a poacher, maybe thought Gray was a wolf?"

"Maybe someone looking for the cougar."

"Did you hear those shots from the other side of the woods?"

"Yup. It was confusing. I heard those distant shots about the same time I heard that pistol. I wonder if Jake or Bennigan got lucky?"

Sam turned and peered into the underbrush, but his light was swallowed up in darkness 10 feet out. They waited for another 2 minutes, but heard nothing.

"We're coming out. Don't shoot!" Sam said.

They waited awhile longer, but didn't hear anything.

"Let's keep moving through these woods, back toward the cars," Sam said.

And then they crept quickly through the dark, all three bunched together, wary.

As the three stumbled out onto the turf lot, they could see two people in headlamps behind Jake's truck—Bennigan and Jake. As they got closer, they watched one of the men, maybe 50 yards out, move around to the side of the truck, get in behind the wheel, and start the engine. Headlights switched on, illuminating the field in front of the truck. The driver got out, came around back, and the two men could be seen dragging something heavy around front. As Sorenson, Sam, and Gray approached, they could see it was a mountain lion.

"They got him," Sam said.

Sorenson started running.

Gray wanted to take off after Sorenson, but when Sam just kept walking, he heeled, peering at the illuminated scene . . . and the cat.

"You got him," Sorenson said.

"You bet we got him," Jake said. "Look at that animal. A damn cougar." He was breathing heavily from dragging the animal.

"Who got him?"

"The great white hunter here, CO Tom Bennigan."

Tom wasn't talking and he, too, was a little winded from dragging the animal around the truck. And from dragging the cougar out of the woods.

"I was pretty close to the cars, actually," Bennigan said.

Sam and Gray approached. Gray eyed the cougar warily, moving in for a closer sniff. But even Gray could smell death and didn't do much more than sniff.

"That's a beautiful specimen," Sam said. "And it looks young and healthy."

Sam bent down and had a look. First he checked its sex. A male. Then he spent a minute or two examining the rest of the animal. Its long, tapered body rippled with muscle, now flaccid in death. Its fur was a beautiful taupe, the color of the rock outcrop on Mable Swenson's cattle ranch. When Sam pulled back an eyelid, a yellow eye peered back, most of its pupil rolled back into the skull. Sam checked its mouth and saw its incisors were all healthy and intact. *What are you doing in Minnesota?* he thought.

CO Bennigan talked about how the coonhounds had tracked and treed the animal. When he'd come upon it and shone his light up into the tree, seeing that big cat nearly made his heart stop. He'd spent some time looking around the tree, but the dogs were carrying on so much he couldn't get them quiet. And they were spooking the cougar. He looked like he was going to jump any second. So Bennigan had finally figured out the best shot and taken it. The first shot hit him in the flanks. The second brought him down.

The lion was a young, fit male. From what Sam could tell, its belly looked pretty full, so it must have recently fed. Its claws, like its teeth, appeared healthy and intact, nothing out of place. By all appearances, the cougar looked to be in great shape.

If this was the mountain lion that killed Jack McGregor, it must have mistaken the speeding cyclist for a deer. But given Jack's bright-yellow garb and the white bike, it still didn't make sense.

At least, Sam thought, a DNA analysis would tell them if it was the same cat. The idea that there were two cougars in the

Minnesota River Valley hadn't occurred to him until he'd examined those prints. Now they would know for sure.

Sam helped them photograph the cat. They wanted one with all of them, but Sam wasn't interested, and Gray sat off to the side, contemplating cat and men. The group took a half hour trading cameras and getting different angles, to be certain they had plenty of images.

Sam stopped twice to check on Gray, but he was fine and the nick on his back had stopped bleeding.

By the end of the photo session, Sam was weary of the lift, focus, shoot, and flash.

Bennigan and Jake piled the big cat into the back of the DNR pickup. Bennigan had already called the coroner's office, and the night staff was waiting to receive it. Ole had called the sheriff and let him know. The wheels were already turning. There was going to be a 9 a.m. press conference, which would give the media time to get there. The sheriff briefly thought about having the cat in the conference room, but knew if the cameras picked it up, with him standing over the dead animal, the tree huggers might get ticked off and the photo op could backfire. A handful of distributed photos should suffice.

Sam needed to get Gray to a vet, have that cut on his back examined. It had stopped bleeding, but it might need some stitches. Sam had also bagged some of the animal's fur, enough to FedEx to Tracy McDonald at USFW forensics. He'd get it off later tonight. Tracy could do the analysis and share the DNA records with the university.

It was nearly 10 when the group disbanded. Sam was tired, but the only thing he could think about was Gray. When he'd heard the shots and saw Gray's shadowy figure fall, the adrenaline took him into overdrive and he didn't have a chance to feel. But in retrospect, his stomach had dropped and he had felt intense pain in the top center of his chest—heart pain. And rage. Sudden and visceral . . . at least until he checked Gray and determined he was OK. And Gray was fine; even now, getting into the jeep, he didn't seem to notice the scratch.

As soon as they were in the jeep, Sam called Diane and gave her the news.

"I need a photo," she said.

"I've got about 100 on my phone," he said. Then he told her about Gray.

"Oh, no," she said, shocked. "Is he OK?"

"He's fine. It's just a scratch."

"Rivers. Get him to a vet. Tonight."

"That was part of the reason I called. Can you look up an emergency vet clinic? My reception isn't great out by the highway and I need to find one, this side of the Cities, if possible."

He waited while she looked it up. There was one in Eden Prairie and she gave Sam the directions.

"I'll meet you there," she said.

"He's OK," Sam assured her.

"You two might need some help," she said, and hung up.

At first, Sam appreciated her concern and thought maybe it meant something. But then he knew it was really about Gray, not Sam. And he understood that perspective. But still . . .

CHAPTER TWENTY-THREE

By 10:30, Jared Sparks was at the CVS off Judicial Road, looking for another pack of gum, trying to appear like a legitimate shopper. He bought the gum, went to the bathroom, came out, and took the rear exit, on his way to the nearby trail behind Carla's house. Just like last night, except tonight the twisted knots in his gut had grown tighter. He'd phoned Carla three times, as the tennis pro following up with a client to reschedule a game. He'd tried the legitimate route because Carla didn't like him to use the other. But she never answered and her silence made him wonder. When he felt certain she'd be home, he tried again. No answer.

Finally, he tried Urban's phone. But she never picked up.

Now he had only one recourse. He turned into the black woods off Judicial Road. He pushed into the tree branches, waited until his eyes grew accustomed to the increased darkness, found the start of the game trail, and took it. In spite of his inner turmoil, he crossed the wild corridor carefully, until he stood hidden behind one of the tall arborvitae bordering the back of the McGregors' property. He pushed his hand through the side of the straight branches, made a small opening, and peered up at the windows of Carla's kitchen.

And that's when he saw them. Carla was there with someone he had never seen and didn't know.

His turmoil ticked up a notch and became some kind of inner storm. He thought about what to do, but for the first time in his adult life, regarding women, all he could feel was rage. He'd wondered why she hadn't answered his calls. And now he knew. There was a man in Carla's kitchen and all Jared could think of was murder.

He slipped around the edge of the tree and hustled to the back side of the house. There was an elevated deck off the kitchen. He stood below the deck, thinking, but had no idea what to do. He needed to get closer, to hear them. The late-summer night was in his favor, and he thought he'd seen a rear window cracked open.

Jared took 5 minutes to creep up the long flight of deck stairs, soundless. Near the top, he peeked his head up enough to view the inside of the kitchen.

The guy wore a uniform. Some kind of officer. They were facing each other across the granite-topped center island. There was a cracked window along the back through which he heard voices, but he was too far away to hear them clearly. From the shadows of the stairs, he watched and waited.

Carla was drinking wine. The officer, nothing. But it appeared to be more than a courtesy call.

Jared watched and waited. One more sip and Carla finished the glass and turned toward the bottle near the sink, her back to the windows. The officer followed her as she moved to replenish her glass.

Jared hustled up and managed to cross the deck until his back was to the solid wall, to the side of the opened window. He listened.

"What about John?" Carla said.

"What about him?"

As soon as he heard the man's voice, he was stunned. Benedict! But the officer looked nothing like the long-haired hunter with a mustache. This guy's head was shaven to nubs.

"Do we need to do anything?"

"Already have," Benedict said.

"What do you mean?"

"The tools. His prints are all over them."

"So what?" Carla said. "What good are the tools?"

"They're at his place. Hidden."

"He let you hide them there?"

"He doesn't know about it. And he won't find them. But if we need them, an investigating officer will find them."

"So what will Chief Deputy Leif Anders be investigating?" Carla asked.

The son of a bitch was an insider, Jared thought. Worked in the sheriff's office!

"Not me," Benedict . . . Anders said. "Somebody else. Maybe Deputy Sorenson, the sheriff's nephew. That'd make the sheriff proud and all the more willing to accept what he's discovered."

"So when the police find them, what do you think John's going to say? He did it all by himself?"

"John won't say anything."

There was a long pause, during which Carla absorbed Benedict's words, and understood how his plan could work, if they needed it. Others had seen her with Jared Sparks. Others may have even noticed his growing absorption, his preoccupation. Like today, when he called her three times from the Club. Someone at the Club could have seen it. The switchboard would have registered it. She'd been discreet about her Jared connection, but it's hard to be discreet when a tennis pro like Jared Sparks is guiding your body through the motions of a serve in front of everyone having lunch at the Club's deli, looking out over the court.

Women had talked about Jared's touch, and Carla was sure those women had talked about her. Her and Jared.

There could also be a note, if they needed it. She had chosen the young pro because he was inexperienced and attractive. Later, she had seen what could be done, how he could be useful. But she had always considered him expendable. There had always been an expiration date with Jared. Maybe now she knew when it was.

"He's getting crazy," she said. "I can feel him. He tried to call me three times today on the regular phone, from the Club. And then he called me on the throwaways."

"Did you answer?"

"Of course not."

"Where were you?" Benedict asked. He had wondered about it, when she hadn't answered his morning call to warn her about Sam Rivers's visit.

"Running errands. It's not easy to lay your hands on that much cash," she said, indicating the thick envelope in front of him. "I can't take it all out of one place at one time."

Benedict considered it. Reasonable. But he didn't trust Carla. He reminded himself to keep an eye out.

"Keep an eye out," he said, talking about Jared. "If we need it, we got insurance. And if they somehow figure out it wasn't a cougar, they find their killer."

"So the police would find the tools investigating John's accident," she said.

"Something like that."

"Maybe . . . suicide," she said.

Benedict thought about it. A spurned lover? Someone crazy enough to call Carla four times in one day? Three of them on record. "Maybe," Benedict said. "But then again, maybe we won't need any of it."

The more Carla thought about it, the more she liked the plan's symmetry, if they needed it.

She turned out of the kitchen and walked the chief deputy to the door, thanking him for checking on her.

The chief walked out to his cruiser, started the engine, and clicked into dispatch.

"Mrs. McGregor's OK. I checked the house and the premises, and there wasn't anything. Maybe she heard a raccoon."

Dispatch confirmed he was back online.

The chief deputy spent some time thinking about a circuitous route to his place—roundabout, but quick enough to let him run in, find a place to put his fat envelope, and be back on patrol before anyone at the sheriff's office had any idea. He appreciated the heft of the first installment, knowing there would be more.

From the corner of the house, Jared watched the cruiser pull out of Carla's drive and turn up Wannamake Circle. He thought, briefly, about breaking into Carla's house and killing her. With his fists. But he was smart enough to know it was a stupid play. He'd spend some time looking for those tools. But he also remembered his recordings. Carla didn't know they existed. And the audio was clear enough to hear everything. Her suggestions, her planning, the names, everything.

He made his way back into the wild darkness behind Carla's house. Jared had insurance of his own.

PART III

September 25

CHAPTER TWENTY-FOUR

Half conscious, Sam rose out of a deep sleep. He'd been dreaming, but he couldn't remember what. And then he remembered and he kept himself quiet, not fully awake, wondering if what he was remembering about the previous evening was a dream.

He and Gray had met Diane at the emergency vet in Eden Prairie. After an examination of Gray's bullet wound, really only a graze, the vet—Dr. Susan Rodriguez—cleaned the wound and sewed it with two stitches. She was young and not what he would have expected in a vet. Diminutive. But she had a way of being around Gray that Sam appreciated. Gray had actually let her stitch his back. And she admired the hybrid, noting his heterochromia and confirming what Sam had already suspected: Gray still had some growing to do. He wouldn't end at 90 pounds. More like 120, she guessed.

She gave Gray something for the pain, and handed Sam the bill.

Susan Rodriguez. Vets weren't always good with Gray, but the petite Latina was superb. Her bill, however, was not so small.

Out in the lot, Sam told Diane he had to drop off the fur sample at a FedEx that was on the way to the Quality Inn.

"You had anything to eat?" she asked.

"Didn't have time," Sam said.

"Me neither. Working on stories. How about some Chinese?"

"I need to get Gray back to the hotel room, let him rest."

"I can bring over some takeout."

"That'd be nice," Sam said, reaching for his cash.

"On me," Diane said. "You've spent enough money for one night."

And so he had. "Thanks."

Sam dropped off the overnight package to forensics. Back at the hotel, he fed and watered Gray, and got him bedded down. And then Diane appeared at his door with an order of moo goo gai pan, General Tso's chicken, and a pair of egg rolls. And a bottle of akvavit, the clear, Northern European liquor Sam had last tasted on the Iron Range, with Diane, when it had more meaning and had led somewhere.

The presence of the akvavit made him suspicious, but the only thing Diane said was, "Got any ice?"

He retrieved some ice and while Diane started putting out the dinner, he poured them both a glass of akvavit.

Sam handed her one of the drinks and said, "To catching the mountain lion," and they toasted to it, though Sam wasn't feeling great about killing such a magnificent animal.

They talked through dinner, comfortable, periodically looking over at Gray. But Gray was tired and lay on his side, on a blanket, dozing. Before midnight, Sam got the call about needing to be at the 9 a.m. press conference. He said he'd be there. So would Diane.

Sam finally voiced his concerns to Diane about the mountain lion and where they'd found it, miles from McGregor Industries.

And it appeared to be well fed. The only thing he could figure is that after attacking Jack McGregor, the animal made its way by daylight nearly 20 miles to the Savannah Swamp, where it may have killed a deer and fed. And that's where they found it. But it wasn't normal mountain lion behavior and, like other things in this case, didn't make ethological sense.

"What other things?" Diane asked.

"McGregor was killed 2 hours before anyone found him. He was killed at dawn, which is a typical hunting time for cougars. But the cougar didn't feed on its kill. And there was plenty of time. If it took the trouble to kill, why didn't it feed?"

"Someone scared it off?" Diane said.

"It's possible, but the place is posted NO TRESPASSING. Marlin Coots said people trespass down there all the time. But if someone scared off the cat right after it killed McGregor, wouldn't they have found his body and reported it?"

"Maybe. Unless they were trespassing and knew they'd be prosecuted."

"Oh, come on," Sam said. "I think trespassing is a misdemeanor in Minnesota. You're saying someone wouldn't report a murder because they didn't want to face a misdemeanor?"

"I'm playing devil's advocate," Diane said. "Was there something else?"

"Here's another thing," Sam said. "The only prints they found at McGregor's kill site had claw marks sticking out. Cougars—in fact, all cats—are very particular about their claws. They only have them out if they are killing or feeding."

"But it *was* killing," Diane said.

"If it killed McGregor, it would have used its claws only for the attack. Once its victim was dead, it would have retracted its claws, at least until it fed. But this cat didn't feed on McGregor."

"*If* it killed McGregor," Diane said. "What else could have happened to the man?"

"I admit, the evidence, troubling as it is, points to one conclusion. But there are a lot of anomalies."

"What else?"

"When I set Gray on the trail of the cat, he led us right back to the road where a car had been parked. And then later, the coonhounds did the same thing. What were they sniffing?"

"Maybe the cougar headed out that way?"

"And got into a car?" Sam said. "And then the lion traveled almost 20 miles during the day? If it was the lion they shot last night, it appeared young and normal. But traveling that far during the day, with some of the river valley running right through Shakopee, would be incredibly unusual mountain lion behavior."

They both considered it. Sam took a sip of his drink and Diane did the same, thinking.

"Maybe we're thinking about this the wrong way." Diane said.

"What do you mean?"

"Set aside the evidence of a cougar kill for a minute. It seems to me there are a lot of people who wanted to see McGregor dead. Isn't there motive all over the place?"

"All over the place," Sam agreed. "If I had the time, I'd look a little more carefully at Carla McGregor, Madeline Baxter, and Jared Sparks, for starters. None of them passed the smell test, and they all had reasons to see McGregor dead."

"Wouldn't everyone working at McGregor be a suspect?"

"Not really, if you think about it. The CFO and the treasurer were both going to make good money from the sale. And the two analysts were young, good with numbers, and would also make some money from the sale. They'd all want to see the sale go through without complications. So I think we can cross them all off the list."

"Unfortunately, I don't think you're going to have the time to look into those others—McGregor's wife, Maddy Baxter, and Jared Sparks," Diane said.

They were on their third glass of akvavit, and it was having an effect. Both of them were beginning to think less about suspects, and more about each other. Though neither admitted it.

"You're right," Sam said. "Now that we've found the mountain lion, Magdalen will be wanting me back in Denver. But before I go, I need to check out that swamp again. I'd like to see where they shot that cougar, and I'd like to check out where Gray got shot, see if I can find anything."

Diane looked at him. Then said, "Rivers, I think before you head back to Denver, one of us has to man up."

Sam looked at her, wondering if they were finally going to have the discussion about his abrupt departure last February and his hinky call to her, two weeks later, telling her he couldn't be involved. He was just about ready to start in with an apology and a discussion about how he still needed time to himself, but before he could speak, Diane set down her glass, stood up, came over to where he was sitting, leaned down, and kissed him.

Damn, he was stupid. And lucky.

Now, in the morning, he noticed the early light coming in around the hotel room window and was certain it was no dream. Because Diane lay beside him, breathing heavily.

Sam remembered their coupling, which had been careful, intimate, at times a little awkward, but satisfying. What happened last night was a *coming together*. Mutual respect, admiration, and pleasure. But . . .

Sam slid out of bed quietly, careful not to disturb her. He padded to the bathroom, avoiding eye contact with Gray. The big hybrid was still on his side, eyes narrow slits. Sam didn't want the rangy hybrid stretching, standing, wagging his tail, and waiting to go out. He needed Gray to stay quiet.

He entered the bathroom, closed the door carefully, and flipped on the light, squinting in the sudden illumination. He glanced in the mirror and thought, *What are you doing?* Then he had a back-and-forth conversation with himself about how it had been her idea and he had just gone along (*wasn't that easy, Rivers, since it absolves you of any responsibility?*), and then he told himself guilt was so typical for him, a killjoy who couldn't seem to have a good time and park the agendas to the side, just for one minute, or a few, or maybe one evening? But he told himself nothing had changed. He was going back to Denver, sooner rather than later, now that the lion had been caught and killed.

His head hurt. And not from the akvavit. They hadn't drunk that much. It was from the whiplash he was giving himself over last night.

Finally, he washed his face, brushed his teeth, and tried to come out of the bathroom without disturbing anyone, including himself. He flipped off the light, coaxed open the door, and saw Diane bent over Gray, cooing to him. She was in her underwear, and a gauzy undershirt hung over her back like gossamer.

"Did you sleep well, Gray?" she asked.

The hybrid's tail flap-flapped on the carpeted floor.

Then she stood up and turned, and Sam smiled, standing there in his red boxers. She looked good in the diaphanous light. It was hard not to notice the shape of those breasts and how the thin cloth was almost sheer, not leaving much to the imagination.

Sam swallowed, just for a moment as dumbstruck as a deer in headlights.

"And how's Sam Rivers?" Diane said, coming forward to hug him.

He returned the hug with affection.

"I'm going to make us some coffee," she said. "After I use the bathroom. I have to wake up, and then we both have a 9 a.m. press conference."

"I can get us some coffee. I've gotta walk Gray," Sam said.

Diane nodded, and then she was gone.

Gray had stood up when the two of them hugged. Now he waited while Sam greeted him. Sam recognized it; he was looking for attention and the leash.

"OK, buddy. Can I put on some clothes first?"

He admitted he wanted to take his time about dressing, just to watch Diane walk out of that bathroom and move across the room. But the dog needed to go out, and Sam needed to get them coffee, and he was hungry. Besides, he was already thinking about his day.

He and Gray walked into the vacant lot behind the Quality Inn. The weather was starting to change. It was warm again, but there was a slight breeze that felt like it was coming out of the northwest.

While Gray did his business, Sam pulled out his phone and checked his messages. Nothing on voice mail, but Marlin had reviewed those prints and sent him a note.

"I'm no expert," Marlin wrote. "But if I had to guess, I'd say the cougar who killed the white-tail earlier this month was a different animal from the one that killed Mr. McGregor. But does that make sense?"

No, it doesn't, Sam thought. But at least he and Marlin agreed.

Sam shot back a note of thanks, told him about killing a mountain lion last night and that they'd talk later.

After Gray was done, they walked over to the hotel lobby. Sam tied Gray to a NO PARKING sign, where Sam could keep an eye on him through a window and where Gray was unlikely to frighten a guest. In the lobby, there was a continental breakfast: coffee, hard-boiled eggs, oatmeal, cinnamon rolls, bagels, toast, jams, jellies, peanut butter, and more.

Sam's hunger intensified, looking at all the food. He filled two large cups with dark brew, wondering why cheap hotels and chain restaurants scrimped on coffee, which looked more like tepid tea than his preferred black tar. Still, the price was right.

He got a tray and picked up hard-boiled eggs in a bowl, salt and pepper packets, some oatmeal, two bagels, strawberry jam, and cream cheese, and then added another hard-boiled egg to his cache, for Gray.

Back in the room, Diane was sitting up in bed, waiting for coffee with her clothes on.

"I wondered where you'd gotten off to."

"Some provisions," Sam said.

He brought the tray over to her, and she took a bagel and one of the large cups of coffee, setting them on the table next to the bed. Sam carried the rest around to the other side, where he set it down. Then he took one of the hard-boiled eggs and cut it up, added it to Gray's kibble, mixed in some canned food, put it all under warm water, stirred, and set it in front of the hungry hybrid, who was starting to drool.

He was just about ready to settle into breakfast when his cell phone rang.

"We're working on a press release," the sheriff said. He sounded excited. Sam guessed the lion's death had put a lift in the sheriff's gait. "Working title is 'Savage Man-Killer Caught in the Savannah Swamp.'"

"Good title."

"I thought so. That was Ole. He's got his mother's artistic gene. I'm wondering if we can quote you about the animal? Saying something like 'Cougars are so rare in Minnesota, we're pretty certain we've bagged the killer.' Something like that?"

"Ah . . ." Sam thought about it. "OK," he said. "Why don't you add something about adult mountain lions being solitary animals?"

"Good idea."

Sam guessed the sheriff's pleasantness was what happened when your crime was solved, the killer apprehended, and your campaign was about to get the kind of boost incumbents only dreamed about in the middle of the night, out of deep REM.

Because of the print comparison, Sam thought there might be another mountain lion on the loose. But he didn't want to share that information with the sheriff because it wasn't definitive and it didn't make sense, and even if there was another lion, he still didn't believe anyone had to worry about it. If there was another mountain lion in Minnesota, it was just passing through. There were too many people in the metro area for a solitary creature like that.

"When will the coroner be done with the lion?" Sam asked.

"I think he's just about done now. I pulled in a favor, wanted him to get me what he could before the press conference. He's testing for any trace of McGregor. Maybe some blood under the cat's claws."

"Any problems with me taking a look at the animal when he's done? I'm just curious. I'd like to see if something was wrong with him. Inside."

"That'd be fine."

The coroner's name was Warren Sap. The sheriff told Sam where to find him, and reminded Sam to be at the press conference at least 5 minutes early.

CHAPTER TWENTY-FIVE

All the media who attended the first conference were present at this one, with one or two new additions. The CEO's death by mountain lion had been big news, and the capture of the killer even bigger. From McGregor Industries, the only person present was Maddy Baxter. Phil Traub and Spencer Higgins were apparently too busy with the sale.

Deputy Sorenson handed out a press release, which was now subtitled "Sheriff Rusty Benson Closes Case on Tragic Accident."

Sam wasn't surprised the sheriff's name had worked its way into the headline. And judging from the ebullient Benson, breezing through the door when everyone was assembled, the sheriff was leveraging the media opportunity like a Hollywood star promoting his recent hit movie.

Sam was quoted in the press release: "Given that cougars are extremely rare in Minnesota and that it was caught in the same area, this is definitely the man-killer that took Jack McGregor's life."

Sam had no one but himself to blame. He wouldn't have been so definitive, he wouldn't have used the phrase *man-killer*, and if he had a chance, he might set the record straight. But he was pretty certain Sheriff Benson wouldn't give him that chance. And there were still some last-minute details he needed to address that might require the sheriff's OK, so he decided to be civil and play along, provided it didn't cost him too much.

The press release also reminded readers of other cougar predations and that cougars were extremely territorial animals. These cougar facts considered in total gave further validation to the sheriff's assertion about the accident.

"Terribly tragic and unfortunate," Benson was quoted as saying. Several other quotes from him were sprinkled throughout the press release.

The cameras needed to get it all on tape, so the sheriff did a good job reiterating the key facts and his overall statement, passing around some photos of the dead cougar, letting them know digital copies were available. The sheriff also included reference to their cougar expert, on loan from the USFW out of Denver. One camera focused briefly on Sam, but only for a moment. For the most part, they remained trained on the sheriff.

Conservation Officer Bennigan talked briefly and shyly about the difficulty of tracking the animal with dogs through the Savannah Swamp in the dark.

There were a few questions, but they were softballs, pitched with such an easy arc that Bennigan and Benson knocked them out of the park. They stood together, shoulder to shoulder, both in uniform. A few cameras flashed and whirred. It made for a good photo and good footage. Sam figured the media had at least nailed the iconic image, even though the case's facts were in dispute. But he kept those to himself.

Then it ended and everyone started packing up.

Diane was present, but she only nodded to Sam, as though they were acquaintances instead of two people who had spent last night in bed together.

She and three other newspaper reporters were asking the sheriff some follow-up questions. Behind the loose gaggle stood Maddy, waiting to speak with the sheriff. Sam had a hunch he knew what their conversation might be about.

He was getting up to leave when the sheriff approached him.

"Rivers," he said. "I need a word."

The press conference was over and Sam followed the sheriff into his office. Benson motioned Sam into a chair across from his desk and Sam took it. The sheriff sat down behind his desk. There were knickknacks and lots of papers strewn around.

"Madeline Baxter told me you were still trying to see two of her employees," the sheriff said.

There was no reason to hide it. "Yeah," Sam said.

"What for?"

"I just wanted to see if they had any questions about the kill, to assure them it was rare and there was no reason to worry."

The sheriff looked skeptical. "Were you planning on doing that with all the McGregor employees?"

Sam shook his head no.

"So that's it?" he concluded.

"That's about it," Sam said.

"Maybe you should leave the follow-up visits to me," the sheriff said.

"Sure," Sam said. "I was just trying to help."

"Have you been helpful in any other ways?"

"What do you mean?"

"The chief deputy thought he saw your jeep up near the McGregors' neighborhood yesterday afternoon. You weren't bothering Carla McGregor, were you?"

"I did stop by to see if she had any questions about what happened."

"Rivers," the sheriff said, not happy about his visit. "Now that we've found the killer, we're done. We really appreciate your help and consider ourselves lucky you were in our neighborhood at a time like this. But I think you can return to Denver. You understand, Agent Rivers?"

Sam nodded.

"No more visits to anyone."

"It's OK if I examine the cougar at the coroner's office?"

"That should be fine," the sheriff said, irritated. "Then you can have a safe trip back to Denver."

Sam reached up and took the sheriff's hand and shook it, nodding.

"Thanks, Sheriff. If you're ever in Denver . . ." Sam said, but didn't finish the sentence. He was trying to be friendly, but considering their history it struck the wrong chord, and Sam dropped it. And so did Benson.

As soon as he was in the car, he phoned Diane.

"Where are you?" Sam asked.

"Heading back to my room. I need to write up the startling conclusion to the man-killer of Savage."

"How would you like to visit the Savannah Swamp? See the haunts of the man-killer's last hours?"

She paused. "That's about the second-best offer I've had in the last 24 hours."

Sam smiled. That was a nice way to put it.

Five minutes after he parked his jeep, Diane's blue Datsun pickup pulled into the remote parking area. Their vehicles were the only two in the gravel lot. Sam was studying the map when Diane came up beside him and peered at the network of trails. There was a big circular border trail marked in red, with several crisscrossing paths inside it.

"Here," Sam said, pointing to the top of the circle. "This is about where Bennigan shot the cougar."

"That looks close," Diane said.

"Probably about a half mile in."

"You think you can find it?"

"We should be able to follow their trail. They dragged that cat out with four dogs in tow. I suspect they left plenty of signs."

Sam slipped into his camera pack and started across the hard-packed lot. Gray was happy to be back in the woods. They bushwhacked across to the perimeter path and picked up the trail left by Bennigan, Jake, and the dogs as they dragged the mountain lion out of the woods. Gray followed it easily, and 30 minutes into the woods, they came to a large river maple with lots of debris stirred up around it.

"What are you hoping to find?" Diane asked.

"Not sure. I'm hoping to see some tracks. Just one or two good ones. I'd like to compare them to the photos taken at the deer kill behind McGregor, and where Monday's incident happened."

"Just to make sure it's the same cat?"

"That's right."

Other than the torn-up ground, there was no sign of cougar.

"Can you imagine this scene after dark?" Diane said. "The dogs must have been crazy."

"Looks like it," Sam agreed.

Sam peered through the shadowy understory. "My hunch is that cat was probably prowling around down here, hunting in the dark, when he heard those dogs and made for this tree. Which would mean there have to be tracks around here somewhere, leading up to it."

They both examined the area beyond the debris under the tree. Sam thought he spied some turned-over leaves, off to the southwest. He walked over to have a closer look.

"With all these leaves on the ground, I'm not sure we're going to find a clear print," Diane said.

Gray was sniffing along the trail Sam had spotted.

"Yup," Sam said. "And a big cat hunting would be careful where it stepped."

"But not a big cat running from dogs," Diane said.

"That's true, but runners don't leave good prints," Sam added. He looked over the ground and said, "Here's where he came from." He pointed to some scattered leaves that had been tracked over in a hurry. If you peered at it carefully, you could see where the cougar had placed its anxious paws.

"I see it," Diane said.

"Gray, heel," Sam said, and the big hybrid came in beside him. Sam reached down and rubbed his head. "I don't want you to get out ahead of us and step on any tracks. But I do need your nose."

They started off slowly, backtracking over the mottled leaves. The farther they hiked away from the cat's last perch, the harder it was to find its trail. They tracked for another half hour, moving in a twisted direction through the river-bottom woods. The cat's last path had been meandering. They came to a small feeder creek with a thin strip of water running through it. And there, in a small spit of sand beside the creekbed, were two perfect front paw prints, close together. Sam told Gray to stay. Then he moved in to examine the impressions.

It appeared as though the big cat had been steadying itself. Sam imagined the cougar moving its paws together for support and then dropping its well-muscled head and neck to lap at the cool water. The extra weight and pressure accentuated the two prints and gave them a clearly defined outline.

"Wow," Diane said.

The prints were flawless. The ground here was a mix of clay and sand, and it had been damp. And there were no leaves. But there would be soon.

Sam set down his pack and took out his camera. Diane, too. Gray stayed in an obedient sit.

"I guess we found what we wanted," Sam said.

"I guess. But no claw points."

"Yup. Not even a pinprick."

Sam set the camera to wide-angle macro and snapped off three or four close-ups. For his last shot, he set his boot down a foot from the prints, for scale.

"These'd look good in my article," Diane said, peering into her viewfinder. "One of the cat's last drinks before its last stand."

"Wish we could get some rear paw prints, just to round it out."

They kept at it, searching through the woods, backtracking the animal's final trail. Fifty yards from the creekbed, they found one good rear paw print. Both of them snapped photos, Diane with her smartphone. Several of them. No claw points.

They were quiet in the woods. Gray was careful to obey Sam's signals. He loved hiking through the trees, the air pungent with leaf decay. Gray was the one most able to follow the trail, once he had the cougar's scent in his nose. It was Gray, 15 minutes later, who found the partially covered remnants of a fresh white-tail kill. It was recent—probably two, maybe three days old. The big hybrid grew excited by the find. For a moment, it appeared Gray was going to challenge Sam for the prize, but after three or four commands he backed off and sat.

"Incredible," Diane said.

The light was muted under the maple canopy. It was a lovely day, and it was interesting to contemplate the rare cougar's final moments. But after examining the dead deer, Sam said, "This looks like it was killed last Sunday or Monday."

They couldn't find any distinct tracks around it, but the ground was dusted up and riled with lots of scraping and covering. The cougar had fed on the kill and then buried it in a shallow grave, covering it with a thin film of leaves and dirt. Without Gray they never would have found it.

"I don't get it," Sam said.

"What?"

"McGregor was killed two days ago. This animal was killed around that same time. Maybe a day earlier. And you can see it was eaten. At least most of it. It appears to have been fed on at least twice."

"So?"

"After a kill like this, no mountain lion's going to wander far. This would be its food source for at least a week."

"That sounds awful," Diane said, thinking about the big cat feeding on rancid meat.

"I know," Sam said. "But that's what they do. They kill, feast, usually on the internal organs, and then cover over what's left to hide it from other scavengers. But they hang around the area just in case. If you spend that much time and energy killing something this big, you want to make the most of it."

"So what do you think? We must be at least 10 miles from McGregor Industries." Diane observed.

"More like 20," Sam said.

"Didn't you tell me mountain lions have territories that range more than 200 miles?"

"That's true," Sam said. "But they're not going to wander over that territory after making a kill like this one. They're going to hang around and guard it. And feed on it awhile."

"Which means we might have two lions?"

"I don't know. That's unlikely. But that could be the case. For starters, we can compare these prints to the prints Marlin took down by that other deer, the one killed earlier in the month behind McGregor."

"And the prints around Jack McGregor?"

"Those were the ones showing claws. And I think they were larger."

"Meaning two big cats?"

"Maybe," Sam said, doubtful.

"The sheriff isn't going to like hearing there are two cats," Diane said.

"Which is why I haven't shared any of my suspicions with him. Until I get more information, the sheriff isn't going to hear anything," Sam said.

After photographing the scene and the carcass, they made their way through the river-bottom woods to where Gray had been shot. Sam had the log from his GPS, and it was easier than he expected to find the spot. They found boot prints near the tree where the shots had come from. Sam took a few photos, tracked the prints for a while, but finally lost them in the thick leaf bed. They spent the next half hour letting Gray pick up the boot scent and track it. Eventually, he led them out of the woods to a minimum-maintenance road that was hard-packed turf. There was no way to discern a clear tire track. A blur of tracks indicated the road was in occasional use, and that whoever had used it was obviously gone.

They turned and started back toward their vehicles. Back in the parking lot, Sam used an old towel and brush to wipe down Gray and tease the burs out of his fur, moving carefully over his rear bandage, which the hybrid didn't seem to notice. Gray was happy for the attention. Diane got in behind the wheel of her Datsun.

"I'm heading back to my room. I have to get this article done before dinner," Diane said.

Sam paused over Gray. He stood up and walked over to Diane's pickup.

"You're not going to write about two mountain lions, are you?" Sam said.

"And I thought you were coming over to say something else entirely."

"Ah," Sam paused. "I'm still a little preoccupied with this whole thing."

"You didn't seem preoccupied last night."

Sam looked at her. He knew he should respond with something poignant, but his mind was filled with cougar and then memories of last night, and his brain just couldn't think that fast.

"For now, it's a story about the death of a man-killer," Diane said.

"I've got to see a coroner about a cat," Sam said.

"Let me know what you find out."

"So maybe the USFW should buy you dinner tonight."

"That could work," Diane said, though she thought it was typical Sam, pretending the date was more about the USFW than him.

"Deputy Sorenson told me about an Indian restaurant down off 13. The Taj. Said the food was excellent," Sam said.

"That sounds good. Maybe something vegetarian," she said, remembering the deer carcass.

"Beer and wine are vegan," Sam said.

"Maybe that too," Diane said. Then she turned her key and the Datsun's engine broke the still afternoon. Before pulling away, she said, "And I might be able to help you sort through some of the issues that have come up in the last couple days."

Watching her taillights drive away, Sam thought, *I don't deserve it, but I sure appreciate it.*

CHAPTER TWENTY-SIX

During the drive to the coroner's office, Sam thought about the mountain lion and its peculiar hunts, so close to an urban area. The deer kill he could understand. In Colorado, there were studies about urban areas and how deer figured out cities were safe havens with plenty of tasty greens where humans didn't hunt them and natural predators usually didn't wander. But it didn't take long for lions to figure out where the deer were grazing, and sure enough, they began coming out of the hills and hunting in backyards. This lion, he reasoned, was just like those outside of Boulder and LA.

On the trip over, Sam couldn't help but reconsider the issues. Again. He found himself wondering about the McGregors. What was it Sam had heard quoted by a Minnesota writer? *The rich are different.*

Maybe it was OK with the McGregors that they each had flings. Sam had heard about swingers but didn't know any. Sexual relationships, Sam believed, were always a mercurial business, even if all the parties involved were candid, forthright, and in full agreement. And because the McGregors' extramarital activity was a wild card, it was one of those details he couldn't ignore.

Then there was the sale of McGregor Industries for mega-bucks. Money, like sex, could be a drug. Everyone made sacrifices to make money. The question was, how far would you go? Sam wasn't the most politically savvy agent in the service, but even he had pulled punches with superiors rather than rock the boat or risk losing his job.

But Sam's willingness to compromise was well within conventional boundaries. Murderers, sociopaths, and even simple felons easily crossed the customary boundaries, often for pleasure, sometimes for money. To some, the almighty dollar was like a dynamite fuse. The willingness to set it off was largely dependent on who held the match.

If he thought about everyone associated with Jack's death, the money angle didn't entirely make sense. Everyone who had been in on the sale of the company was already in line to benefit from it. It was obvious some of them didn't want the sale, but now it was so far along not even Jack's death would alter its course. The one person who benefited the most was Carla McGregor. But once Jack sold the company she was going to share in the riches.

The more Sam thought about it all, the more he felt like he was chasing his tail. Better to set it aside for now, he guessed. Which is what he did. At least for the moment.

Over the phone, Coroner Warren Sap had a clear baritone's voice. In person he looked like Wilford Brimley, with pop bottle–bottom glasses and a bushy mustache.

"Damnedest thing," Warren said, turning down the hall to the examination room.

"What's that?" Sam said.

"A cougar. I've never seen one before this close up. Beautiful animal. Stunning. Looks like one big killing machine," Warren said, turning to Sam with raised eyebrows that made his eyes look twice their normal size, particularly under those eyeglasses.

"They *are* stunning animals," Sam agreed.

Warren opened the door to the room and both of them entered. There was a white sheet over a stainless-steel table and plenty of glass cupboards and instruments. Beside the table was another small stainless-steel table on wheels carrying an assortment of strewn instruments, including some gauze in forceps, shiny chest cutters, what looked like sterile pliers, and other items. There wasn't much blood and the room smelled of formaldehyde, but not enough to make Sam's eyes water.

When Warren pulled down the sheet, Sam saw that the animal was beautiful. Its coat was still shiny and soft, except for where the bullets entered its flanks and then its side, chest high. Its belly had been opened, giving it a gaunt appearance, at least in the hind quarters.

"I checked its stomach. Found some deer hair and what appeared to be organ meat, but not human. I'm double-checking just to be sure. And I wiped down its claws," Warren said.

Sam turned to one of the big, stiff rear paws. The claws were completely retracted. "You checked them all?" Sam asked. He pulled the toe skin back and was able to surface one of the claws. It was big and sharp and came to a deadly pinpoint, like a miniature Yemeni dagger.

"I'd hate to be on the receiving end of that," Warren said.

That made them both pause, knowing Jack McGregor could have been killed by these claws. "You didn't find anything?"

"Nothing. Not a trace. Not even a little dirt. This animal kept himself pretty clean," Warren said.

"See anything else inside? Anything that might look like disease?"

"Nothing internally. I've been at it all morning, on account of the sheriff wanting something definitive. But I had to take a little break. I'll open up the head later this afternoon. But if I was a judge of animal flesh, I'd say this guy was about as healthy as an animal can be."

Sam agreed. He reached up and lifted the left-side lip, exposing the large, knifelike incisors. "Teeth look pretty good too."

"I don't know how old this animal is, but I'd guess it was in the prime of life. I was surprised by the teeth because I thought I might find something there."

"Like what?"

Warren turned, walked over to a corner desk, and stepped around to its back side. Sam heard a bottom drawer open and the coroner pulled out a quart-size mason jar with a brass lid. When he returned with the jar, he unscrewed the lid.

"Mind you," he said, "I wouldn't want this getting around. But since we're all friends here, I think I can share this with you in confidence?"

There was an odd assortment of items in the bottom of the jar. Sam recognized what he thought were a few bullet slugs. There were a couple nickel- to quarter-sized pieces of metal that looked like shrapnel. There were some small stones, what looked like a 1-inch ball of steel wool, and other miscellaneous artifacts.

Warren was peering through the glass jar, looking for something. Sam hadn't responded to his comment about "confidence," which made the coroner pause in his search. He brought the jar down and looked at Sam out of those magnified eyes. "What's said in my examination room stays in my examination room, unless I say otherwise. That understood, Agent Rivers?"

Sam nodded. "Sure. And call me Sam." He liked Warren Sap. The coroner was quirky.

Warren brought up the jar and peered into the jumble of items, shaking them a little. "This here is what I call my old curiosity collection. These are some of the very odd things I've taken out of people over the years." He lifted the jar up and peered through the cylindrical, clear glass bottom. "Ah, there it is."

Sam couldn't tell what he was looking at. Could have been anything. "I see some slugs," Sam said.

"Those are common," Warren said. "I'd have a lot more if the sheriff and the local police didn't need them for cases. These here are extras." He smiled and brought the jar down, tilting it so he could reach in with one of his fingers.

Sam watched Warren's index finger move in and separate items, surprisingly adroit for such a large hand. Then it settled onto something, and he slid it up to the rim.

Warren coaxed what appeared to be a piece of bone onto his palm. "Got it," he said. Then he opened his hand and displayed his find. "Know where I found this?"

It looked like a nearly 1-inch piece of fang tip. It was almost like one of those shark teeth he'd seen people wear on necklaces when he was a kid, only more tapered and thin. "Where?"

"Jack McGregor's C5 vertebra."

Sam was a little fuzzy on the numbering scheme. "I'm guessing that's near the top of the spine?" he asked.

Warren nodded. "That's right. It's near the bottom of the cervical vertebrae. They're the ones at the top, directly beneath the skull. They're numbered from C1 to C7. C5 is near the carotid."

"It's a fang tip?" Sam asked.

"I thought so. The way it was embedded, it looked like it was new. But it was odd, almost as though it was fused to the top of that vertebra. I thought it might be a bone spur, but it was too big and there was too much bruising around it. A spur this size would have caused Jack McGregor to crawl out of his skin in pain. And there was nothing in his medical records about it. So then I thought whatever killed him broke it off on his bone. These animals," Warren said, nodding to the cougar on the table, "are killing machines. I can't believe they'd lose their teeth when they killed. Unless they were old and infirm, which this one isn't. But ultimately I thought that was the only logical explanation, which is what I put in the autopsy."

He moved his palm toward Sam. "Here," he said.

Sam cradled the small ivory piece and had a closer look, while Warren set the jar down on his instrument table. It definitely looked like a carnivore's tooth, or at least part of one.

Warren walked around to the head of the table and turned the cougar's head so its mouth was facing toward the ceiling, into the overhead examination lights. "Look at this." He pried open the mouth, revealing two sets of perfectly formed teeth, sharp and deadly, all intact.

"Deadly," Sam said.

"Perfect," Warren said, shutting the mouth. "If my kids had teeth like those, I wouldn't have sent them to the orthodontist."

Sam smiled.

"I was told there couldn't be two cougars in this valley, so now I'm back to bone spur, or maybe it was broken off of the victim's spine when the big cat struck. But I couldn't find anywhere on McGregor's vertebrae where it might fit."

Now Warren was staring at the white, almost porcelain-like piece in Sam's hand.

"I'm thinking we should have it tested," Sam said.

"DNA?"

"Yeah," Sam said. "Can you have it tested?"

"Sure," Warren said. "But it'll take a while."

Sam thought about it. "What would you think if I shipped it out to Fish & Wildlife forensics in Oregon? They could have it by tomorrow and we'd probably know by tomorrow night."

"They'd ship what was left back?"

Coroners could be an odd bunch. Warren liked collecting curiosities from his cadavers, and he was apparently reluctant to give up his prize.

"I'll make sure of it," Sam said.

CHAPTER TWENTY-SEVEN

On his way to FedEx, he thought about Tracy McDonald at USFW forensics, wondering why he hadn't heard anything. He decided to give him a quick call. It was after 10 in Oregon. And from what he remembered, Tracy was an early riser.

"Tracy. What'd you find out?"

"I'm not sure what we found out, which is why I haven't gotten back to you before now. It's unusual. It's definitely a mountain lion."

"So you got the hair sample?"

"I got it all. The tail tip. The DNA records from the crime scene, from the local guys in Minnesota. I would have called you earlier, but the results were so bizarre we had to check them twice. Then I called Minnesota, just to make sure they were following protocol. Those guys clearly know what they're doing. Gives you hope for law enforcement."

"What's bizarre?" Sam said.

"You sure the tail tip came from an old wall mount?"

"Yeah. It was in some guy's drawer, up where the trophies were stolen. In northern Minnesota."

"Any chance someone could be playing a joke on you?"

"What do you mean?"

"I mean the samples are from the same animal."

Sam didn't understand. "They're from the same cougar?"

"That's right. Specimen 1470. Thanks for that, by the way. Another cougar for our UC DNA database. And it's good to have some historical data."

Sam still didn't understand. "So let me get this straight. You got the tail tip?"

"Yeah. The package is still here on my desk. Let me see . . ."

Sam could hear shuffling. He'd been to forensics in Ashland. He'd seen Tracy's desk. It scared him.

"From Grand Ma-race," Tracy said.

"Ma-ray," Sam corrected.

"What?"

"Nothing," Sam said. "So the tail tip from up north was from a mountain lion's tail?"

"That's right. Specimen 1470."

"And you got the hair from the BCA?"

"Not the hair," Tracy corrected. "We got the records. The DNA results. It's the same cat: 1470."

"Specimen 1470," Sam said.

"That's right . . . 1470."

That didn't make any sense. "The hair that was collected at the scene? The scene where the man was attacked and killed by the cat?"

"That's my understanding," Tracy said. "I double-checked with the BCA guys, just to be sure. They had control of the cat fur from beginning to end, no doubt about it. And their analysis is by the book."

"It was from 1470 too?"

"That's what I said," Tracy said. "They're both from the same cat."

Sam laughed. "I think you got your samples or your results mixed up. Something."

"I'm an evidence guy," Tracy said, a little irritated.

Sam caught himself. "I'm just saying, Trace, if what you say is true, a lion that has been on a wall for the last 50 years got off that wall, walked down to Savage, Minnesota, and killed a guy."

"I'm not saying anything," Tracy said. "I'm just telling you what we found."

It was absurd, Sam knew. The tests were in error. He was just about ready to tell Tracy to rerun the tests and that he was sending him another sample, the fang tip, so he could test it, too.

And then suddenly, he understood. Or thought he did. It was starting to make horrible sense. And just as suddenly, he began to worry.

Sam spent another 5 minutes making Tracy repeat all the details. They backtracked over the origin and testing of each specimen. Sam wanted to make sure there was no way they could have mixed up the samples. Tracy became slightly annoyed, then irritated, but he confirmed there was no way they could have confused the results. For starters, the BCA result came from a different lab, in Minnesota. Then the tail tip was tested by the day staff, yesterday. In fact, Tracy had thought it was strange, so he'd already double-checked—actually, triple-checked—the results.

It gave Sam pause.

But not for long.

He agreed with Tracy, told him it was definitely strange and unusual and he'd need to think about it, but meanwhile he was going to FedEx him another sample, this time of what he thought was a tooth.

"Another mountain lion?" Tracy asked.

"I think so."

"We'll see."

"For now, Tracy, this doesn't go any further than you and me."

Sam had one more thing he wanted him to do. He wondered if Tracy's crew had some time to examine some boot prints, tell him if there was anything peculiar or that stood out about them. There were those photos taken from around the minimum-maintenance road gate, behind McGregor Industries. Probably nothing, but now he wondered about them. There had been eight or nine prints, he remembered, which seemed excessive for the number of people who had been down the road that morning.

Back in his hotel room, Sam emailed the boot print photos to Tracy. Then he phoned Diane.

"I'm on deadline," she answered.

"Can you just look something up for me? That burglary up at Rushing River. When did it happen?"

"Rivers, can't this wait?"

"No," Sam said.

"Just a sec," she said, irritated. "Saturday, September 7."

Five days after the mountain lion first appeared behind McGregor Industries.

"How much time do you have left on the article?"

"I'm just about done."

"I may need a favor," Sam said. "I'll call you back."

"Fine," she said, but she didn't sound fine.

Sam called Marlin and he picked up.

"Do you ever sleep?" Sam asked.

"All morning," Marlin said. "Just woke up."

Sam checked his watch. It was 1:15 p.m. "When people work on Saturday, do they have to check in?"

"Yeah. We scan their IDs."

"Do you keep a record of it?"

"Sure."

"So you could tell me if anyone was working on Saturday, September 7?"

"Uh-huh," Marlin affirmed. "I'd have to use the security database at work, though. I could check later tonight. Who did you want to know about?"

"Baxter, Traub, Higgins, Connelly, and Sweet. Were any of them working?"

Sam thought he heard paper shuffling. A calendar page turning.

"I don't know about Connelly or Sweet," Marlin finally said. "But I can tell you Baxter, Traub, and Higgins were in Arizona, with Mr. McGregor."

"What were they doing in Arizona?"

"Some kind of executive retreat. That was when I really began to worry something important was going on. Because Mr. McGregor had a place in Phoenix, in some kind of big-buck neighborhood. Camel something," Marlin said.

"Camelback?" Sam said.

"Yeah. That's the place. Some kind of club place where he and Mrs. McGregor would go every winter, sometimes for long weekends."

"And how long were they down there?"

"They were down there from that Friday through the next Wednesday. We had to charter a private plane."

"You guys do that?"

"Not very often, but since so many people were going down, it was cheaper to rent a plane."

"Who went?" Sam asked.

"McGregor and the three I mentioned. I heard them talking about some others they were meeting down there, but I don't think they were from McGregor."

"What about Mrs. McGregor?"

"Yeah, she went. She almost always went when they visited the place. It was over a weekend."

"And you're sure the ones you've mentioned were all there?"

"The only thing I'm sure about is they all got on a rented plane that took off for Phoenix Friday afternoon, and they returned the following Wednesday," Marlin said. "That would be . . . the 11th. Same group. Same thing—on a rental, if you can call it that."

"An expensive rental," Sam said.

Marlin agreed.

Sam reminded Marlin to call him later about Connelly and Sweet, whether they were working that Saturday. Marlin said he would and hung up.

So that takes out Carla and the McGregor execs, Sam thought. They couldn't have gone up to Rushing River because they were 1,000 miles south. The young financial analysts could still be involved, but why? Didn't make sense.

Sam thought for a full minute, contemplating how best to find out about the whereabouts of the Club's tennis pro on Saturday, September 7.

Then he thought of something worth a try.

Sam called the Club and when someone answered, he said, "I'd like to arrange a private tennis lesson with one of your pros."

He was transferred and a young woman came on the line. "Tennis desk," she said.

"A few Saturdays ago, my girlfriend was there with a friend, playing tennis. She saw one of the pros teaching someone. She said the guy looked really good . . . I mean, tennis-wise, and I wanted to surprise her with a lesson. But she didn't tell me the guy's name. Would you know who was teaching tennis that Saturday, in the afternoon? I think it was around 3 or 4."

"Yeah. I think I can tell you. Which Saturday?"

"September 7," Sam said.

"Sure," the woman said. "Just a minute. I have all our pros' schedules. Did she tell you what he looked like?"

"Not exactly," Sam said.

"Here it is," she said. "Let's see. That afternoon we had Stan Brewster and . . . was it a guy or a woman?"

"It was definitely a guy," Sam said.

"Usually we have Stan and Jared Sparks all day on Saturdays, but Jared called in sick that day. So it looks like Bernie Carruthers was subbing for Jared. Do those names sound familiar? Stan Brewster or Bernie Carruthers?"

Sam told her they didn't. "Geesh. Maybe it was Sunday. That name, Sparks, sounds familiar. Was he on that Sunday?"

"Sunday the eighth?" the receptionist asked.

"Yeah," Sam said. "The eighth."

"Usually he works the entire weekend, but let's see. . . Here it is. Oh, he was out sick Sunday too. It was Carruthers and Brewster again."

Sam asked a few more questions, stuff to make his request sound legitimate. Then he said he'd just have to ask his girlfriend for more information. He thanked her and hung up.

Jared was gone . . . called in sick . . . the entire weekend.

Sam called Diane back. It rang four times before she picked up.

"Rivers," she said, impatient. "I'm just about finished here. Can't this wait?"

"No. I need that favor."

"Favors can wait."

"Not this one."

Then Sam explained he needed her to go over to the Club and find something with Jared Sparks's scent on it—maybe an article of clothing—get it, and meet him at the road behind McGregor Industries.

Diane asked if he was crazy and told him she wouldn't do any such thing.

So he gave her more background, explaining about the DNA analysis and how it answered a lot more questions than whether or not the fur had come from a mountain lion; it had begun to lead to a logical explanation for the anomalies in mountain lion ethology he'd been struggling to understand.

Then he told her about Jared's absence on the weekend of the Rushing River Lodge theft.

Once he laid it all out for Diane, she said, "All right. I'm in. But I want exclusive rights to the story."

"Exclusive," Sam said.

"You think he acted alone?"

"No idea. But I'm not sure who would help him."

"How about the wife?"

"I wondered about it. But she was down in Arizona the weekend of the thefts."

"That doesn't mean anything. She could still be involved."

"Yeah. But I don't have anything else on her. And the sheriff thinks she's innocent."

"I thought you'd heard otherwise."

"I have," he said. "For now, it doesn't matter. If it was Jared and we got more evidence on him and cornered him, I think he'd give up any others who were involved."

"Bargain?"

"Wouldn't you?"

She said she'd figure something out, some way to get something of Jared's, and let him know.

Sam had spotted the FedEx store and was closing in on it when his cell phone went off. He glanced at the number and recognized the sheriff's office. He wondered if the sheriff might have heard him thinking.

"Find anything?" the sheriff said.

"At the coroner's?"

"Yeah. Anything odd?" he asked.

"Ah, not really," Sam lied. He needed time.

"Good. So I've spoken with your boss."

"Kay Magdalen?"

"Yup."

The sheriff sounded a little like the Cheshire cat.

"I told her how much we appreciated your participation and support," the sheriff said.

"Thanks, Sheriff."

"Don't mention it," the sheriff said. "I also told her now that the official investigation was over, we no longer needed to keep you away from your regular job and you could return to Denver."

It was a preemptive strike, Sam thought. The sheriff was trying to move along Sam's departure because he suspected the USFW special agent might still be curious about some things.

"Thanks, Sheriff."

"Don't mention it," the sheriff repeated, a little more pointedly. "You have a safe trip back."

Sam had pulled into a parking space in front of the FedEx. The fang tip was beside him. But things were happening fast and he had to think.

If Jared's scent item took Gray from the prints at the kill site back to the road, to the same place both Gray and the coonhounds had gone earlier, then given everything Sam had, all the evidence, he thought the sheriff might be interested. The next logical step would be a search warrant for Jared's house, to see if they could find any cougar parts.

But Sam worried about the sheriff. The case was closed and the sheriff had received an incredible media boost, and it was all starting to settle.

CHAPTER TWENTY-EIGHT

Diane called the Club and they told her Jared Sparks had called in sick for the day. She asked if she could leave a message on his voice mail, and when the receptionist transferred her, she hung up.

And then she started thinking.

When she rolled into the Club parking lot, the first thing she noticed were the cars. All expensive. She parked near the lot's outer edge—didn't want to taint the Mercedes with her rusted-out blue Datsun pickup—and walked across the lot through the big glass doors.

"This is quite a place," Diane said.

When the receptionist asked if she could help her, Diane explained she was thinking about joining a health club and had heard good things about this one. Within 2 minutes, sales assistant manager Casper Anthony greeted her at the front desk, ready to answer her questions and show her around.

It was a shockingly luxurious health club. Granite countertops in a deli that served all the latest vitamin waters, protein powder shakes, marinated tofu, organic whole-grain sandwiches, and, for the decadent, kettle-fried chips. And while you were enjoying the deli, you could gaze out over the tennis courts and watch people play.

"It's a nice place to work," Casper said.

During the tour they passed by Jared's office. The door was open, but it was dark. As they passed, Diane glanced inside. It was a windowless closet with what looked like a desk no one ever used. His name was on the open door, but the room itself looked like someone used it for a tennis equipment dumping ground. There were clothes all over the place, some still in boxes. A tennis shirt and warm-ups hung over a chair. They both appeared to have been worn, she noticed.

There was also a nearby bathroom.

The tour lasted about 20 minutes. At the front desk, Casper said goodbye, gave her his card, a membership application form, and told her to call him with any questions. It was a soft sell. He was a very nice guy.

After he walked away, Diane asked if she could use the bathroom. The receptionist pointed down the hallway and then turned to greet three Club members who had just walked through the door. In the bathroom, Diane pulled four sheets of brown paper towels out of a wall dispenser. Then she pushed back through the door, glanced down the hallway, and headed to Jared's office.

Five minutes later, Diane returned to her pickup. She used two of the paper towels to pull a damp white tennis shirt and wristband from her shoulder bag and dropped both into an oversized ziplock bag.

CHAPTER TWENTY-NINE

Sam, Diane, and Gray walked around the yellow crime scene tape, skirting the outside edge of road.

"How do you do this?" Diane asked.

"First we let Gray sniff the clothing. Then basically I tell him to follow it."

Sam placed Gray in a sit. He brought down his day pack, opened it, and pulled out the ziplock bag containing Jared's tennis shirt and Wilson wristband. Sam examined them through the plastic in the fading light.

"You sure these were worn?" he asked.

"I know they were worn. And they were in Jared's office. Unless someone borrowed his wristband and shirt, they're Jared's. Wait until you open the baggie. They were both still damp."

Sam pulled on a pair of surgical gloves and lifted the items out of the bag.

"What if he doesn't find anything?" Diane said. "It's been, what, three days?"

"Yeah. That's a while, even for a dog with a nose as sensitive as Gray's. Scent deteriorates. But at least it hasn't rained, the weather has been pretty stable, and there hasn't been much wind. All ideal for maintaining a scent trail."

"The mild weather helps?" Diane said.

"It does. And the temperature has dropped every night. That's all good. So if Jared was here, Gray should be able to find something."

Diane moved behind the hybrid, trying not to disturb him.

Sam pulled out the bagged shirt and wristband and had Gray smell one, then the other. When the hybrid leaned forward, Sam said, "That's it. That's it, Gray. Find!"

Gray liked to work. He liked to be productive, and it was as though the big, young hybrid knew he was a key player. It was another reason Sam knew he'd be an asset to the service.

"Find it, Gray. Hunt it up."

The hybrid spread out over the road, moving back and forth, trying to locate the thin ribbon of scent. He moved back. He moved forward. He moved to the side. He spent a while around the huge oak trunk, staring up into the branches. At one point, his nose led him in a meandering path all the way back to the edge of the road overlooking the old deer carcass. Then he put his nose in the air, scenting the deer, Sam thought. But he only paused, staying on top of the road.

Then he turned back around, winding back and forth along the road until they came to the spot where McGregor had bled out. Sam could tell the big hybrid was finding something. He was still in search mode but getting excited, as though he'd scented the thread.

Instantly, the hybrid's nose went to the ground.

For a full 10 seconds, he didn't move. Sam and Diane could hear him sniff hard, pause, breath in deep. Once, twice, five or six times. And then he stepped back toward them. He moved around the blood-soaked earth. He barely varied his nose hunt, shifting from side to side, sniffing hard. He kept pacing forward, returning along the minimum-maintenance road.

"He's going back," Diane said.

"He is," Sam agreed.

They followed.

Gray remained focused on the dual road ruts, keeping to the right rut. His nose shifted back and forth as he stepped forward, but he kept moving, staying in that right rut.

The three of them made their way along the road rut, all the way back to the main gravel road. Then Gray made a sharp left, nose still down. It was similar to the path he'd made the day McGregor was killed. He followed almost a straight line for 50 yards. And then he stopped, looked around, sniffed up and down and back and forth, but the scent trail had disappeared.

Sam and Diane came up behind him. When Sam approached, he remembered the tire tracks, saw them again.

"They got into a parked car," Sam said.

"And drove away," Diane said, following the tracks as they pulled out of the deep shoulder, angled across it, and disappeared into the main lane of the gravel road.

"Probably drove up over that rise ahead," Sam said, indicating a small right turn up ahead, behind thick ditch growth and some trees.

"Good boy," Sam said, thumping Gray's side in an appreciative gesture Sam knew the big dog liked.

"Now what?" Diane said.

"We need a little more evidence. And I think I know where we
might be able to find some."

In the late afternoon, they made their way to Judicial Road, parked
in the CVS parking lot, on the back side, and got out of Sam's
jeep. He brought his camera bag out and they crossed the lawn
bordering the route. Sam remembered what Emma Winetraub
had said about seeing a man come up through the trees behind
the McGregors' house. If it had been Jared, as she suspected, he
might have left some tracks. Worth a try, anyway.

They walked quickly up the other side of Judicial Road and
determined the point where they were probably opposite the
houses at the bottom of Wannamake Circle. Then Sam took out
Jared's wristband and brought Gray into a sit, so he could smell it.

The same thing as before: Gray got excited and started wandering around, dodging into the tree edge until he finally found
something and disappeared. Sam called him back, and it was hard
getting the hybrid to stop. His tail was making short, excited wags.

Gray had found the start of a small-game trail, just the other
side of the tree edge. They started walking it, and after just a few
steps discovered a shoe print. There were several, made at different
times, all the same. Sam thought the tread pattern looked familiar
but didn't know for sure. He found two clear prints and used the
camera to take close-ups. Then the three of them retreated the way
they'd come.

By the time they returned to Diane's hotel room at the Travelodge, it was nearly 5. Three o'clock in Ashland.

Sam connected his camera to Diane's computer to view the photos. They were in order by date taken. First he found the photo of the footprint he'd snapped less than an hour earlier and dropped it into a temporary folder on Diane's hard drive. Then he worked back through his photos until he came to the site where the cougar had been killed, and then back to the dead deer, Monday's dried carcass, the site where McGregor was killed, and finally the photos he'd taken of footprints around the shot-up NO TRESPASSING sign marking the start of the minimum-maintenance road. Diane recognized the tread pattern as soon as it appeared.

"There," Diane said, pointing.

Sam double-clicked on the image to enlarge it. "Gotta be the same print," he said.

"Let's look at the other one."

Sam double-clicked on the photo he'd taken that afternoon, just off Judicial Road, behind Carla's house. The two prints were in different-colored dirt. The maintenance road was black with bits of cinder or gravel, but powdery enough to yield a clear, complete print. The other print, the one Sam took from the clearing in front of the trees, was in damp earth. It was perfect for an impression, but the earth was brown. Regardless of the different backgrounds, the prints appeared identical. Both of them were right feet. Both had worn outside edges. And both had an interesting design Sam hadn't seen on any of the footwear he'd ever worn.

"That's different," Diane said.

"What do you mean it's different? It's the same print."

"Yeah, I know. It's the same print. I mean, the pattern of that shoe's bottom. It's a weird zigzag with very narrow lines, almost as though it was drawn by a Navajo silversmith."

"Navajo silversmith?" Sam said.

"I mean, I bought some silver in Santa Fe once, and it had a pattern on it like that shoe," Diane said.

"Let's call Tracy, see if his team's come up with anything," Sam said. He pulled out his phone and started dialing. "If this turns out to be a tennis shoe, I'm thinking we just might be able to convince Rusty Benson to go for a warrant to search Jared's house."

"What would you look for?"

"The shoes that made these prints. And cougar parts, from the cougar up north."

"The murder weapons?"

"If we're right. If the fang tip came from the Rushing River Lodge, they could have used the animal's jaw to fashion some kind of weapon. Used it, along with some of the fur. If we find what's left of it, we hit pay dirt."

"You think Sheriff Benson will go along?"

"I don't know. Right now he's got this crime solved and his reelection bid is on the rise. Why upset the applecart?"

"Because it's murder."

"It's still not definitive. And if we don't find any evidence . . ." Sam trailed off, not wanting to think about it.

"Because it's murder," Diane repeated.

But Sam still wasn't sure if Sheriff Benson would play along.

Sam took a minute to email the print image to Tracy. Then he texted him about it.

Five minutes later, Tracy called and said, "It's a high-end tennis shoe, pretty well worn. And by 'tennis' I mean it's used by people who play tennis."

When he paused, Sam said, "Is that it?"

"Nope. I'm just sorting through my notes. It's a 'he,' of course. These are 10-and-a-halfs. He pronates his step, walks on the outside of his foot. We can't tell for sure because we didn't see a complete pattern, but it appears he has a pretty straight, maybe slightly pigeon-toed step. And here's the interesting thing," Tracy continued. "It's not a cheap shoe. It's specifically designed for tennis and you can't buy it for less than $200. It's called a David Beckham Forest Hills Mid shoe—comes in black and white.

"Whoever wore it weighs probably 180–190, but in spite of what you read in Sherlock Holmes, there are a lot of variables in a footprint and it's tough to get the actual weight. And anyone who gives you height off a footprint is full of horse pucky."

Sam thanked the forensics expert and said he'd buy him a drink the next time they saw each other. Today, at least, Tracy had made a difference. A very big difference.

Sam called the sheriff's office and asked for Benson.

The receptionist told him Benson was out on calls and she expected him in around 6, before he left for the day.

Sam asked for Sorenson, and after a minute the deputy came on the line.

"Sorenson," Sam said. "It's Sam Rivers."

"You headed to Denver?"

"Nope. Still here. Something came up and I need to speak with Sheriff Benson. And you."

There was a pause. Sorenson was wondering about it. "He's not in."

"You think he'll be in by 6? It'd be great if I could see you both then, before you go home," Sam said.

Sorenson thought about it. "Just a minute. Let me check his calendar."

After a brief hold, Sorenson came back on the line and said, "Yeah, I think he has time then. Can I tell him what it's regarding?"

"I just need you guys' help on something."

There was another pause. "Everything OK?"

"As good as it can be," Sam said, trying to be upbeat.

After hanging up, Sam phoned Mac McCollum and spent a few minutes bringing Mac up on current events.

"So what's the plan?"

Sam told him he was going to meet with the sheriff and wondered if Mac could see if the judge who had presided over Angus Moon's extradition hearing was around. They might need her, depending upon the sheriff's perspective.

"If the sheriff doesn't go for it, the service could back you up," Mac said.

"I appreciate that, but it would be more legit coming from the investigating officer. And since the sheriff's been spearheading the investigation, he's the logical officer to request it."

"He's too political," Mac said. "I'll bet you dinner he says no."

Sam knew Mac might be right. But he liked a good bet and he held a strong conviction in his own abilities to persuade. "It's a bet," he said. But Sam knew it was a wager that could fall either way because Sheriff Benson's lack of imagination was more than equal to Sam's intuition about crime.

CHAPTER THIRTY

The receptionist waved Sam into the same room that had housed the press conference. In less than 5 minutes, Deputy Sorenson entered with Chief Deputy Leif Anders, who told them the sheriff was on the phone but would be there shortly.

"What's this about?" the chief asked. He didn't look friendly and he didn't sound interested. Sam couldn't read Sorenson's look, one way or the other.

"Some additional information has come to light that I think you guys should know about. I'll explain when Benson gets here."

"About McGregor?" the chief said.

Sam nodded.

"What kind of information?"

"Something pertinent to McGregor's death. I think it's important."

The chief frowned.

There was a reason he was called the Iceman, Sam thought.

After a couple more minutes, Sheriff Benson entered the room. He was blustery and preoccupied, and Sam immediately worried about his wager with Mac, for dinner.

"I thought you had important business back in Denver, Agent Rivers," the sheriff started. "Seems to me I spoke with your boss just this morning and she needed you back pronto."

"After you talked with her, Magdalen and I spoke," Sam lied. "When I explained there were one or two outstanding matters that still needed my attention, she agreed. She's one of the most thorough investigators I've ever known. If there's still a stone to turn over, she likes to see what's underneath it." Another lie. The prevarications were starting to pile up.

The sheriff paused, gazing at Sam. He wasn't happy, but Sam wasn't there to lift his spirits.

"The funny thing about rocks," the sheriff said, "is once you start turning them over, something's bound to slither out, whether it's related to the accident or not."

"Not sure I'm following," Sam said.

"Agent Rivers," the sheriff sighed, "it's not like we've never investigated a crime before. And when we start asking questions, they're about people, not skunks or ducks or snakes."

Sam waited.

"So I seriously think it's time for you to head back to Denver and continue policing the great outdoors. I can tell you from more than 20 years of law enforcement that this was a terrible accident. It's been examined by some of the best investigators in the business, and everyone agrees: it was a tragedy. Period."

"I appreciate that, Sheriff." Sam paused. "But some snakes you just can't ignore."

The sheriff glanced at his fellow officers. There was a flash of get-this-jerk-out-of-my-sight. And he would have uttered the dictate if he hadn't already experienced Sam's persistence. The sheriff thought Sam was a pissant nuisance, and he cared less and less about concealing it.

"What kind of snake are we talking about, Agent Rivers?" the sheriff finally asked, with derision.

"It's not just one," Sam said, with conviction. "It's a lot of things that don't make sense."

And then he laid out his concerns, in large part the way they had unfolded. He had worked out the evidentiary details ahead of time, discussing them with Diane. He reiterated the anomalies he'd already shared with the sheriff. There was the absence of blood around the rear claw marks, indicating the victim had been scratched after he'd been killed. Then the mountain lion hadn't cut McGregor open to feed. And there were the prints showing the animal's claws fully extended. All of these facts pointed to extremely peculiar cougar behavior.

The sheriff stared, remembering the details, more unimpressed now than he had been the first time.

Then Sam talked about the additional evidence collected at the site. There was the fur and the fang tip Warren Sap had dug out of McGregor's C5 vertebra. The sheriff knew about the fur. It was the first he'd heard about the fang tip. But so what? It only corroborated the fact it was a cougar kill.

Then Sam talked about Gray's behavior, how Sam was training him to be a scent-tracking dog, and how the hybrid was proving to have a remarkable nose. He'd asked Gray to follow a footprint at the site, follow a scent, and Gray tracked it all the way back to the

314 | CARY J. GRIFFITH

gravel road where a pair of tire tracks indicated a parked car had pulled away from the shoulder. Later, Jake Massey's coonhounds had done the same thing.

The sheriff's eyes didn't waver. So far, Sam knew, he hadn't heard anything that couldn't be explained somehow. So far there were snakes, but none of them were poisonous. At least not yet.

Then Sam mentioned the photos he'd taken of footprints around the rusted gate near the start of the minimum-maintenance road, when he'd first come onto the scene. Deputy Sorenson had been impatient, but Sam had carefully focused on and snapped several photos of the different prints.

The only indication the sheriff was beginning to track with Sam's ultimate thesis was the pressure Sam thought he sensed, building behind the officer's eyes.

Chief Anders was stone-faced.

Deputy Sorenson was the only one who appeared interested in what Sam had to say, but he was trying to conceal it.

Then Sam told him about the theft of the trophy up north, at the Rushing River Lodge. He explained about the tail tip and the reason they'd had the DNA analyzed. Ostensibly the sample provided more data for the UC mountain lion database. But Sam had had a feeling about the tail tip. A suspicion. And then he laid out his most significant piece of evidence: the DNA from the tail tip was identical to the fur taken from the kill site, and probably the fang tip pulled out of McGregor's spine, though they wouldn't know for certain until late tomorrow.

When Sam paused, letting it sink in, the sheriff flinched, but it only appeared to increase his bad temper.

"You mean to tell me," the sheriff finally said, "the cougar stolen off a wall mount from a lodge up north is the same cougar that killed Jack McGregor?"

"The DNA seems to indicate that."

"Bullshit," the chief said, standing up out of his chair.

The sheriff glanced at Sam and said, "Agent Rivers, have you gone batshit crazy? Because unless I missed something, we tracked down the killer and bagged it in the Savannah Swamp and it wasn't some trophy that'd been hanging on a wall for the past 50 years."

"Unless the mountain lion you killed in the Savannah Swamp wasn't the killer at all," Sam suggested.

The sheriff was just getting started. He turned away and hissed. "You ever heard the simplest explanation is probably the correct one, Agent Rivers?"

"Occam's razor," Sam said.

"What?"

"There's a principle that says simpler explanations are, other things being equal, generally better than more complex ones. I think it's called Occam's razor."

"I don't know about any razors. But the simple explanations aren't just better. They're the right ones."

"But the evidence indicates otherwise," Sam said.

"What in the hell was killed in the Savannah Swamp, then— Puss in Boots?"

"It was definitely a mountain lion, just not the one that killed Jack McGregor."

"Now hold onto your shorts, Agent Rivers," the sheriff said. There was color in his cheeks. "You and all the papers and our own experts at the DNR have told us cougars in Minnesota are incredibly rare, especially near the Cities. Isn't that correct, Agent Rivers?"

"That's right."

"And you've also mentioned they are solitary animals. They don't have partners. They don't travel in packs."

"That's right," Sam said.

"And now you're telling me there are two of them?"

"I'm telling you the one killed in the Savannah Swamp didn't kill McGregor. The one that killed McGregor, from the DNA evidence, was the trophy up on the wall of the Rushing River Lodge."

The sheriff and the chief appeared dumbstruck.

"I'll tell you what it is," the sheriff finally said. "It's bad DNA testing. That's what it is."

"I double-checked. Triple-checked it, in fact."

"So you're a DNA expert now?"

"I mean, I didn't triple-check. But our experts in Oregon did."

The sheriff made a *pfffft* sound, as though *USFW DNA experts* was an oxymoron.

"I think someone stole that trophy and used its teeth and claws to fashion some kind of killing instruments to use on McGregor. I know it sounds incredible, but that's where the evidence leads."

The sheriff stood up and huffed, looking away and rubbing his face with his hands.

The chief was staring at Sam with the same startled disbelief. Deputy Sorenson was sitting back, taking it in.

Sam reminded himself he'd had more time to consider his theory than they'd had, and he knew it sounded like some bizarre made-for-TV mystery.

"That's just plain bullshit," the sheriff said. "They screwed up the tests. Mixed up the samples. It wouldn't be the first time. Did you consider that?"

Sam explained where and how the samples were taken and tested. The hair on the scene was even collected and tested by a different office, the BCA. The rest of it was tested by USFW forensics.

"Screwed up the samples," the sheriff insisted. "The only logical explanation."

But Sam continued. When the sheriff heard he'd found a footprint behind Carla McGregor's house, his face turned purple. Sam explained that it was identical to a print he'd found on the minimum-maintenance road, near the rusted gate and the start of the rutted trail where McGregor was killed. They were expensive, well-worn tennis shoes, the kind professional tennis players buy. He shared his suspicions about Jared Sparks, Carla's tennis coach. He mentioned how Emma Winetraub thought she'd seen Jared behind the McGregors' house. Then, finally, he explained about the clothing items they'd obtained (he didn't say how) and how Gray had recognized Jared's scent at the kill site, how he'd tracked it back to the car tracks on the gravel road's shoulder, about 50 yards from the rusty gate, just like the two prior times.

Then the sheriff laughed. And he repeated Sam's chain of evidence. Every step of it. Every damn stone. But with increasing incredulity and derision.

Sam just took it because there was no other play to make.

When the sheriff came to the tire tracks from the parked car beside the gravel road, Sam said, "Yes, that about covers it."

"And so what are we supposed to do about this, Agent Rivers?"

"I was hoping we could get a warrant and search Jared's house, see if we can find the murder weapons."

The sheriff was even more flummoxed.

"Uh-huh," he said, nodding, sarcastic. "You are a regular Sherlock Holmes. I knew it that first day I met you at the kill site." Then the sheriff gazed at the chief and Deputy Sorenson, shaking his head. "Let me tell you what we got, Agent Rivers. We've got a cougar at the site three weeks before McGregor gets attacked and killed by one. I don't know about the behaviors that aren't typical cougar behavior, but then typical cougars aren't going out every day and killing people. Some cougars maybe get some kind of loco, and I'm guessing this was one of them. And you yourself told me there were incidents in which cougars attacked and killed mountain bikers, which is what McGregor was doing the morning he was killed. And you also explained how cougars patrol their kills. And there was an old kill right there, less than 50 yards from where McGregor was attacked. This is the first I've heard about that theft up north, but it doesn't matter. That's botched DNA evidence. That's all that is."

Sheriff Benson was just getting warmed up. "Now if I'm hearing you right, it sounds like maybe the young and beautiful Carla McGregor could be having an affair with her tennis coach. I haven't seen this guy, but I'm thinking he's pretty damn lucky, if it's true. And you're not the first person to suggest the woman was not exactly a nun. You might be surprised to know we did a little asking around, and sure enough, it sounds like the woman isn't exactly Snow White. But so what? If it's true, it's not too surprising, given the age difference between Carla and her late husband and the amount of free time she had and he didn't. Who knows? Maybe the McGregors liked to partner up with other people. You ever heard of swingers?!"

"What about the print?" Sam asked. "And the scent trail?"

"Oh for Christ's sake," the sheriff blew. "If anything, that supports the idea of an affair, nothing more. Carla knew about that trail. And if she was having an affair with this guy, maybe she wanted to share a beautiful nature walk with him. Hell, maybe she got her jollies doing it in the weeds?"

"But the fang tip," Sam said. "The one they found in McGregor's vertebra. There wasn't any broken fang in the lion killed in the Savannah Swamp."

"You're a wildlife dentist, Sherlock? Because unless you have a degree in wildlife dentistry, I don't think you're qualified to judge what you found or didn't find in a cougar's mouth!"

"Let's get someone qualified to take a look," Sam offered.

"Look where? We had that cougar cremated . . . should have happened this afternoon. Right, Deputy Sorenson?"

The deputy nodded. "Should have already happened."

Now Sam was angry. And he could feel where it was taking him. He knew it wasn't the right place to go, but he couldn't help himself. "So, Sheriff," Sam started. "I understand the way things currently stand; this tragic accident has been completely explained and the case is closed. It was a present, really, considering the effect it's having on your reelection bid. But is that what you're really about, Sheriff Benson? You want to take the easiest path, the solution that admittedly is the simplest and appears the most likely, in spite of what we've found? I think any judge would be willing to consider our evidence, and probably grant us a warrant." Sam could tell he was getting through because the sheriff's face color was leaning toward boil. "Is that what I'm hearing, Sheriff? That you're letting your own personal interests interfere with an investigation?"

"There is *no* investigation, Agent Rivers," the sheriff said, point-blank. "That's what I've been trying to tell you." He stared at Sam out of those flinty gray eyes, above his handlebar mustache. "It's over," he said. "It's time for you to get the hell out of town."

And then he walked out of the room, followed by the chief.

Deputy Sorenson only raised his eyes, otherwise expression-less. Sam knew Sorenson would stick with family, and sure enough, he, too, turned and left without a word.

But Sam was thinking, *It isn't over. It's just getting started.*

CHAPTER THIRTY-ONE

❝Plan B," Sam said, when he and Diane were settled into Sam's jeep. Gray was in back, staring between them through the windshield. When Sam peered into his rearview mirror, he was faced with Gray's piercing eyes. One startling blue, one topaz yellow.

"That bad, huh?" Diane said.

"He doesn't want to rock the boat. I thought he'd be more open," Sam said.

"So, the politician is getting the best of the law officer."

"I'd like to say I can't blame him, given how nicely this whole episode has unfolded for him. But I think 20 years in the job has made the sheriff lose his center."

"And we helped make him look good," Diane said.

"Like players on the sheriff's stage."

"So, Plan B?"

"We're about to plumb the depths of Mac's judicial connections," Sam said.

When Mac answered his phone, Sam said, "Dinner's on me."

"I knew it," Mac said.

"You think you can persuade Judge Stalter to get us a warrant?"

"It'll take both of us."

"Can you set up an appointment, like right now?"

"Can you be there by 7? She's staying late for us," Mac said.

Sam smiled. For an old man he was full of surprises. "Did you tell her what it was about?"

"Of course. Whether the request comes from the sheriff's office or Fish & Wildlife, we're still asking for the same thing."

They talked about what pieces of evidence to surface and how to lay it out. They agreed they could sequence it in a way that identified the tennis pro as the prime suspect. He had motive, and the warrant could be used to look for both the murder weapons and the expensive pair of elite tennis shoes.

"I think the judge liked Gray," Mac said.

"Good," Sam said. "Because Gray was instrumental in leading us toward Jared."

Sam told Mac he'd meet him at the courthouse before 7. Mac told him to comb his hair, shave, and make sure he was in his khaki greens. The uniform would help.

Sam took Diane back to her hotel.

"If we get this subpoena," Sam said, "I want to move on it quickly."

"I want in," she said. "I've been in it from the beginning. I helped you collect evidence. There's no reason for me to stay back in the nickel seats."

Sam thought about it. Having the media involved would make Sheriff Benson apoplectic. But more importantly, they could use another body executing their search. It would be unorthodox, but at this point everything they were doing was from a story line they were making up as they went along.

"That'd be good," Sam finally said. "Mac can corral a couple other agents in his office. You and I and Mac and the two agents and Gray should do it. I'm really hoping Gray will find what we need." Sam reached back and stroked the hybrid's neck. Gray was still staring into the mirror, listening.

"We're going to have a tail tip for you, buddy," Sam said, remembering the second 2-inch tail tip he had received from the proprietor of the Rushing River Lodge.

Gray whined.

"Let's just hope it leads to more of where it came from," Diane said.

Back at Sam's hotel room, he finished getting ready. He showered, shaved, combed his hair, and stepped into his official khaki greens, all in about 10 minutes. Then he looked at himself in the mirror, considering the Boy Scout garb.

"How does the service expect anyone to take us seriously?"

Finally, he donned the oversized Redwings with the waffle-pattern sole. At least his boots would be genuine Sam Rivers.

On his way out, he grabbed the envelope containing the double-bagged tip. If they got lucky, they'd be ready.

Sam drove down to the courthouse with Gray. He parked two blocks from the main entrance, on a side street. The weather had cooled enough, so Sam only cracked one jeep window.

"Be good," Sam said, hoping their time in the Savannah Swamp and down the McGregor road had worked enough tucker into the animal to keep him from tearing apart a headrest.

At almost 7, Sam was waiting in front of the courthouse. It took Mac another 5 minutes to arrive. The man was perpetually late.

They made their way through security and then up to the judge's floor, where they were ushered into the judge's chambers. Her office was just large enough for two people to sit across from the judge's desk.

Mac said hello to Judge Stalter and she nodded to both of them, cool.

"Whadda we got?" the judge asked.

Sam took the lead and laid out the trail of circumstantial evidence that would get them their paper. He explained about the prints. He explained about Gray's role.

The judge appeared interested when they talked about Gray. Otherwise, she asked some pointed questions, but not too many. When she finally heard the entire story, she looked at both of them and said, "That's about the craziest thing I've ever heard. Let me see if I've got this right."

And then she reiterated the chain of evidence, practically word for word, in the order in which Sam and Mac had laid it out. She was smart and tough, Sam thought. He didn't think they were going to get their warrant.

"Really?" she finally asked.

Sam nodded. "I know, Judge, it sounds unusual. But otherwise, how do you explain the DNA? And what better way to make it look like an accident?"

"So you think this Sparks guy was just waiting to get rid of McGregor and the cougar sighting was the catalyst for the idea?"

"We do," Sam said.

"And you know how crazy that sounds? You know how insane your theory is?"

Sam didn't think it was crazy. He believed in it because his gut told him it wasn't a mountain lion that killed Jack and because the trail of evidence he'd uncovered had led him to this bizarre, maybe even fantastical, theory. "Yes," he said.

"You think she was in on it? The wife?"

Mac and Sam shrugged. "No idea. But judging from the victim's physique, whoever did it, if it happened the way I think, had to have some strength and physical ability to pull it off. McGregor may have been more than 50, but he was fit and strong and by all accounts pretty tough."

"And he liked messing around," the judge said.

She was a straight-talking judge. "Sounds like it."

"Five to one the woman's in on it," the judge said. Her observation came out of nowhere.

Suddenly they knew they had their paper. But only for Jared. If they wanted a warrant for Carla's house, they would need more evidence.

"After she started asking questions, I didn't think we had a chance," Mac said, in front of the courthouse.

"It was Gray," Sam said.

"I'd like to think it was my persuasive personality."

"I think she liked you," Sam said. "We should head over. Right now."

"Sounds about right," Mac said.

They talked about where to meet. Jared lived in Minnetonka. To make sure they all arrived at the same time, Mac suggested meeting in a park-and-ride near Jared's house. Sam could pick up Diane and meet them there at around 7:45, 8 at the latest. Sam had already checked out Jared's address on Google Maps, and it appeared to be in a nice neighborhood with big yards and plenty of mature growth. Good cover, if they needed to approach him quietly.

First, they could all park in the street behind Jared's house. Then he and Diane could scope out the place, front and back. Then he'd bring in Gray.

CHAPTER THIRTY-TWO

After meeting with Sam Rivers and hearing his incredible yarn, Chief Anders and Deputy Sorenson spent some time calming down the sheriff, in his office. The rants lasted for about 5 minutes. The chief just listened, occasionally nodding in agreement. Deputy Sorenson got in "that was crazy" and "I can't believe it," but otherwise the sheriff had the floor. Finally, after the sheriff had spent himself, the chief looked at his watch and said, "I've got to run. We OK here?"

"Yeah, we're good," the sheriff said. "You guys can take off. A sheriff's day is never done."

The deputy and chief left the sheriff's office. Sorenson tried to make a comment about Sam Rivers, really just to make small talk. But the chief ignored him and then turned and headed out the door.

What a jerk, Sorenson thought.

Once in his car, the chief started his engine, put it in gear, and hurried out of the lot. As soon as he was a safe distance from the sheriff's office, he pulled out the throwaway and called Carla.

"What?"

"Sam Rivers knows."

"Knows what?"

"He's working some DNA angle. He knows about the theft up north. And they figured out the fur sample was from the same cougar."

"How?"

"I don't know how. But I was just in a meeting in which he tried to talk the sheriff into getting a warrant to search John's house."

"What?" Carla was alarmed. "What are we going to do?"

"It's time to use our insurance."

"How?"

"You need to call him. Use the John phone. Tell him I'm coming over with some cash. From you."

"He won't like it, coming from you."

"Tell him you've been busy figuring out how to get that much cash without raising suspicions."

That was true enough, Carla knew.

"Tell him you can't be seen over at his house, let alone the neighborhood," said Anders. "It's too dangerous. Tell him in a way that strings him along, lets him know he still has a chance. Where is he?"

She looked at her watch. It was 7:45. "He's at the Club until 8. I'll call him then." She hesitated. "What did the sheriff think?"

"He thought it was crazy. For now, we've got time."

"Good," she said. "Let's use it. Once it's done, his share will be yours."

Anders didn't say anything and hung up.

Carla paused for a minute, thinking. This was not good. She had a very, very bad feeling about it. But it could still all work out, if she played her cards right. For now, the next best step was the one Anders suggested. If he could take care of Jared, that'd take him out of the equation. And if they found the tools at Jared's place, covered with his prints, they'd think it was a murder committed by a crazy kid with a bad past and worse habits. Everyone knew Jared was a player. He'd killed Jack hoping to get Carla and all that money.

There might be suspicions, but she was in Arizona when the trophy was stolen from the Rushing River Lodge. She had alibis.

At 8, she phoned the Club and asked to speak with Jared.

"I'm sorry, Jared called in sick today."

Carla hung up.

That wasn't good.

She used the throwaway to call Anders.

"What."

"He's home sick."

There was a long pause.

"Benedict?" Carla said.

"I heard. So what. Even better. Call him at home. Tell him I'm coming over. What I'm planning will look better if he's in bed."

She didn't think about it. She just hung up and dialed Jared.

It rang four times before he picked up. "This is . . . John."

"John, it's Urban. Are you OK?"

"Ah, yeah. I'm OK."

He had spent the entire day searching through every inch of his house. But he had not found their tools. It made him question what he'd overheard when he'd crept up to the back of Carla's house and heard her and Benedict talking. He thought Benedict had said he'd hid the tools at Jared's place. Now he wondered. But he didn't wonder about betrayal. Now he just hoped he could act well enough to conceal what he knew, while he figured out his next move.

"You called in sick?" Carla asked. "Why? I thought we were going to be normal. Everything was supposed to be normal."

"I really was. Sick. I don't know, the flu maybe. I've been throwing up all afternoon."

Carla thought about it. "You OK now?"

"Better," he said.

"Where are you?"

"Home," he said. He had been in his kitchen, trying to think, when the throwaway had rung. He hadn't moved from the kitchen, but now he added, "In bed."

"OK. I know I missed your calls yesterday. I was taking care of accounts, trying to get the money together, but trying not to make it obvious. But I have something for you." She knew he wouldn't like this, but there was no other way. "Benedict's bringing it over."

"Benedict?" He sounded weak. Maybe he really was sick.

"It's OK. He's just going to drop it off. I couldn't very well bring it over myself."

"No," he said, thinking. "When?"

"Within the hour, I think."

"Yeah," he said, thinking some more. "That should work. Just tell him I'm in bed and I'm still a little weak. It'll take a minute for me to get to the door. Tell him."

She said she would and hung up.

Then she called Anders.

"He's at home, in bed. He said to knock, but be patient. He's weak. He sounded sick."

"You think everything's OK?"

She paused. "I think it will be. After your visit."

Anders thought about it. He'd have to be careful. "OK," he said.

"Let me know when it's done," Carla said.

CHAPTER THIRTY-THREE

At around 8, Sam and Diane pulled into the park-and-ride and found Mac waiting in a nondescript Chrysler, one fellow service agent in the front passenger seat and another in the back—both women Sam didn't recognize. He waved and swung by them and then watched as Mac pulled out behind him and followed. When Sam drove by the place, there were no cars in the street, and the homes looked quiet. And there were a lot of trees. Jared's place was the smallest house on the block, and it had two thick, 7-foot-tall hedgerows on either side marking the yard's boundaries. Perfect.

Diane was dressed in hiking boots, jeans, and a loose-fitting flannel shirt.

"Got your phone?" Sam said.

"Sure."

"I'll park on the back side of Jared's block," Sam said.

"And I'll place my phone in my shirt pocket, walk in front of his place, and tell you what's going on," Diane said.

Sam, surprised, said, "You done this before?"

"Not in an official capacity."

On the back side of the block, Sam pulled over and parked. He sent Mac a text message. "Let's just sit tight for a sec. Let the dust settle."

"OK," Mac texted back.

Mac's Chrysler was behind Sam's jeep. Sam glanced at Diane and then looked in his rearview mirror. Gray was peering at him. "Almost showtime," Sam said to Diane. "You ready?"

Diane looked at him and said, "It's not like a walk down the red carpet. So, yeah, I'm ready."

Sam smiled, but said, "Nothing crazy. Just walk around the block, keep your phone on and the microphone part sticking out of your shirt pocket, and talk to me."

"That'll work," she said.

Sam texted Mac and let him know Diane was about to check out the front of Jared's house, that he should sit tight.

There were lights on in some of the houses on this side of the block, but it was getting to the point on a Wednesday evening when everyone was winding down in front of their TVs. The only chance of alarm was if there was a bored dog looking out a window. If one of them saw Gray, all bets were off. At least for sneaking up on Jared.

Diane walked to the end of the block and turned. It took another minute to walk the block's short side, during which she dialed Sam. When he came on the line she said, "Just about to Jared's street. I'll turn the mic up in my pocket and keep you posted."

"Perfect," Sam said.

In another minute, she said, "I'm on the street," continuing forward, looking like a neighbor out for a stroll. Halfway down the block, she passed in front of Jared's house. The place looked dark, except for some faint light coming through the front-door window.

"It's dark," Diane said. "Front is dark. I see some ambient light coming through a front-door window. Maybe someone's in a back room? Maybe in bed?"

Sam said, low, "Walk to the end of the block and hang out."

When she neared the corner she said, "OK. I'm here."

Sam texted Mac and told him he'd cut between the two dark houses and come up behind Jared's. Once he checked it out and found out where Jared was, if he could, he'd be back and they'd surprise him and show up in force, with Gray.

"10-4," Mac texted.

Gray looked worried.

"It's OK," Sam said. "I'll be right back."

Sam cut through the houses. There was a rear hedge behind Jared's place. Sam bent low and walked awkwardly to the hedge-row, keeping out of sight. Once at the hedge, he peered up over the bush and saw a man in green khakis peering into one of the rear windows.

What the? Sam wondered.

He ducked down and waited, thinking.

When he looked again, the man was gone.

From the street corner, Diane was glancing in the direction of Jared's house when she thought she saw movement at the near corner of the house. It was a man. He came around the side and started walking toward Jared's front door. Diane started to cross the street, to get a better view of the front of the house, at the same time saying, "Somebody's out front, moving to his front door."

Then Sam thought he heard a knock, on the other side of Jared's house—someone knocking on the front door.

Sam continued watching from the rear.

Diane said, "He's got company. Man went in."

After a few moments, there was some movement in the house. Then barely discernible voices, from the front. From the rear of the house, Sam saw a small middle window light up. Judging from the opaque glass, probably a bathroom.

Sam's phone vibrated, He looked down and saw a message from Mac that said, "Ready?"

Sam ignored it. He was riveted now. Then he thought he heard someone in the bathroom. Then there was a toilet flush. Then the light went out. And then the bathroom door opened and there were two gunshots, fired one right after the other.

Jesus, Sam thought.

"Shots fired," Diane said. She was still down near the corner.

Sam texted Mac. "Everybody armed? Your guys carrying?"

"Yeah, all of us," Mac texted. "Did I just hear gunshots?"

"Someone shot inside the house," Sam texted. "Come quick. Leave Gray."

Then he spoke to Diane in a terse whisper. "Stay put."

Within 2 minutes, Mac and the two female agents were beside him. Sam indicated Mac should take one of the agents and go around the left side of the house. He and the other agent would go around the right. "Be careful. Somebody's armed and shooting."

While Sam and the agent were making their way around to the front of the house, they heard what sounded like window glass being broken. They both hunkered down. The agent's gun was out, ready. They waited, but nothing.

Sam peered around the corner. He saw Mac come around the garage, the other agent behind him.

Finally, Sam stepped carefully to the front of the house. Someone had definitely kicked in the door. Inside, Sam thought he saw a man through the front-door glass, leaning over a body. The man had a phone in his hand.

"Police, please, hurry," he heard the man say. "I think I just killed a burglar."

Sam ended the call with Diane. Then he texted her. "Stay put. If you saw anything, text it to me."

By the time the police arrived, Sam was already talking to Jared. He could see he was shaken, so he waited for the local police. Then he explained who they were—Mac, the female agents, and Sam—and what they were doing. He thought he saw Jared's face fall an octave.

But Jared stuck to his story. This man had come in, kicked down his door, and started waving his gun around.

And sure enough, there was a body on Jared's hallway floor, spread out over a pool of blood. The man was dressed in khakis, had long brown hair and a mustache. A 9-millimeter pistol lay near the body. Something about the man looked familiar, but as soon as the police appeared, they called in the crime scene guys, who took over the body.

It was a mess. All of it. The house, their warrant, everything.

But Sam did the best he could to navigate it.

Diane thought about what she saw, wondering if what she saw after the gunshots was accurate, because it didn't make sense. Regardless, she texted Sam, then stayed on the corner, looking like a nosy neighbor.

When Sam had a moment, he checked his phone. From Diane, he read, "After gunshots man came out front of house, closed the door, turned around and kicked in the glass. Then went inside."

Sam wasn't sure he understood. He texted back. "Thanks. Can you go get Gray from the jeep?"

After the body was gone and the police had taken Jared's weapon and his statement, they stuck around, to assist when Sam executed the warrant. Diane came around the corner with Gray.

Sam pulled the mountain lion tail tip from the double bag and put Gray onto the scent, then turned him loose in the house.

The place looked like a bachelor's residence. Dirty dishes lined the counter. The sink was filled with food-encrusted plates, silverware, glasses, and pans. A half loaf of bread sat on the countertop in front of a toaster, its bag hanging open. Crumbs from various meals were scattered across the Formica top. There was a jar of peanut butter with the lid tilted on top of it like an off-kilter hat. There was a half-finished jar of strawberry jam beside it.

Gray searched all of it.

There was nothing on the main floor. The entryway to the basement was off the kitchen. When Sam opened the door, he saw old basement steps and a concrete floor, and it smelled dank. He descended the steps and found a 15-year-old furnace, a water heater, open rafters, cobwebs, and a corner with a couple of old suitcases, two boxes of junk, and a set of golf clubs. There was fresh cement around the basement wall's perimeter. Sam guessed a contractor had recently sledged up the floor and put in a drainage system. It all ended in the far basement corner with a 3-foot-square lid covering what Sam assumed was a sump pump. Sam lifted the lid to be sure.

Must have had some flooding, Sam thought.

Other than the sump pump installation, it appeared as though no one ever entered the basement, except to use it for storage.

Upstairs, Mac and his two agents were going through rooms, but so far had come up empty. The living room had a sizable collection of porn videos. The tall, dark-haired agent popped a couple in and hit play, just to make sure they were the real deal.

"Ah," she said, as if it figured.

Mac came in and said, "Nothing in the spare room."

"Basement's empty," Sam said. Gray had finished searching the house, but hadn't smelled any cougar.

The agent placed the porn DVD back in its jacket, shaking her head.

In the bathroom, there was a *Hustler* next to the porcelain bowl.

"This guy is a creep," the other agent said.

"Anything else? Anything?" Sam asked.

"Just the kind of stuff you'd figure in a bachelor pad."

The other agent came in from the master bedroom. "Found the shoes, I think," she said. Sam followed her into the master bedroom and the agent walked over to the closet. There was a pair of black tennis shoes on the closet floor with an Adidas logo on the back and some dirt still caked around the edges.

"Looks about right," Sam said. He kneeled down, took out a pen, and coaxed one of the shoes from the back of the closet, into better light. There was a faded "David Beckham Forest Hills Mid Black" in the inside bottom. "That's it," Sam said. He lifted the one shoe out with the pen and dropped it into a black garbage bag the agent held open. They fished the other out and did the same thing. Gray watched from Sam's side, interested, but only in smelly shoes.

Sam came outside to where Jared sat on the curb. Two plain-clothes officers stood near him, looking in Sam's direction.

Diane stood to the side.

Sam walked over to Diane and said, "You saw someone come out of the house, kick out the glass, and go back in?"

"Pretty sure it was Jared," she said.

Then Sam thought he understood. Jared must have known someone was coming over. A murder? And he was waiting. With the gun.

"Did you find anything?" Diane said.

"The shoes."

"Nothing from the cougar?"

"No."

"Did you check the garage?"

The moment Gray entered the garage, his attitude changed. There was a big plastic container in the corner of the garage marked "Christmas," piled up near some rafters, against the wall. Gray walked over to it, raised himself up on his paws and sniffed at the container, interested.

"What you got, Gray?" Sam asked.

Gray whined.

Sam clipped on Gray's leash and handed it to Diane. "Hold him," he said.

Sam went over and pulled down the container. It was big. Heavy. Mac helped him get it down.

Gray was watching and whining with his eyes totally focused on the plastic bin, as though he was disappointed Sam would be the first one to open it.

Sam took off the lid, and under several strings of Christmas lights found three heavy plastic bags, two containing what looked like paws with foot-long two-by-twos attached to them. The other held what appeared to be hedge clippers with the cutting ends refashioned with two cutout jaws, spiked with fangs, top and bottom. They were all carefully wrapped in plastic.

"Wow," Mac said, peering into the bin.

"Keep him back," Sam said. "We need to get these out carefully."

Diane gripped the leash and pulled the straining hybrid away from the bag.

One of Mac's agents opened a large plastic garbage bag and handed it to Sam. Sam placed the clipper jaws into it. He placed the two poles with claws into another garbage bag. Then he handed the bags to the agents. "Hope we can find some prints," Sam said.

"Wow!" Mac repeated.

One of the agents held up a garbage bag and said, "What is this thing?"

"That's a killing device," Sam said. Then, "Good boy, Gray."

He reached over and stroked Gray's head.

Gray kept staring at the bags.

CHAPTER THIRTY-FOUR

S am, Diane, Mac, and the two other agents walked out of the garage, carrying the cougar parts in two black garbage bags like they were a dozen eggs.

"What now?" Diane asked.

"We arrest him. Technically we're law enforcement officers. And I was more or less deputized to examine McGregor's death. Arresting Jared happened as a result of my investigation."

"What about the sheriff?" Mac said.

"What about him?"

"You calling him ahead of time, or what?"

"We could take Jared to the local police. Minnetonka," Sam suggested.

"They don't have any history with this," Mac said. "We'd have to explain it to them. And you know how they are about the service."

There were plenty in law enforcement who thought the USFW was only about wildlife enforcement, that their officers weren't capable of tracking down real criminals.

Sam considered it. "I don't want the sheriff screwing anything up. I think we take him to the sheriff's office. I can call him en route and explain what we need and why he should participate."

"That's a conversation I'd like to hear," Mac said.

"He'll participate," Sam said, looking forward to breaking the news to the sheriff, like blowing a hole in a pressure cooker. "I'll use the politics angle. If he doesn't participate, we'll share his reluctance to pursue the investigation with the media, now that Diane's along. He'll lose his job."

Jared took one look at Sam, saw what the agents were carrying, and his face turned pale.

"What's that?" he said.

"Jared Sparks, you're being arrested for the murder of Jack McGregor," Sam said, and read him his Miranda rights.

"I don't know anything about it. I don't know Jack McGregor." But his face turned paler.

Jared was just beginning to realize he might be caught. For two murders, once they figured out who had been lying on his hallway floor. For just one second, Sam thought he saw a flash in Jared's eyes, contemplating a run. But the remaining agent flared out to the side of Sam and with Mac behind him and the Minnetonka cop, it would have been impossible.

The tennis pro let them cuff him. "I don't know anything about this," he said, without turning.

Sam glanced down and noticed the pro's shoes. Black, with an Adidas logo on the heel.

"Nice shoes," Sam said.

Sam started walking him to the curb.

"This is far enough," Sam said. "I believe you give tennis lessons to Carla McGregor."

"Carla?"

Sam nodded. "Carla."

He thought for a moment. "Yeah," he said. "She's a client."

"We need to bring you in for some questions."

"I know Carla. But I don't know anything about Jack McGregor."

"It's hard for me to imagine you don't know about his death. Being attacked by a cougar?"

He paused. "I might have heard about it, now that you mention it. But I didn't know the guy and don't know anything about it."

"Why are there cougar claws and teeth in your garage?"

"They're not mine," Jared said.

There was a little whine in his voice, as though he was beginning to recognize the depth of his predicament.

"We'll take them down to the lab and check them for prints and blood," Sam said. "But it doesn't look good, Jared."

Suddenly Jared exploded forward with a shoulder blow to Sam's chest, slamming him into the agent behind them. Sam and the agent both went down. Sam spun on his side, vaulted up, and watched Jared sprinting away down the sidewalk. He was running as best you could with your hands cuffed behind you.

"Go!" Diane yelled, taking Gray off leash.

Gray seemed to instinctively know he should run down the cuffed man, which is what he did, knocking him to the ground.

Sam was up and sprinting down the sidewalk, and by the time he reached him, Jared was cowering in front of the hybrid, Sam, and then Diane coming up fast.

They put Jared in one of the black-and-whites, cuffed and locked so he couldn't run. Mac gave his car keys to one of the agents and got in the front seat of the black-and-white. They would all meet at the sheriff's office.

Once Sam, Diane, and Gray were in his jeep, Sam called and asked for the sheriff but got Deputy Sorenson.

"Agent Rivers," Sorenson said.

Sam could hear it in his voice. They were putting up the official wall.

"Sorenson," Sam said. "I think you should find the sheriff, even if he's home and in bed, and conference yourself in, put me on the speaker. This is something he will want to participate in."

There was a pause. "The sheriff's out, Agent Rivers."

"Well, you'd better find him in the next 5 minutes because I'm bringing in Jared Sparks and three murder weapons."

Judging from the long silence, the deputy was weighing his options.

"Unless," Sam added, "the sheriff wants me to take them to the Minnetonka police, since we were technically in their jurisdiction when we pulled the murder weapons from Jared's garage."

"Uh," Sorenson said, "can you wait just a minute?"

"Tell him I'm 10 minutes out, and unless he wants me to strike a match to a media firestorm, he'd better get on the phone in the next 60 seconds."

Thirty seconds later, Sheriff Rusty Benson came on the line. Diane smiled.

"What in the Sam Hill is going on, Rivers?" the sheriff said.

He sounded a little angry, for someone who should have his hat in his hands.

"Sheriff Benson. We just arrested Jared Sparks for the murder of Jack McGregor. We have evidence. We collected it from his home. Parts from a dead mountain lion, as I suspected. All I need from you is your interrogation room and an operational tape recorder. Do you think you can help us?"

Sam wondered if the sheriff's face reddened.

"What the hell are you talking about, Rivers?"

Sam walked the sheriff through it from the top, how the USFW managed to get a warrant from Judge Stalter, and what they found at the tennis pro's house. And there had been a shooting, which Sam thought was somehow related, but he hadn't yet figured it out.

"Did you read him his rights?" the sheriff asked.

"Of course," Sam said,

"Now you listen here, Rivers," Benson started.

Sam hung up. He was seriously contemplating turning around and heading to the Minnetonka police department. While he was thinking about it, his phone rang. He saw it was the sheriff's office and answered.

"Agent Rivers?" the sheriff asked.

Sam could still hear anger, but it was ratcheted down a couple notches.

"Sheriff, you're on speaker. Diane Talbott is with me."

"Who?"

"A reporter."

There was a muffled expletive while the sheriff took stock of his situation and apparently realized he was in that rare place where his official status didn't mean squat. He was trying to regain his composure.

"Your interrogation room and a tape recorder and your cooperation or I'm turning around and heading over to Minnetonka," Sam said. "And don't screw around because I have a paper trail to back up my story."

There was a pause.

"For the *Chicago Tribune*," Diane said.

When Diane's comment was met with more silence, Sam hung up.

This time there was no call back.

"I guess he finally got the message," Diane said.

"Let's hope so."

Sam phoned Mac.

They were 5 minutes behind him.

"Tell Jared we're the only ones who can offer him any deals. I don't want him talking in front of the sheriff."

"You got a room?" Mac said.

"I think so. If I don't, I'll let you know before you get there and we'll go someplace where we can get a room, even if we have to get a tape recorder from Best Buy and rent a hotel room."

"10-4."

By the time Sam arrived at the sheriff's office, he was ready to go a few rounds with Rusty Benson, provided the sheriff was up for it. But he wasn't. He sent out Deputy Sorenson, who ushered Sam into the interrogation room, where there was an operational tape recorder sitting on the table. There were three chairs in the room. Otherwise, it was nondescript, gray and cold.

"Perfect," Sam said. "Just tell the sheriff to stay in his office."

"I don't think he's planning on coming out for a while, Agent Rivers."

"Sorenson," Sam said. "Call me Sam."

The black-and-white pulled up to the door 5 minutes later. Mac got out of the car and helped a docile, cuffed Jared Sparks get out of the back seat.

Jared looked up and saw Sam and must have recognized him as the person in charge. "It wasn't me," he said.

"Just keep your mouth shut until we get inside."

Jared swallowed hard and nodded. He was ashen and frightened and looked like he was going to lose his dinner.

They pushed through the station doors and Sorenson led the way to the room. Sam walked up beside Sorenson and said, "You think you could get us a wastebasket for that room? Something with a plastic bottom? A pail would work too."

Sorenson nodded. Once Sam, Jared, and Mac were in the room, Sorenson brought in a pail and then left, closing and locking the door.

For the second time, Sam read Jared his Miranda rights. This time he was recorded and when Jared nodded, indicating he understood, Sam said, "You need to tell us. The machine doesn't pick up head nods."

Sam didn't care about the tennis pro. He didn't care what he said. They had him. He suspected when the BCA analyzed the cougar parts taken from the garage, they'd find more evidence. Prints. Blood. And Sam knew Jared knew it. The only thing Sam was interested in was how much it was going to cost to find out if anyone else was involved.

When all the cards were finally on the table, Jared told them he had the whole story and could share it with them, and he had the proof to back it all up. But he reiterated it wasn't him who killed Jack McGregor. He said he helped carry the murder weapons to the scene, but it wasn't him that used them.

"Then who?" asked Sam.

He paused, looking sideways. "It was Chief Deputy Leif Anders."

Sam and Mac both appeared stunned.

"The chief deputy?" Sam said.

Jared nodded. "The sheriff's chief deputy."

Sam remembered the man on Jared's hallway floor. He thought he'd recognized something about him, about his face? Even though the man was dressed in khakis, had long hair and a mustache, it was the chief. In disguise. Jared had assumed they knew.

Jared took some time filling in the details. He explained about Carla McGregor, how it was her idea, and that he didn't know it was the chief deputy until last night. The chief had always worn a disguise. But last night Jared had overheard the chief and Carla plotting to frame him with the weapons and then kill him. But he, Jared, had been waiting for the chief. He had let the chief in and told him he needed to go to the bathroom, that it was urgent.

Earlier he'd put a gun in the bathroom. When he came out, the chief pointed a gun at him and told him to get into bed. That's when Jared shot him. Self-defense.

Jared was willing to plead to anything that would get him a lower sentence, say 10 years with the possibility of parole after 5? He knew he was guilty and would have to pay, but he wasn't the guy. He was just a bit player. And shooting Anders had been self-defense. Anders had come over to kill him.

Sam played dumb, explaining how they were the USFW and couldn't make deals in criminal matters, but that he would speak with the prosecuting attorney and the judge and that there was no doubt his testimony would hold a great deal of sway in a matter like this. Depending upon what part he played in the crime, Sam might be able to get a reduced charge of involuntary manslaughter.

"With involuntary manslaughter you'd be looking at that kind of time," Sam said. "Probably more than 10 years, though, since you participated."

"With some chance of parole after some time was served?"

Sam shrugged.

Jared looked at him, still ashen. He was dealing, but he looked like any moment he was going to throw up. "I thought the recorder didn't pick up gestures," he said.

"Oh, yeah," Sam said. "There will be some chance of parole after a certain number of years are served," Sam said, noncommittally.

Jared nodded, said he'd tell them what he knew if they could guarantee it.

And that's when Mac came out of the shadows with a bad-cop routine, explaining if they didn't reach some kind of understanding in the next 30 minutes, the Scott County attorney's office would be on them like stink on a bear, and once that guy got there—a law-and-order guy named Marone—Jared would be lucky to get accomplice to murder and 30 years without the possibility of parole.

"Marone?" Sam asked.

"Marone," Mac said, ominous.

"Not Marone," Sam said.

It took a while longer, but Jared finally decided to play along.

Sam explained they didn't need to draw up any documents. At this point, the recording would suffice as his statement of record.

Over the next half hour, Jared sang out with all the choking rancor of a crow at dawn. He repeated it was Carla McGregor. And the man he shot on his hallway floor was Chief Deputy Leif Anders, who was the one who murdered Jack McGregor. The chief was trying to set up Jared for the murder, and when all the ballistics came out, they'd see his shooting of the chief was self-defense.

Carla had planned the entire thing, Jared said. He assured them he was an innocent bystander. Well, mostly innocent. He told them he had proof of her involvement: recordings in which they would hear her plotting the entire scheme. The man referred to as Benedict in the recordings was Chief Deputy Leif Anders.

"Where are the recordings?" Sam asked.

Jared looked shifty. "I've got 'em," he said. "But you'll never find them. And I won't tell you where they are until I'm sure we've got some kind of deal."

They badgered him for a while, reminding him that once Marone showed up they weren't sure they could help him. And did he really want to see Carla walk free? Because if it was a "he said, she said" type thing, people like Carla could afford the best attorney in the country. The world, for that matter. Without evidence, she would walk.

He continued looking pale. But he didn't budge. And finally he asked for an attorney.

Sam and Mac finally came out of the room.

"What do you think?" Sam said.

"I think we've got plenty. I think we use that warrant to go back over to his place and tear it apart. Find those recordings."

Sam thought about it. "Maybe."

"What are you going to do about Carla?"

Sam thought about it. Then he asked Sorenson to keep an eye on the room and headed for the sheriff's office.

The sheriff was sitting behind his desk, looking uncharacteristically contrite and reserved.

"He's implicated Carla McGregor. We need to bring her in."

"Mrs. McGregor?" the sheriff said. He didn't look happy. He could only imagine the political fallout. Sam thought letting the sheriff sweat a little would be good for Rusty Benson's soul. It might even be better if Sam turned a screw.

"The first thing we do is call Judge Stalter and with this new evidence get a warrant to search Carla's house."

"Now?"

"The judge is aware of the possibility Carla might have been involved. Now that Jared has accused her, we have reason to bring her in for questioning and search her house."

"These people aren't nobodies, Rivers," the sheriff said, though his tone was even.

Sam returned the sheriff's look. The man was in no position to argue. "You're right, Sheriff. Jack McGregor appears to be the victim of a homicide. And his wife, if we can believe the tennis pro, arranged his murder. And your chief deputy was the executioner. So I guess the McGregors weren't your typical super rich."

The sheriff frowned. He'd already received word that a car registered to Anders was found near Jared's house. The fallout couldn't be worse. He was beginning to think maybe he should resign. But all he said was, "I'll call the judge."

"Loan me Deputy Sorenson and we can go over in one of your squad cars and bring her in. While we're there, maybe you can get some of your guys and the BCA to check out the house."

"That's a lot to do in the next 30 minutes."

"I'm certain Rusty Benson can manage it."

The sheriff nodded. "OK," he said.

"Good," Sam said. He started to push out of the room.

"Agent Rivers," the sheriff asked, politely. "How exactly is this going to end?"

"I don't know," Sam said. "It's a mystery."

CHAPTER THIRTY-FIVE

Almost an hour after Sam first entered the sheriff's office, he and Sorenson turned onto Wannamake Circle.

The sheriff beeped them on the cruiser radio. "We're on our way," he said. "There's three of us, and the BCA is giving us another three. We should be in and out in 3 or 4 hours."

Sam and Sorenson would give him notice, once they had Carla in custody and were on their way to the office.

"Just make sure the BCA and your guys stay well out of sight until we get her out of the house. There's a CVS pharmacy off Judicial Road, about a quarter mile behind the house."

The sheriff wasn't used to taking orders. He sounded irritable.

"We just better find something," he said.

Humility was coming hard to Sheriff Rusty Benson.

"I don't get it," Sorenson said as they approached the McGregors' mansion.

"What?" Sam asked.

"She had all this. And she throws it away for a tennis pro?"

"I bet the tennis pro wasn't part of Carla's long-term plan," Sam said. "I bet Jared Jared and your chief deputy were just a means to an end, and maybe Jared was a little fun. I'd guess once Carla came into her wealth, she'd play around with the pro long enough to let him know it wasn't for keeps, then cut him loose. My sense of the chief is it was a money thing. He seemed too cold and smart to be seduced by someone like Carla. Carla would pay them both well. But I'm sure the chief was promised plenty, at least in money."

"But they could blackmail her."

"With what? Anything they said would implicate themselves."

"I just can't believe it," Sorenson said.

"I can," Sam said. "She wanted it all. And she's young enough to have put it to good use."

Carla was dressed in black spandex, with the bottoms of her skin-tight pants cut mid-calf. Her top was ruby red and fit so snug, Sam thought, she could barely breathe. But she looked good. She always looked good.

"Agent Rivers," she said, greeting them. "Deputy Sorenson."

Sorenson nodded. He had that deer-in-the-headlights look.

"Ma'am," Sorenson managed.

"What can I do for you gentlemen? I was just about to do some late-night exercise on my treadmill. Lately I've been having trouble sleeping."

"Some things have come up about your late husband's accident. We need to ask you some questions, back at the sheriff's office."

"What things?" Carla asked.

Who wears makeup to work out on their treadmill? Sam wondered. "I think there's been some question about how exactly he died."

"Oh?" she appeared genuinely concerned. "What kind of question?"

"Now the sheriff's thinking there was some foul play involved. Before the media picks it up, we need to talk to you about it."

She hesitated. Sam thought he saw a flash of mild concern, but not much.

"I appreciate that, Agent Rivers. But if it's OK, I can stop by in the morning."

"The sheriff's pretty sure this is going to hit the media sooner rather than later. It would be better if you came over right away. It's important," Sam said.

She had two options, Sam knew. She could play along, or she could run. Sam bet she'd play along.

"Oh? Well, I suppose. But there's no way I'm going in that squad car," she said, making a tight smile. "What would the neighbors think?"

"Doesn't look like any of your neighbors are in," Sam said.

"Oh, they're in," Carla said. "And they're nosy. I'll follow you over. Just give me a sec," she said, and closed the door.

Sorenson looked at Sam with a question. Sam nodded, turned, and started back to the car. Once inside, Sam said, "No sense in making a scene, unless we have to."

"You going to let her follow us?"

"Sure," Sam shrugged. "Why not?"

"What if she takes off?"

"If she takes off, we got her. She drives a brand-new red Mercedes convertible. She'll stick out like a rocket," Sam said. "Besides, why would she take off?"

In a couple minutes, the garage door went up.

Sorenson put the patrol car in gear and drove to the end of the drive.

Sam glanced over and saw Emma Winetraub's front curtains sway shut.

Sorenson waited until Carla appeared behind them. Then he started up the street, and the red two-door followed.

At the top of the cul-de-sac, Sorenson turned right onto Chester Drive. As soon as he saw Carla in his rearview mirror, he clicked the radio and got the sheriff on the line.

"We're on our way," Sorenson said.

"10-4," the sheriff responded, and then clicked off.

"I hope they find something," Sorenson said.

"I don't want to be around if they don't," Sam said. "But it would be fun to watch your boss turn purple."

At the sheriff's office, Sam held the door open for Carla, who wore a light black windbreaker over her ruby-red top. Her hair was perfect, like her face, Sam thought, following her into the station.

"There's a room down here," Sam said. He ushered her into the interrogation room and told her he'd check on the sheriff and be right back. Then he closed the door.

Sam waited 5 minutes and then knocked on the interrogation room door and went in. The air was comfortable, maybe a little cool.

Carla was still wearing her light jacket, though she'd unzipped it halfway down her chest. Her décolletage beamed across the table like neon. She was sitting back in the chair with her legs crossed. She looked bored and slightly irritated.

No matter what kind of cheap chair you put that woman in, Sam thought, she still looked like a million bucks. Fifty million, now that he thought about it. He glanced up and said, "The sheriff had to step out. I just spoke with him, and he has authorized me to tell you what we know."

"Is this the station's interrogation room?" Carla asked.

The tape recorder was sitting in the center of the table.

"Does it look like one?"

It was just the two of them. This room didn't have mirrored windows, and the tape recorder wasn't recording. They were alone.

"It does, Agent Rivers. And unless I'm mistaken, I smell a rat."

The comment surprised Sam. He wasn't sure he heard right, or if he did, what she meant.

"Sorry?" he said.

"I smell a rat, Agent Rivers. I'm not sure why I'm here, but I don't think it's only to share news about Jack's death. I think you're fishing," she said.

Sam was startled, but he didn't show it. It was probably time to read her her Miranda rights. Sam turned on the recorder and recited Miranda as casually as possible. Carla didn't react.

"Do you understand your rights?" Sam said.

"Oh yes, Agent Rivers. I watch TV."

She smiled, but Sam ignored it.

"Fishing for what?" Sam said.

"I have no idea," she said.

Carla straightened up in the chair and unzipped her thin black jacket. She opened it up until it hung at her sides. "It's a little warm in here," she said.

But it was hard not to notice her gesture, as cheap as it was. Maybe she really was warm, but Sam didn't think so.

"So what is it you wanted to tell me about my husband's death?"

There was a sudden stillness in the room. Sam had felt it before. A blue heron hunting an anole lizard, a snake hunting a mouse, a raptor hunting a rabbit . . . it was the same kind of concentrated stillness. Predatory.

"We think your husband was murdered, Mrs. McGregor."

"Murdered? Really?"

She didn't have a surprised reaction. Moreover, she looked as though in the three days since his death she had put her late husband behind her.

"I guess we more than think it," Sam said. "We have evidence, and we have a confession."

"Who?"

"Jared Sparks."

"I thought I smelled him."

"Sorry?" Sam said.

"I thought I smelled Jared," Carla said. "You don't sleep with a man and not become familiar with his scent."

"I wouldn't know."

"Yes, you would. I can smell a woman on you, Agent Rivers. It's not only the smell, Agent Rivers. I've got a sense about these things."

"Do you know what Mr. Sparks told us?"

"I have no idea," Carla said. "We weren't that close."

"I thought you were sleeping with him."

"We were sleeping together, if that's what you want to call it," Carla said. "These euphemisms for sex are so banal." She paused. Before Sam could respond she said, "Don't you think?"

Sam ignored the comment. "Mr. Sparks told us you hired him and Chief Deputy Leif Anders to kill your husband. That you promised to pay them both well. That you maybe made more promises to him."

Carla laughed. "I can hardly honor that with a response," she said. "Of course I had sex with Jared. He has a nearly perfect body. And knows how to use it."

"We went over to his house and searched it," Sam said. He waited, watching her face for anything. But she was unfazed. "Before we got there, Anders tried to kill Jared, but Jared shot him first. He's dead."

Sam watched her reaction, but there was only calm.

"We found what we are pretty sure are the murder weapons," Sam continued. "And when we confronted Mr. Sparks about them, he admitted they were the weapons used on your husband, by Chief Deputy Anders. And that you were the one in charge. It was all your idea."

"He said it was my idea?" Carla asked.

Sam paused. "That's right, Mrs. McGregor."

She had grown cool. Maybe she was bored. Maybe, since parting her windbreaker was having no effect on him, she had decided to take a different approach. Sam didn't really care.

"Is it true?" he said.

"Of course not. He needs someone to blame. I'm convenient."

"We have his statement," Sam said.

"I'm sure you do, Agent Rivers."

"It was your idea from start to finish. He said that after Jack was out of the picture, you'd be rich and you and he could do whatever you wanted. Go anywhere. Do anything."

"I could have done that with Jack alive. And while Jack and I didn't exactly have an understanding, we were both discreet. And the truth is, Agent Rivers, Jack was pretty good in bed, too. Why *would* I risk the perfect life?"

"Jared thought it was because of what you and he had together."

She laughed. "Men are so vain."

"So you didn't plan it?" Sam asked.

"Really, Agent Rivers? I gave you more credit than that."

"Had to ask," Sam said.

"Well then, no, I didn't. Does that make you feel better?"

"Mr. Sparks says he has recordings. Of you planning the entire thing. Apparently it's pillow talk."

That got her attention, but just barely. "Jared Sparks and I have been fucking for less than a year. Sometimes at his place. Occasionally mine. Sometimes wherever and whenever the itch needs a scratch. If Jared made some recordings of our outings, I bet they'd make for interesting listening. But you won't find anything on them about murder, Agent Rivers."

"So you think he did it on his own? What would he have to gain by your husband's death?"

She shrugged. "Jared thought I was in love with him. I could tell he liked me. He probably did it because he thought I'd marry him and share the money."

"And then he blamed you because he doesn't want to go to prison?" Sam said.

"When there's that much skin in the game, everyone shows their true colors."

"So you have no idea about any of this?"

"None," she said. "You should be careful about trusting the word of a murderer."

Sam looked at her, considering. "For someone who has just learned about it, you don't seem too upset to have found out your husband may have been murdered."

She paused, and finally frowned a little. "Agent Rivers, how I choose to deal with grief is my business. Don't judge me because of the way I choose to live. Jack didn't."

Sam wasn't sure where else to go. He needed more information. Maybe Jared could shake something loose. Something that might unsettle her. "Would you mind waiting for a minute?"

"You mean wait to listen to more lies?"

Sam didn't say anything.

"You know what, Agent Rivers? I'm tired of being accused of murder. So unless you have something more to say, I'll be going."

"I'm not sure we can let you go, Mrs. McGregor. At least not until we get to the bottom of this."

"You're arresting me, Agent Rivers?"

"Not exactly. We can hold you for 24 hours, as long as there's probable cause."

"Now you're making me angry. And you're such a good-looking man. There was a chance . . ." she let it lie there. "But now I need to call my lawyer."

"Be my guest," Sam said.

"I don't want to be your guest," she said, reaching into her purse. "Which is why I'm making the call." Then she looked at him. "I want you to turn off that recorder. And I want some privacy."

Sam thought about it, but she was within her rights. And technically, they hadn't filed charges. Yet. He shut off the recorder and stood up. "OK, Mrs. McGregor. We'll wait outside. Just let us know when you're done."

Her eyes had a look that in the pit viper world would have signaled a venomous strike.

Finally, Sam thought, I must be getting to her. But he didn't smile, and walked out of the room.

Before going to speak with Jared, he told Sorenson to keep an eye on Carla. "When she comes out, escort her to a holding cell." Then he added. "She's going to try to charm you, Sorenson. Just tell her Agent Rivers said we need to hold her for 24 hours. Got it?"

Sorenson looked worried, but also offended that Sam Rivers thought he could be charmed by a murderer. "I got it."

"And can you let the sheriff know what's going on?"

Sorenson said he would, but his worried look intensified.

CHAPTER THIRTY-SIX

When Jared heard about Carla's denials, he said, "Of course she denied it. What did you think she was going to do? Lie down and let you screw her?"

"She has alibis," Sam said. "She was in Phoenix when the mounted cougar was stolen from Rushing River Lodge, and she was seen out walking the morning Jack was killed. So far they are reasonable explanations. So far it's a solo crime."

"Which is why I'm going to share something with you. Something even Carla can't refute. I just need assurances: involuntary manslaughter, 10 years, with the possibility of parole after 5."

"We can't do that, Jared. I mean, I can't."

"Find someone who can."

"To even get someone interested, I'm going to have to know what you're offering."

"Enough to hang her," Jared said.

"They don't hang people in Minnesota. They put them away for life."

"Then life, without the possibility of parole."

"It would have to be very good because Carla doesn't look like a lifer and she's got good explanations for why you're incriminating her."

Jared paused, considering, working it out in his head. "I have the recordings. She planned everything. Some of it's on tape, loud and clear. I can deliver Carla McGregor."

"How many recordings?"

"Carla first proposed offing her husband about four months ago. I thought she was kidding. Then about two weeks later she brought it up again. This time she'd found out about some woman he was sleeping with at work and said she'd had enough."

"But," Sam said, ready to state the obvious.

"I know," Jared said. "She brought it up while we were in bed. There's no accounting . . ." he tried to grin, but there wasn't really any humor in it. "So this time, when she talked about offing him, she didn't smile. And I began to suspect she was serious. I put her off, but she kept bringing it up. I know Carla. I never thought she'd actually go through with anything. I thought she was just angry and tired about the other women. I thought she was blowing off steam. So I humored her, going along.

"Then this cougar thing happened," Jared continued. "And she turned into a totally different person. I still didn't think she'd go through with it, but she knew about that cougar on the wall up north, and she said it was a message from God. That's what she said. And then she got me to go up and get it. It was on the drive back I figured I would help with this thing, but I wouldn't actually kill anyone. I'd just be, you know, the one to go along and help out. Not do the killing. And then she recruited the chief deputy. Only I didn't know who the guy was. The first time we met was 60 miles south at a truck stop off 169. And he looked the way he did when you saw him on my floor. He was in disguise. She told me he'd do all the bad stuff, but he couldn't do it alone. I figured then I'd need some insurance. I'd actually started recording some of our sessions. Because Carla could do stuff, ya know. She was . . ." Jared trailed off, wistful. Then he said, "I didn't know what was going to happen. She made me a little crazy, in the head."

"Where are the recordings? Why didn't we find them during our house search?"

"Because I didn't want you to find them."

"You didn't want us to find your weapons, either," Sam said.

"Not my weapons. Benedict's. I mean, the chief deputy's. He put them there. I thought he was going to destroy them. She told me he was going to destroy them when we . . . when he was done using them."

"But your prints are all over them."

"I handled them because I thought they were going to be destroyed. But it was Anders who did it. He wore gloves, and then didn't destroy them. That's all." He was worried and angry, but mostly worried. "I wonder what she's going to say when you hear the recordings. I have some video, too, but it doesn't show much."

"Are they at your place?"

"Give me some credit. Do you think I'm going to tell you where they are? If you want Carla McGregor, you're going to have to find someone who can deal with me. Ten or so years, eligible for parole after serving maybe five. Something like that."

"They grant parole to model prisoners. I can't guarantee parole," Sam said.

"I'll be a model prisoner. I just can't take a decade."

Sam thought about it. "Let me see what we can do," he said.

The sheriff and his crime scene crew searched through Carla's house with a figurative fine-toothed comb. They were able to uncover a dresser drawer compartment, secreted in Jack's dresser in the master bedroom. It contained a library of porno videos and several sex toys, mostly of the bondage variety. Their only other find was in an unfinished basement storage room, hidden behind some wall insulation: specialized paper, charcoal, and an old leather pouch containing three weird dice. But they had no idea why it was hidden there.

As far as they could tell, the pornos, sex toys, and dice had nothing whatsoever to do with Jack's murder, so at 2:30 a.m. they called it quits.

When the sheriff returned to his office, there was a message from Carl Rodriguez, Carla's lawyer.

"Please call me immediately," Carl said. "Even if it's the middle of the night."

"Oh, God," the sheriff said. He was tired and he had dealt with Rodriguez in the past, whenever some well-heeled person entered into the sheriff's custody. He thought about ignoring the call but knew if he did, Carl would use it against him in front of a judge.

Carl answered after the fourth ring. He sounded tired, but alert.

"You still holding Carla McGregor?" Carl said.

"Yes," the sheriff said. "We can hold her for 24 hours."

Another pause. "I understand you executed a search warrant of her house?"

"We did."

"And I'm guessing you found nothing?"

"That's correct," the sheriff said. No use equivocating, though he thought about mentioning the pornos and sex toys.

"We've got a meeting in front of Judge Stalter tomorrow morning at 9. After which my client will be released."

Rodriguez's tone sounded like a threat. Normally, the sheriff would have gone off on him. But he was tired and frankly he was still predisposed to give the beautiful Carla McGregor the benefit of the doubt, given that the only evidence against her was an accusation by a known scallywag who, more likely than not, was trying to blur the facts. As the sheriff saw it, it was a perpetrator's desperate search for a way out, or at least to muddy the waters.

He'd been shocked about his chief deputy, but if he was a betting man, he would have fingered Jared as the main guy. He'd heard the tennis coach and Carla had some kind of relationship. But in all the times he'd seen the McGregors together, he had never witnessed a tense moment between them. Nothing but happiness and contentment, from the sheriff's perspective. No one knew what went on behind bedroom doors. Maybe they had some kind of agreement? And if all that was true, why would Carla risk everything to get what she was going to get regardless. It made a hell of a lot more sense that a lowly tennis pro was plotting to kill Jack. Once the husband was out of the way, a mourning Carla would be available. And from what the sheriff had heard, the tennis pro was as good with women as he was at tennis.

Besides, the sheriff remembered, the McGregors had been nothing but decent to the sheriff and his campaign.

So, for now, all he said to Rodriguez was, "Tomorrow morning."

Sam was busy until the wee hours. Sorenson let Sam know that Carla's attorney was working on her release and that meanwhile he'd placed her in a holding cell. She wasn't happy about it, but Sorenson said she was much less upset than many he'd put into cells, as though she knew what to expect. Sorenson also told Sam that so far the sheriff had turned up nothing at the McGregors' home, at least with regard to Jack's murder.

Sam wasn't surprised. Besides, he and Mac were working the angle with the county prosecutor. He was looking forward to listening to those recordings.

Sam helped Diane with several details surrounding the first of many stories she planned to write. She'd finished a draft that introduced the double murder, Jack McGregor, and Chief Deputy Anders. She'd identified a suspect in custody, Jared Sparks. The details of the double murder were sensational. The cliffhanger Diane left for readers was "authorities suspect there was at least one additional accomplice as yet to be identified and charged."

After the draft was solid, they had enough time for an akvavit. And then they fell into bed. In spite of being exhausted, they could not help themselves, fooling around for the better part of an hour before both, sated, collapsed.

The sex at the end of such a long day was intense, abandoned, and remarkable. But it also dropped both of them into profound unconsciousness, a deeper sleep than the deepest REM.

By 10:30 the next morning, Sam was finally awakened by the cold muzzle of Gray, who needed to do his business outdoors, and then wanted breakfast. It was late.

Sam took one look at his watch and said, "What?" He couldn't remember the last time he'd slept in until 10:30. But then neither could he remember the last time he'd stayed awake until 3 and then fallen into bed with the likes of Diane Talbott. And then . . . well, he knew it was an experience he would have plenty of time in the future to remember. Right now, he needed to tend to Gray.

When he was outside with Gray, he finally glanced at his phone and saw three calls and one voice mail from Mac.

"Rivers!" Mac said. "Where the hell are you? That's a rhetorical question. I know where you are and what you're doing. But while you dallied, Carla McGregor walked. Her lawyer convinced the judge to let her out after posting $100,000 in bail. He dug up enough about Jared Sparks's character to suggest the tennis pro was a second Charlie Manson. Call me!"

Back in the room, Sam told Diane. "The judge let Carla walk."

"What?"

"She posted a $100,000 bond," Sam said.

"That's nothing to Carla McGregor."

"I know. But the only thing we've got on her so far is Jared's accusation that she was the planner. And Jared isn't exactly a stellar character witness."

"I hope somebody's keeping tabs on her," Diane said.

Sam phoned the sheriff's office. Myrtle explained about the sheriff's late night and that he wasn't in yet. When Sorenson came on the line, Sam said, "Tell me you have someone watching Carla McGregor's place."

"Of course," Sorenson said. "She's home. There's a deputy at the top of Wannamake Circle and one in the CVS parking lot off Judicial Road, behind the house."

"I can't believe she got out."

"She posted a $100,000 bond."

"Sorenson!" Sam said. "In less than a week, they're selling McGregor Industries. She's coming into a lot of money. She probably already has access to millions. One hundred thousand is nothing to someone with Carla McGregor's resources."

"I know. But that was part of her lawyer's argument. Why would she jump bail when she's looking at a $50 million windfall in less than a week? And she and Jack had already purchased tickets and made reservations for a round-the-world trip. They were going to be gone for two months. Does that sound like the plan of a murderer?"

"It sounds like a convenient alibi," Sam said.

There was a pause. "Jared Sparks isn't exactly the best accuser. And, frankly, the sheriff likes Carla. He's always thought she was nice. Said he just didn't see her behind this, so he accepted the judge's bail recommendation as reasonable."

Sheriff Rusty Benson was a terrible judge of character, Sam thought. But he sighed and said, "Watch her, Sorenson. Mark my words: she's gonna run."

"We've got her covered," Sorenson said.

Sam wasn't comforted.

Diane heard enough of Sam's call to opine, "She's not gonna run. She's gonna fly."

Sam called Mac. When he picked up, Sam said, "Where are we with the county prosecutor?"

"Well, Agent Rivers," Mac said, "I hope we aren't interfering with your personal life."

Sam deserved it, but there wasn't time. "Where are we?"

Mac started to tell him about Carla posting bail.

"Where are we with the prosecutor? We've got to hear those tapes. The prosecutor needs to deal."

"Meeting her at 1, if you can make it."

During the meeting with Scott County prosecutor Fanny Pederson, she asked several tough, pointed questions. Sam and Mac answered every one of them, finally convincing her to play along.

"But just let him know," Pederson said, "there better be something on those tapes, or the deal's off."

Sam kept in touch with the officer posted near the top of Wannamake Circle. In the morning, Carla made one quick trip to the local Cub grocery and then returned home. She'd been there all day.

"And she didn't see you?"

"No way," the deputy said.

Sam wasn't so sure. How could he be posted at the top of the circle and not be noticed?

"Otherwise, she didn't move?"

"Not a peep. I watched her come out and get her mail, but that was about it."

Jared Sparks's recordings were made by devices secreted in the massive headboard on his king-size bed. The devices had the appearance of knots in rough-hewn wood. Clever.

Four deputies—two men and two women—began watching two short videos and listening to maybe 8 hours of scratchy audio recordings.

Sheriff Benson came into the office around 4. By that time, they'd reviewed the videos, and 4 hours of audio. The videos were brief, and the angles such that they never saw heads or faces. They heard voices that sounded like Carla and Jared. But there was nothing illegal about Carla's words, most of which were unfit to share or print.

By hour 6 of the audio, they began to hear the suggestions Jared mentioned. They started as complaints about her husband, Jack. Then she opined about what she and Jared could do if they were rid of him. It was pillow talk, heard after sexual encounters so histrionic and intense the atmosphere in which they were spoken was like seeding thunderclouds before a coming storm.

But it was all subtle and gradual, until the cougar sighting behind McGregor Industries on September 2. Hour 7 of the audio contained the first mention of the cougar, the first suggested plans. Then the Rushing River Lodge. By this time, Jared was so mesmerized by his beautiful, rich, and seductive lover, there was never any question of refusal. Best to play along.

And that's when she first suggested Jared begin using the name John, cementing it in place using the name during subsequent sexual encounters. Not long after, she mentioned Benedict.

They needed him, Carla said. A friend from her past had put her in touch. It was Benedict who had suggested the names.

That's when she became Urban. The names were all arranged so that Jared would think she was protecting his identity, that he was on the inside.

It was time to bring her in.

It was well after dark when Sam called the watch at the top of the drive. "Lights on at the house?"

"Lit up like a Roman candle," the deputy said. "She's still there."

Hmm, Sam thought. *Why would she have all those lights on?*

"Somebody's watching Judicial Road, aren't they?"

"Course," the deputy said, incredulous. "Not a peep out of nothin'."

"OK," Sam said. "If she moves, call me."

Everything was happening fast.

Sam was suspicious about Carla. They needed to move on her now. But he didn't feel good about it.

Carla was *just too damn smart.* And he, like everyone else, including her own husband, had been too preoccupied by her beauty to recognize she had a brain.

He radioed the deputy at the top of Wannamake Circle. Carla hadn't moved. He told him to keep an eye out, that they were coming over.

In 15 minutes, Sam and Sorenson pulled a squad car up to the McGregors' front door.

Sam got out and rang the doorbell. He thought he heard the TV inside. But he didn't hear anyone approach the front door. After a full minute, he rang the doorbell a second time and peered through the glass pane beside the door. He thought he saw the TV flicker coming from the kitchen. He rang the bell again.

Nothing.

Then he banged on the door, loud enough to wake the dead.

No footsteps, no movement. Just the TV.

He had a bad feeling.

Then Emma Winetraub's garage door went up. Sam watched her take something to a trash can, a small bag. It was too convenient. He waited until she turned to see him.

"Oh," she said, stepping onto the drive. "How are you, Agent Rivers?"

"Mrs. Winetraub," Sam nodded.

"Are you looking for Carla?"

"Yes."

"I saw her go into the woods about 2 hours ago."

"Into the woods?" Sam said.

"I was fixing an early dinner, and I saw her walk out the back of her house into the woods. Sometimes she does that; cuts across to Judicial Road for one of her evening walks. Or to walk to the CVS. She had a shoulder bag."

"And did you see her return?" Sam said, already knowing the answer.

"I didn't, but I was only at the table for about 20 minutes. She might have returned later. Sometimes she takes long walks. But that was about 2 hours ago. It was just starting to get dark."

A long walk, Sam thought. Probably a very long walk.

"Thanks."

"If I see her, do you want me to tell her you came by?"

"Sure," Sam said. "We just wanted to speak with her."

"Oh," Emma said. And then she said goodnight and retreated into her garage. In a moment the door came down.

Sam went around the side of the McGregors' house, but all the doors were locked, including the rear sliding door. He went up onto the rear deck. There was a back door into the kitchen, the TV blaring. This door appeared less substantial than the front. Sam shouldered it, hard, and the bolt snapped away from the wood. If there was a security system, it had been turned off.

Once inside, he and Sorenson checked everywhere, but she was gone.

"She ran," Sam said. "She figured it out. She went out the back. I don't know where and I don't know how far she can get, but she has a 2-hour head start."

"Shit," Sorenson said.

"Exactly."

"What are we going to do?"

The sheriff put out an APB, but Sam wasn't hopeful. Both of the McGregors' cars were in the garage, so all they could do was describe her, and stress the importance of finding her—that she was wanted for questioning in a murder investigation. They found a good photo of her on her dead husband's bedroom dresser and put it out on the police network, but by 10 they hadn't heard anything or seen Carla. And after a thorough search of her cars and house, with Gray, they hadn't found anything. The TV had been on, but it appeared she'd left without a trace. They couldn't even find missing clothes.

They interviewed Emma Winetraub, who told them all she knew was she saw Carla walk away wearing tennis sweats and carrying a shoulder bag, around 4:30 or 5. The tennis sweats made Emma suspect she was going out for a walk.

"I bet she had a load of money stashed away," Sam said.

"But when would she have gotten it?" Mac said. "We need to subpoena her bank records and check out her transactions. But we won't be able to see anything until morning."

"Maybe she salted some away, just in case."

"Smart *and* beautiful," Mac said.

Sam agreed.

"At least she's hard to miss," Mac said.

"She's too good-looking," Sam said. "If a patrolman picked her up, she'd talk her way out of it."

"Probably offer him something in return."

"Most men wouldn't turn it down."

That got them thinking.

"I just hope she runs into Mark Trail," Mac said. "Mark wouldn't ever accept that kind of favor from a suspect."

CHAPTER THIRTY-SEVEN

September 27

B ut she didn't run into Mark Trail. Apparently, she didn't run into anyone. She disappeared.

The Scott County sheriff's office, the BCA, the entire network of the upper Midwest, and then the nation's highway patrol were issued the BOLO report, along with her photo. Sam could only imagine the comments in patrol headquarters from Tuscaloosa to Timbuktu. Carla was a looker, and that was a good thing. Sam knew they'd keep an eye out.

But nothing ever came of it.

Carla McGregor vanished.

Sam knew the longer they went without any sign or news of Carla, the more difficult and unlikely it would be to find her.

"She could be anywhere by now," Diane said, from her hotel bed that second morning after she went missing.

"She could be in Mexico by now," Sam said.

"Or in Canada. How much did she take out?"

By midday, they'd been able to ascertain some of her financial transactions, and she'd been busy.

"She drained more than $250,000 from their accounts," Sam said. "Who keeps that kind of money in checking and savings accounts?"

"Someone who is the sole owner of a multimillion-dollar business," Diane said.

They'd spent the weekend checking the McGregors' portfolio accounts and found more than $12 million missing or transferred, some of it to offshore accounts in the Cayman Islands, though no one suspected it would end up there. Jack had accumulated a considerable fortune. There was almost $20 million in stocks and bonds and numerous other accounts, just less than half untouched, probably because she didn't have time to liquidate and transfer everything.

For Sam, who blamed himself for not pushing harder and sooner to promote the murder angle, her inability to take it all provided no solace.

Finally, what made the discovery of the raided accounts even worse was what they'd heard on the tapes. Never mind the libertine encounters with her tennis pro. Carla McGregor was a black widow. Poisonous. A black panther, if you considered her torrid affair with Jared, a good tennis player and shockingly handsome young man who didn't stand a chance. Carla had schemed and plotted, and in between the sheets she hypnotized Jared and induced him to play along.

For Chief Deputy Anders, it had always been about the money.

They searched his house and cars and found $100,000 in a thick envelope, probably his first installment from Carla.

She was a one-woman dynamo.

Jared still looked wistful when he thought about her.

But he was true to his word. He'd delivered the recordings, and there were plenty. Carla's sudden vanishing only corroborated what they'd heard on the tapes. Carla had planned everything. Jack had put his blood, sweat, and tears into that business. And then he'd emptied his blood into the earth behind it.

Diane spent the entire next day working on the story. An exclusive. When the *Chicago Tribune* ran the story later that day, the AP picked it up. There was a media firestorm over the incident. Sheriff Benson held several communications meetings with his staff. Everything went through Rusty. He was the spokesperson and the clear lead, and the catchphrase of the day was *damage control*, which he seemed to manage OK.

Knowing Sam was a special agent with the USFW and how he had broken the case, the sheriff could only *suggest* Sam clear all public statements through him. Sam nodded but had no intention of clearing anything through Sheriff Rusty Benson. In practically every encounter Sam had had with the sheriff, up to the point when it was finally obvious what had happened, the sheriff had tried to block Sam. And worse, he'd suggested Sam return to where he belonged, policing ducks and fish.

Sam told the true, complete story to Diane, who put it into a five-day front-page series for the *Vermilion Falls Gazette* and the *Chicago Tribune*. And, again, the stories were picked up by the

AP. The sheriff wasn't happy about some of it, but Sam had told the story in a way that largely left the sheriff out, recalling the old maxim "If you can't say something nice about a person . . ."

He was sorely tempted. But Sam hated to burn bridges because you just never knew.

Finally, Kay Magdalen called Sam home—him and Gray, who was still a candidate in training. Gray earned high marks for everything he'd done on the trail of the Savage killers. But Carmine Salazar learned about his disruption in the courtroom, that first day of Angus Moon's extradition hearing, and used it to neutralize Gray's high marks.

The big hybrid was again in limbo and was supposed to be cleared by a panel before he did any work in the field. Sam largely ignored the dictate, except when Magdalen's superiors were watching. Every time he went out into the field, Gray was with him.

In late October, Sam was spending a rare afternoon behind his desk in the Denver Federal Center, still trying to figure out what he was going to do about Diane. He wanted to call her but knew he shouldn't. He needed more time to process his failed marriage, as well as his relationship with Diane. So far, the idea of distancing himself from his divorce and spending more time trying to figure out his romantic path forward was winning out.

But it was tough to forget Diane's touch, her full, rich self lying beside him, which on more than one occasion gave him second thoughts.

Ah, geesh, he thought. *Why am I such a fool?*

Then his phone rang.

"Agent Rivers?" a woman asked.

The hair on Sam's neck rose. He glanced at the caller ID. "Unknown Caller." But he knew it was Carla McGregor.

When Sam didn't answer, she added, "You're a hard man to find."

"Not as hard as you," Sam said.

"Then you know who this is?"

"Sure, Mrs. McGregor. How have you been?"

Sam was twisting his brain into pretzels, trying to figure out how to trace the call. But he had nothing.

"I've been enjoying myself," she said.

Sam thought he heard something in the background. He thought he heard waves. The ocean?

"You know, it's only a matter of time before we find you."

She laughed, infectious as a snake charmer. "I don't think so, Agent Rivers. First you have to know where to look."

He was sure he heard waves.

"If I was a betting man, I'd guess somewhere warm."

"Could be, Agent Rivers. Truth is, I haven't been to a lot of places in the world, so I'm making up for lost time."

Sam paused. "So why don't you help me out? Which hemisphere?"

She started laughing. "I just wanted to let you know, no hard feelings," she said.

"I wish I could say the same."

Another pause. If he could keep her on the phone long enough, Sam thought, he might be able to pick up something else. He was pretty sure he heard surf.

"That's too bad," she said. "You know what they say about revenge, Sam?"

"They say a lot of things about revenge."

"Before you seek revenge, dig two graves."

"It's not really about revenge, Mrs. McGregor. Not for me. I don't feel vengeful. I feel regret. It's about justice. Something you've managed to evade, at least for now."

"Do you really think you can find me?"

"I know we will," Sam said.

"Don't make me mad, Sam. You know I don't play nice."

"I remember. I just hope we have another chance to play again. We're going to find you, Mrs. McGregor," Sam said. "Eventually we'll chase you down."

"Be careful what you wish for, Agent Rivers."

And then the line went dead.

Sam made the usual calls to the authorities, to let them know she'd called and what she'd said and he'd heard. The surf. But it never went anywhere. There were a lot of places with waves in the world. She could be anywhere. And for all Sam knew, Carla could have been playing some kind of recording of waves.

He just hoped sometime, in the not-too-distant future, she would return to take care of the one loose end that might still give her pause when things go bump in the night: Sam Rivers, Special Agent, U.S. Fish & Wildlife Service.

ACKNOWLEDGMENTS

The book you have in your hands has had an interesting life, in no small part because it has been touched by many hands. I shared the first draft with my wife, Anna, and two sons, Nick and Noah, who all provided valuable feedback. Their input was in part the reason the *Star Tribune* decided to serialize the original version, *Savage Minnesota*.

We Minnesota writers are fortunate to live in a state where the populace is well educated and there are still enough interested readers to support the state's major newspaper serializing a book. According to the *Star Tribune:* "The next Sam Rivers novel was selected by the [*Star Tribune*] as its summer read. It will appear in approximately 100 installments from Memorial Day through Labor Day." After the book was accepted as the newspaper's 2014 summer read, Kate Parry, *Star Tribune* news editor, and Laurie Hertzel, *Star Tribune* books editor, pored over the manuscript and used a couple of deft pens to tighten the work. There were many others at the newspaper—photographers, artists, copy editors, and more—that also had a hand in bringing this title to press. The serialized version of the novel was widely read, and the e-book version sold well.

Unfortunately, the *Star Tribune* has never produced printed versions of its serialized summer books. I'm old-fashioned enough to feel that a book is not truly a book until there's a printed version available. So, five years later, the copyright for the book reverted to me.

Enter Brett Ortler, AdventureKEEN's acquisitions and developmental editor. Brett helped publish *Wolves*, the first Sam Rivers novel. *Wolves* won a Midwest Book Award and was a finalist for a Minnesota Book Award. It sold enough copies to convince AdventureKEEN to issue a new, significantly revised version (*Wolf Kill*) in 2020, and to take on another Sam Rivers novel. Most people in Minnesota have an AdventureKEEN nature guide of one kind or another. I own several. However, recognizing that fiction isn't their normal book genre, the publisher reached out to local novelist, poet, and teacher Mary Logue. Mary, author of nine mysteries of her own, as well as myriad other books, focused her experienced eye on the manuscript and, frankly, improved it. She also suggested a title change.

Similarly, others at AdventureKEEN, most notably Managing Editor Kate Johnson, had a hand in bringing this latest edition to print. Copy editor Kerry Smith took Mary's revised manuscript and, again, worked to make it better.

Hopefully, the parts all these hands have played in producing *Cougar Claw* have made it a satisfying and memorable read. Many thanks for their efforts. I am deeply grateful.

I've always liked Sam Rivers, and though he had a difficult childhood and is flawed, his love of remote places and the solace he finds in the wilderness are passions many of us share. Moreover,

Sam recognizes that a simple walk in the woods can be restorative, is free, and only requires us to be present and aware.

With regard to the book's wildlife biology and cougar ethology, I have tried to be factual and accurate. All of the accounts of cougar–human attacks referenced in the book are true. A simple internet search will retrieve many articles discussing the occasional, albeit rare, instances when cougars encounter people. Similarly, books like David Baron's *The Beast in the Garden: The True Story of a Predator's Deadly Return to Suburban America* not only detail the fatal cougar predation of a jogger, but also explain how and why these encounters are on the rise. Finally, websites like the Cougar Fund (cougarfund.org) and the Cougar Network (www.cougarnet.org) are excellent resources for finding out more about cougars.

ABOUT THE AUTHOR

Award-winning author Cary J. Griffith grew up among the woods, fields, and emerald waters of eastern Iowa. His childhood fostered a lifelong love of wild places.

He earned a BA in English from the University of Iowa and an MA in library science from the University of Minnesota.

Cary's books explore the natural world. In nonfiction, he covers the borderlands between civilization and wild places. In fiction, he focuses on the ways some people use flora and fauna to commit crimes, while others with more reverence and understanding of the natural world leverage their knowledge to bring criminals to justice.

DISCUSSION QUESTIONS

1. *Cougar Claw* opens with Jack McGregor pedaling through the early-morning darkness, heading toward his mountain biking trail in a remote section of the Minnesota River Valley. During his ride, how does what he senses, encounters, and thinks presage his murder in the Minnesota woods?

2. Approximately one year earlier, Sam Rivers and his wolf dog, Gray, were investigating a cougar–calf predation on Mable Swenson's cattle ranch. In what ways is Sam's review of that predation different from, or similar to, the cougar–human predation in the Minnesota River Valley?

3. Sam Rivers's understanding of cougar behavior causes him to question how the victim, Jack McGregor, died. What are some of Sam's ethological findings that do not support the idea that Jack's death was the result of a cougar attack?

4. As Sam begins to investigate Jack's death, he learns of the pending sale of Jack's business for approximately $50 million. For some, that kind of financial windfall could be a motive for

committing murder. Are there others who may have different motives for seeing Jack dead?

5. Sheriff Rusty Benson and other law enforcement officers are certain Jack was killed by a cougar. In addition to clear cougar signs, there is DNA evidence supporting their perspective. Are there any reasons Sheriff Benson's willingness to accept that conclusion could be considered a rush to judgment? What are some of the sheriff's motives for making this an open-and-shut case?

6. In what ways do reporter Diane Talbott's research efforts help Sam's investigation?

7. A few different relationships are described in the novel. How is Sam's relationship with Diane different from Jack and Carla's marriage? Does Sam's relationship with Diane contribute to his understanding of what may have happened in the Minnesota woods?

8. Sheriff Benson refuses to follow the investigation wherever it leads. Moreover, at numerous times he tries to impede Sam's probe into what may have occurred. Based on the preceding, Sam could have been much more critical of the sheriff than he was. Do you think the way he handled the sheriff was correct? Why, or why not?

9. At the end of the novel, Sam gets a call from Carla. How do you feel about that phone call, their conversation, and what it might presage for Sam's future? As a reader, how do you feel about Carla?

10. Author Tom Clancy said: "The difference between fiction and reality? Fiction has to make sense." Do you think the end of the novel violates Clancy's maxim? Why, or why not?

READ ON FOR AN EXCERPT FROM CARY J. GRIFFITH'S NEXT NOVEL

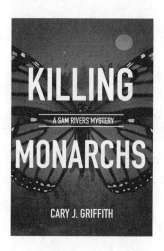

Praise for *Cougar Claw*

"From the first page to the last, *Cougar Claw* blends high suspense with the quiet observations of the predator's predator, Sam Rivers. Between Griffith's descriptions of Minnesota's natural beauty and the human nature of his characters, this is a book you won't want to end."

—Debra H. Goldstein, award-winning author of the Sarah Blair mystery series

AVAILABLE SUMMER 2023
WHEREVER BOOKS ARE SOLD

CHAPTER 1

There were three in the car. Domina drove, Jon Lockhart sat in the front seat, and Tiburon, the muscle, in back.

They traveled north on Minnesota Highway 169 to the Highway 7 exit. At this hour of the morning, the streets were empty, but Domina approached the top of the exit carefully, signaling a left well in advance of the light. As she approached, the light turned yellow, and rather than risk it, she slowed to a stop.

"You could have made that light," Lockhart said.

"No reason to push it. We got time."

"How long?" Lockhart said.

"Five minutes to the drop-off. Take you another five to get into position behind those bushes. Then Tibby and me circle the block, park, and knock on Jerry's door."

"Tibby" was Tiburon, hunkered in the backseat, staring into the rearview out of two obsidian eyes.

Domina wore a pair of custom-made Gaspar black driving gloves and a lightweight jacket with a dark sheen. Her jet-black hair was long on top and shorn butch on both sides, in the style of certain women she hung with in Morelia, south of the border.

"What if he's early?" Lockhart said.

"Jerry Trailor wouldn't show up early to a clusterfuck of beauty queens."

"You sure about the bushes?"

"I checked." Domina remembered them from previous pickups and had scouted the place. "No way Jerry's going to see you back there. It's a blind spot."

"Just make sure he doesn't look around," Lockhart said.

"Jerry's not the kind of guy to look," Domina said, remembering. "Jerry rolls."

Lockhart sniffed and said, "Just make sure."

Lockhart wore a light gray hiking shirt over a black tee, faded jeans, and a pair of Keen hiking shoes. There was a wide-brimmed hat on the seat beside him and a black day pack balanced on the floor between his legs. He'd acquired the gear from an outlet outside of Dallas 8 hours after crossing the Mexico border. The left side of his face and ear looked like he'd been caught between two surgeons having a skin fight. Otherwise, he could have easily passed for a tourist heading out Highway 7 to Minnetonka or Deep Haven or farther west to check out wild country. But the hiking disguise had been unnecessary because in two days' driving they had not been stopped. And now, less than a mile from their destination, Lockhart swore he could smell something like wet iron, something like blood. But maybe it was the idea of watching Jerry Trailor die.

Domina exhaled, waiting for the light. "Jerry's going to tell you whatever you need to know. But Jerry doesn't know jack about your money."

After a pause during which Lockhart was careful not to betray his intentions, he said, "We'll see."

A crescent moon hung off the eastern horizon like a sickle waiting to drop. The way west, where they were headed, was a cavernous maw.

The light changed and Domina turned. Two blocks from the school she pulled to the curb. "Five minutes."

Lockhart opened the car door and said, "Tell him to be careful with the pack."

"Tibby grew up with stingers," Domina said. "He'll be careful."

Inside Ms. Mansfield's sixth-grade classroom, Jerry Trailor stared at the 2-pound brick of brown heroin, trying to think. Twice a year he fielded shipments from Las Monarcas, the Monarchs, a Michoacán drug cartel. But before, it had always been meth.

Yesterday afternoon he'd only had time to tuck the shipment into Ms. Mansfield's refrigerator, careful to change the lock. Then he'd gone out to Walmart and picked up a bottle of Johnson's Baby Powder.

Every six months he got a little freebie, courtesy of the Mexicans. He'd carve out six, maybe seven good hits and replace the ground crystal with baby powder, nobody the wiser. Stealing from Monarchs was risky, but no way they could track so little replaced so well. And they hadn't.

After getting the Johnson's he'd texted his old pal Suthy.

"Coming into a little extra jack. Maybe we should head over to Shakopee and get some rooms at the casino, do a little partyin'?"

Suthy was in.

But now Jerry stared at the brick of heroin and thought, *Baby powder will show up on this stuff like snow dust on sand. No way I should touch it.*

But Jerry knew plenty of girls who would jump at a chance for a taste. Jump and kneel and do just about anything else he could imagine, which was plenty. The idea caused a hot fog to swirl below his solar plexus, clouding his mind.

Think . . .

Nobody'd miss a couple, three, maybe four good hits, nicked off at the corners. Two for me. One for Suthy. And a half each for the chiquitas.

He stared at the brick the way a kid stares at a birthday cake with sweet buttercream frosting, candles, and well wishes. It was a gift. A hot-girl gift.

But he had no way to conceal it.

But on a brick this size, who would notice?

Think . . .

He glanced at the clock's minute hand, same clock on the classroom wall when he was a kid. Same goddamn black on white marks he stared at before recess and end of school and last day, waiting for that minute hand to tick, waiting for that freedom bell to ring. Now it clicked onto the black 4, telling Jerry he'd better decide. In 10 minutes he had to be at the school's side door, looking relaxed, fist bumping his old friend Domina, business-as-usual, just more product passing through.

Jerry knew the smart move. Jerry always knew the smart move. He just had trouble making it.

Lockhart hustled up the street through the dark, approaching the school from the rear. He crossed through shadows to the remote side entrance and crouched behind the row of bushes.

The morning was still and black. An hour before dawn was supposed to be the coldest time of the day, but it was already 70° and humid, crazy climate for Minnesota three days before Memorial Day weekend. It was as though he had walked across the street to his colonial *casa* in Morelia, Mexico, instead of the dark side entrance to Hopkins Elementary.

When he had imagined his homecoming, he had always imagined it cold—the iceman cometh. But now Minnesota had gone all global warming on him and he was going to have to improvise. Now, he thought, the devil rides a hot wind, bringing grim reckoning.

The idea did nothing to assuage the throb that spread across his scarred left cheek. He reached up to rub it and thought, *Fuckin' Minnesota.* The irony of a perfect Twin Cities spring making his burn scar ache should have made him smile. But Lockhart wasn't the kind of man to smile, about anything.

He heard Domina's car approach along the dark side street.

There was a faint click from inside the school's side door. It pushed open 6, maybe 7 inches.

Lockhart remained still, his back pressed against the red-brick wall. The door's narrow opening faced a small walkway that stretched 30 feet to the side street.

The door narrowed to a 1-inch crack.

The car pulled to a nearby curb, and the idling engine turned off. A pair of car doors opened and shut. Then steps started up the walk. When they grew close, the door swung open and Jerry said, "Hey, Doms. You bring this heat from Mexico?"

Even though it had been five years, Lockhart, hidden behind the bushes, recognized Jerry's voice.

"The only thing I bring from home is these guns," Domina said, turning her arm and flexing her bicep.

Domina and Jerry laughed, familiar.

Doms was short and solid through the shoulders. Beneath her driving jacket, her stout arms were covered with tattoos, one of them a crucifix with a highly stylized image of Jesus, hands and feet weeping blood. She wore black jeans, a black Madonna T-shirt, and an oversized dark blue hat with *A's* emblazoned above the bill, for Oakland. The bill was turned off-center, resting on ears with black steel horseshoe earrings piercing the cartilage.

Tiburon was half again bigger and wore a dark blue Twins baseball cap with the bill turned sideways. His Jack Daniel's T-shirt was too tight for his ample chest and belly. The pack hung over one shoulder, riding on his back like Quasimodo's hump.

Jerry thought Tiburon's hat, turned sideways, made him look stupid. But he didn't know the man, so he only nodded and said, "*Hola, compadre. ¿Que pasa?*" like a wannabe Mexican gangster.

Tiburon shrugged.

"How ya' been, Jerry?" Doms said. Doms had been raised in Iowa by Mexican immigrants, so she sounded Upper Midwest. But if she wanted, she could effect an accent as thick as a Michoacán *Monarcas*.

Doms reached out, and she and Jerry did some kind of handshake thing, slapping each others' palms.

"I been hangin'," Jerry said.

"Tiburon's my mule," Doms said, pointing to the pack.

"Damn straight," Jerry said, holding out his fist toward the big man, ready to bump knuckles. But Tiburon only stared.

"He's not so good with the English," Doms said.

Jerry dropped his fist and shrugged. "No problemo. I ain't so good with the Mexican."

The three disappeared inside and the door swung shut.

Lockhart waited 30 seconds. Then he pushed off the wall and hurried to the side entrance, reaching into his pocket for a key. He put his good ear to the metal and heard voices echo down a hall, turn a corner, and fade.

Once inside, Lockhart saw a long, poorly lit hallway with rows of lockers down either side, ending at a pair of closed glass doors. In front of the doors was an opening, and down the left he heard Domina talking, and then someone—Jerry—laughed.

Lockhart followed without a sound.

"Here it is," Jerry said, stopping in front of a classroom door with MS. MANSFIELD posted on the wall. Jerry's chrome chain hung almost to his knee. His long-sleeved work shirt was rolled up to his elbows, revealing the start of tattoos that ran to his shoulder, one of them an ornate cross, just like Doms's, from their time in the Arrowhead Juvenile Detention Center in Duluth, when they thought the shared Jesus would keep their gang safe. Jerry made a kind of flourish, pulling on the chain until the keys jangled out of his pocket.

"What happened to the piercings, Jerry?" Doms asked.

A long time ago, when they were both in juvie, Doms presided over Jerry's first piercing. His left cheek. One of the kids in the yard held a match to a 2-inch shingle nail until it turned white-hot. Doms could still remember how Jerry had tried to act tough about it, like he could handle the pain. And for 5 seconds, while the hot metal burned through his cheek, he kept still. But as soon as they pulled the nail out, Jerry howled and danced like a jumping bean. A half dozen onlookers howled like a pack of hyenas.

Before they got out of juvie he did it two more times; once in the lip, once in an ear lobe.

But that was more than four years ago.

"Policy, man," Jerry said. "The school district won't hire you with face piercings or too many tattoos. These tats are bad enough," he added, nodding to his arms. "Gotta wear a long-sleeved shirt during the day so the brats don't see." Jerry inserted the key into the door and let them in.

Amber Mansfield's sixth-grade classroom was dark and empty. The ambient streetlight revealed three rows of seats, each with a writing surface, pointing toward the front of the room. A recessed ceiling light bathed a large teacher's desk in half glow. Behind the desk, an oversized poster titled *The Miracle of Metamorphosis* was taped to the wall. The poster contained four large close-ups: a Monarch butterfly egg, a caterpillar, a pupa, and an adult butterfly, wings open, resting on a yellow flower.

"*Es un signo, puta,*" Tiburon said.

Jerry fished his iPhone out of his breast pocket, flicked on the flashlight beam and said, "What'd he say?"

"He likes the poster," Doms said. "He thinks it's a sign."

Doms and Tiburon were members of the Monarchs. It was about being kings, but it was also the name of the large orange butterfly that overwintered in the mountains of the Mexican state they called home.

"Oh," Jerry said, remembering the affiliation. Jerry was only a contractor.

"¿Que le diría?" Tiburon said.

"El Milagro de la Metamorfosis."

Tiburon didn't know *metamorfosis*. But he said, "Si. Somos milagros chingones."

"What?" Jerry said.

"He said, 'We're badass miracles.'"

"Damn straight," Jerry said, turning to acknowledge Tiburon's comment. But the big man was considering the poster. "The fridge is down here."

"Damn, Jerry," Doms said. "I never thought you'd bow down to the man." It was a joke because whenever possible Jerry took the path of least resistance, played the angles, maximized personal benefit and minimized pain.

"Sometimes you gotta give an inch," Jerry said.

"I guess," Doms said.

"Because later you take a mile," Jerry added and stopped in front of the half fridge.

"I hear that," Doms said. Then Doms turned to Tiburon, and even though Tiburon didn't understand English, some kind of acknowledgment passed between them. But Jerry didn't see it.

Jerry sorted through his keys, found the right one, and crouched. There was a lock on a clasp, and once it was opened Jerry pulled on the fridge door and extracted a cardboard box. On the side was printed "Monarch Butterfly Preserve, San Isidro de las Palomas, Michoacán, Mexico. Fragile. *Frágil.*"

Jerry returned his keys to his pocket and placed the box on the counter next to the fridge. Then he pulled a white plastic trash bag out of his pocket and said, "We gotta be careful. We don't want any of these ugly little bugs damaged or there might be questions."

Jerry used a box cutter to slice through the plastic tape. Then he opened the flaps, took off the thin cardboard covering, and shined his light on a sea of green Monarch butterfly pupae. Each of them was about the size and shape of a finger digit. They were a deep, shiny emerald, with a black stripe near their top center, along an edge marked by tiny gold dots—iridescent and startlingly beautiful, if you forgot they were alive.

"Creepy little mothers," Jerry said.

Doms glanced into the box and said, "Not if you think about what they become." Then she noticed something about the box— the edge of tape—and picked it up to have a closer look.

"I guess, but looks like money to me," Jerry said. "The kids can't get enough of this shit. The school district pays to have these ugly bugs shipped from Mexico, and you guys get to move a little product. Easy peasy." He handed Doms the white plastic garbage bag, but Doms didn't take it.

"You already open the box, Jerry?"

Jerry shrugged and said, "I had to look, Dommy."

"You shouldn't have opened it, Jerry."

"It felt a little funny. Heavier. I was worried, so I had a look. But I didn't touch nothin'."

Domina's face turned cold and still.

Jerry smiled, a little nervous, and said, "You didn't tell me it was heroin, Dommy." He was still holding the white bag for Domina to take, which she did, slowly.

Then Jerry carefully gripped the box, tipped it, and poured the pupae into the bag. "They're definitely disgusting," Jerry said.

When the pupae were all out of the box, Domina said, "Damn, bro. You shouldn't have done that," still talking about Jerry opening the box.

Once the emptied box was back on the counter, Jerry reached in and took out a thin piece of cardboard. Under the false bottom, the 2-pound brick lay wrapped in heavy plastic.

"No biggie. It just didn't feel right. I wanted to make sure, in case there was a problem."

"How long we been doin' this?" Domina asked.

Jerry shrugged. "Four years."

"We ever had a problem?"

"We never moved 2 pounds of heroin. It was always meth, and only a pound."

"What difference does it make?"

"Street value, Dommy. This much heroin is worth a lot more than meth."

"So what?"

"It's just a lot of jack. A lot more than a meth shipment. Especially on the street."

"What we get on the street shouldn't make any difference," Domina said. "To *you*."

She wasn't happy, but Jerry continued. "Just sayin', given the merchandise, maybe my payment's a little thin."

Domina looked at him until Jerry glanced away.

"Just sayin'," Jerry said.

After an uncomfortable silence, Domina said, "Let's get these bugs back in the box. Then I gotta check out this shipment. Somewhere safe. You got a place . . . out of the way?"

"Yeah," Jerry said. "I got the dungeon. Nobody goes to the dungeon. But are you thinkin' I took something?"

"Just sayin' I gotta check, now that I know you opened it."

"Sure. Check," Jerry shrugged. "But I'd never take nothin'. You know that, Dommy."

"Gotta check, Jerry." Domina knew Jerry; he was a liar, a cheat, and a punk. But he was one of those guys you liked because he made you laugh. "If everything's OK, we can talk. Maybe we got something else for you."

Jerry nodded. "OK."

They wadded newspaper and used it to fill the space where the heroin had been. Then they reinserted the cardboard square and carefully poured the pupae on top of it. They closed and retaped the box and returned it to the fridge.

While Jerry was locking the fridge, Tiburon opened his backpack and carefully slipped the 2-pound brick inside, beside two different-sized jars. Something alive scuttled inside the jars. Tiburon's hand jerked out like he'd stuck a fork in a wall socket. But Jerry didn't see it.

After the fridge was shut and locked, Jerry led them out of the classroom and down a very long hallway into a stairwell. They walked down two flights of stairs into shadows. On the right, there was a metal door marked UTILITIES.

Jerry unlocked the door and said, "Welcome to the dungeon," and walked in.

It was a narrow room with low pipes overhead, maybe 7 feet, and a huge boiler near the right back wall. The boiler had been replaced long ago by more modern HVAC technology.

Down the left side of the room was a workbench with tools strewn haphazardly on racks and across the workbench surface. Jerry walked down and made space on the bench and said, "You can check it out here, Doms. But I'd never take nothin'."

There were two old wooden school chairs sitting at a scarred wooden table that held an ashtray filled with butts.

"Have a seat, Jerry, while I take a look," Domina said.

Jerry let out an irritating sigh and sat down. He reached into his breast pocket, pulled out a pack of Kools, opened the box, took out a lighter and cigarette, and lit it. Then he inhaled and filled the space with smoke.

Domina unzipped the backpack and carefully extracted the brick.

"They let you smoke in school?" Domina said.

"Nobody comes down to the dungeon."

Domina was careful with the plastic, peering closely at the folded, taped ends. Through the clear plastic she examined the brick and noticed what appeared to be small nicks at the corners. *Jerry, Jerry, Jerry,* she thought, without betraying her suspicions.

The corners could have been nicked in shipment, even though care was taken with biological cargo. There was no way to tell for sure. She was still hoping Lockhart was just going to scare her old friend. Scare the hell out of him, get some information, and then they'd all walk. Jerry would learn a lesson, and Lockhart would understand Jerry didn't know shit about Lockhart's money.

But Domina didn't know Lockhart, and over two days driving the only thing she knew for certain was that the man trusted no one and was a son of a bitch, a real *hijo de puta*. If Lockhart thought Jerry had stolen any product, however insignificant, Domina's old friend could be enduring a whole lot more than pain.

So, for now, all she did was look up and nod to Tiburon and say, "*Está bien. Listo.*" OK. Ready.

Then the big man walked back to the dungeon door and opened it.

Jerry, startled, watched a man with a hideous half-face walk into the room.

"What the hell?" Jerry said, standing.

The guy was about Jerry's height, 5 foot 9, but with the left side of his face and part of his ear looking like melted candle wax. And he entered the room like he'd been expected.

"What the hell?" Jerry repeated.

"Sit down, Jerry," Lockhart said. "We need to talk."

Jerry didn't sit because the moment he heard Lockhart's voice he remembered it. When he was a kid, he believed there were fiends in the world who could do a lot more than scare you. When he turned 17 and started working for Lockhart, helping him peddle meth in Isanti County, he knew he had finally met one.

Jerry stepped away from the table.

"Sit down, Jerry," Lockhart repeated. "We don't want any trouble. We just need to talk."

Tiburon came up beside Lockhart and pulled a long black handle out of his front jean pocket. He squeezed and a blade popped out of it like a glittering tusk.

"I guess you remember me?" Lockhart said.

Jerry looked at the blade and managed a slight nod. "What gives, Doms?" Jerry said, a tremble in his voice. But he didn't look in Dom's direction. He kept glancing between Lockhart and Tiburon's knife.

"Lockhart says he knows you, Jerry." Then she turned to Lockhart. "It's all here."

"Sure it is," Lockhart said. "Jerry wouldn't steal from Las Monarcas, would you, Jerry?"

Jerry shook his head, too frightened to answer.

"It's OK, Jerry," Lockhart said.

But it wasn't, and everyone knew it.

"Griffith's prose makes you feel the winter chill . . . and the twisty plot delivers a chill down your spine. This is a Minnesota mystery with razor-sharp teeth."

—Brian Freeman, *New York Times* best-selling author of *The Deep, Deep Snow*

"*Wolf Kill* is a terrific read! The writing is so good that you can feel the frigid winds blowing through this dark and masterfully crafted novel even as the suspense heats up. And the wolves are as magnificent and frightening as you could hope.

—David Housewright, Edgar Award–winning author of *What Doesn't Kill Us*

"In northern Minnesota, winter is full of dangers that can kill: hard cold, hard men, and hungry wolves. Cary Griffith brings the menace of all three into play in his riveting new thriller. Returning to the childhood home he fled 20 years earlier, Sam Rivers finds himself battling a group of scheming reprobates and struggling against an avalanche of painful memories. Griffith's intimacy with the territory he writes about comes through in every line. I loved this novel and highly recommend it. But I suggest you enjoy it under a warm blanket. Honestly, I've never read a book that evokes the fierce winter landscape of the North Country better than *Wolf Kill*."

—William Kent Krueger, Edgar Award–winning author of *This Tender Land*

"The deep freeze of a Minnesota winter meets the chilling underbelly of a small Iron Range town in Cary Griffith's fantastic *Wolf*

Kill. I loved meeting Sam Rivers, the wolf expert and USFW field agent assigned to protect the nation's wildlife and can't wait to follow Rivers on his next adventure."

—Mindy Mejia, author of *Leave No Trace* and *Strike Me Down*

"Up here in the North Country, we have a bounty of fine mystery writers. Krueger, Housewright, Eskens, Freeman, Mejia, Sanford . . . Add to that list Cary Griffith, whose *Wolf Kill* thrills for its plotting, superb writing, and unforgettable characters, not least the brutal Minnesota winter. Sam Rivers is not only a fine sleuth, but a complicated man with a complicated history and a fair family grudge. Taken together, he's a force, both on the page and long after you finish reading his story. Good thing there's more of him to go around, and I'll be first in line for the next Sam Rivers novel."

—Peter Geye, author of *Northernmost*

"Cary J. Griffith defines the savage, howling beauty of a Northern Minnesota winter in this taut, compulsively readable mystery. I want more Sam Rivers!

—Wendy Webb, author of *The Haunting of Brynn Wilder*

"I love books where I go on a great adventure but I also learn something along the way. *Wolf Kill* does all this and more—it's the beginning of a series featuring a smart wildlife special agent who takes us into the wilderness and safely out again. A deeply satisfying read."

—Mary Logue, author of Claire Watkins mysteries and *The Streel*

"Fans of Paul Doiron's *The Poacher's Son* or the Joe Pickett books will appreciate this descriptive novel with an intriguing plot and well-written characters."

—Lesa Holstine, *Library Journal*

PRAISE FOR *WOLF KILL (continued)*

"Involving, fast-paced . . . [Cary J. Griffith's] writing is so vivid the reader wants to bundle up and enjoy the beauty of the landscape, even at 20 below zero."

—Mary Ann Grossmann, *Pioneer Press*

"The latest from accomplished Minnesota author Cary J. Griffith brings us a new North Woods hero to join the ranks of William Kent Krueger's Cork O'Connor and Allen Eskens' Max Rupert. He even gives Brian Freeman's Minnesota-to-the-core Jonathan Stride a run for the money."

—Ginny Greene, *Star Tribune*